Sign up for our newsletter to hear
about new and upcoming releases.

www.ylva-publishing.com

Other Books in the
Norfolk Coast Investigation Story

Collide-O-Scope

Under Parr
(Book #2; Coming Spring 2017)

Collide-O-Scope

Andrea Bramhall

Acknowledgements

To everyone at Ylva Publishing, Astrid, Daniela, and Gill in particular, thank you. For showing me the doorway to new opportunities and fresh challenges. And then taking the chance with me when I decided to jump. Your patience, guidance, and faith in me are so very much appreciated. I do so hope that I can do you all justice.

R.G. Emanuelle, for your editing skills and guidance, thank you. And I swear, I'm working on those pesky, bloody apostrophes.

Now, while all the characters and most of the places in this story are fictional, I do live on the North Norfolk Coast, and my partner and I do have a campsite there. I've been told I have to tell you all that she has never considered murdering me and leaving my body on the marshes. And that the entirety of this story is a figment of my imagination. (Darling, will you let go of my arm now please? It's not meant to go so far up my back!) So, a great big thank you to Norfolk, for all the inspiration, the wonderful years we've spent living and working there, and to all the great people we've met there.

Dedication

Louise, you said that without Deepdale we wouldn't be where we are today. I think that we'd have found our way here eventually, no matter what. Some things are just meant to be.

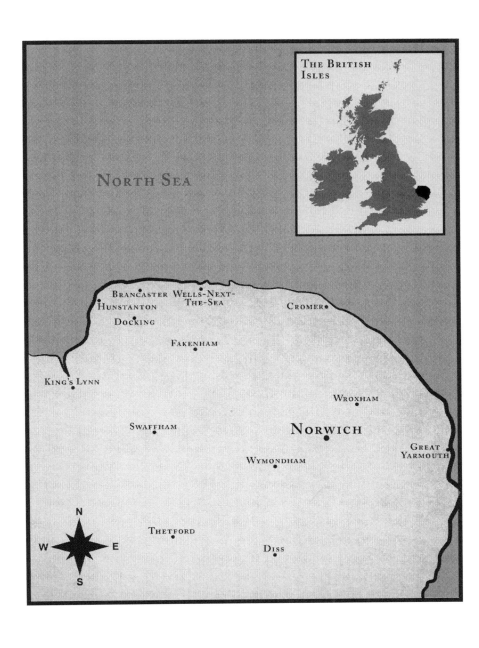

THE BRITISH
ISLES

NORTH SEA

BRANCASTER   WELLS-NEXT-
HUNSTANTON   THE-SEA
DOCKING   CROMER

FAKENHAM

KING'S LYNN

WROXHAM

SWAFFHAM   NORWICH

GREAT
YARMOUTH

WYMONDHAM

N
W   E
S

THETFORD

DISS

Prologue

A chill wind blew across the barren-looking marsh. Connie tugged her collar up around her ears and pulled the zipper closed. She blew on her hands to try and warm them before tucking them under her armpits and stomping her feet to get the blood flowing. The late October chill made promises of a harsh winter, with snow, roaring fires, and mulled wine—promises that Connie hoped Mother Nature would keep.

She eyed the horizon, smiling as the first hints of pink muscled their way into the expansive indigo sky. The *clink clink* of steel ropes clattering against the masts reached her from the harbour less than a mile from where she stood. A sound too soft to be heard in the light of day, where the hustle and bustle of the tiny fishing harbour clamouring with tourists, sailors, and walkers, swallowed the tiny sounds of the night. Green and red lights flickered in the harbour. Fishing boats hauling their wares drifted on the current of the North Sea, as the wind died to nothing and the stars blinked out of sight. The eternal battle between night and day lost for another cycle, they no longer cast their ethereal sparkle across the glistening water filling the creeks that surrounded her as the tide continued its journey inland.

As the water continued to rise, it spilled over the banks of each shallow creek and swallowed huge swathes of samphire and heather-covered land. The flood plain known as The Saltings was already underwater as the highest spring tide of the year continued to rise. Connie was glad there was no wind. The last time they'd had a tide such as this, combined with a strong wind, it had led to half of the homes in the village being flooded.

A gentle nudge against her boot reminded her of her companion. She looked down at the dirty stick that had been deposited for her. The hopeful look on her beloved dog's face made her smile as she reached for the object of Merlin's desire. Her blue eyes were alert, and her dappled grey body was all set to dive into action and chase it wherever she threw it.

"Are you ready, girl? Are ya?" She prepared herself and flung the stick like a boomerang, laughing as Merlin bounded after it as fast as her legs would take her. Her body was soon hidden by the long grasses and bramble bushes that lined the Coastal Path. Connie chuckled, sighed out a long breath that fogged as it left her lips, and turned back towards the sea. The darkness was starting to give way to the daylight and she lifted her camera, quickly checking the aperture and shutter settings before clicking off a few shots. She reviewed them on the LCD screen as Merlin deposited her stick by her boot again.

Another distracted toss and she zoomed in as tight as the lens of her Nikon D5300 would let her. Eighteen millimetres to 300 millimetres gave her the best options for her two greatest photography passions, landscape and wildlife. Today she wasn't trying to shoot either. Today she was trying to capture images of an entirely different animal plaguing the North Norfolk salt marshes. She ground her teeth and focused the lens tight on the lobster pots being hauled out of the North Sea. She clicked and reviewed the image. Too dark. She checked her settings, the aperture was already wide open, she'd just have to wait for the sun to rise a little more.

She rounded the steep steps that led down the embankment to the overflow and glanced out towards the hectares of arable fields covered in pink-footed geese feeding on the recently ploughed sod. A loud bang caused her to flinch and look around for Merlin as a flock of geese hundreds strong took to the air. Merlin cowered at her feet and watched the birds with suspicion as they squawked indignantly and flapped and made their way to quieter feeding grounds. Every field in the vicinity had them. Bird scarers. Noisy machines that sounded like a shotgun and were far more reliable than the scarecrows of old. After a while you stopped hearing them. They faded into the background of bird song, rustling leaves, cars, and people.

Connie shook her head at her canine's cowardice and bent to collect her stick. She threw it in the hope of distracting her from the scary birds and walked a little farther down the path as Merlin took off after her prize. She moved beyond the long shadows of the houseboat that bobbed in the foreground of many of her pictures. Merlin ran ahead, branch clenched between her teeth. She stopped a short way away and looked back to make sure Connie was still following and hadn't stopped again.

"I'm coming, Merlin. Good girl."

An egret flew across the marsh heading for Scolt Head Island, just the far side of the creeks and the other side of the raised sea defences she walked along. Normally, it was a shot she'd love to get—the long-legged and white-bodied bird she had once mistaken for a heron in her early days as a photographer. She chuckled to herself again. A twitcher she was not, but she'd learned a lot over the past six years. A lot about the wildlife, the geography, the politics of small village life, and more and more about the locals themselves.

"More than I ever wanted to know." She lifted the camera to her eye again and refocused. The light was much better and the shots showed the detail she needed them to show. "Think you can threaten me?" She zoomed out a little. "Well, we'll just have to see who's bluffing, won't we?"

Merlin dropped the stick at her foot again. She looked down from the viewfinder and kicked the stick into the shrubs. The rustle was the only sound she could hear, not a breath of wind ruffled the rising surface of the sea. Every boat and cloud was reflected perfectly in the still water. She set herself again for another shot and her camera exploded in her hand.

CHAPTER 1

Kate Brannon zipped her black leather jacket closed, climbed out of her car, and made her way down the mud track. Rain splatted through the tree canopy and quickly became a heavy shower as she emerged from the trees and glanced out at the grey sky and sodden-looking marshland in front of her. She flashed her warrant card at the young PCSO, Police Community Support Officer, standing at the perimeter of the cordoned-off area. He lifted the tape to duck under while he held a dog lead attached to a visibly distraught animal.

"The duty officer and the DI are up there." He waved down the muddy path.

She pointed to the dog. "What's going on?"

"Dog was with the body, ma'am. The crime scene guys say they need to examine it for evidence, 'cos it was all over the body when they got here."

She gazed at the poor animal. It was whimpering and barking, trying desperately to break free, seemingly intent on returning to the crime scene. Kate wanted to bend down and stroke it, try to soothe it a little, but that wasn't a good idea. Not until the evidence on its coat was recovered. "Who called it in?"

"Couple walking the path, ma'am. They didn't go near. Said the dog wouldn't let 'em."

"Has it been vicious?" She frowned at the dog. It's pleading blue eyes moved quickly from her face to the lead in her officer's hand and back to its owner.

"No, not at all. Just didn't want to let anyone near the victim."

"Does she have a name?"

"I don't know. I haven't been up there—"

"I meant the dog."

"Oh, right, sorry. Collar says 'Merlin,' but she's a girl."

Kate chuckled. "Right. Better call ahead and get a vet on standby. There's no way they'll be able to examine her while she's awake. Poor thing."

"Right-o, ma'am."

She patted him on the arm then glanced up and saw the white tent being hastily erected farther down the path. One thing less to worry about—losing any more evidence to the rain. She nodded to him and made her way through the mud. She wrinkled her nose against the wind, salty with a tang of iron in it.

She approached the uniformed man obviously directing the whole affair as he issued orders, his arm waving and people scurrying around at his behest.

"Sir," she said as she approached. "Detective Sergeant Brannon."

"Inspector Savage." He held out his hand for her to shake, his grip firm. "Thanks for getting here so soon. On your own?"

"I was at home when my CO called. I only live in Docking," she said, referring to the village just six miles inland from their current location. "My partner will catch up."

"Jolly good. You new?"

"Moved to King's Lynn from Norwich about three weeks ago."

"Promoted at the same time?"

She nodded. "Yes, sir." A loud voice from down the embankment caused them both to turn and watch as a young police community support officer stood still, eyes fixed on the ground as a ruddy-cheeked man offered him some sound advice. Loud enough for everyone to hear.

"This is a crime scene, you bleeding imbecile. You do not, I repeat, do not come wandering over for a look without taking precautions. Do you hear me, boy?"

"Yes, sir."

"And why do you not come wandering over to take a little look at the scene without taking precautions?"

"So that I don't contaminate the scene."

"Or destroy evidence."

"Or destroy evidence, sir."

Kate could see the spittle flying from the corners of his mouth as he continued to dress down the young man.

"The five building blocks of an investigation, lad. Tell me?"

"Sir?"

"The five building blocks. Come on. You went through the training. Tell me."

"Sir, I'm not sure—"

"I'll give you a hint. Number one. Preserve life." He pointed to the tent that was almost fully erect now. "Can we do her any good?"

"No, sir."

"Right. So what's next?"

"Preserve the scene, sir?" His voice was timid. Asking a question rather than answering.

"Halle-fucking-lujah. Then what do we do?"

"Secure evidence." The young man responded with more confidence. "Identify the victim and then identify the suspects."

"Brain of Britain you are, mate. Brain of Britain." He tapped the guy on the cheek. "So where in that little list does it tell you to walk through my crime scene with no overshoes, no coveralls, and touching any bloody thing you like on the way?"

"Nowhere, sir."

"Exactly." He leaned back. "Now get the fuck out of my sight, off my crime scene, and hope like fucking hell I don't take this to your CO and enjoy watching you issue parking tickets for the rest of your natural. Are we clear?"

"Yes, sir." The young man clambered up the steep embankment and headed away from the scene, almost as though he were heading out to sea, but Kate knew what lay in that direction. It was a path she'd walked several times over the last three weeks. There was a turn-off to a small village a half mile or so farther on. She figured he'd been assigned to prevent walkers heading towards the crime scene. The ruddy-cheeked man watched him go, shaking his head and muttering under his breath.

"Your CO? Detective Inspector Timmons, right?" Savage asked, turning to Kate.

"That's right." Kate wondered if he'd take offence at Timmons dressing down his officer. He must have caught the look on her face because he just shrugged.

"Saved me having to read him the riot act and actually assign him to parking tickets for the rest of his natural." He smiled and winked at her. "Is he going to be SIO on this one?"

"He will. Have you not spoken to him yet?" Kate thought it unusual for the Senior Investigating Officer to have not introduced himself to his uniformed counterpart.

"Not yet. It's been bedlam so far, as I'm sure you can imagine. Not sure when he arrived to be fair."

"Can you put us up for the duration?" She offered him what she hoped was a winning smile, and judging by the softening around the eyes, it worked. "We can run the investigation from here, then, rather than too-ing and fro-ing to King's Lynn all the time. Stands to reason that the suspects will most likely be in the local area. Doesn't make sense to base almost thirty miles away."

"Fair point." He nodded. "How many of you?"

"Say five of us, if you can lend us a hand with the witness interviews. Timmons, me, and another sergeant, plus a couple of DCs."

"Sure." He snorted a sardonic laugh. "Not like we don't have anything better to do." He sighed and pointed to the trees where she'd come from. "Well, I've cordoned off the Coastal Path for five hundred yards in either direction. I've got a PCSO on each entry of the pathway to stop anyone coming down until we're done here. If they can manage to stay put, mind." He pointed to the tent just as Timmons looked up the embankment, clearly spotted her, and beckoned for her to join him. She indicated she was on her way with a quick wave of her hand and nodded back to the inspector beside her.

"You coming down?"

He shook his head. "I've seen it already. We've got an unidentified female with a single gunshot wound to the face."

"No ID on her?"

"No. Nothing on her but a phone and a set of keys. The dog's tag says 'If found, please call my mum, Connie.'"

"Well, that's a start."

"Yeah. I've got the crime scene boys in there now looking for anything, but I've got to say there's a lot of contamination from the dog, and probably just as much lost from the rain."

Kate looked up and nodded. She'd seen the amount of blood covering the dog. She wondered if the forensics team would actually be able to get anything useful at all. They stood in the middle of nowhere, not a CCTV camera in sight. *Welcome to rural policing, Brannon.* "Mind if I take a look?"

"Nope. I'm getting some bodies here to help the coroner get the body up the embankment. Tell Timmons I'll have the kettle on when he gets to the station. Hope you've not eaten yet."

She didn't answer him. There was no need to. Instead, she made her way down the steep embankment and pulled a pair of white overshoes out of her pocket and slipped them on. The Coastal Path sat atop a flood defence barrier. On the sea side the embankment rose up almost five feet, on the back side it dropped down a good six or seven. The water channels cut along the boundaries of the fields, a system of irrigation that had been utilised for a couple of hundred years. Along the steep side, brambles were well established, and the route down to the marquee was somewhat treacherous.

She pushed her hair off her face, noting it was about time she got it cut, and took a deep breath. She prayed she wouldn't land on her arse and make a fool of herself as she made her way down. Or even worse, destroy vital evidence as she did so.

Timmons waited for her. "Lovely day for it."

The drizzle was getting harder, or maybe she was just saturated now. Either way, it was bloody lousy. "Is that what you're calling it, sir?"

He chuckled. "Did he fill you in?"

She followed his gaze towards Inspector Savage as he spoke to an officer she didn't know. "Yes. Unidentified female, deceased, gunshot wound. Suspicious."

He snorted. "Well, that certainly sums up the pertinent facts." He flicked his hand in the direction of the tent. "Shall we?"

She nodded and stepped towards the structure as the PVC fluttered and crinkled against the wind.

"Ma'am," said a young man dressed in a white coverall, safety glasses, and a face mask. Kate waded through the long grasses and rushes, and the young man held back the door of the newly erected canvas structure.

"Safe to go in?" Kate asked.

"Yes, ma'am. Dr. Anderson is already examining the body."

She nodded and ducked inside, Timmons on her heels.

"What've we got?" Kate squatted beside another white-clad figure.

"And you are?"

"Detective Sergeant Kate Brannon." Kate held out her warrant badge, her picture clear for the examiner to see.

"Ah. Welcome to North Norfolk. I'm Doctor Anderson. Nice to meet you."

"Thank you, Doctor," she said. "And this is—"

"Detective Inspector Timmons," Dr. Anderson said. "We've worked together before."

"All right, Ruth," Timmons said and pointed to the body. "So?"

"Female, Caucasian, approximately thirty to forty years old. Fatal gunshot wound to the face."

"Savage said there was no ID," Kate said.

"Correct. And I don't have a picture for you to flash around to try and find someone who recognises her. Not without facial reconstruction anyway."

"That's okay. I've got a couple of ideas. You're going to need a vet to knock the dog out when you collect the evidence from her. I'll get them to check her chip and see if we can get a name and address from it."

Anderson smiled. "I like the way you think, Detective."

"Thanks." Kate peered over her shoulder to make her own observations.

There was little left of the woman's face to identify her. Long, dark hair framed her head in a tangled mess, lumps of brain matter and blood clumped indiscriminately. There was a small mole on the right-hand side of her neck. Jeans, stout hiking boots, and a thick purple coat covered the rest of the body. Her right arm was flung out, lying flat on the ground. Barely far enough from the edge of the narrow creek for them to get the tent over her without having to go into the water.

"What kind of weapon would cause that much damage? A shotgun?"

Anderson shrugged. "Maybe. But I wouldn't bet my licence on it. There's something in the wound that doesn't look like it belongs there." She leaned closer to the body. "Light's crap here though. I can't tell what it is until I get her back to my lab and have a good look."

"Fair enough."

"Are you planning to attend the autopsy, Detective?"

"Wouldn't miss it, Doctor." Kate quirked her lips. In all honesty, she'd love to miss it. There was nothing more clinical and dehumanising than watching victims being reduced to the sum of their parts in an attempt to learn what had happened to them. But it wasn't something she planned on missing. It also wasn't something she had to attend very often either. Small villages didn't throw that many suspicious deaths their way, after all.

"Do you have an ETD for us to start working with?"

"Given the temperature out here, her core temp, very little insect activity, I'd say she's been dead about four hours now. I'll have a better idea when I examine stomach contents if you can get me an ID and the time she last ate, but four hours looks about right at the moment."

Kate checked her watch. Eleven o'clock. "Around seven?"

"Approximately."

"Sunrise. Well, almost."

"And high tide today," Timmons said.

Kate nodded. "Nice time to walk the dog."

"Hmm. Unfortunately, that fur ball's done more than enough to contaminate my scene." Anderson waved in her assistant and together they manoeuvred the victim into a body bag. "The wound's been licked, the beast has got tissue, bone fragments, and brain matter all over it, and I couldn't tell you from the surroundings if someone else was with her or not. All the grass is trampled with paw prints." She dusted off her hands and pulled her face mask down. "Then there's the rain."

Kate looked around again, committing the surroundings to memory. "So what you're telling me is, don't expect too much."

Anderson laughed. "That'll be about the size of it, yes."

"Well, it could be worse," Timmons said, chuckling.

"How do you figure?"

"Another foot and she'd have ended up in the water." He pointed. "Don't know about you, but I find late October a bit cold for swimming around here."

"Fair point, well made, Inspector." Anderson offered a quick grin.

"I'm going to ask around and see if I can get a bead on an ID. Do you have a number I can get you on in case I get something?" Kate asked.

"Sure." Anderson quickly recited the number as Kate tapped it into her phone before tucking it back into her pocket. "Thanks. I'll let you get on, Doctor. See you at the morgue later."

"Thanks."

"No problem." Kate ducked her head as she left the tent and spent a couple of minutes looking around, memorising as many details as she could, while Timmons answered his phone. She wanted to be able to remember everything she could see and feel, every sound and smell. What was the victim doing out here? Walking the dog? Who was she? Local? Kate had to assume that was likely. Most of the cars parked in proximity to the path access were patrol vehicles, an ambulance, and her own car. Not a single driving visitor, so the victim must have lived, or was staying, within walking distance. How many "Connies" were there going to be in this village with a dog like the one they'd found with the body?

The doctor closed up the back of the van and waved as she climbed into the front seat. Kate looked over at the petrol station, lights shining brightly, cars moving on and off the forecourt. She grabbed her phone and clicked a quick picture of the dog before sending the PCSO off with her. No harm in trying a couple of things while she waited for the vet to get information from the dog's chip, right?

Across the road was a row of shops, a cafe, as well as the petrol station with a convenience store inside. She'd eaten breakfast at the cafe just a couple of days ago. Nice bacon, free-range eggs, and strong coffee. It'd be worth a return visit in the near future.

Kate looked back over at Timmons, who was still on the phone and gesticulating wildly. She gestured at him and when she caught his attention, indicated that she was heading over to the shops and she'd be back in ten minutes. He nodded. Then she crossed the road, went into the petrol station, and walked straight up to the cashier. "Hi, I'm wondering if you can help me."

The young woman behind the desk popped a big bubble and nodded. "Sure."

Kate showed her the picture of the dog. "Do you know this—"

"How've you got a picture of Merlin?"

Bingo. "She's been found on the marsh. Do you know who her owner is?"

"Well, yeah. She's Connie's dog. Isn't it on her collar?"

"Connie who?"

"Connie Wells." The girl pointed towards the far end of the shop. "She owns the campsite at the end of the row of shops. She'll be frantic. That dog's about all she cares about." She wiped her woolly-gloved hand under her nose, wrinkling it as she did so.

"You know her well?"

"Used to work for her." She sniffed. "For about three days. Bitch said I wasn't cut out for working with an upper-class clientele, so being her secretary was never going to happen."

"Was that recent?"

"No. About six years ago. When she first took over. I worked for the people who they bought it off."

"They?"

"Her and her girlfriend."

"Right. And they own the business together?"

"Humph. For now."

"Excuse me?"

"Ah hmm."

Kate turned around at the soft cough behind her. An elderly lady with a heavy shopping basket stood waiting. "Oh, I'm sorry." Kate reached for the basket. "Here let me help you with that." She put the basket in the well at the counter. "Thanks for your help," she said to the cashier. "I really appreciate it."

She tucked her hands into her pockets as she exited into the cold air again and turned in the direction the young woman had indicated. The sky-blue and white italic "i" for the information centre was hung above the door, and flashing multicoloured rope lights blazed underneath the sign. She pushed open the door and stepped inside. A poster behind the desk told her she was in the right place. The grey-and-white dog with the blue eyes grinned into the camera while she leaned against the side of a woman with long dark hair, green eyes, a mole on the right side of her neck, and a warm smile. And with the exception of having a face, she looked remarkably like the victim she'd just seen zipped into a body bag.

"Hi, can I help you?" The blonde behind the counter smiled.

Kate flashed her badge. "Detective Sergeant Brannon. Do you recognise this animal?" She showed the woman the picture on her phone.

"Sure, that's Merlin." She pointed to the picture behind the desk. "She's Connie's dog and the campsite mascot. She has her own blog and everything." The woman chuckled.

Without holding out much hope, Kate asked the logical follow-up question. "Is Connie around?"

"No. She hasn't been in yet."

"Is that usual?"

The woman shook her head. "No, not really. She practically lives here, usually."

"Where does she live?"

"Just in one of the cottages on the other side of the farmhouse. Why?"

"How well do you know Connie?"

"Pretty well. I've worked here for two years."

"Seasonally?"

"No, full time."

"And your name is?"

"Sarah. Sarah Willis."

"Are you the manager here?"

"No. That's Gina. I'm just a tourism assistant."

"I see. Is she here?"

"She's in the office."

"I need to speak to her."

"Has something happened?"

"I'm afraid so. Please, can you ask Gina to come talk to me?"

"Of course." Sarah picked up a small handheld radio and pushed the button. "Hi, Gina, can you come down to reception, please?"

A short crunch of static before a soft voice said, "On my way."

"Thank you."

"What's happened?"

"I'm afraid I'm investigating a suspicious death. This dog was found with the victim."

"Oh, my God. What happened? What victim? Connie?"

"That's what I'm trying to find out."

She frowned. "I don't understand." She pointed to the photograph. "This is Connie. Was it her or not?"

"Are you aware of any identifying feature that Connie has?"

"Like what?"

"A tattoo, maybe. A scar. Something like that."

"She had an operation last year," someone else said.

Kate turned towards the back door. A woman had one hand holding the handle of the door and the other stuffed deep in the pocket of a down-filled jacket. Shoulder-length dark hair peeked out from under a red beanie hat, and wide blue eyes stared at her.

"Where?"

"Appendix."

"Thank you. Are you Gina?"

"Yes. Georgina Temple. And you are?" She offered her hand.

"Detective Sergeant Kate Brannon." Kate took the proffered hand, her fingers wrapping securely around warm flesh as a jolt of electricity radiated between them. A tingle ran up her arm and her gaze locked onto beautiful eyes. They reminded her of the sea the last time she'd been holidaying on one of the Greek islands. She shook her head, aware that she was still holding onto her hand. "Thank you for coming."

"No problem."

"Can you excuse me for one moment? I just need to relay that information." Kate held her phone up.

"Of course."

Kate quickly pressed the buttons and asked for Dr. Anderson.

"You caught me just as we stopped, Detective. What can I do for you?"

"I have a possible ID on the victim."

"Fast work."

"Distinctive pooch."

"So distinguishing features, right? What am I looking for?"

"Appendectomy scar."

"Hold on."

Kate heard the sound of a zipper and rustling as the doctor checked.

"Yep, got one. Probably about twelve months ago, I'd say. So who is this?"

"I believe she's Connie Wells."

"I'll proceed accordingly. Keep me updated if you find anything different and I'll be starting the autopsy at two. If you can get me anything for a DNA comparison, that'd be good."

"Understood." She disconnected and turned back to Georgina. "Sorry about that."

"Connie's dead?" Georgina's hands trembled.

Not going there until the next of kin's notified...and we have a definitive ID, of course. "I'm sorry, but I can't comment on that right now." *Like she's going to swallow that line of crap.*

"I'll take that as a yes."

See? Sometimes Kate hated the procedures that went along with her work. But they were there for a reason. Well, some of them were. Georgina's face paled and she seemed to sway backwards a little. Just enough to make Kate think she was going to collapse on her. Kate saw a chair positioned at a computer terminal. "Please, sit." She turned the chair and gently guided Georgina towards it. "Miss Temple, I'm really sorry, but I do need to ask you some questions. Is it possible to close the shop for a little while, or can we go somewhere more private?"

"I'll lock up," Sarah said and scurried around the desk, fishing a key from her pocket as she did.

Kate focused on Georgina. The tall, willowy brunette sat shivering in the chair. Her eyes downcast, tears welled and slipped easily down her cheeks. "She was a good friend of yours?" Kate asked.

Sarah sniggered. Kate glanced over her shoulder.

"Yes," Georgina said. "We'd worked together since she moved here. We became friends over the years."

"I'm sorry."

"Thank you." Georgina's voice was quiet, the tremble distinct.

"Do you mind answering some questions for me?"

She shook her head. "Anything. What happened to her?"

"That's what I intend to find out. Was Connie often out on the marshes in the early hours? Around sunrise time?"

"Yes. High tide was early today. Seven, I think. And sunrise not long after, she'd have been out there today. Walking Merlin, maybe taking pictures if it looked like it was going to be a nice morning."

"There wasn't a camera with her."

Georgina shrugged. "Maybe the light wasn't good." She pointed to some of the pictures hanging on the walls. "They're all hers. The postcards too."

Kate looked at the beautiful landscapes, colourful sunsets and sunrises over the marshes, boats on the water, birds in flight, a beach with half-rotted posts sticking out of the sand, rocky outcrops, and a windmill poking out of the mist looked down at her. "She was very good."

"Yes."

"Did she usually walk alone?"

"Yes, just with Merlin."

"I understand she owns the campsite with her girlfriend. Is she here?"

Sarah snorted. "Not bloody likely."

Georgina shot her a look. "I'm afraid this is probably the last place you'll find Leah right now."

"Leah?"

"Leah Shaw. Connie's ex."

"Ah."

"Yeah." Georgina flicked her eyes up to Sarah and back to Kate. It seemed as if she didn't want to air Connie's dirty laundry to the staff. Fair enough. "Do you have a key to Connie's home?"

"Yes. There's a spare set in the office," Georgina answered. "Why?"

"I need to locate something with her DNA on it. A hairbrush or toothbrush, something like that. Would you mind taking me to her house?"

"Of course. I'll go and get the keys."

"Thank you."

Kate watched Georgina leave.

Sarah cleared her throat. "Can I get you anything, Detective?"

"I'm fine, thank you." Kate smiled. "Was Ms Wells a good boss?"

Sarah shrugged. "I've had better, had worse. You know?"

Kate nodded. She'd learned over the years that often keeping quiet and letting other people fill the silence was more illuminating than asking questions, so she waited. She didn't have to wait long.

"She was planning to leave." Sarah spun her finger in the air, indicating the entire information centre. "She wanted to sell up and go back to where she came from, but she wasn't going to wait until it sold. She was going to close up after the October school holidays were finished. End of this week." She sighed and sat down. "She'd have closed and gone ages ago though if we hadn't already had bookings in for the holiday."

"What happens to you when this place closes?"

"Out of a job. Get lost, goodbye." She shrugged. "It's not much, but you know, some of us live here too."

"What do you mean?"

"I'm onsite staff. I live in the hostel as well as work here."

"So you don't have anywhere to live either?"

"Not unless I go back to my mum and dad's."

"Is it just you?"

Sarah frowned.

"Living in?"

"Oh, no. There's William, Rick, and Emma too. Rick and Emma will probably go to Rick's parents. They've got some caravan or something in the garden that they'll move into. It's William I feel really sorry for."

"Why?"

"He's got no one. He's literally going to be living on the streets when she closes—I mean when she was going to close this place."

"Wow. He can't find something else?"

"He's trying." She shrugged. "He's not had much luck."

"Sounds like it'll be rough for him."

"Yeah."

"What'll happen now?"

She shrugged. "No idea. I guess it's up to Leah." She rolled her eyes. "She'll probably keep it open. Leave Gina in charge of everything."

"How come?"

She glanced from side to side and dropped her voice. "She didn't want to sell in the first place, but Connie holds—held—the purse strings. Nothing Leah could do about it. She put up the money for them to buy this place in the beginning."

Kate frowned as the door opened and Georgina walked back in.

"Shall we?"

"Sure. Thanks for your help, Sarah."

"My pleasure. If you need anything else, you know where to find me."

She smiled and followed Georgina out of the door.

CHAPTER 2

Gina checked the road before leading Kate across the driveway.

"What's the story with Leah?" Kate asked.

Gina glanced at her and pushed her hands deeper into her pockets. "You don't waste any time."

"We both know I'm trying to find out how your friend died. Do you want me to waste time?"

"No, I guess not." Gina fought back the tears that threatened to fall again, instead focusing on the sticky subject that was Leah and Connie's relationship. "Well, it wasn't a good break-up."

"Is there such a thing as a good one?"

She snorted a short laugh. "Good point."

"What was so bad?"

"Connie didn't tell me everything. She said she couldn't deal with Leah's crap any more. That she was sick of bailing her out."

"What did she mean by that?"

Gina shrugged. "I don't know."

"You've worked with her as long as Connie, right?"

"Yes."

"So give me your opinion."

She sighed and turned the corner. "Fine. Leah was always the more...rash of the two of them. Hot headed, quick tempered, you know?"

Kate nodded.

"She never seemed happy either. Always needed more. Bigger, better, more than everyone else."

"Sounds like a prize."

"She was also creative, generous, friendly, and much more of a people person than Connie ever was. They complemented each other in a lot of ways. Compensated for each other's weaknesses."

"So what happened?"

"How do you mean?"

"I mean, you're right, everyone has their strengths and weaknesses, but if they complemented each other, something had to change to split them up?"

"I guess so." Gina didn't want to go into depth about her suspicions as to why Connie had finally thrown Leah out. Her suspicions were just that anyway, suspicions. Connie had never actually told her what had happened, what had finally been the end of the road. The detective would speak to Leah and be able to form her own opinion. It's not like Leah can hide her problems anymore.

Gina led her up the garden path and unlocked the door to the three-bedroom semi-detached house. Like many in the area, they had been built for farm workers more than a century before, and the flint and limestone walls of the traditional building style had always reminded her of the sandcastles she'd built as a child, decorating them with shells and pebbles. "This is...was...Connie's house."

"Thank you, Miss Temple."

"Gina. Only my daughter's teachers call me Miss Temple, and I'm sure that's to remind everyone I'm not married."

Kate smiled and Gina was struck by how it changed her face. The deep frown line on her forehead smoothed out and a dimple creased her right cheek. Wisps of auburn hair curled gently around her jaw and green eyes shone with apparent mischief as she pulled her lower lip between her teeth.

"Biting your lip, Detective?"

"Better than my tongue."

"Really? And what is it you don't want to say?"

"If I was going to tell you, I wouldn't be biting my lip. So, tell me about Connie."

Gina arched her eyebrow and waited. Kate mirrored her expression and cocked her head to one side.

Christ, she looks damn sexy like that. And that's not even counting the leather jacket. "Fine." Gina caved. "Connie was fastidious, quite shy and quiet until you got to know her, and she was pretty difficult to get to know." She took a picture off the mantle shelf and held it out to Kate, sucking in a quick breath when their fingertips brushed, and heat shot through her body. Again. "That's her." Her voice sounded breathless to her own ears, and she could hear her own heartbeat pounding inside her skull. *Jesus, what's going on with me?*

"Sarah said she was going to close it down and sell up?"

"That was her plan."

"Why?"

"During the winter, a business like this haemorrhages money. Between utility bills and wages, it loses thousands over the winter period. By closing, you minimise some of that. Since she wanted to sell it on, she saw no reason to suffer the loss. By closing, she'd cut wages and bills to practically nothing, she'd only have to cover rates and whatnot. By the time the new owners took it on, it'd be after Christmas and the place starts to earn its keep again."

"But surely it's worth less when it's closed."

"Grey area with a seasonal business. But it was more than worth any potential loss to her."

"Why?"

"She said to maintain her sanity."

"Where was she planning to go?"

"She wanted to go to the Lake District. Somewhere around Keswick, she said. Buy a little cottage, sell her pictures to make ends meet."

"Does she have family up there?"

"No. Her gran passed away about six or seven months ago. She was the only family Connie ever talked about. I think her passing had a profound impact on Connie. She was never the same after that."

"How so?"

Gina licked her lips as she thought of how her friend had changed all those months ago. Naturally reserved, Connie seemed to crawl inside herself even more. Getting her to talk was like trying to get blood from a stone, and she couldn't remember once seeing her cry. She knew that Connie's gran had raised her from being a young child. She was more mother than grandmother to her, but Gina couldn't remember one occasion where she'd seen Connie grieving. It was like she was numb instead, or maybe there was just too much pain for her to process. "She shut down, really. I think it was then that her relationship with Leah really started to fall apart. I think she gave up on her."

"Depression? With the grief?"

"I think so. But she'd never got to the doctor to get help. By the time she came out of it, or started to figure her own problems out," Gina said with a shrug. "Leah was lost to her."

"In what way?"

"She refused to say." She kept her fingers crossed that Kate would move on to her next topic, because Leah and her newfound hobby was not something Gina wanted to talk about in any way.

"How big an impact would the closure have on the village?"

"Over the winter? Minimal. If it stayed closed, it would be huge. The village of Brandale Staithe has forty year-round residents." She shook her head. "Thirty-nine now. It has two pubs, two clothes shops, a cafe, a grocery shop, garage, a post office, fish mongers, two chandleries, and a gift shop. With the best will in the world, thirty-nine people cannot sustain those businesses. During the season, the houses that sit empty fill up with tourists and the village population swells to four hundred."

Kate whistled. "That's a huge difference."

"Yeah, but the campsite holds six hundred people per night. Without the income from the tourists, none of those businesses could sustain themselves throughout the winter. If the campsite were to be closed over one season, the impact would affect the whole village."

"What were the chances of the business being sold over the winter?"

"Well, Connie had a buyer lined up already. But Leah managed to wreck that. Leah doesn't want to sell, so I guess the chances weren't great." She could practically see the thoughts whirling around Kate's head. Motive, motive, motive.

"Sarah said that Connie held the purse strings and Leah didn't have a say in the selling of the business."

Gina sighed. "That's true. On paper, everything was in Connie's name. Leah had some financial problems in the past. She didn't go into details, but I think she'd been made bankrupt at some point. Connie had inherited money when her father died years ago. She used it to buy this place, but because of Leah's history it was only ever Connie's name on the paperwork. Leah couldn't legally stop her selling, even though she wanted to."

"How did Leah wreck the deal then?"

"She sent letters to the buyer telling them that she was suing for half the business and that it was going to be tied up in court until the matter was settled. She managed to make it sound as though she had a case, which she legally didn't, and they'd get embroiled in it all if they bought." She shrugged. "She made it unattractive enough to them to back out. Connie was livid."

"How many people knew Connie was selling?"

Gina laughed. "Everyone did. Leah told everyone in the pub weeks ago. And I'm sure you know what it's like in a small village."

"Yeah, she may as well have put an advert in the parish news or something."

"Exactly."

"Do you have another job lined up?"

Gina shook her head. "No, Connie was keeping me on to keep things ticking over when she left and meet with prospective buyers. Show them round, the books, etc. Then hopefully stay on with the new owners."

"You live close by?"

"Next door." She pointed to the adjoining house.

"Handy for work."

"Yeah. And for Sammy's school."

"Your daughter?"

"Yes. She's nine. She goes to Brandale Primary School."

Kate nodded and glanced around the room. "You mind if I just have a look around?"

"No, not at all."

"Thanks." Kate left the room and Gina heard her talking, presumably on her phone, requesting people to come and secure and search the property.

She looked around. The fire was laid, ready for Connie to light it when she got home later that evening. A habit Gina had often teased her about, but Connie had told her how much she loved curling up in front of the fire, Merlin settled against her side, head on her lap, while she read one of her books. The snap and crackle of the twigs soothing her after a day dealing with disgruntled locals, or tourists, sometimes both. She ran her finger over the spine of the book that was set open across the arm of the chair. The overstuffed, cream leather acting as book mark instead of a turned corner, or the scrap of paper that Gina usually used. It was the new one that she'd gotten in the post just yesterday. Marian Keyes. She'd promised Gina she would lend it when she'd finished it.

"Oh, Connie." Tears spilled over her eyelids and she quickly swiped them away. She sat down and stared about her, unable to take in the details of a room she knew almost as well as her own. She'd lost count of the number of nights she'd sat on the sofa, the two of them putting the world to rights with the aid of a nice bottle of Shiraz, or just a bottle if the nice one wasn't on sale. Connie had been the first person Gina had confided in when she'd finally accepted she was gay. She smiled as she remembered how Connie had wrapped an arm around her shoulder, poured more wine in her glass, and told her women were fucking crazy and she'd best remain single. Made life simpler, she'd said. She already had the kid and a cat, what more did any rural lesbian really need?

Gina chuckled through her tears.

"Something funny?" Kate asked, as she wandered back into the room.

"Just remembering a conversation with Connie from years ago." She smiled sadly.

"Care to share?"

"She'd been here about eighteen months then. We were friends, but I was kind of holding her at arm's length. Heck, I was holding everyone at arm's length. Always did, I suppose. But I knew I could trust her, so I'd decided to tell her something that I haven't told anyone before or since."

"Sorry, I didn't mean to pry into the happy memories of your friendship. It's just that I have no idea right now what is pertinent and what isn't."

For some reason Gina trusted her too. She waved away Kate's concern. "It's okay. I don't think you're going to go blabbing to all and sundry."

"No, I listen far more than I talk," Kate said.

"Well, I bit the bullet and came out to her." Gina grinned. Saying it again after so many years felt...weird. Kinda naughty in a sexy sorta way. *Gina, you make no fucking sense.* "Anyway, we got drunk. Damn good bottle of Rioja, if memory serves, and I told her I was gay. She told me that women are crazy and it's simpler to stay single."

Kate chuckled. "She might be right."

Gina laughed. "Well, well, well. Another gay in the village, what will the vicar say?"

"More tea?" Kate sniggered.

"Oh, my God. I refuse to be pulled into rehashing Monty Python sketches."

"But they're classics. Besides, how do you know the vicar isn't one of us?"

"Because I know his wife. Scratch that. That would be enough to turn anyone homosexual." She gasped and clasped her hand over her mouth, wishing she could pull back in the uncharitable words.

Kate burst out laughing. "No, no, don't hold back. Tell me what you really think, Miss Temple."

"Oh, that was awful. I'm so sorry."

Kate waved her hand. "Don't be." She tapped the side of her head. "Note to self, stay on Temple's good side."

Gina giggled and found herself unable to stop. Every time she looked at Kate, the bubbles of laughter rippled up again and erupted from her lips. She knew it was a form of shock, some sort of hysteria, but try as she might, she couldn't stop herself. She covered her eyes and rested her elbows on her knees, trying hard to quell the ridiculous urge. "I'm sorry. That's so inappropriate, I don't know what came over me."

"Miss Temple, I've seen people react in pretty much every way possible to the death of a loved one. Anger, denial, hatred, uncontrollable weeping, running away, screaming, you name it. Now I can add giggles to my list. And I've got to tell you, this is by far one of my favourites." She held up two plastic bags, one with a hairbrush in, the other a toothbrush. "I need to get these over to King's Lynn and I need to secure this house before I leave. Can I walk you home?"

"I only live next door."

"I know. That's why I offered. Not far to go."

"Thanks, but I'm sure I can manage." Gina hauled herself to her feet and pulled open the front door.

"Do you happen to know where I could find Leah Shaw?"

"Of course. She's staying with Ally the Cat."

"Excuse me?"

"Oh, sorry. Ally Robbins. We call her Ally the Cat for several reasons."

"Which are?"

"One, she's a tramp who'll sleep with anything that doesn't say no. You know, like a nasty, old tomcat?"

"Right, got it. And?"

"She doesn't like cats. She shoots a pellet gun from her bedroom window at any that go in her garden, so they don't kill the birds."

"You're joking?"

"I wish I was. Half the village had to stop letting their cats out."

"Where does she live?"

"Other end of the village, two down from the entrance to the harbour."

"Okay, thank you, you've been a great help."

"No problem. Anything I can do. Connie was my best friend."

"Can I get your number? I'm sure I'll have lots more questions."

"Oh, sure." Gina quickly recited the number, as Kate scribbled it down in her note pad. "Again, I'm really sorry about the giggles before. I'm sure it's shock or something."

"Don't worry about it." Kate glanced at her watch. "I've really got to go now. See you again, Miss Temple."

"You too, Detective." Gina pulled open her front door and watched Kate turn up the collar on her jacket and head back to where she was no doubt parked. Head down, shoulders braced, she walked into the wind, her black jeans clinging to her tight arse, and tucked into a pair of soft leather boots. Damn sexy.

CHAPTER 3

Timmons was buckling his seatbelt when Kate arrived back at the entrance to the Coastal Path.

"Anderson said you were getting DNA samples," he said out of the window.

"I've got them." She held up the sealed bags.

"Excellent work, Brannon."

"Thanks. Problem?"

"Yes. I've got another crime scene."

"Related to this one?"

He shook his head, frowning. "Unlikely, but I've got three dead girls in the middle of King's Lynn, possibly drug related. I'll know more when I get there." He handed her a piece of paper with three names and telephone numbers on it. "This is the rest of the team that was going to work this case with us. Stella Goodwin is an experienced sergeant. I'm putting her as lead on this, but you'll both report directly back to me. I'm still SIO, but I can't be in two places at once."

She got it. Three dead bodies versus one. Town centre versus the middle of nowhere. Politics and money. If he wanted to keep his current level of funding for King's Lynn's Criminal Investigation Department, he needed to play the political game and keep the powers that be sweet.

"Goodwin's good." He winked at her. "You'll do all right." He put the car in gear and pulled away from the kerb.

"Right." Kate glanced down at the page in her hand. It was a massive opportunity for her to show what she could do. Huge. *Better not fuck it up, then.* She ran her fingers through her wet hair and jumped back in her car. She turned west out of the cul-de-sac heading towards King's Lynn and the mortuary.

The Queen Elizabeth Hospital at King's Lynn was a sprawling mass of two-storey buildings hastily erected in the late 1970s, and first opened its doors in 1980. Prefabricated walls, with pasty yellow panels, loomed over her as she walked through the main doors and navigated her way down long corridors towards the mortuary. As always, the very thought of where she was going did more to make her skin crawl than the actual act she was preparing herself to witness. The fact that she knew—well, suspected—who she would see on the slab now, made it more important that she find out what happened. She wanted to give Gina that peace of mind.

She buzzed the intercom to gain access to the mortuary and took what would be her last deep breath for a while before she pushed open the door.

"Detective, right on time. No Timmons?" Dr. Anderson stood over the steel table, the body laid out, naked and ready for the post-mortem.

"No. He's been called to another crime scene."

"The dead girls in Lynn?"

Kate nodded.

"Like buses."

Kate frowned. "Excuse me?"

"Murders. Haven't had one round here for bloody ages. Now we get four in a day." She picked up her scalpel and set it poised in her hand. "Like buses." Dr. Anderson must have decided to forego any further pleasantries, as she set to work with her blade. She was efficient, methodical, practiced. Each stroke of her hand was mesmerising in its clinically horrific dissection, every cut reducing Connie from human being to a collection of evidence. Every organ weighed transformed her from person to cadaver before Kate's eyes. More than the sight of the blood, it was this that made Kate feel queasy—the dehumanisation of a woman who had lived and breathed, loved and laughed just a few hours before.

Kate hated this final act of desecration. Intellectually, she knew they needed to know everything they could possibly learn from the body. Every miniscule iota of information could make the difference between understanding what had happened to Connie and failing her again. But emotionally, she felt the violation of the victim deep in her soul. This may be her first big opportunity to show what she was really capable of, but it wasn't the first suspicious death she'd worked. It wasn't the first autopsy she had been a part of. And she suspected she'd never feel any differently about it. A part of her even wondered if she'd want to. Wouldn't that be more worrisome? Wouldn't lack of feeling, empathy, connection to the victim she was trying to find justice for be more of an issue for her?

Techs had long since taken the hair and toothbrush from her to begin harvesting DNA for comparison, to make sure, once and for all, that this was the body of Connie Wells, but Kate was in no doubt. She could see the small mole on the victim's neck that she'd seen in the photograph on Connie's mantelpiece, and the necklace that had been around her neck was now sitting in an evidence bag on a steel table along the wall on the other side of the room. The distinctive downward-pointing triangle, with stones around the perimeter representing the rainbow flag, hung on a leather thong that had been tied around her neck. Perhaps there was some story behind it, some significance for Connie—besides the rainbow insignia—some meaning. A gift, maybe?

"Any idea yet what it is that's in the wound, Doctor?" Kate asked when the preliminaries of the autopsy had been completed.

"Let's take a look." She pulled on magnifying glasses and gripped a pair of tweezers. Digging into the mangled flesh, she managed to fish out a few particles of something hard. Even Kate could see that they weren't bone fragments.

Light reflected off the part of the surface that wasn't covered in blood, refracting the light and casting a tiny prism onto the white floor.

"Glass?"

"Apparently." Anderson placed several particles into a petri dish, then sealed and labelled it before retrieving another sample and placing it on a slide.

"Can you tell what it's from? I don't remember seeing any broken bottles at the scene."

Anderson pushed the slide under the microscope and adjusted the lenses. "The glass does have a slight tint to it, perhaps some sort of UV coating."

"Sunglasses?"

"Mmm. Maybe, maybe not. It doesn't look that dark to me and it wasn't exactly sunny at the crack of dawn this morning. I can't see why anyone would be wearing sunglasses at seven a.m. in October in England."

"Fair point." Kate acceded.

Anderson looked up and nodded to the petri dish. "We'll get that off to analysis, find out exactly what the glass came from."

Kate nodded. "Anything else?"

"No. She was a fit, healthy young woman. Cause of death was a single gunshot wound to the head and it would have been instantaneous."

"Could it have been accidental?"

"Well, anything is possible, I suppose. But frankly, I don't see how. The weapon used was a high-powered rifle. Without knowing what interfered with the bullet's trajectory, I can't really get you a range or angle, or even where to look to retrieve the round, as it isn't in the skull. I'd suggest the water, but let's face it, pulling a bullet fragment out of that would be like tracking down dobbyhorse shit, if you'll pardon the language. The water looks like my coffee in a morning, but doesn't smell half as good."

"So, even if I find a gun, you won't be able to match it?"

"Not right now, no."

Kate sighed and regretted it as the acrid smell of formaldehyde and blood invaded her nostrils. "How long for the DNA results?"

"Tomorrow, lunchtime. I should have analysis on the glass by then too."

"Great, thanks."

"Now, I get to go play with a sleeping dog."

"Have fun. What'll happen to the dog afterwards?"

"Don't know. Does she have any family to take the dog?"

"As far as I know, she lived alone, recently broken up with her girlfriend, was getting ready to up sticks and move on in a couple of weeks."

"Well, if the ex doesn't want the dog, then it'll probably end up going to a shelter."

Kate shook her head. "Poor thing."

"You want to watch this?"

"Nah. I think I'll go and pay a visit to said ex and see if she wants the dog. If she didn't kill her girlfriend, of course."

"Of course." Anderson winked at her. "Later, Detective."

Kate pushed open the door and headed for the exit. She knew she was grinning, but what the hell. Flirty pathologists did that to her. She stopped at the hospital cafe for a coffee and managed to beat the parking attendant to her unticketed car. She pulled out of the parking bay while still pulling her seatbelt across her body and slipping her cup into the holder in the centre console, sloshing hot liquid over her hand.

"Shit."

"Serves you right." The parking attendant shouted through the glass.

"Yeah, yeah," she whispered under her breath. "Bite me." She shook the last drops of coffee from her hand and picked up her Bluetooth earpiece, hitting the speed dial on her phone as she flicked the stem over her ear.

"Timmons."

"Sir, I've just come out of the autopsy and I'm heading back to Hunstanton now, to get the ball rolling with the team."

"Anything interesting at the autopsy?"

"Massive head trauma from a single gunshot is COD as we knew, Anderson found something in the wound. Looks like glass, but there wasn't anything at the scene that fit. No broken bottles, sunglasses, or anything. She's sent it for analysis."

"Do you have a definitive ID yet?"

"Awaiting DNA results."

"Due in?"

"Tomorrow, lunch time."

"Okay, until then?"

"I'm working on the victim being Connie Wells. Local business owner, recently ended a relationship, was closing down her business that was one of the most influential in the local area."

"So, a number of potential suspects already."

"Yes, sir."

"Good work. Next step, Brannon?"

"Check in with the team at our incident room, and then I want to talk to the ex."

"Good. Goodwin's expecting you. I want you and her to work as a team. Like I said before, she's experienced. She's also bloody efficient, and good with the details, the paperwork, running the books, and organising the facts. I want you out on the ground. You've seen the scene, you've already got a bead on the vic, and potential suspects. That's good work, that's fast. Keep it up and keep me informed. Take Jimmy Powers with you, and I've got another PC who'll be with you this afternoon to partner up with DC Brothers by the name of Collier."

She could hear scratching and rustling down the line. Like he was searching through the pages of a book for the information. "Newbie. That's why I want him with Brothers. This is his first case."

"Got it." *You don't want the newbie DC with the newbie DS.*

"Just don't let him fuck up."

She chuckled and read the warning for herself in the words. "I won't."

"You'll all be fine. Good people, all of 'em."

"I'm sure, sir. Thank you." She hung up.

The A149 followed the length of the coast from King's Lynn to Cromer—sixty miles of open skies, blue seas, and sandy beaches to the left of her. Well, on a good day it was. Today wasn't a good day. Today was a day of tractors, non-stop drizzle, and brown-grey water that looked as inviting as dysentery. The twenty-odd miles to Hunstanton dragged by slowly, and Kate tapped her fingernails on the steering wheel as she inched forward.

She pulled into the car park at Hunstanton Police Station and turned off her engine. She swallowed the last mouthful of her coffee as she opened the door, and tossed it into the rubbish bin just inside the door. She tried to shake off her impatience and restlessness and smiled at the desk officer.

"DS Bran…"

"Brannon, I know." He smiled and offered his hand. "I'm PC Noble. Inspector Savage told me to expect you. The rest of your team are upstairs setting up the incident room."

"Thank you."

"You're welcome, ma'am." He pointed to a door. "Stairs are right over there. I'll buzz you through."

She nodded and pushed open the door when she heard the raucous buzzing. The solid metal rail was cold beneath her hand and her boot heels clicked against the concrete stairs, but she could hear noise and banter ahead of her. Her team. Well, sort of. Shared…ish. Okay, so it was mostly Goodwin's team, but she was of equal rank and this was her first real opportunity to step up and prove herself. At any point, Timmons could step in and actively control it all, but his priority had to be elsewhere right now. Three dead girls in the town centre. Most of King's Lynn CID was going to be tied up with that investigation. She could ask him to step in if she didn't think Goodwin was up to it and she couldn't carry the load. But she knew it'd be a cold day in hell before she did that. If she could get a quick solve on this one, she'd show them she had what it took to go all the way. Inspector, chief inspector, superintendant, chief super. Fuck it, why not commissioner while she was at it?

Oh, shut up and focus on what you're doing before you fuck it up already.

She pushed open the door and looked around at their new incident room. The room was long and narrow, maybe ten feet wide and fifteen feet long. A guy in his late twenties, floppy dark hair obscuring his face, was busy setting up monitors at one desk, the other monitors already in situ. A blonde woman sat at one of the fully operational stations, diligently working away at what Kate assumed was the murder book. It was a detailed account of the investigation they would carry out, a catalogue of every decision made, why they made it, and what result it netted them. As far as Kate was concerned, the woman was writing the Bible.

A squeak drew Kate's attention to the whiteboard that was suspended on the wall at the end of the room. The final member of the team was shaking a pen and trying to get enough ink to the tip to get it to write, but all it did was play a tune.

"Stella, you got another pen hiding somewhere?" he asked the blonde woman.

"Tons of 'em, chick. Want a pink one?" Stella asked.

"Ha bloody ha—" He stopped short at seeing Kate. "Sergeant, didn't hear you come in."

The young guy setting up the monitors straightened up, cable in his hand, and banged his head on the underside of the table. "Ow." He rubbed the spot and scrunched up his face.

"Well, you were all hard at it," Kate said.

The man with the pen problem tossed the dried-up pen in the rubbish bin and strode across the room, hand extended. "I'm DC Brothers. Tom." He smiled warmly, his strong features creased with the signs of a lot of time spent in the outdoors, and a faint hint of tan lines around the eyes. She couldn't stop herself from thinking that he looked a little like a panda in reverse. "The lad over there's Jimmy."

Jimmy, still rubbing his scalp, held out his hand. "DC Powers." He was tall, with a wiry, long-legged build that made him look younger than he probably was. Kate had no doubt that the goatee was his way of compensating. At least it was neatly trimmed and well kept. Beards made her itch. Her father had grown one when she was a child, and seeing bits of food stuck in it had made her feel sick.

"Nice to meet you," Kate said.

"Stella Goodwin." Stella got up to greet her.

Kate shook her hand. "Kate Brannon." She looked around the room. "Settling in?"

"Yes, the boys here have made themselves useful, and I think we've got everything we need."

"Excellent. Let me fill you in, then." She grabbed a pen from the pot on Stella's desk and crossed to the whiteboard, quickly giving the details she had and drawing a simple line diagram of the crime scene. "That'll have to do until we get the crime scene photos."

"I've got the tide and sunrise times." Stella read them off, and Kate added them to the diagram.

"We're waiting on DNA confirmation of ID, but given the confirmation of distinctive features, I'll eat my jacket if it isn't Connie Wells."

Chuckles went around the room.

"So, what's the plan of attack, boss?" Tom asked, looking at Stella. She in turn looked at Kate with eyebrows raised, clearly offering her the floor.

"I want to speak to the ex-girlfriend first, and we need to get SOCO round to the victim's house. I left a PCSO at the door and left a message on the number I had for SOCO, but no one's got back to me yet."

"I'll chase that. You head out to the ex's." Stella picked up the phone and punched numbers from memory.

"We need to talk to everyone in the village," Kate said.

"Everyone?" Jimmy asked.

"Yes. Without Ms Wells, there are thirty-nine year-round residents. From what Miss Temple said, every one of them had some reason or other to dislike our victim," Kate said.

"Sure," Tom said, "but not all of them will have had opportunity."

"Exactly. Right now we need to start ruling people out."

"Door to door?"

Kate nodded, still frowning at the board. "Yes, does anyone know Ally the Cat?"

Tom and Jimmy both sniggered.

"I'll take that as a yes. Do you have an address?"

Jimmy passed her a piece of paper, the writing barely legible.

"Why?

"Apparently, Leah Shaw is staying with her."

"Really?" Tom's eyebrows arched. "Didn't think our Ally swung that way too."

"Just because she's staying there, doesn't necessarily mean they're sleeping together," Kate said.

Tom sniggered again. "You haven't met her yet."

"I'll bear that in mind."

"That was Wild," Stella said, hanging up the phone.

Tom let out a shrill wolf whistle. "Number four," he shouted pointing to the ring finger on his left hand and winking at her.

"Fuck off," Stella said, throwing him a caustic look.

"Who's Wild?" Kate asked.

"Head of the forensics team working with us," Stella said.

"Lover boy." Tom whispered loud enough for everyone in the room to hear.

Stella glared at him. "He's a happily married man, fuck wit. He's not interested in me. I'm not interested in him. We work well together, and his wife's lovely. Now get back to bloody work."

"Hmm. What crawled up her arse?" Tom asked and ducked under the pen that was launched at his head. Kate chuckled.

"SOCO'll head over there when they finish at the crime scene. They reckon a couple more hours out there." Stella tossed Kate a card. "Plug that into your phone. Always best to go straight to the organ grinder, and Wild's the best one they've got over there."

Kate fished her phone out of her pocket and added the contact. "They find anything interesting?"

"No. That's why they're sticking with it."

Kate shrugged. "You guys want a lift to the village?"

"I'll stay here and start going over the statements the PCSO's and PC's dropped off," Stella said.

"The walkers who found her?"

"Yes."

"Okay. Timmons said that we'll be getting another body this afternoon. Collier."

Tom and Jimmy groaned.

"Pack it in." Stella warned them. "At least it means you'll outrank someone, Jimmy." She chuckled evilly.

Kate sniggered at the crestfallen yet smug look that slipped onto Jimmy's face. "Right, enough chitchat, ladies. You two with me then." She inclined her head towards the door as the two men followed her, grabbing heavy jackets as they went.

CHAPTER 4

Gina pulled a thick Aran jumper over her head. She couldn't get warm. Her hands felt like blocks of ice, and the hairs on her arms stood on end. She wrapped her arms around herself and chaffed at her biceps. She'd decided to close up for the day, sent Sarah home, and locked the office she had shared with Connie, certain the police would want to see it at some point. *It only makes sense, right?*

She filled the kettle and put it on to boil, hoping that a cup of tea would thaw the chill from her bones. Leaves rustled outside the kitchen window, drawing her attention to the ivy bushes that covered most of her garden shed, something she'd promised to take off several years ago. Now the wood inside was so rotten she was pretty sure that the ivy was the only thing keeping the shed standing. Her garden was long, but relatively narrow. The old wooden shed stood next to the solid brick utility room that extended off the kitchen, and there was a border of shrubs halfway down the garden. Beyond that was almost wild. It was Sammy's playground. She smiled at the thought of her unruly nine-year-old daughter. The thought of having to tell her that Connie was dead made her shiver anew.

Whilst she wouldn't say that Connie and Sammy had been close, there had always been a weird understanding between them. Connie talked to Sammy like she was an adult, and Sammy had always responded to her with a respect she rarely showed anyone else. Connie was the one person in the village that she knew Sammy truly didn't want to piss off. It had been amusing to watch them both together. Both wary but curious.

A shadow crossed the edge of her vision, catching her attention before disappearing. The leaves shook again, but not a breath of wind disturbed the bare branches anywhere else in the garden. *What the hell?*

She went to unlock the back door, only to find it already opened. Her heart pounded. She always locked it and kept the keys on a hook under the cupboard next to the sink. More to prevent Sammy having an easy escape than from fear of anything else. She was sure she'd hear if Sammy had to climb on a chair to get the keys in the night. But they were gone, and hanging in the back door.

What the hell was going on? Connie dead. Her backdoor unlocked. Brandale Staithe was in the middle of a crime wave! She shook her head. She must have forgotten to lock it when she put the bins out or something. Simple as that. Still, she couldn't shake the uneasy feeling and pushed on the handle as quietly as she could. She pulled the door open and listened before she put her head around the door jamb.

More rustling leaves and a scraping sound, like metal rasping against stiff plastic, accompanied a sniffling sound that seemed to be coming from the roof of the lean-to.

"Goddamn it, you piece of shit bastard thing, it's all your bastard bloody fault."

Gina stepped out of the doorway, hands on her hips as she looked up at the roof. "Samantha Temple, get your scrawny little backside down here right now and tell me why you're on the roof using language like that!"

Sammy stared down at her with red-rimmed eyes, tear-stained cheeks, and the most perfect "Oh shit" expression on her face that Gina had ever seen. Even better than Sammy's dad's when she'd told him she was pregnant.

"'S'nuffink, Mum." She wiped her nose on her sleeve while trying surreptitiously to tuck something under the leaves with the other.

"Well, since you're supposed to be in school, you're swearing like a sailor, and you're crying—"

"I'm not crying."

"Okay, while you look upset, I think something is going on. So get down here, with whatever you have there, and tell me."

"I can't."

"Of course you can. I'm your mum, you can tell me anything."

"I can't, Mum."

Gina heard a creak and envisioned the ivy-covered building that Sammy was half on top of giving way beneath her. She held her hand up. "Just give me whatever you were trying to hide." Sammy's face paled and she shook her head. "If you don't, I'm going to have to come up there and get it myself. Then the building will collapse on us both and we'll probably die. Not a good plan. Sammy, sweetheart, what is it?"

Tears rolled down Sammy's cheeks as she buried her face in the crook of her elbow. She said something, but Gina couldn't make it out. She quickly grabbed the ladder from inside the utility room and leaned it up against the lean-to, as far from the shed as she could and still be able to reach Sammy.

When she climbed up, she stayed on the ladder and saw that Sammy was still trying to hide her air rifle. The one her bloody father had given her last Christmas. The child had practically slept with it under her pillow ever since. Gina hated it. Didn't want it in the house to begin with, but Matt was a farmer and had been brought up with guns and rifles his whole life. He saw no harm in taking a nine-year-old out on the marshes with him to hunt rabbits, rats, and God only knew what else. It's only an air rifle, he'd said, can't do any harm to no one. *It will when I fire it straight into your bloody testicles, you stupid piece of shit.*

"Sammy, pass it to me." She held her hand out and smiled reassuringly. Whatever was going on, it was something huge for Sammy to be crying. Her jeans were covered in muck and grime, her coat had a rip down the right arm. Another one, Gina thought. She wiggled her fingers.

Sammy gingerly handled the gun, making sure she handed the butt to Gina and kept the muzzle pointed away from her body.

She's afraid of it. What the hell happened? "Good girl. I'm going to climb down now, and I want you to follow me, okay?"

Sammy nodded. Gina slung the strap over her shoulder and started down the ladder.

"And don't even think about running off, Sammy. We need to talk about this and making me hunt you down will only make it worse."

"Yes, Mum."

Gina put the rifle on the table and pointed to a chair. Sammy sat down, wiping her eyes, her little face looking resigned to whatever her fate would be. Her feet swung as they didn't touch the ground.

"Your dad was supposed to drop you off at school this morning. What happened?" Gina set a cup of tea on the table for herself and a glass of milk for Sammy.

Sammy frowned, obviously wondering why she was being given sustenance before the firing squad. "We got up early and went on the marsh. Dad was on geese duty and he said I could go with him."

"Okay." Gina knew that Matt often took Sammy along in the early morning, setting the scarers going to keep the geese off the crops was far from the worst thing that Matt had ever done with Sammy.

"He said I could take that gun and see if I could catch him something for his tea tonight."

Gina sighed.

"So I went on the Coastal Path so I could walk to school afterwards."

"With your gun? Surely even your father can't—"

"He said he'd meet me at the gate to take it home for me."

"And where was he?"

"Dunno. One of the fields over near Top Wood."

In other words, more than two miles away from where Sammy would be shooting. Gina tried to rein in her anger at Matt's irresponsible attitude. Leaving a nine-year-old unsupervised with a weapon was a recipe for disaster. Christ.

"So what happened?"

"I was trying to get a hare. He said one in stew was good. So I was waiting and waiting, but it wouldn't come close enough for ages. When it did, I got excited and tried to remember everything Dad told me about shootin', but I was too excited. I closed my eyes when I pulled the trigger and I lost the hare." She sniffed and wiped her nose with her sleeve. "But Connie was on the path and she fell down when I pulled the trigger. She fell down the embankment and never came back up." Sammy was sobbing. Her head buried in her hands, elbows resting on the table. "I went to help her. I did. I went right round the path where she was and Merlin was licking her, and whined at me.

But her face was gone, Mum." She looked up with horror-filled eyes. "It was all gone. And I didn't mean to kill her."

Gina swallowed down her revulsion as the image of Connie sans face resolved in her mind. *No wonder that detective couldn't identify Connie from a picture.* "Oh, sweetie, I'm sure it wasn't your fault."

"It was, Mum. There was no one else around. No one at all."

"But your little gun shoots pellets, sweetheart. It can't make someone's face explode."

"It's Dad's gun." She pointed to the rifle on the table. "It's Dad's, not mine."

Gina looked at it and saw that Sammy was right. It wasn't the powerless air rifle she'd gotten used to seeing. It was the .22 rifle that Matt hunted with, not the little plastic air gun that he'd given Sammy. Gina had seen what she expected to see rather than what was really in front of her. *I'll fucking kill him. No wonder he was going to meet her to take it home. I'll wring his scrawny fucking neck and then...* Gina took a deep breath. She needed to be calm, she needed to think clearly. *Oh, fuck.* Sammy killed Connie. She wanted to throw up for the second time that day. Her hands trembled as she pulled Sammy into her arms. *She's nine years old.*

"Then what happened?"

"I went to the school and hid near the gate to wait for Dad." A shadow of anger crossed her face.

"He didn't turn up?"

Sammy shook her head. "So I walked home."

Jesus. What next? "Sammy, it's miles."

"I know. I went the long way too. I didn't want to be on the Coastal Path. I didn't want to go past her again." Sammy sobbed and Gina pulled her into her arms again.

"It's okay, baby. It's okay."

"I didn't mean to, Mum. I didn't mean to."

"I know." She kissed the top of Sammy's head. "It was an accident."

"Yeah."

"This is why I don't like guns. You understand that, right?"

Sammy nodded. "I don't like 'em no more, neither."

"Okay. So no more playing with guns. Ever. Okay?"

"Promise." Sammy sniffed and pulled away. She stared up at Gina, her little blue eyes a replica of Gina's own, so sad, so solemn. "Will I have to go to jail now?"

"No, sweetie. We'll explain what happened and the police will know it wasn't your fault. It was most definitely your dad's fault."

"I shot her, Mum. Not Dad."

"Your dad should never have left you alone with any gun, never mind a dangerous one. The authorities will have a field day with this. They'll stop you from—" *Oh fuck.* They'd stop Matt from seeing Sammy. He'd been negligent to the point of endangering not only Sammy's life but other people's as well. Social Services wouldn't let him see her, the police would charge him—may be even with manslaughter or unlawful death, or whatever it would be called. But whatever they called it, Connie was dead, and Sammy shot her because Matt was an idiot. And she let Matt see Sammy. She knew he was a pillock, and she still let Sammy stay with him. Would Social Services deem her an unfit mother? Would they take Sammy away from her? It was Gina's greatest fear. Losing her daughter. If the authorities got involved— and they would, they had to—they'd say she was a bad parent. Her daughter had just shot someone, after all. They would take Sammy away from her. She pulled Sammy back into her arms. She wasn't going to let that happen. No way. She couldn't help Connie now. She was already dead, but there was no way she was going to risk losing her daughter for it.

"Mum, why are you crying?"

Gina swiped at the moisture on her cheeks, not even realising it was there. "I'm just sad about Connie."

"I'm sorry. I'm so sorry, Mum. I know she was your friend."

"She was. But you're my daughter. I love you. Now, you have to promise me something else, okay?"

Sammy nodded.

"Never, ever, tell anyone what you've told me today. Not your friends, not your dad. No one."

"Not even Dad?"

"Especially not your dad."

"But what if he asks me about his gun?"

"Don't worry about that. I'll take care of it. If anyone asks why you weren't at school today, you were at home, being sick. Okay?"

"But you told me not to tell lies."

"I know, sweetie. And you never, ever, tell lies to me. Promise?"

"Promise."

"But this one time, you have to tell this fib."

"But you said I won't go to heaven if I tell fibs."

"Sammy, this time it's okay, because I said it is." Sammy opened her mouth to object again, Gina put a finger over her lips to quiet her. "I'll take the blame with God."

Sammy's jaw closed so quickly her teeth clicked and she nodded. "Okay. Sick. Puking. Got it."

"Good. Now I have to call the school and tell them why you aren't there, and tell them I forgot to call earlier because of everything that's happened at work today. Go upstairs and get a shower, put your pj's on, and bring your clothes down."

"But why?"

"You're grounded, kiddo. And don't argue with me. You've skipped school, you were up on the roof swearing like a sailor, and shooting a real gun without an adult to supervise. Do I need to go on?"

Sammy's head dropped to her chest. "No."

"Good, now scoot. I need to tell some more lies and hope I can still get into heaven after all this."

Gina watched Sammy walk out of the room with a much lighter step than she'd had earlier. She picked up the phone and called the school, blaming Sammy's tummy bug and Connie's death for her late call and letting them know that Sammy wouldn't be in tomorrow either. Slowly, it was actually starting to sink in. Her daughter, her sweet, mischievous little girl, had accidentally killed her boss, her friend, her confidante. And now she was going to make sure she got away with it.

And maybe, just maybe, I'll kill Matt in the process.

CHAPTER 5

Kate knocked on the door of the small wood-clad building. It had the appearance of an aged shack but she'd seen the wall-to-ceiling windows on the rear side that overlooked the harbour and out to sea. One bedroomed it may be, but like they say, location, location, location. Kate was pretty sure the property was worth at least half a million pounds. She wondered what Ally the Cat did with her life, besides sleep around and shoot a pellet gun towards the marshes, but she'd not thought to ask before Tom had set off to knock on doors and she and Jimmy stood waiting for this one to open.

She could hear scuffling sounds inside, but it seemed no one was heading towards the door. Kate knocked again and listened closer. She could hear muffled swearing, a pitiful groaning, and the sound of breaking glass. But still no answer seemed forthcoming, so she knocked again. This time, she shouted through the door too.

"I'm Detective Sergeant Kate Brannon, and Detective Constable Powers is here with me. I need to talk to you about Connie Wells."

"Fuck off." The voice on the other side of the door was gruff and cracked, like it didn't belong to a person.

Kate snorted, cast a quick glance at Jimmy, and knocked again. Harder. "Not going to happen."

"For fuck's sake." The disconnected voice shouted and the angry sound of furniture scraping across a wooden floor reverberated through the door. The barrier swung away as Kate raised her fist to knock again. Instead, she stood face to face with a very naked, very dishevelled blonde. Her short hair was stuck up at odd angles, and her blue eyes were red rimmed and clearly having trouble focusing as she squinted at the light. The room beyond the door was in darkness. The smell of stale beer, slumber, and morning breath caused Kate to wrinkle her nose slightly as she tried to figure out if it was coming directly from the woman in front of her or farther inside the room.

"What the fuck does the bitch want now?" the woman asked.

"Are you Ally or Leah?"

"Why do you want to fucking know?"

"I'm Detective Sergeant Kate Brannon. This is Detective Constable Powers," she said, waving her hand towards Jimmy, "and we're investigating a murder that occurred on the Coastal Path this morning. Are you Ally or Leah?"

"What the fuck?"

"Don't make me say it again. Ally or Leah?"

The woman stared at her like she was still trying to understand English. "Leah."

"Thank you. Do you think I could come in and you could put some clothes on while we talk?"

She moved away from the door, leaving it open in her wake. "What do we need to talk about?"

"We suspect that the victim was Connie Wells."

Leah dropped to the floor like the pins had been pulled from her knees. "What the fuck?"

Kate mentally shook her head but didn't speak again. Instead, she peered through the dimly lit room and caught a good look at a small empty wrapper of foil on the coffee table next to a mirror and a rolled up £10 note. Well, at least now Kate knew why no one saw her around the campsite and possibly why Connie wanted rid. It also gave Kate reason to have her taken in for questioning. She looked at Jimmy to make sure he'd spotted it too, and wasn't just staring at the very naked woman in front of them. He nodded to indicate he'd seen what she had. Kate grabbed what looked to be a sweatshirt off a chair and flung it at Leah. "Put that on and sit on the sofa."

"You can't treat me like that. You've just told me my partner's dead."

"Ex, Leah. I'm well aware of the fact that your relationship with Connie was over and that the split was far from amicable."

Kate could see the moment the penny dropped and Leah realised that Kate suspected her. Her mouth formed a perfect circle, her eyes widened so much that Kate could see the whites completely surrounding the irises...well, they should have been white. Instead, the bloodshot eyeballs gave her a really freaky appearance.

"Wait a minute—"

"Sit there," Kate said pointing to the sofa, "and start answering my questions."

Leah stared at her, clearly weighing up whether or not trying to incapacitate Kate in some way and make a run for it was a feasible option. Kate squared her shoulders and straightened up to her full height. Not so much to ready herself in case of an assault, more to show Leah that she'd be bloody stupid to even try it. Apparently, Leah saw the folly in her assessment and instead hoisted herself gracelessly onto the sofa, sweatshirt draped over her knees where she picked at the lint that covered the fabric. She ran a hand through her hair and then reached across the coffee table for a pack of cigarettes. She paused as she pulled one from the pack, and Kate knew Leah had spotted the wrapper and mirror when she visibly swallowed and her hand began to tremble.

"That shit's not mine." She put the cigarette between her lips and snatched at the lighter, scraping the dial and flicking the flint, trying to get a flame to appear with hands that shook far too much to be effective.

"Of course it isn't," Kate said, knowing full well they were both lying. She took the lighter from Leah's hand and quickly stroked it to life. "But that doesn't mean you wouldn't have a lot of explaining to do if I took you down to the police station, now does it?"

Leah stared at her, then shook her head as Kate's point seemed to sink in.

Kate held the flame close enough for her to light her cigarette. "So tell me where you were at seven this morning."

Leah looked around her. "Here." She pointed to the sofa. "I was asleep till you woke me up."

"Alone?"

Leah nodded. "Well, probably Ally's upstairs, unless the boat's gone out."

"Boat?"

"Yeah. Ally works on one of the fishing boats out of the harbour."

"Which one?"

"The *Jean Rayner.*"

Kate tossed the lighter back onto the coffee table and strode across the room to the spiral staircase against the back wall. She quickly ran up and poked her head into the single room. It was clearly empty but she crossed to the bathroom just to be sure.

"What time does the boat go out?"

Leah shrugged. "I don't know. They have to make the most of the tide, so I think they usually go out as soon as the water comes into the harbour. About two hours before the high tide. If they're running a short day then they're out no more than four hours. On a long day they won't come back in until the tide's almost out. About a sixteen-hour day."

"I'm guessing they do long days in summer and this time of year they're on shorts. Right?"

"I don't know." She pulled in a long drag. "Probably."

"So if high tide was at seven, the boats should be back in by now."

Leah glanced at the clock on the DVD player under the TV. Almost five. "Yeah. Should be."

"And you've been asleep all day?"

Leah shrugged and blew out a smoke ring. "I've not been sleeping well at night." She flicked her ash onto the table, not even trying for the ashtray. "I've been going through a tough time."

Kate pointed to the empty cans that littered the floor. "Do the sleeping aids not help much, then?"

Leah snorted. "No. Not that it's any of your fucking business."

"Right now, Leah, it is."

"I didn't kill her." Her eyes flicked from Kate to Jimmy, seemingly pleading with each of them in turn. "I didn't."

It was Kate's turn to shrug. "You've got no alibi, you've got a turbulent recent past with the victim, and you've been heard threatening her. Convince me."

"I still loved her."

"More people kill out of a misguided sense of love than hate." As much as it sounded like an oxymoron, it was true. Jealousy, possession, and fear of losing loved ones drove more people to kill than hatred did. Domestic violence, jilted lovers, crimes of passion were all far more commonplace than premeditated acts of violence. It was the disturbing truth Kate had had to face years ago.

"Yeah, well, I didn't do it. She was a bitch, she was doing everything she could to ruin my life, but I wouldn't do that. I couldn't." Leah stubbed her cigarette out on the foil wrapper and ran a hand through her hair again. Her fingers still shook but she seemed much more stable now. More awake. "I loved her. I still love her."

Something niggled at Kate but she couldn't put her finger on it. "Do you have any idea what she might have been doing on the marshes at that time in a morning?"

Leah wiped her face with the back of her hand and shrugged, but Kate thought she saw something. A shadow of...concern, fear perhaps...flickered across Leah's face. But then it was gone. "Walking the dog probably. Maybe taking pictures."

What was that about? She glanced at Jimmy, his frown told her that he, too, had caught the look on Leah's face. "Did you worry about her walking out there so early?"

"What? God no. She's always done that. Taking her bloody pictures."

"Then what?"

"What do you mean?"

"When I asked what she could have been doing out there, you looked scared. Why?"

"I don't know what you're talking about."

"Yes, you do."

"No, I don't. I'm upset. You just told me the woman I love is dead. I'm upset. I'm in shock."

No, you're not. "Right." Kate looked around her again. "Merlin was with Connie at the scene. They're collecting evidence from her and then she'll be released. Do you want to collect her or should I have someone bring her here for you?"

Leah shook her head. "Can't have a pet here. Ally doesn't like 'em."

"Okay." Kate could have predicted this outcome, but it didn't stop her heart aching at the callousness and indifference she saw. *Still loved Connie? My arse. If you did you'd hold onto that dog like it was the last part of her left on this earth.*

"Besides, she was Connie's dog, not mine. She never even liked me."

I wonder why? "So do you want her to be put in a shelter?"

Leah nodded. Not looking up from the grubby looking carpet. "Yeah. That's probably for the best."

"Fine." *Like hell.* "I may need to speak to you again."

"What for?"

"Background information about Connie. So you have to inform me if you're planning to go anywhere." Kate handed her a card. "Will you continue to stay here?"

Leah tossed the card on to the table and nodded. "I've got nowhere else to go."

Kate left her with her head in her hands, elbows braced on her sweatshirt-covered knees. The sobs started as Kate pulled the door closed behind her. Kate couldn't be sure if Leah was her killer or not, but she was damn sure she didn't like the junkie she'd just met. She wondered if she'd always been a user or if this was the change that had caused the breakdown in the relationship. She hadn't bothered to ask Leah, as there was no way she'd get an honest answer. She needed to get those answers from someone else first. Maybe Gina. But if she knew that, why hadn't she mentioned it earlier? She turned right out of the gate as Jimmy pulled it closed behind him, then they turned right again and followed the dirt path down to the harbour. The flat-bottomed boats sat on the mud, the water long gone and yet to return. The *Jean Rayner* sat next to the dock, her light blue hull showing signs of age as the rust ran down one side. The paint was chipped and flaking away, and the wind rattled the chain links and steel cables against the mast and wheelhouse. She looked tired, old, and shabby.

"So what did you make of that?"

Jimmy snorted. "I'll eat your jacket if she's the killer."

"Watch it."

He laughed. "No way would she be able to shoot anyone." He held his hand out in front of him and shook it wildly, grossly imitating Leah's tremor. "No way."

"Accident?"

"In what scenario do you have a junkie, her ex, and a gun out on the marshes at the crack of dawn and a gun accidentally blowing off said ex's face?"

"Stranger things have happened."

"No, they bloody haven't." He laughed again. "Seriously, I think she was right where she said she was. Passed out on that stinking sofa."

"Probably right."

The scent of salt, mud, and diesel hung in the air, making Kate feel slightly green as she wandered past the surprisingly small vessels. Lobster pots were stacked on the dock—ten, twelve high in places—and a conveyor belt ran to a bagging machine on the far side of the dock. Mussels were sorted, tossed, and bagged in quick order as practiced eyes watched, and experienced hands worked tirelessly to prepare the catch for sale. The harbour had the look of old and new smashed together with little regard for the aesthetic appeal of either. Like a city of two halves. Old ramshackle huts with rotten boards and rusted corrugated steel roofs had been patched with new materials, the difference in colour and amount of rust being the main indicators to the work that needed to be done, had been done, and still needed completing. Everything done as quickly and cheaply as possible. A proper, working harbour.

Everyone wore waterproof overalls, wellies, and big heavy coats. Hats obscured faces just as well as the bulky clothes obscured bodies and Kate knew she'd never spot Ally if she were among this crowd. She walked over to the first person she saw.

"I'm looking for Ally."

A wizened, elderly man looked up from the lobster pot he was mending, his agile hands continuing with the intricate knots he was tying, even as he looked her up and down. He didn't stop but nodded towards one of the shacks at the far end with his head. "Second from the end. She's in there."

"Thank you." Kate smiled and turned away as a shrill whistle pierced the air, gaining everyone's attention.

"Ally? Lady here to see ya." The old man's voice was strong and carried across the din of machinery, clanging steel, and the wind as it tore ashore. She nodded her thanks to him and watched as a figure approached from the direction he had indicated.

"Yeah. Who wants me?" The woman was grinning, she was easily in her mid-forties with salt-and-pepper hair sticking out from under her beanie hat. Brightly coloured waterproofs covered what Kate assumed were many layers of warm, bulky clothes, including a pair of full length waders with straps over her shoulders. She was tall, heading for six feet, and broad in the shoulders. More than that, though, the bulk of material made it impossible to tell. She was grinning, but Kate could see that the amusement didn't meet her eyes as she wiped her hands on a rag that looked just as dirty as the meaty hand she held out to Kate.

"Detective Sergeant Kate Brannon. Detective Constable Powers," she said, gesturing at Jimmy.

Ally froze for a split second before grasping Kate's hand and pumping it. "Ally Robbins." She let go and stuffed her hands in her pockets. "What can I do for you?"

"I'm investigating the death of a woman on the Coastal Path this morning. Can you tell me what time you were out on the boat, please?"

"Death? Who's dead?"

"Please, can you answer the question?"

Ally frowned. "Well, high tide was seven so we left just after five. I was here about an hour before that with the lads getting the pots on the boat."

"And what time did you get back in?"

"About nine, maybe five past. I can get the log book if you like."

"That would be great, thank you." Kate wasn't sure what made her want to see it. Maybe just plain curiosity because she'd never seen a ship's log book before, but she agreed before she over thought the impulse. Ally headed towards the boat, and Kate suddenly realised how quiet the harbour had become. Only the wind and the clattering of steel cables against steel masts disturbed the awkward silence that filled the air. She wondered if she'd grown a second head for a moment but knew instead how insular communities like this could be. Anyone unknown was an outsider, and when people worked difficult jobs like these people did, they grew closer than family. They had to rely on each other in the worst of conditions, when their lives were on the line. And here she was questioning one of their own. She was grateful when Ally returned holding out a heavy ledger.

"That's today's entry." She pointed.

"Do you mind if I take a picture of it?"

Ally frowned but nodded her head.

Kate quickly positioned her phone and shot a few pictures to make sure she'd have at least one where you could read the various numbers, shorthand codes, and seemingly nonsensical squiggles. "Are you the ship's captain?"

"No. My dad is. Cedric Robbins." She pointed behind Kate to the old man she'd spoken to earlier.

"Ah, right. And do you all work on the same boat?"

"No. Dad captains, and me and my brother, Adam, work our boat. The rest of these guys work the other boats in the harbour." She pointed her thumb over her shoulder to indicate the eight or nine guys behind her.

"Was it a good catch today?"

Ally smiled, and Kate was struck by the fact that this one seemed genuine. "We met all our targets today." The guy she'd pointed to as her brother, Adam, sniggered as she said this.

"What does that mean?"

"Exactly what I said. We had targets to make today, quotas to reach, and we met them. So, yes, I guess that means you could say it was a good day on the water."

"I understand Leah is staying with you?"

Ally frowned and nodded again. "Yeah, ever since her bitch ex threw her out."

"How long ago was that?"

"Four, maybe five months now."

"That's a long time for someone to crash on your couch."

"Yeah, well, she's got nowhere else to go."

"So, she does sleep on your couch?"

Ally's eyebrow's rose. "Where else would she sleep?"

"With you, perhaps."

"What? Oh, hell no. No offence to her, but I'm not a muff diver. She's a mate. Crashing on the couch. End of story."

"And what's your policy on pets?"

"Hate the fuckers. Allergic."

"I stopped by your house before I came here. Lovely place."

"Thanks."

"I met Leah."

"You mean she was awake?" Adam spoke almost too quietly for Kate to hear, but the look Ally shot his way told Kate that she hadn't missed it either.

"She's going through a rough time."

"I'm sure. You might want to be careful about what your house guests get up to in your home. You could get yourself into a lot of trouble on their behalf."

The look of dark anger that skittered across Ally's features told her that she knew exactly what Kate was talking about. Then it vanished and was replaced by a look of mock innocence. "I'm sure I don't know what you're talking about, Detective."

"Thanks." Kate handed her a card. "I'll be in touch."

"You didn't say who was dead."

"Thanks for your time, Ms Robbins."

Kate and Jimmy walked away and the hushed conversation at her back was too low to hear. The fact that it started as soon as they turned their backs, the look that had swept across Leah's face, the anger that had darkened Ally's...it all told her one thing. There was more going on in this sleepy little fishing village than she had thought.

CHAPTER 6

Gina half filled her glass with delicious looking red wine. She held the bottle up to the light and inspected what was left before pouring the remainder into her glass. There were barely two millimetres to spare.

"Waste not, want not." She slurped noisily at the liquid, determined not to spill a drop, though the task was becoming increasingly difficult. She put the now empty bottle on the floor beside the sofa and leaned back. She held the glass up to the picture on her mantle. It was one of Connie and Sammy playing with a kite on the beach. She'd taken it last summer, and it was one of the few times last year she could remember Connie being truly happy. They'd had a picnic and ventured down to one of the creeks where the seals had a small colony. They'd watched them lazing on the sandbank in the middle of the creek, watching everyone who was watching them. It had been a blissful day.

She couldn't believe Connie was gone. She really couldn't. And she couldn't believe how...who...she swallowed a hearty gulp, determined to forget. Usually, a full bottle of Rioja made her forget her own name, but apparently not tonight. Tonight it made the scene that much clearer so that she could now actually picture her nine-year-old daughter pointing the gun at her best friend and "blowing her away." She shook her head to dispel the image and succeeded only in dispelling wine from her glass to her hand. She cursed as she sucked the drops from her skin.

"What the fuck am I going to do?"

Sammy had seen Connie's body and knew she was responsible for it. She'd seen her dead, face blown off, and she'd no doubt see that image in her head for the rest of her life. Gina could barely imagine the horror. How it must feel to know that she'd done that. *How the hell do I help her come to terms with that?*

She took another large mouthful.

If it weren't for that fucking Matt, Connie would still be alive. How could he be so stupid, so irresponsible, so reckless? How could he put Sammy in danger like that? Did he not even think? "I could fucking kill him. I really could."

She didn't understand how his brain worked. Scratch that, it clearly didn't. And now she had to protect him to protect Sammy. "I will not lose my daughter because you're a fucking dickhead."

Gina polished off the last mouthful in her glass. She knew she was going to regret this in the morning, but right now she didn't care. All she'd wanted was to turn off her head. Epic fail. Momentous fail. Now her whole world was spinning out of control, and the whole world was spinning too. She hated that feeling. As though any moment she was going to fly off into space never to be seen or heard from again. On second thought, she kinda liked that idea.

A soft knock at the door startled her. The sudden jolt causing her to drop the wine glass that she still held in her hand. "Shit." She quickly pulled open the door and waved her guest inside without looking. "I just broke a glass, come in while I grab a dust pan and brush."

She ran to the kitchen and returned in time to find Kate bent over picking up the now broken glass.

"Christ, what an arse."

"Excuse me?" Kate looked over her shoulder before straightening up. Gina paled. *Oh shit, oh shit, oh shit, oh shit.* "Erm...I'm drunk."

Kate smiled. "Really?"

"Yep. Definitely."

Kate chuckled and held up the broken glass. "Bin?"

"I'll take it."

"Oh no, we can't have you drunk and in charge of broken glass. That's a disaster waiting to happen. I might even have to write you up for that one."

Gina cocked her head to one side. "You're taking the piss now."

Kate widened her eyes, a look of mock innocence on her face. "I don't know what you're talking about." She nodded down the hallway.

"Bin in the kitchen, right?" She started down the hall and Gina decided to just go with it. The damage was done. She could feel her cheeks burning. As Kate came back in the room Gina was hit by another round of spinny world. She reached out for the arm of the sofa, but Kate caught her first.

"Careful there." She helped her up and set her safely onto the sofa, before Gina could say a word.

"So, Detective, what can I do you—" Gina frowned and tried again. "What can I for you—" She shook her head.

Kate chuckled again. "Don't worry, I'll come back tomorrow and ask. If I can just ask one thing. It'll be a yes or no answer."

"Yes."

Kate smiled at her and leaned forward on her knees. "Did Connie and Leah split up because Leah's a drug addict?"

Gina nodded.

"Why didn't you tell me earlier?"

"Secret."

"Who's secret? Leah's?"

"No. Connie's."

"I don't understand. Was Connie using drugs too?"

"Connie was using drugs? Really?"

Kate shook her head. "No, that's what I'm asking."

Gina frowned. "What?" She couldn't follow what Kate was asking of her, and she was terrified that she would say something to lead them to her daughter. Her head spun again as too many thoughts and emotions flew around. She could feel her heart pounding so fast and so hard, it reminded her of the sound a woodpecker makes, pecking against a tree. *Rat-a-tat-tat.* Like a machine gun going on and on in her chest.

She held up her hand, determined to put it on her heart to slow down the escalating beat, but she couldn't reach it. Instead, her chest seemed to get farther and farther away from her hand even as she moved it closer. How can that be? She could hear her own breathing. It was too fast. Far too fast. Like all she was doing was dragging air into her body without being able to expel anything and the oxygen was building up and fogging her brain even more than the Rioja had. She looked at Kate, her lovely green eyes had widened in alarm. Gina put her hand out to let her know everything was all right, but her fingers had locked into talon like claws. Stiff and unbending as she stared at them. Her vision tunnelled and everything blessedly shut down.

Kate caught Gina as she pitched forward on her way to the floor. She didn't know what had triggered the panic attack, but she recognised one when she saw it. She cradled Gina's head and held her fingers against the pulse point in her throat, glad that her heart beat was slowing down. Her breathing had returned to normal as soon as she had passed out and now all Kate had to figure out was what to do with the unconscious woman in her arms. She suspected her blackout would soon morph into a sleep that was going to last all night.

She slipped her arms under Gina's knees and tested her weight. Her working theory was that if she could at least get her laid on the sofa, she could find a blanket and let her sleep there. She'd called round to ask about Leah, and to check on Gina and see if she was completely honest. Now she was really glad she had. As she lifted, she found that she was able to get Gina onto the sofa quite easily, and she turned her on her side. She propped some cushions in front of her to stop her from rolling off. And just in case, she pulled the cushions off the other sofa and laid them on the floor as a crash mat. She looked around for a blanket or throw to cover her with, but couldn't see anything suitable. She looked up at the ceiling and sighed.

It took less than a minute to locate the master bedroom but she was unable to find anything but the duvet covering Gina's bed, partly due to the fact that she didn't want to go snooping through her cupboards and drawers. She was reluctant to invade Gina's privacy. And Kate had long ago learned to follow her instincts.

She folded the duvet up and walked back onto the landing. A young girl stood staring at her, silently watching, her eyes curious yet wary.

"Who are you?"

"I'm a policewoman." The girl's eyes widened and she clutched a stuffed bear to her chest. "Are you Sammy?"

The girl nodded.

"Good, your mum's fallen asleep on the sofa, so I'm just going to cover her up with this."

"Is she okay?"

"Yes, why?"

"She never sleeps downstairs."

"Well, she had some wine and I think she's upset about Connie, so she just fell asleep."

Tears rolled down Sammy's cheeks and she disappeared back into her room, closing the door quietly behind her.

"Looks like your mum isn't the only one upset about Connie dying." Kate stood at the top of the stairs, unsure whether or not to look in on the child, who was clearly crying, or leave her be. But now she was seriously starting to regret her decision to pop round on her way home from the station. *I wish I'd picked up my own bottle of something after leaving the station.* It was gone eight o'clock after all, but no. Instead, Sergeant Brannon's got a case to solve on her own, if at all possible, and now she was staring at the door of a sobbing nine-year-old, while her mother was in a coma on the sofa. *After admiring my arse. Fabulous plan, Kate. Fabulous.*

She stared at the door for a long time and wished Gina would wake up and come see to her daughter. "Shit." She put the duvet over the banister and knocked on the door. "Sammy, can I come in?"

She took the lack of response as a positive one and pushed open the door. It was dark, except for the tiny, blue LED on the front of a wall-mounted TV screen. Kate let her eyes adjust and found that it was more than enough to make out the large shapes in the room. She moved steadily towards the snuffling lump in the bed.

"Connie was your friend too, huh?"

Sammy cried harder and Kate pulled the girl into her arms.

"It's okay, kiddo. It's okay." She held her gently and sat down on the bed with her. "You want to talk about it?"

Sammy shook her head.

"That's okay. It's hard to lose someone you care about." She pulled the covers over Sammy's legs. "When I was little and got upset, my gran used to sing to me." She chuckled. "But she wasn't a very good singer, and I used to pretend to be asleep so she'd stop."

Sammy chuckled.

"I know. Mean, huh?"

"Little bit."

"Want me to sing to you?"

"Do you sing like your gran?"

"Worse."

Sammy laughed. "No, thanks."

"Okay. Want me to leave you alone?"

Sammy gripped her harder and shook her head. "I don't want to be alone."

Kate could feel the damp spot developing on her shirt as Sammy's tears began to fall again. "No problem. I'll just wait right here until you're ready for me to go," she said and rocked the girl until she fell asleep.

Kate found herself wondering at the kind of woman Connie must have been. Besides Gina and Sammy, everyone else she'd met that day had been extremely negative about Connie. Most had called her a bitch or some equivalent. Even her ex-lover had had more than one negative thing to say about her. Yet here were the two nicest people she'd met, crying their hearts out over her loss. Grieving genuinely for the loss of their friend. It seemed Connie was one of those people you either loved or hated, with nothing in between.

Kate tucked Sammy snugly under the covers and closed the door behind her. She gathered up the duvet and went back to the living room. Gina hadn't moved. She unfolded the cover and spread it over the slumbering woman. The gorgeous, slumbering woman. The gorgeous, slumbering witness, her cop brain supplied. Yes, witness, not a suspect. She checked Gina's pulse one last time and, satisfied that she was just sleeping, Kate sat down in the chair to keep an eye on the Temple girls. She couldn't put into words why she felt the need to stay, she just knew she wouldn't be able to rest if she left Gina in the state she was in.

Maybe I can get some answers in the morning. She looked at the empty bottle of wine. *Okay, maybe I can get some answers by lunchtime.* She tucked her coat around her shoulders and closed her eyes.

CHAPTER 7

Gina wasn't entirely sure how much money she had in the bank at that moment, but she'd gladly give every penny if someone would bring her a bucket of water. And shoot the elephant that was tap dancing on her head with a bad case of the farts. Farts that were making her feel more nauseated than she could ever remember feeling before. She opened her mouth to groan and realised the fart smell was actually something dead in her mouth. She couldn't be sure, but the dead thing may have been her tongue. She turned over and bumped into a mound of something soft and squishy, and very unlike her bed. She cracked open one eye just a fraction—she knew that would be more than painful enough—and saw that, despite being covered in her duvet, she was actually snuggled up on her sofa.

"What the hell?" A frog belched up from her throat. She sat up and looked around, hands holding her head to prevent it falling off, and saw Kate sleeping peacefully in the armchair across the room. Her leather jacket was tucked around her shoulders, pulled up under her chin.

What the fuck happened? Gina racked her memory, but she couldn't even remember Kate being in the house. She swung her legs gingerly off the couch and groaned pitifully. Kate stirred but didn't wake. Gina watched, a smile crept onto her lips unbidden as she put together the pieces of the puzzle. Kate must have shown up and Gina passed out on her at some point. *Christ she must have been worried about me to stay. How much did I drink anyway?* She spied the empty bottle on the coffee table. She swallowed and hoped that Kate had at least helped her with some of it. Given how her head felt, though, she doubted it.

She slowly eased her body off the couch and stumbled out of the room, bouncing from wall to wall down the hallway and into the kitchen. She grabbed a glass from the drainer and held it under the tap, then downed two glasses before she reached into the top cupboard for the small medicine box she kept out of the reach of little hands. She popped two pills out of the blister pack, swallowed them, then popped a third for good measure, hoping that her stomach didn't reject them. There was nothing she hated more than throwing up. She filled the kettle and put it on to boil before downing another glass of water.

"Good morning."

Gina put her hand to her chest as she whirled around and met the sleepy, slightly creased-looking Kate smiling at her gently.

"Sorry, I didn't mean to startle you."

"It's okay."

"How are you doing this morning?"

"Hung over."

"That all?"

"Erm, yes. Why?"

Kate tipped her head to the side and frowned slightly. "Don't you remember what happened last night?"

Gina stared at her. *Oh shit, what happened?* "Erm, no. I remember deciding to have a drink. I was upset about Connie, and I thought a glass would help me switch off a bit."

"A glass. By the time I got here, you'd gone through the whole bottle."

"Oh, God. No wonder I feel like I'm dead." The kettle finished boiling. "Coffee?"

"Please. Milk no sugar."

"Can you get the milk out of the fridge, please?"

Kate handed her the bottle. "What else do you remember about last night?"

Gina shook her head and regretted it. "Nothing. What did I do?"

Kate took the coffees and put them on the table. "Well, you complimented my arse and had a panic attack."

"I what?"

"You had a panic attack. Hyperventilating, the works. Then you passed out."

"I meant the other bit."

"Oh, right. Well, you broke a glass when I knocked and I bent down to pick it up. You seemed, erm, impressed." Kate grinned, a sexy mixture of cocky and coy.

"I'm sorry."

"What for?"

"Well, by the sound of it, everything."

Kate flapped her hand to wave it away. "Don't worry about it. I just didn't want to leave you in that condition, and Sammy woke up at one point. She was upset too, so I didn't feel comfortable just abandoning you both and heading home."

Christ, now she'll think I'm a terrible mother, as well as a drunk and a floozy, practically throwing myself at her.

"I'm sorry to have put you to so much trouble."

"No trouble. You've got a pretty comfy chair there. Trust me, I've had much worse nights." She smiled. "Sammy's a great kid. She seems to have taken Connie's death really hard. They must have been close."

Gina shrugged. "Yes. Like I told you yesterday, Connie was my best friend. We spent time together, and Sammy really looked up to Connie." She sighed. "Sammy seemed to respect that Connie never treated her like a child. She spoke to her like everyone else and Sammy really flourished under that."

"I'm sorry to be insensitive, but I have to ask. Was there anything more? Between you and Connie?"

Gina stared at her. "Not like that, no. We were best friends. Closer maybe. I always thought of her as the big sister I never had. But there was nothing romantic between us, if that's what you mean."

"I'm sorry, I had to ask."

"Why?"

Kate shrugged. "I need to know everything I can about Connie's life if I'm going to find out who killed her."

"Is that why you came round last night? To ask if I was having an affair with her?"

"No, I came to ask you about Leah, actually."

Gina frowned. "What about her? I wasn't having an affair with her either."

Kate chuckled. "I didn't think that for even a second. When I went to visit her, there was drug paraphernalia visible. I couldn't see any actual drugs, but I'm certain she's a user. Is that why she and Connie split?"

"Ultimately, yes, I believe it was. There was more to it than just that. But I think Leah's refusal to get help, and her deterioration as she got more and more hooked was, I think, the straw that broke the camel's back."

"Why didn't you mention this when we spoke yesterday?"

Gina looked at her for a long moment and tried to get her alcohol-soaked brain to work. She'd watched plenty of crime dramas and knew that the spouse or the ex was always the top of the suspect list. Add to that formula Leah's drug use, her unreliability, and the threats that everyone would attest to having heard Leah make, she had to be looking pretty damn good for this right now. A few words and Gina could certainly help prod Kate along that direction. It wouldn't be hard. She wouldn't even have to make anything up. But could she live with herself if she did? What if Leah couldn't prove it wasn't her and she went to prison for the crime? A crime Leah didn't commit.

Could she live with that on her conscience? Could she do that to another human being? Could she do that to Leah? Yes, Leah was a junkie and time in prison might actually help her get off the drugs and sort herself out, but not if she went down for a murder she didn't commit. Even if she wasn't convicted, if she was the only suspect, how would that affect her life from here on out? Could Gina subject someone, anyone, to that?

Sammy appeared in the doorway. "Mum, can I have a drink?"

Gina held out her hand and pulled her close when Sammy scooted in towards Gina's body. She wrapped her arms around her and wished none of it was happening, but nothing was more precious to her than the child in her arms. Nothing was going to separate them. She'd make sure Sammy wouldn't make a mistake like this again. And it was an accident. A stupid, mindless, senseless, Matt-induced accident.

"What do you want, baby?"

"Milk, please."

"Okay. Then back upstairs, okay? I need to finish talking to Detective Brannon."

"Okay."

"How are you this morning, Sammy?" Kate asked.

She shrugged and wiped her nose on her sleeve. "Fanks for last night."

"You're very welcome, kiddo. I'm glad I could help."

Sammy got her drink and her feet echoed on the stairs as she made good her escape.

"What happened with Sammy last night?"

"I told you, she woke up."

Gina nodded.

"She got really upset, so I cuddled her while she cried until she fell back asleep."

"She cried with you?"

"Erm, yes. Is that bad?"

"No, no. It's unusual. Sammy usually only cries with me."

"Oh, well, I think it was more about missing Connie than me."

Gina blinked. "I'm sure." She sipped her coffee.

"You haven't answered my question."

"I'm sorry, what question?"

Kate laughed gently. "I asked why you didn't mention Leah's drug use yesterday."

"Oh, right." Now or never. Could she tell a lie to point the finger of suspicion elsewhere? Did she need to? Who in their right mind would actually conceive of the scenario that had happened? Child alone with a gun shooting at rabbits accidentally kills mother's best friend. Who'd even think of it? Seriously? Did she really need to redirect suspicion?

Then there was the lovely DS Brannon to consider. She was conscientious and tenacious, and all that other good cop stuff. Why else would she have slept in a chair last night to make sure they were both okay? So, could she lie to DS Brannon and deflect any possible attention that might come her way? *Now or never, Gina.* She shrugged.

"It wasn't something Connie had really spoken about, and I wasn't one hundred percent. Most of what I know about that is through rumours around the village, if truth be told. I listened to them and put two and two together. It wasn't until you told me that, that I knew I'd got four, rather than twenty-two. Do you know what I mean?" *Never.*

Kate nodded. "Yes, but I did ask you for your opinion."

"I know. But I guess I'm a firm believer in if you can't say something nice, don't say anything at all."

Kate sighed. "I understand. I even like the notion. But I'm investigating the murder of your best friend here. Please, I need you to tell me everything about her. I need to know what you know, to find who killed her. Will you help me find her killer?"

Gina closed her eyes and willed away the tears as she made a promise she had no intention of ever keeping. "Yes." *Now. This is the now part.*

"Thank you." Kate finished her coffee and put her cup in the sink. "I should get going. I need to head home before I go to the station."

"Thank you for staying here last night, for helping me and Sammy. I can't tell you what that means to me."

"You don't need to thank me." She reached over and squeezed Gina's arm. "It was the most interesting evening I've had in while."

Gina laughed and winced. "Then you need to work on your social life, Detective."

Kate laughed. "I probably do."

Gina pulled open the door for Kate and found herself staring at the dirty, unshaven face of Sammy's father.

"Matt, what are you doing here?"

"I need to see Sammy." He stared at Kate. "Who are you?"

"Detective Sergeant Kate Brannon. And you are?"

Matt swallowed hard and Gina took a perverse pleasure in watching him squirm. "Matt Green."

"Matt is Sammy's father." Gina added to explain his presence. Kate glanced at her quickly, one eyebrow raised. Gina felt as though she were looking right into her soul, before she nodded to them both and stepped out of the door.

"Thanks for your help, Miss Temple. I'm sure I'll have more questions later."

"I'll be here all day. I'm not opening up the office and Sammy's staying home today. She's not up to school."

"Of course. I'll know where to find you, then." She nodded at Matt. "Mr Green."

Was it my imagination or did she emphasise our different names to make some sort of point?

She waited until Kate was in her car and gone before she turned her attention to Matt. "What kind of fucking moron are you?"

"Excuse me? You can't talk to me like that."

"Watch me." She slammed the door shut behind her.

"I just need to see Sammy and get something, then I'll be out of your way and you can go back to doing...whatever the fuck it is you do, Gina."

"I'll just bet you need to see Sammy. You need to see her so much that you couldn't turn up to meet her at the school gate like you promised her you would. You need to see her so much that you waited more than twenty-four hours to turn up again."

"Wh—what are you talking about?"

"Your fucking gun. That's what I'm talking about. The one you left in the hands of a nine-year-old. Fully loaded. While you were more than two miles away. The one you didn't turn up to collect at school as you promised. The one you left in her possession to walk home with after your irresponsible arse didn't do what you promised."

"I was working. I got busy. You know what old Ed's like when he gets on one. It's all 'do this and do that or don't bother coming in tomorrow.'"

"I don't give a shit if God himself ordered you to do something. That is the last promise you are ever going to break to your daughter."

"I know. I'll never let her down again. You have my word."

"Your word doesn't mean anything to me, Matt. But mine will damn sure mean something to you. If you ever, ever, come near Sammy again, I'll take that gun to the police and tell them that you left that loaded weapon with her, and left her. She could have killed herself with that thing."

"You can't do that, Gina. She's my daughter too."

"No, she's a toy you pick up and play with when you feel like it. You're not capable of being a father, Matt. You're still a fucking child yourself."

"I'll take you to court."

"Try it. I'll tell them exactly what kind of man you are."

"What are you talking about?"

"I'll tell them everything, Matt. I'll tell them about you giving a gun to a nine-year-old and leaving her alone."

Anger contorted his face. "You won't do that."

"Won't I?" She smiled at him. "I guess you'll have to try me, then, won't you?"

"Don't do anything stupid, Gina."

"Then stay away, Matt. Stay away from Sammy, and stay away from me."

"You can't do this."

"You did this to yourself. Giving her a bloody rifle and leaving her." She shook her head. "What did you think was going to happen?"

"She knew what she was doing with it."

"She's nine years old!"

"You can't take her away from me."

"I'm not. I'm protecting her from bad influences and stupidity." She pulled open the door. "Now get out and don't come back."

CHAPTER 8

Kate shook her head as she drove away. The picture of Matt staring at Gina lingered behind her eyelids every time she blinked. She didn't know the story behind them, but no part of her could see her and Matt as a couple. But they had a child together. Kate shuddered and tried to shake it off again. It took her five minutes to reach her small, chalk-and-flint fronted cottage in Docking with the ivy climbing up and over the front window and door. She made a mental note to contact a gardening service to come and strip it back.

She parked her metallic, sky blue BMW Mini in the driveway and dragged the wheelie bin back into the garden, before unlocking the door and kicking off her boots in the hallway. She stripped as she made her way up the stairs, tossed her clothes in the hamper, and turned on the shower.

The hot water soothed the ache in her neck from the night spent sleeping in a chair, and the scent of the orange body scrub invigorated her, clearing the cobwebs from her brain and readying her for the day ahead. She scrubbed at her scalp as she formulated her plan for the day.

She grabbed her mobile when she stepped out of the shower and punched the number for the incident room. She started to towel herself dry while she waited for an answer.

"Incident room."

"Goodwin?"

"Yes. Is that you, Kate?"

"Yes. You're there early."

"Thought I'd make a start on going over those interviews from yesterday."

"Good plan. I've just been talking to Gina Temple again. I'll fill you in when I get there. Are the boys in yet?"

"En route. Brothers swung by to pick up Jimmy. His car's broken down."

Kate sniggered, knowing full well the young DC was going to take some stick for that little cry for help. "Okay, I'll be there in twenty." She leaned down and tugged a sock on her still damp foot.

"Don't drive like a lunatic."

"Me?"

"Yes. Your, erm," she said and coughed, "talent behind the wheel is already legendary."

Kate grinned. "I'm not sure whether I should feel complimented or insulted, Stella."

The older woman laughed. "Your choice. See you in twenty."

Kate finished getting dressed with a smile on her face and grabbed a cereal bar as she headed back out the door. The road between Docking and Hunstanton was one of her favourites to drive. As long as she didn't get stuck behind a tractor. It was long and straight, but with hills and blind dips that belied the notion that Norfolk was a flat county. They made Kate's stomach flip when she crested each hillock and put air beneath her tyres. It's certainly not bloody flat when you're cycling this bastard. She grinned and lowered her window. The soft rain tickled her skin as she stuck her arm out of the window and imagined it on her face.

The station was quiet when she pulled the door open, and she had to wait for the desk officer to appear and buzz her in. The biscuit crumbs the poor chap dusted off the front of his shirt gave away his earlier location.

Kate took the stairs two at a time and pulled open the door to the incident room. Stella was pointedly ignoring the boys and looked to be reading over the transcripts of the interviews as Tom mercilessly teased Jimmy. An even younger looking man, presumably one DC Collier, was laughing heartily at his colleague's misfortune.

"Look, next time the battery's dead, I'll call someone else."

"Next time, don't be a dickhead and leave the lights on all night."

"Good morning, everyone," Kate said.

"Morning," they all chorused.

"Any news on the samples yet?" Kate asked looking at Stella.

"They said anytime in the next two hours."

"Good. So fill me in on who you spoke to yesterday." She looked at Tom.

"I talked to Helen Tidewell, landlady at the Jolly Rogers pub. She corroborated everything Gina Temple and the girl, Sarah, said about Leah having spilt the beans in the pub about Connie's plans to sell, and she also confirmed that Leah had threatened to kill Connie if she didn't give up on this plan to sell the campsite and move away. Said Leah made it clear that she expected Connie to take her back when she calmed down and got over herself." He curled his fingers around the last three words, making air quotes.

"Good."

"Does that make Leah our prime suspect?" Collier asked.

Kate pursed her lips. "It should, but when we spoke to her yesterday I got the impression that she'd been out of commission for quite some time. Her hands shook so badly she couldn't light a cigarette, and I got confirmation from Gina Temple this morning that Leah is a drug addict. I have a hard time putting her, in that state, being able to pull something like this off."

"Maybe she did it while she was drug fuelled," Collier said. "It's not exactly unheard of for a junkie to kill while under the influence."

"Very true," Kate said.

"But you didn't see her," Jimmy said holding out his hand and doing his trembling impression again. "She didn't even seem to notice that she was stark naked while we talked to her." Collier's mouth dropped open a little while Jimmy nodded his head. They looked more like boys in the school playground than police detectives.

"All right, boys, all right. Also a point to consider is that junkie crimes are usually crimes of opportunity. The victim is there while they're high and someone loses control. For this to have been Leah, she would have had to go out and find Connie, while armed, and then have the presence of mind to cover her tracks." She shook her head. "I don't see her being able to plan that far ahead in the state she was in. Connie wasn't with Leah. Ally confirmed that Leah was at her house all night and passed out on the couch when she left for work, where I found her later that afternoon."

"That's a big time gap, Kate," Tom said. "Ally left at around five a.m., if not earlier, and you didn't see her until after four p.m. Anything could've happened in that time."

"I know. And we'll keep looking for anything that puts Leah at the scene, but I don't think we're going to find it. I think she was as high as a kite on Ally's sofa when this happened."

Stella shrugged. "Then who do you think did this?"

"Good question." She picked up the whiteboard pen and started writing. "We've got a lot of people with a lot to lose when Connie closed down the hostel and campsite." She wrote the name "William" on the top of the board. "He worked for Connie and lived in the staff accommodations in the hostel. When the place closed under Connie, he was going to be homeless, as well as jobless, with apparently nowhere else to turn. I want to know more about him and where he was."

"Do you have a second name?" Stella asked.

"No, but we should be able to get it from the records at the campsite. Gina's closed down the office so we can have access whenever we need."

Stella nodded. "Want to look ourselves first, or send in SOCO straight away?"

"Have they finished at Connie's house?"

"Not yet."

"Then we might as well take a little scout around before they start. Hopefully, William's in the hostel anyway."

"Makes sense. Right, I want the rest of the interviews finished and a list of suspects compiled by the end of the day," she said to Tom and Collier. "I'll chase up the DNA and particulate samples." Stella made notes in the murder book as she spoke. "You and Jimmy head over to Connie's office and see if you can find this William."

Kate glanced at the whiteboard. "And if we can find them, we'll talk to the rest of the staff that worked for Connie."

Stella completed her notes.

"Can you let me know when you get the results?"

"Of course."

"Do you guys want a lift?" Kate asked.

"Erm, thanks, we're good," Tom said.

Jimmy laughed. "What he's trying to say, ma'am, is that it may be beneficial if we have our own vehicle today. In case they have to be separated."

"Right," Kate said. "Chicken shits."

Tom and Collier looked aghast, but Jimmy just chuckled. "Yes, ma'am."

Kate's hands itched inside the latex gloves as she carefully leafed through the pages in Connie's many files. Financial documents, bank statements, contracts, receipts, owner's manuals for TVs and microwaves, all carefully stored and filed away. Easy to find at a moment's notice. Clearly, Connie was an excellent record keeper and an exceptionally organised businesswoman. It was quite easy for Kate to see why she had made the business a success and why the staff was concerned at the prospect of Leah taking over. The condition she was living in and the lack of concern for her own nakedness was enough to make Kate certain of the fact that Leah would not take the kind of care Connie had of the business.

Kate made copious notes about the current and recent staff members from Connie's files. Recently dismissed staff crept up Kate's list of suspects when she discovered one staff member had been fired for smoking pot in the staff dorm. Drugs again. Kate was beginning to suspect that rural life had just as much of a drug problem as she'd faced in the inner city. Something she hadn't counted on. She'd always imagined that living in such beautiful places would make people happier and less likely to turn to crutches like drugs and alcohol. It seemed not.

Besides William Clapp, Gina Temple, and Sarah Willis, there were two other full-time staff members at Brandale Backpackers and Camping. Twenty-one-year-old Richard "Ricky" Pepper and his nineteen-year-old pregnant girlfriend, Emma Goose. Both had limited prospects and seemed to be looking at a future living in a caravan in Rick's dad's garden.

There was nothing outstanding in the work history of the staff currently, no significant disciplinary issues, and the only one who seemed to be facing real hardship at the closing of the hostel was William. She noted, though, that Connie had made a point to say that as long as he helped Gina out with any issues, he'd be allowed to stay in the staff dorm until he found himself another place to live and work. So not quite the heartless bitch that Sarah had painted her to be. Perhaps she just wasn't privy to all of Connie's plans.

She wondered if William knew of this possibility. If not, he was still high on the list of general suspects. If he did, then he was slipping off fast.

Her mobile buzzed in her pocket. She fished it out and touched the screen to answer. "Brannon."

"DNA results are back. It's definitely Connie Wells."

"Right, thanks, Stella. Anything on those particulates from the wound."

"Yes, I waited for those to call as the DNA wasn't much of a revelation."

"And?"

"It seems it's glass from a lens."

"A lens? Like a pair of glasses?"

"No. Too thick for that. Plus, it has a specific coating that's used on camera lenses. Wild, my friend over in SOCO, gave me some fancy scientific name, but apparently it's used as an ingredient to coat Nikon lenses."

"There was no camera."

"I know, but it does make sense with what every interviewee has said. She was always out on those marshes with the dog and her camera."

"True." Kate bit her lip. "Okay, call SOCO and find out if a camera was found in the house."

"Already done. Lots of camera equipment, tripods, flash guns, light reflectors...you name it, it's in there. But no camera."

"Okay, so either the killer took the camera with them or it's somewhere at the scene."

"SOCO said they combed every inch of that ground and found nothing. Not even more fragments of glass."

Kate closed her eyes a second and called to mind the crime scene. The trampled grass, the position of the body. They way it looked like it had been flung backwards. She remembered thinking how lucky they were that it hadn't landed a little farther or they'd be in the creek. Shit. "Did they dredge the water?"

"Excuse me?"

"Did SOCO dredge the water nearby? Connie's right arm was outstretched and only about two or three inches from the edge of the water."

"If that's the case, won't the tide have washed it away?"

"No. The water on that side of the dyke isn't tidal. It's brackish and stationary. Like a pond. They need to get back there and get in the water."

"Will they need divers?"

"I don't think it's that deep. Waders and long gloves should do it. Fingertip search, Stella. We need that camera. Maybe then we can figure out what kind of weapon killed her, and where the killer was when they fired the shot."

"On it."

Kate rubbed her hands together and peeled off the gloves, scratching gleefully at her powder-covered skin. Time to go and see what Jimmy had found in the information centre. She stuffed them into her pocket and closed the office door behind her. A thin, blonde guy walked across the gravel-covered courtyard, hair brushed to one side, styled and fixed in place with wet-look gel. A diamond earring—probably fake—glinted in his left ear, while sweatpants with a hole slashing across one knee were tucked into scuffed wellies. He had a cigarette stuck between his lips and a rake under one arm as he pushed a wheelbarrow in front of him.

"Excuse me," Kate said. "I'm looking for William Clapp."

Blue eyes assessed her warily. "What do you want him for?" The uncomfortable edge to his stance and the unconscious leaning away told her she'd found the person she wanted.

"Just a couple of questions about Connie Wells. You know she was killed yesterday, don't you, William?"

If he was surprised at her using his first name, he didn't show it. He just nodded his head, flicked ash from his cigarette, and tucked it back between his lips.

"I'm Detective Sergeant Kate Brannon. Did you know she was planning to close this place down?"

He snorted. "Whole village knows that. It weren't no secret."

"Someone told me that it would mean you ending up on the streets. Is that true?"

He pulled a deep drag on his smoke, took it from his lips, and fished a tiny fleck of tobacco off his tongue. "People say a lot of shit."

Kate smiled and tried to sidestep the plume of smoke. "Does that mean you weren't going to be out on your ear?"

He flicked the butt to the ground and crushed it beneath his heel. "Connie said I could stay in here once this place closed, but the heating would be off. She said if I helped Gina keep on top of the place I could stay until I found somewhere else to live. If Gina said I had to go, though, then I had to go or they'd call the cops in to get rid of me."

"I'd be pissed if someone said that to me."

He shrugged and fished a small packet of tobacco from his pocket. His fingers deftly rolled another smoke and he tucked it between his lips. "Nah. At least she was giving me time. She could've just told me to get lost." He shrugged again. "That's what usually happens to me."

"Did you like Connie?"

He stared at her. She could see him carefully weighing his options on what he said next. "She gave me a chance. Only person around here who did. She said I would either prove myself or not. She was fair and she knew this place inside and out. There wasn't a job here that she hadn't done. And whether or not you liked her, you respected her for that."

"Did you like her?"

He lit his cigarette and tucked the lighter back in his pocket. "Yeah. She done right by me. Well, as best she could given the circumstances."

"You mean Leah?"

He spat on the ground. "Yeah."

"Most people I've spoken to seem to hate her."

"Who?"

"Connie."

He laughed. "Most people here never got to know Connie. She wasn't an easy person to know. You know?"

"How do you mean?"

"She didn't talk about herself much. Didn't put herself forward in a crowd. She was happy enough to let Leah do that."

"She was shy?"

He frowned. "Not so much shy as private. She didn't like people to know what went on in her head."

"I see."

"So people had to work to get to know her. They had to put in the effort." He sucked on the skinny roll-up. "If you did, she was cool. If not, she could be pretty cold."

"Who do you think would have done this to her?"

"Isn't that your job to figure out?"

"Yeah. But you knew her, and you know the people around here. If you had to bet, who would you be putting your money on?"

"Well, I'd be asking myself who had the most to lose from this place being closed."

"I have been."

He grunted. "And that led you to me?"

"Yes."

"Think higher up the food chain, lady. Connie owned the land here, the buildings, the business. Who owns other businesses in the village that would be in danger if this wasn't here to help sustain them?"

"Who?"

"Try the Sands."

Kate frowned. "Who?"

"Edward and Rupert Sands." He pointed to the cluster of farm buildings and barns overlooking the campsite. "The local landowners. They own all the land around here, contract it out to the farmers. More than a thousand acres of it. Everything except this campsite. Rupert tried to get planning permission a few years back to do his own campsite." He pointed across the road. "Over on the marshes. Wanted to diversify. Farming's not what it used to be. At least that's what the farmers all say. Anyway, he wanted his own slice of the tourists." He snorted a laugh. "Not that he doesn't have enough. He owns half the houses in the village, and most of them are holiday rentals. Planners knocked him back. Said there was no need for another one in this area. Prick."

"I take it you're a fan."

"Love 'em to death," he said, a sarcastic sneer curling his lip.

"Why?"

"They think they own the village. Lord of the manor. Think they're better than everyone else, and expect us all to kiss their arses and shine their shoes. No, thank you. They treat everyone like they are only here at their whim and at any moment they could send them all away." He sniggered. "They couldn't do that with Connie. She was in charge and they knew it. After their plans were derailed, rumour has it they wanted to buy this place, but she refused to sell to them. Connie and Rupert had more arguments and fights than anyone else in the village. Lifelong enemies, those two."

"Why?"

He stubbed out his second cigarette. "Ask Gina. She might know."

"I will."

"Do you need me anymore?"

She shook her head and held out a card to him. "But don't go anywhere, I might need to talk to you again."

He took the card, touched it to his temple, and saluted her as he walked away, fishing his tobacco from his pocket again.

"The Sands, hey?" She stuffed her hands in her pockets. "Let's go see what you've got to say about all this, then."

CHAPTER 9

The farmhouse was large, but the Georgian architecture and smooth stone walls were out of step with every other building in the village, which were made of flint and chalk. The high windows offered the passerby a view into rooms with vaulted ceilings, enough paintings for a museum, and in one room Kate could clearly see that the love seat was more than a little thread bare. She wondered if it was one antique piece that was suffering the effects of time or if it was indicative of the state of the Sands' affairs.

"Do you know these guys, Jimmy?" Kate asked.

"By reputation, and I know that they're about as far up the arse of the local member of parliament as you can get and still breathe oxygen instead of methane. But that's your lot I'm afraid."

She chuckled. "Nice imagery. You been taking lessons from Tom?"

He buffed his nails on his shirt. "It takes work to be this good, Sarge. A lot of work."

She laughed and rang the bell, then waited. She half expected a servant of some description to answer, but instead a wiry, elderly man yanked open the door. A scowl painted his features behind the oversized glasses perched on his nose. Very short, grey hair was stuck at odd angles, and his skin had a sallow and shrunken look. His cheeks were concave, hugging his cheekbones so closely that it made his teeth seem overly prominent beneath his thin lips. The stubble on his chin was patchy, like it only grew in certain places on his face, and added to the look of a man who didn't seem well.

"What do you want?"

Kate held up her warrant card. "Mr Sands?"

"Yes."

"I'm Detective Sergeant Kate Brannon. May I come in?"

"I suppose this is about that ghastly business on the Coastal Path yesterday."

"Yes. I'm investigating the murder of Connie Wells."

"Murder, you say?"

"Yes."

A small smile flickered across his lips, then disappeared. "Well, you should be talking to that woman, then, not bothering decent folk."

His appearance had made her worry for his health, but his attitude rankled. She was pretty sure he was talking about Leah, but she wasn't sure why he considered her not "decent folk." Something told her it had nothing to do with the drugs, so she decided to call him on it. "What woman would that be, sir?"

"Her bloody girlfriend, Leah." The distaste in his voice made his opinion of them and their "girlfriend" status perfectly clear.

"Well, sir, right now I need to talk to you and your son, Rupert. May I come in?"

He let out a clearly aggravated sigh and held the door open for her. "Fine. We're in the parlour." He led the way to the room with the love seat, hollering up the stairs for Rupert as he passed. The room had a rack of hunting rifles mounted on the wall. She counted six weapons. Two double-barrelled shotguns and four rifles. Above the fireplace was the stuffed head of a stag, his antlers twisting towards the ceiling. Her own dislike for the man in front of her grew. Even if he hadn't killed the beast, the display of its carcass as a point of honour was more than enough to turn her stomach.

Rupert bustled into the room and couldn't have been more opposite to his father. A thick ruff of beard covered his cheeks and neck, in a vain attempt at hiding some of the superfluous skin and flab that clung to his neck and jaw, like a child clings to its mother on the first day of school. His mousy coloured hair hung over his ears like the greasy strings of an overused mop head. His rotund physique made his father seem even smaller, even more frail, and Kate was convinced that the old man was sick.

"What do you want?" Rupert said.

"I take it you are also aware of yesterday's events, Mr Sands?"

Rupert nodded. "And?"

"I wanted to talk to you and your father about some information I've come across. I understand that you expressed an interest in buying the campsite and hostel from Ms Wells. Is that correct?"

Edward cleared his throat. "We're businessmen, Detective, we're interested in buying a great many things."

"I appreciate that, but were you specifically interested in this one?"

Edward paused before answering. "Yes."

"Thank you. Is it also true that she refused to sell to you?"

"Bitch," Rupert whispered under his breath, earning him a sharp look from his father.

"Yes, it was."

Edward stared at her. She just waited, knowing that Rupert would speak if Edward didn't fill the silence.

"Everyone in the village knew that. Leah screamed it in the pub, for God's sake."

"How would you describe your relationship with Connie, Mr Sands?" She looked at Rupert.

He narrowed his eyes. "I don't like your tone."

"I'm very sorry to hear that, Mr Sands, but I do require you to answer the question."

"I'm not required to do anything for you."

"I'm a detective investigating the murder of someone known to you. Are you refusing to help the police with their enquiries, sir?"

"Rupert." Edward's voice was low, warning his son to tread carefully.

He glared at her, his red, puffy jowls shaking as he struggled to contain his temper. "We didn't get along very well," he ground out.

"May I ask why not?"

"She was rude, arrogant, and argumentative."

Is that you or her you're describing? Kate nodded towards the guns. "Who's the hunter?"

"We're country folk, Detective. We shoot grouse, pheasant, quail, rabbits, and such like often. For food."

"And the deer?" She nodded to the stuffed head. "Was that dinner too?"

Edward smiled. "Yes, he was. A magnificent venison stew we had that night."

"Where were you both yesterday morning between six a.m. and eight a.m.?"

Edward smiled again. "On the farm. I had breakfast with my wife between six and six thirty, then I showered, and I had a meeting at seven with the farmhands to task work for the day. After that, I spoke with the foreman for about half an hour."

"Who's the foreman?"

"Matt Green."

"And what were you talking to him about?"

"He was a little late for the morning meeting, so naturally I had to have a word."

"How late?"

"I don't remember exactly, but we were almost through and the meeting usually takes half an hour or so."

"And you?" She turned to Rupert.

"I was here getting ready for a business meeting in Norwich."

"What time was the meeting?"

"Eleven."

"Was there anyone else here with you?"

"No."

"He was here when I got back from talking to the lads," Edward said. "I can vouch for him."

"And what time did you see him?"

"Well, I got back here about eight fifteen. You'd just got out of the shower, hadn't you?" He turned to Rupert.

"Yes, that's right," Rupert said.

Kate's ears pricked up. Shower, eight fifteen, no alibi prior to that. She tried to gauge the distance between the farmhouse and the location on the marsh where Connie's body was found. There was more than enough time for Rupert Sands to have made it from there and back without any one missing him. Was there enough reason to suspect him? There was opportunity, motive, and on the wall behind her, there was possibly a murder weapon. But there was still no evidence.

"Thank you for your time. We'll be in touch if we have any further questions." She followed behind the elder Sands as he led her out of the house and slammed the door closed behind her without a further word. "It was a pleasure to meet you too, and good luck to you both in the future." She shook her head and made her way back to the car. She needed evidence. She needed something to make Mr Rupert Sands either her prime suspect, or just another villager with a grudge.

Instead of getting back in her car, she crossed the main road and took the small cul-de-sac that led to the dirt path and the marshes. She walked under the tree canopy as she had done the previous morning and stepped out onto Brandale Staithe marsh. The SOCO team were on the path to her left. The ramshackle old houseboat in front of her bobbed gently on the receding tide, its paint chipped. The gangplank walkway up to the door was covered in chicken wire so that one's boots could attain purchase when walking up or down it. But as unloved as it appeared when she looked closely, she noticed that the roof was in good condition. There were curtains up, and every window was well maintained. The boat looked water-tight and used. She wondered who owned it, as she made her way towards the scene's crime officers.

"How's it going?" Kate asked the tall overall-covered man standing on the embankment.

"Wetly." He laughed. "Sergeant Wild, ma'am. We didn't have the pleasure yesterday."

"Detective Sergeant Brannon." She smiled. "Sorry about this." She pointed down at the two overall-clad figures standing in the black water of the creek, fishermen's waders fastened up to their chests as they plunged their rubber-covered arms into the dark water and moved along slowly.

"No need to apologise. If we'd known we were looking for a camera, we'd have gone in yesterday."

"What do you think the chances of finding it are?"

"Well, there's no movement in the water. It's only twenty-four hours, so sediment shift should be minimal. I'd say that if it's in there, we'll find it."

She nodded. He didn't need to say that if the killer was close enough to take it with him or her, then those guys were getting wet and cold for nothing. "How long have they been at it?"

Wild lifted the elasticated cuff of his overall and glanced at his watch. "About half an hour now." He tucked his hands into his pockets. "Any leads?"

"Not much to go on so far. Hoping this camera will help." She ran her fingers through her hair and gathered it at her nape, twisting it to try and keep it from blowing on to her face for, well, maybe ten seconds. "Anything interesting at the house?"

"Depends on what you call interesting."

She chuckled. "Okay, how about useful?"

"Not sure. I sent the inventory over to Stella and a couple of things that need chasing down. I do have a couple of things in the car to give you, though."

"What?"

"A diary and a weird key."

"Fabulous." Kate hated digging through the treasure trove that was a victim's diary. Like an autopsy, it was just one more intrusion into the victim's personal life. As helpful as diaries could be sometimes, they could also be a distraction. "Does she tell us who killed her?"

He snorted. "I had a brief flick through, and there's a lot of shit about the ex. You focusing on her?"

"I'm asking questions about everyone at the moment."

"Hmphf. One thing caught my eye, though."

She waited for him to continue while she watched the shivering men in the water inch their way through the mud.

"Entries were steady and regular, four to five times a week on average, until June. Then there was only one entry after that."

Kate understood why this would catch his eye. "What changed?"

He shrugged. "It was a few weeks after they split up, and she writes about a cat hanging around the marshes fishing. Very different from the tone of the other entries I scanned. Read more like a kid's story or something. Then the last entry was just a series of numbers."

"What kind of numbers?"

"Haven't the foggiest. But it's a fair old list of them. I'll grab it for you before you go."

"Sarge, we found something," one of the techs called from the creek as his colleague raised up a twisted chunk of metal and plastic. Weed clung to it as water poured and dripped out.

"Right-o lads, fetch it up here, then, and we'll get it bagged."

Kate watched as they recorded the find and sealed it in an evidence bag. "Do you think you'll be able to figure out what kind of weapon was used now?"

Wild studied the remains of the camera. "Yes. It'll take me a day or two, mind."

"Is there a memory card in there?"

He flicked open a small flap with the camera still sealed in the bag, peered through the plastic, and then closed the flap again. "There is, but after twenty-four hours submerged, I wouldn't hold out much hope of getting anything off it."

"I won't. But if you can, I'd be forever grateful."

"I'll see what we can do." He stood up and started walking. "Let me get you that key and diary. See if you can make anything of those numbers."

CHAPTER 10

Gina put the plate down in front of Sammy and sat down to her own lunch. The girl sniffed, wiped her nose on her sleeve, and picked up a square of cheese on toast.

"Use a handkerchief, not your sleeve."

"Don't got one."

"You don't have one, and, yes, you do," Gina corrected. "You have several, in fact. Hidden somewhere in your bedroom. After lunch you will go and find one."

"But—"

"Do not argue with me, Samantha."

Sammy's lower lip quivered and she poked at the melted cheese with a grubby finger. Gina sighed, Sammy hadn't left her room all day, but somehow she'd still managed to get dirty.

"What's wrong?"

"Nuffink."

"Don't lie to me, Sammy."

Sammy dropped her uneaten piece of toast back onto her plate. "I heard you tell Dad to leave me alone."

Gina sighed. She hadn't been looking forward to this conversation. As much of a prat as Matt was, Sammy idolised him. Not surprising, since he spoiled her with guns, take-aways, and sweets at every opportunity.

"Yes, I did. Do you know why I did that?"

Sammy nodded. "'Cos I killed Connie." She pushed her plate away, folded her arms on the table, and laid her head on them. Sobs racked her body, and Gina slid from her seat, kneeling next to her, she tugged a reluctant Sammy into her arms.

"No, sweetie. I didn't tell him to stay away to punish you." She rubbed her back to soothe her as she had since she was a small baby.

It was an action that was comforting to both of them. "I don't blame you for what happened yesterday."

"Then why can't I see him anymore? He's my dad."

"Yes, he is. But he's not a good influence for you. After yesterday, you can understand that, right?"

Sammy nodded against her neck. "But I love him."

"I know. And he loves you too. That's a good thing. And maybe when you're older you can spend time with him again."

"When?"

"I don't know, sweetie. When you don't have to be dependent on him to look after you if you're with him."

"So when I'm like, ten or something?"

Gina smiled. "Maybe a bit older than that. Maybe sixteen or twenty-one."

"Mum, that's a million years away."

"No, it's not." She tugged Sammy away from her and looked into her eyes. "Your dad should never have let you use his gun. He should never have put you in the position where yesterday could have happened. Do you understand that?"

Sammy nodded, fat tears rolling down her cheeks.

"But he did. Then he should have met you like he promised. But he didn't. Instead he left you to deal with a situation you couldn't possibly be expected to deal with on your own."

"He didn't know."

"I don't care. He should have been there like he promised. It's just one more in a string of promises he's broken to you. One more time he's let you down. But this time, he can't make this mistake right. He can't make this up to you. He doesn't protect you, so I have to. Right now, you're not old enough to protect yourself." She ruffled Sammy's hair. "That's my job."

"I'm not a little kid anymore, Mum. I can look after myself."

"I know you think so—and I know you're not going to like this—but, no, you can't. You're nine years old, and I intend for you to remain a child as long as possible. So, until you can keep yourself out of the trouble he can get you in, he can't be around you."

"So you're punishing him not me?"

Gina thought about that for a second. Was she doing this to make Matt suffer? Did she want to make him pay the price of his stupidity, given that she and Sammy were going to have to live with the consequences of his poor choices for the rest of their lives? Maybe. Could she admit that to Sammy? Hell, no. "No, sweetie. I'm doing this to protect you. It has nothing to do with him. It's all about protecting you. I would do anything to make sure that nothing ever hurts you, or makes you feel sad, or bad." She wiped the tears from Sammy's cheeks. "I didn't do a very good job of protecting you from your dad."

"But I love him."

"I know, sweetie. I know." Doubts plagued her constantly. Was she doing the right thing by keeping Sammy and Matt apart? Her head said yes, but her heart ached as she cuddled Sammy. What Sammy had described to her was an accident. Would Social Services really take her away for that? She couldn't be sure. One thing she was sure of is that the investigation would delve into every aspect of her life. Of Matt's life. And they would keep her away from Matt anyway. That's if he didn't end up in prison. Holding her daughter like this was the only moment's peace she felt. The only time she felt certain of the choices she'd made. She only hoped her choices weren't as bad as the ones Matt had made yesterday.

CHAPTER 11

Kate stared at the diary page until her eyes began to hurt. She rubbed them and squinted back at the scrawled jumble of letters and numbers. She shook her head, picked up the book and a pen, and walked over to the whiteboard to copy what she was staring at.

LN353, 03.06.15, MK52 UXB, 54.4, -3.03, 20
YH971, 10.06.15, KL51 KLD, 54.4, -3.03, 25
LN353, 12.06.15, MN02 MRS, 54.4, -3.03, 15
LT554, 19.06.15, MK52 UXB, 54.4, -3.03, 30

"What the hell is all that?" Brothers asked.

"Not sure," Kate replied. "It's part of the last entry in Connie's diary."

"It's a code," Jimmy said, earning him a swiftly tossed paper ball at the head for his trouble.

"Yes, I got that, Jimmy. Any idea what it means?"

Stella got to her feet and walked over to the board. She drew a box around 03.06.15 down to 19.06.15. "Those are dates," she said, pointing at them. "Third of June down to the nineteenth."

"Yup." Kate drew another box around MK52 UXB down to MK52 UXB. "And those are registration numbers." She pointed to the rest of the board. "What's the rest of it and why the hell did Connie put it all in her diary?"

"Not sure," Tom said. "Want me to run the registration numbers?"

"Please," Kate said, distracted. "And put those dates in the computer while you're at it. Let's see if anything pops up."

"Looking for anything specific?"

Kate shook her head. "No, but we've got so little to go on right now, I don't want to rule anything out. She's written these dates down for a reason." She tapped the board. "I want to know why."

"On it."

"Anything on that key?" she asked Stella, while still staring at the code.

"I've got a serial number on it, but so far nothing. I'm running it through all the databases we have, but it looks like it might be a padlock key."

"No padlocks at the house?" Kate asked.

"None that it fit."

"What about padlocks at the campsite?"

"Wild didn't check that."

"Well, perhaps we should." Kate turned to her and held her hand out. Stella tossed her the evidence bag with the small key inside it. The blade was thicker than most keys she normally saw, and the head was rounded, not flat. The cuts and profile contours were quite subtle but the collar and shoulder were quite pronounced. If it was a padlock key, it was the weirdest one she'd ever seen. "Jimmy, want to join me?"

"Erm, yeah, sure," he said, lifting his coat somewhat reluctantly from the back of his chair. Tom sniggered and Stella wiggled her fingers in farewell as he headed for the door, as if it were the walk to the gallows.

"Need me to take it slowly for you?"

He chuckled nervously. "No, ma'am."

She clicked open the car and checked her mirror as he climbed in and secured his seat belt. "You know, Jimmy, I've never had an accident, a speeding ticket, or a parking ticket. I'm a good driver."

"I'm sure you are, ma'am. I'm just a nervous passenger."

Kate threw her head back and laughed. "Sure you are." She gunned the engine and chuckled, as he gripped the handle above the passenger door, before backing slowly out of the car park.

"Any news on your car?" she asked.

He sighed. "Yeah. Wasn't the battery after all. The cam belt's snapped."

"Ouch. Much damage?"

"Yup. The mechanic said it'll cost more than the car's worth to fix it."

"Uh oh."

"And the insurance is only third party."

"Not your day, Jimmy."

"You can say that again."

She sniggered and said, "Not your day, Jimmy."

"Ha bloody ha." He fidgeted in his seat and seemed to relax a bit as she kept to a moderate speed along the sixty-miles-per-hour section of the road. "So who are we going to see now?"

"We're going to the campsite." She lifted the evidence bag out of her pocket and tossed it to him. "See if we can figure out what this opens."

He looked at it, a frown forming on his brow. "You think this opens something at the campsite?"

"Not a clue. But it's the only other place I can think to look, as it didn't fit anything at her house. Why would you have a key if not to open a lock?"

"True, but my mother has a drawer in the kitchen that's filled with all kinds of junk. She's got keys in there from bike locks we don't even have anymore, and even my grandad's old house, and she sold that ten years ago when he died."

"Glad it's not just me then."

"So how do you know this isn't the same thing?"

"I don't. But the SOCO guys said it wasn't in a drawer, it was hung up with all the other keys on the rack. All the others there fit something. House, car, safe, office, and so on. So it stands to reason that the keys there were all ones that she regularly used."

He grunted. "Still don't think it looks like a padlock key."

"So what does it look like to you?"

His frown deepened. "Does she have a boat?"

Now it was Kate's turn to frown. "Not that I know of. Why?"

"Well, it looks a bit like the key for my dad's boat. Same kind of round head and thick blade."

"What kind of boat?"

"Oh, he lives on a narrow boat on the broads. Gorgeous sixty-footer."

"Your parents live on a barge?"

He shook his head. "Just my dad and his dog. They split when I was a kid."

"Oh, I'm sorry."

"Don't be. They were better parents when they were apart. Together all they did was fight. Me and my sister hated it."

"Older or younger?"

"My sister?"

Kate nodded.

"Younger. She's at uni at the moment. Studying to be a vet."

"Admirable career."

"Yeah." He stared out of the window. "What about you?"

"Only child."

"Mum and dad?"

She clenched her teeth. "My mum died when I was a baby. My dad worked on the oil rigs, so I went to live with my gran. She brought me up."

"I'm sorry about your mum."

She nodded. What else could she say?

"You close to your gran and your dad?"

Kate hated answering the questions she knew would come if she told Jimmy the rest of her story. The words *Piper Alpha* and cancer were blights on her history that she couldn't erase. But it was her history and one she was happy to keep to herself for a while longer. The looks of pity that accompanied the truth were something she could easily live without. She pulled into the gravel car park at the back of the campsite information centre and jumped out of the car before Jimmy could wonder at her lack of answer.

The lights were off and the door locked as she approached. Then she remembered that Gina had said she would remain closed today. She detoured immediately round to the farm cottages, Jimmy close on her heels, scuffling pinecones across the road as he stepped.

"Pick your feet up, Jimmy."

He laughed. "I don't need another mother."

"Good, I have no intention of being one." She knocked on the door and waited for Gina to answer as Jimmy caught her up. She reached over and jovially fiddled with his tie, cinching it a little tighter about his throat. He slapped her hands away and loosened the knot, scowling at her for good measure as the door opened.

"Good afternoon, Miss Temple. How are you?" Kate asked.

Gina smiled. "A hell of a lot better than I was feeling when you saw me this morning." She opened the door wider and swept her arm towards the kitchen. "Come on in."

"Thanks." Kate stepped inside and made her way down to the warm, sunny room at the back of the house.

The large, south-facing windows and today's sunshine made the room warm and bright. The smell of coffee and toast hung in the air, and the radio imported the sounds of Jeremy Vine on his Radio 2 talk show. Gina turned it off as she walked into the room.

"This is Detective Powers." Kate pointed to Jimmy as he held out his hand to Gina and exchanged pleasantries.

"How can I help you, Detective?"

Kate held out the evidence bag. "We found this key next door and wondered what it opened. We thought perhaps something at the campsite or hostel. Do you have any idea?"

Gina took hold of the small plastic bag and examined the key carefully before shaking her head. "It's not a key we use onsite."

"You're sure?"

"Positive. I have a bunch of keys here. Spares for every lock over there. You can take a look." She retrieved three huge sets of keys. All different shapes and sizes hung off three climbing karabiners. "This one is for the office, storage barn, and laundry area." She handed over the largest set of keys to Kate. "This one's the hostels and information centre." She handed those to Jimmy. "And these are for the toilet block, bin areas, and store cupboards on the campsite." She held up the smallest set, flipping through them. Each of them sorted through bunches of steel, brass, and iron.

Kate could see quickly that none of them fit the key they had, the rounded head a dead giveaway. "It didn't fit any lock in Connie's house or car. Do you know of anything else she would be holding keys for?"

Gina ran her fingers through her hair. Kate and Jimmy handed back the keys she had given them. "I don't think so." She studied the key again before handing it back. "I'm sorry, I don't know what this is for."

Kate took hold of the evidence bag and tried to ignore the tingling in her fingers when her skin touched Gina's. "Powers here thinks it reminds him of a boat key."

Gina frowned and shook her head. "Connie didn't have a boat. She didn't sail."

"What about Leah? Could the key be hers?"

Gina shrugged. "I guess it could be, but I'm almost certain Connie packed all her things and sent them to her or put them in storage." She slowly pulled her hand away from Kate's and Kate immediately felt the loss. "I suppose the only way to know for sure is to ask Leah."

"Of course." Kate stuffed the key into her pocket. It was time to leave. To move on to the next set of questions, the next witness, or suspect. But Kate didn't want to go. She wanted to stay talking to Gina. "How's Sammy doing?"

"She'll be fine. It's hit her hard."

"She's a tough kid."

Gina laughed and leaned on the back of her chair. "That she is."

"And she has you." Kate wanted to tell her what a difference a mother made to a child going through a tragic loss. She wanted to tell her that Gina's love would get her through to the other side of this and she'd be so much stronger. That they'd be stronger. She found herself wanting to find a way to erase the sorrow and grief from Gina's face. "Thanks for your time."

Pathetic!

Gina smiled sadly and walked them back to the front door. "Anytime, Detective. You know where to find me."

She could feel Jimmy staring at her as they got back in the car but, thankfully, he didn't say anything. Little bastard didn't need to. The grin on his face said it all. *Bollocks.*

Kate knocked on Ally's door. The curtains were closed and she could hear raised voices from inside. Great. Looked like Leah wasn't alone. She knocked again, louder, hoping to be heard over the row. The shouting stopped and the door opened quickly. Ally scowled at them.

"What?"

"Is Leah in?"

Ally sighed and opened the door for them to enter. "Leah, you've got company."

"What? Who?" She stood up and poked her head around the kitchen door. "Oh, for fuck's sake. What do you want now?"

Kate smiled, grateful Leah was wearing a T-shirt this time. It was grubby, hung off one shoulder, and was one she had obviously been wearing for a while, if the smell was anything to go by. "Nice to see you again, Leah. Mind if we sit down?" She addressed her question to Ally.

"Help yourselves," Ally said as she dropped down onto the only clear seat in the room. The sofa was strewned with bedclothes, an armchair being used as a magazine stand, and the dining chairs all had numerous articles of clothing on or draped over the back of them.

Kate gathered the magazines, dropped them on the table, and sat down, leaving Jimmy to fend for himself. "I need you to take a look at something for me and tell me if it's yours or if you know what it's for." She looked at Leah closely. Her blonde hair needed a good wash. The dirt and grease had made it stick to her head in stringy strands that fell to her shoulders. The room's odour was testament to her unwashed state, and Kate tried valiantly to avoid wrinkling her nose.

"What?"

Kate held out the evidence bag. "Do you know what this is?"

Leah took it and Kate noticed the track marks on the inside of her elbow and forearm.

"It's a key." Ally sniggered.

Kate closed her eyes briefly. "I know that. We found this key in Connie's house, but we can't locate what it locked. Do you recognise it? Is it yours?" she asked Leah.

"No." Leah held it out to Kate.

"Mind if I take a look?" Ally asked.

Kate glanced over at Jimmy, standing close to the door. He gave a tiny shrug. If she hadn't been looking right at him, she wouldn't have seen it. "Sure." Kate waved the key in Ally's direction. This was the first time she'd seen the woman not covered in bulky overalls, sweaters, a massive coat, and a hat that had hidden more of her face than was on show.

She took the time Ally used to study the key to study her. She had strong-looking hands and equally strong features. Her jaw was on the square side, lips wide and full. Her nose was straight but had a small bump about halfway up, no doubt the result of a break at some point. Her salt-and-pepper hair was short, but cut in a flattering no-fuss style that complemented her angular jaw and prominent cheekbones. Grey eyes looked keenly intelligent and wary at the same time. She was attractive, Kate could see that, but Ally had a reputation that seemed out of proportion. Perhaps it was unjustified after all, and gave the locals something to talk about. Ally cocked her head to one side as she examined the key from all sides.

"It's a boat key," she said. "I see keys like this all the time down at the harbour." She fished a set of keys from her pocket. "Even got one of my own." She tossed the small bunch to Kate. "See?"

Kate did. The key was almost an exact replica of the key on Ally's keyring. There were obvious differences in the cuts on the blade and the head had a red plastic cover over it. She looked at Leah. "Did Connie have a boat?"

"No." She scratched at her arms as she perched on the edge of the sofa. "She didn't sail."

Exactly what Gina had told them. Kate frowned. Why would a woman who didn't sail have a key for a boat hung up with all her other important keys? "Do you have a boat, Leah?"

Leah shook her head. "I don't like the water. I went out on a boat with Ally once."

"Yeah, and all she did was throw up," Ally added. She laughed, but there seemed something forced about it to Kate, like she was trying to make funny something that really wasn't. Having suffered on a ferry crossing to Ireland once, Kate was well aware of how little humour there was to be found in seasickness.

"Sorry to hear that." She retrieved the key from Ally. "Thank you both for your help."

Ally let Kate and Jimmy out the door, and they both remained silent until they had closed the car doors.

"Did you see those track marks on her arm?"

"Yes." Kate pulled her phone from her pocket and dialled. "Hey, Stella, I need you to focus on that serial number on the key. It's a boat key. That should help narrow down the search."

"Will do."

"Thanks." She hung up and started the engine, then drove towards the harbour to turn around. The boats were all docked at the quay, the keels sitting in the soft, muddy bottom that only filled with water as the high tide approached. Lobster pots were stacked high on land, and the steel cables clattered against the masts.

"What do you think's going on there?" He pointed to the house they'd just left.

"What do you mean?"

"Between them two. Do you think they're a couple?"

Kate laughed. "No."

Jimmy looked at her curiously. "How do you know?"

"Trust me, Jimmy, I know. Ally's not interested in Leah one little bit. Even if she wasn't a junkie who's about as broken as I've seen, Ally's not interested in women."

"How do you know?"

Kate shook her head. "I know."

"Ah, I get it." He smiled looking more than a little smug, and turned to look out of the window as Kate pulled onto the main road.

"What do you get?" Kate asked.

"It's one of them gaydar things, right?"

"Seriously? You're going there, Jimmy?" She wondered if he'd have the guts to ask.

"My sister's a lesbian. She and her girlfriend have been together for three years now. We go out sometimes and she'll point out this person or that person. Giving me pointers." He chuckled. "I still can't spot when someone's gay or not."

"Oh, I don't know, Jimmy." She smiled at him. "I think you're doing all right."

He grinned back at her. "Really?"

"Yeah. Really." Kate turned on to one of the back roads.

"Where are we going now?"

"Mission of mercy."

He frowned. "I don't understand."

"You will." She gunned the engine and watched his face pale. Just a little. Just enough to keep him from asking any more questions.

CHAPTER 12

"You sure you want to do this?" Wild asked as he led Kate down a corridor at King's Lynn's police station.

"Why wouldn't I?"

"She's been, well, temperamental."

"Meaning?"

"We've had to put her in a cage because she started chewing on the desk legs. Now," he said and pushed open the door, "she won't stop barking."

The barking was deep, loud, and obviously distressed. "Are you surprised?"

"Excuse me?"

"Well, she doesn't know where she is, she doesn't know what's going on, and she's being ignored." She shrugged and knelt down to open the cage. "Not to mention what she went through the other day." She pulled open the door and held out her hand for the dog to sniff. The barking stopped and the dog backed up against the far end of the cage, tail tucked between her legs, ears down. Everything about her posture screamed submission and fear. Kate just sat back on her heels and waited, hand extended. Slowly the dog inched forward and sniffed her fingers. Then she backed up a little and whined.

"It's okay, pup. You're fine." She kept waiting, watching, as the dog slowly approached again and took a longer sniff before crawling closer. Kate slowly stroked her face, the top of her head, and scratched gently around her ears, smiling as the dog relaxed a little more and stepped out of the cage to her. She glared up at Wild and growled low in her throat. Kate chuckled. "I don't think she liked you putting her in there, Sergeant."

"Apparently not." He backed away a step and the dog immediately relaxed and seemed to lean into Kate's touch. "Looks like you've got yourself a friend, though."

"She's got nothing bad to associate with me. Just good stuff. I'm taking her out of the cage she doesn't like." She continued to stroke the dappled grey fur and whisper nonsense to the frightened animal. "Do you have a lead for her?"

"Erm, no. The collar and lead she was wearing are evidence now, Detective."

"Right. Well, have you got anything I can use temporarily?"

"I can probably find you a bit of rope."

"Christ." She rolled her eyes. "Do me a favour, will you?"

"What?"

"Go out front and find my car. Jimmy Powers is in there." She tossed her car keys at him. "Tell him to go to the pet shop and get a collar and lead for a collie. I'll pay him back later."

He grinned. "Right-o."

"And tell him to bring my car back in one piece."

Wild laughed. "Will do."

The dog lay down next to her and rested her head over Kate's thigh, staring at the door, eyes flicking from one moving figure to the next. Kate could feel the tension thrumming through every muscle in Merlin's body, she trembled as she remained on high alert.

"Is there a back door with a yard or something?" she asked one of the passing officers.

"That way," the young man said, pointing to a door at the end of the room. "Smoker's shed out there."

"Right. Thanks." She patted the dog's head. "Well, it's better than nothing. Let's see if you need to go." She stood up and took a step towards the door, the dog was right on her heels. The "smoker's shed" was definitely an apt description. There must have been so many people inside that the fumes from the toxic little sticks were trying to escape through every gap they could find in the cheap pine box that offered shelter from the rain. Just. The yard was about six feet wide and ten feet long, plus the shed at the end that ran the width of the yard. It wasn't much, but it seemed that Merlin had quickly become accustomed to this being her outside space while at the police station. She sniffed around and seemed happy enough exploring.

Kate watched her while she thought about the case. She hoped Stella had managed to find some information on that boat key by the time she got back to Hunstanton. If not, she had no idea where to go next with this case. All leads seemed to lead nowhere, and she was guessing at who the killer was. Wild joined her after a few minutes.

"Well, I can't say the lad looked happy. But I think it was fear of damaging your car rather than anything else." He chuckled. "Shouldn't be long."

"Thanks." She smiled when the dog returned to her side, growled at Wild, and leaned against her leg, head almost reaching Kate's hip. "Anything on the camera?"

"I've got the computer guys trying to pull some images off the SD card. It was badly damaged but they think they've got some whizz-bang, shit-hot software that can do magic with it, so we'll see. They said tomorrow morning at the earliest."

"And the actual camera? Can you tell what kind of weapon was used or anything from it?"

"I've got a few ideas, but it's pretty tough to put this all together. I'm meeting with Dr. Anderson and one of these tech guys later this afternoon to see if we can work up a realistic scenario as to what happened."

"Care to share your ideas?"

"Well, to get anywhere, I have to make a few assumptions. That's where I want to collaborate with Anderson and this guy in tech, Grimshaw. If I assume she was on the bank walking the dog and taking pictures, it would make sense and fit with her usual routine. Correct?"

"Based on all witnesses, friends, and even those who didn't like her, yes. That's a very logical assumption," Kate said.

"It also stands to reason that she'd be facing the harbour to take pictures. It's far more picturesque than the other direction. And the sunrise, even though it was behind her, would be colouring the sky. Reasonable?"

Kate nodded.

"So, based on that, we can start to work up where it most likely was that the shot was fired from."

"Excellent. What about the type of weapon?"

"I found a few slivers of metal that didn't belong to the camera embedded inside. They're being analysed now, and I'll know more when we get the results tomorrow."

"Anything?"

"Well, it was definitely high powered. Not shot at close range, and given that the tide was in, I'd say maybe the best part of three to four hundred yards. It was a spring tide so the whole marsh nearby was flooded. The nearest land mass big enough to support human weight for long enough to take that shot would be at least that far away."

"Seriously?"

"Yup."

"So you're talking a sniper rifle, from long range."

"Around a quarter of a mile away."

"That kind of shot takes skill."

"And knowledge, and patience, and it is not something that happens by accident."

"So the killer was waiting out on the marsh somewhere with what?"

"Like I said, I'm waiting for the report, but if I'm right, the round was a 7.62 by 51 millimetre NATO round, which is pretty standard for a lot of European sniper rifles. I'll get you a list of potential guns, but this isn't a common weapon around here. The farmers around here carry .22s and double-barrel shotguns for hunting and shooting vermin. This is a big, powerful weapon that is designed to do nothing but kill things from a long, long way away. The kind of person who can make that shot is someone who has been around guns for a long time. Someone who's spent a lot of time practicing to become that good."

"Maybe a member at a gun club?"

Wild smiled. "Maybe, indeed." He handed her a piece of paper.

"List of gun clubs close to Brandale Staithe, by any chance?"

He chuckled. "Guess that's why they pay you the big bucks and gave you the fancy title."

She laughed with him and lifted the page in his direction. "Thank you."

"A pleasure. I gotta tell you, I'm enjoying this case."

She cocked an eyebrow in his direction, not entirely sure she had heard him correctly.

"I know it's not the right thing to say, and it's a damn shame a woman was killed, but every now and then, you need a case like this to get you fired up. To put the old brain matter to the test. You know what I mean?"

She did, but she liked to think that that was something she gave to every case. Not just the interesting ones, or the ones with special victims. She nodded anyway. No sense in alienating a colleague that was proving to be quite resourceful and full of information.

"So are you going to keep the animal?"

Kate cast her eyes down to where the dog sat at her side. "See how it goes. Supposed to be a temporary thing. The rescue place is looking for a permanent home for her."

He grunted and looked at his watch. "Gotta go. I'm meeting with Anderson and Grimshaw in twenty minutes."

"I look forward to hearing about the results."

He nodded and pushed the door open behind them. A high-powered sniper rifle. She recalled Leah's shaking hands and her inability to light her own cigarette, and felt her certainty in the woman's innocence solidify. Even if Leah owned such a rifle, had waited out on the marsh to take the shot, Kate seriously doubted that she would have been able to hit a double-decker bus at that distance, never mind the camera lens held to the face of the target. Nah, she wasn't buying that one. So who did that leave? Rupert Sands? He was the only one who didn't seem to have an alibi. There was certainly a gun culture going on there. Just because they didn't have a sniper rifle on display didn't mean he didn't have one somewhere else. Was he callous enough to commit that kind of crime? Or was it just plain greed?

What motivated a killer to commit this kind of crime? It was remote, impersonal, as if it hadn't anything to do with the people involved. It was just business. It was almost transactional. A means to an end. But what end? Connie's intention of closing down the campsite would have affected many of the business owners in the village. Yes, Rupert Sands would be affected—the loss of amenities in the village would eventually work its way down to affecting his holiday home business, but he was by no means the only one. Others would be affected worse than he. Perhaps not in the amount of lost revenue, but simply because they could afford to lose so much less than Rupert Sands could. The rich would lose money, the poor would lose their entire livelihoods. Businesses would go bankrupt, individuals would lose their jobs, their incomes, and maybe, as a result, their homes. Their security. Was that enough to make them kill?

People had killed for a lot less.

Or did it come down to some sort of maniacal temper tantrum? I can't have it so I'll stop you having it too? Was a grown man capable of such a feat of stubborn stupidity? Specifically, was Rupert Sands capable of it? He was certainly stubborn. He'd demonstrated a temper, he didn't like being questioned, and given what she'd seen and heard, he seemed to have a problem with women having power or authority over him.

Kate didn't like him. She doubted many people did. But did that mean he was a killer? A bully, maybe. But bullies are usually too cowardly to put themselves on the line the way a murderer would have to.

"I just got black because I didn't know what colour you'd prefer." Jimmy slapped a scrunched-up plastic bag against her arm, distracting her from her musings.

"That's great, thanks." She fished the dog collar from the bag and used her teeth to break off the plastic tag. She squatted down and fitted the collar around the dog's neck, who in turn rewarded her with a long, pink tongue up the length of her face. Jimmy laughed as she wiped her face and buckled the collar in place. Merlin's jaw hung open a little, her tongue lolling to the right in a satisfied doggy grin. Kate clipped the lead in place and walked out of the station, Merlin at her side, and Jimmy trotting behind them.

Once Merlin was settled in the back seat of the car, Kate handed the sheet of paper to Jimmy. "Do you know where any of those are?"

He looked at the page in his hand. "The first one's just a couple of miles away."

"Direct me."

"Sure. Turn left out of the car park and then left again at the lights." She followed his directions for the next five minutes and pulled up at the first gun club on Wild's list.

"So what're we doing here, boss?" he asked.

"We're going to see who could make an amazing shot at this club and if any of those names are on our suspect list."

"How amazing a shot?"

"Pinpoint accurate at about a quarter of a mile."

Jimmy whistled.

"Does that qualify as amazing?"

"Yup. And then some." He followed her out of the car and laughed. Merlin jumped out and followed at Kate's heels despite her not having hold of her lead.

"You're supposed to wait in the car," Kate said to the dog. She pointed back to the vehicle where Jimmy held the door open, but the dog just looked up at her blankly. Jimmy sniggered. Kate repeated her command, with no change in the standoff. "Fine. But do not bark, do not chew anything, and do not pee on the carpet."

Merlin whined as though she were telling Kate that she wasn't stupid. Jimmy laughed outright and slammed the door closed. Kate locked it and picked up Merlin's lead.

"And don't go wandering off either."

"Me or the dog?"

Kate glared at Jimmy but didn't respond to the jibe. She pushed open the door of the rather run-down-looking prefab building. The pebble-dashed render on the outside was covered in graffiti—cartoon images of penises, exceptionally well endowed women, and several graphically portrayed sexual positions were depicted. Kate couldn't help but think that the imagery was much more suited to a strip club than a gun club, but teenagers were teenagers and a wall was a wall at the end of the day.

A middle-aged man sat behind a desk, newspaper spread open in front of him. He glanced up at them. "No dogs. This isn't the place to train gun dogs." He turned the page.

"I'll bear that in mind. In the meantime, I was hoping you could help us." Kate held out her warrant card and badge. "Detective Sergeant Brannon. This is Detective Constable Powers. Can we see the manager, please?"

He eyed them warily. "That'd be me. Don Howe. What can I do for you?"

"I'm in need of the help of a sharpshooter."

"A sharpshooter, you say. Well, I know pretty much every one of my boys here considers themselves to be a pretty sharp shooter." He chuckled. "What specifically are you looking for?"

"Someone who can hit a camera at four hundred yards."

Don whistled. "You don't want a sharpshooter. You want a marksman. And a pretty decent one at that. You don't find many of those outside the forces."

Kate nodded. "I didn't think so. I guess you don't know of any here at this club, then?"

Don shook his head. "The only person I know who could've made that shot was me." He pointed to a photograph on the wall of himself in uniform. "Special forces. Two tours of Afghanistan." He shook his head. "Now I can't even pick up a weapon without my hands shaking." He held out a hand that was already trembling. "PTSD's a terrible thing for a man to live with."

"I'm very sorry, sir." Kate looked him in the eye, hoping she conveyed the depth of her appreciation for his service. "If you do think of anyone who can help us with our enquiries," she said, handing him a card, "please give me a call."

"Sure, sure." He nodded. "But that kind of range, you need to be looking at clubs with an outdoor range, not indoor ones like this."

Kate put her piece of paper on the counter. "Can you tell me which ones I should look at?"

He put a star next to three of them. "Those are the closest ones, but there are two others farther out towards Norwich. You can try them too." He wrote the addresses beneath her printed list.

"Thank you for your help, Don."

"No problem." He smiled. "I hope you find what you're looking for."

Three hours later, they had visited the five ranges and now had acquired a list of the people across Norfolk who could have made the kind of shot that killed Connie Wells. Of those, four were known to them.

Matt Green, Adam Robbins, Ally Robbins, and Rupert Sands.

"Are we going to arrest him?" Jimmy asked as they made their way back to the station.

"Who?"

"Sands."

"Rupert?"

"Yeah. Everyone in the village hates them."

"Right." Kate frowned. Nothing had changed. Everything they had against Sands was still circumstantial. They had nothing concrete. No evidence.

"Are we?"

"I don't think we should."

"Why not? He's got motive, opportunity, now we know he has the skill required to pull this murder off. We should arrest him."

Kate dialled Timmons and filled him in.

"Do you think you have enough to arrest him?" Timmons asked.

"No. Everything we have is circumstantial right now, and we have almost as much on three other suspects." She chewed her lip. "I think that if it is him and we move too early he'll get his fancy brief in and we'll lose our advantage."

"Another possibility if it isn't him, the jungle drums will start and the real killer will ditch the weapon if they haven't already. You know what the gossip's like in small villages."

"Of course, sir."

"I think you're right to wait until you get the results back tomorrow. In the meantime, I'd be running a check on them all to see what firearms they have registered."

"Already in the works, sir."

"Good work, Brannon. Anything else?"

"No, sir."

"Good, carry on, then."

Kate looked at Jimmy, who sighed as she started the engine and drove back to the station. She wanted to look at the code again and see if Stella had found anything out about that bloody key. It was driving her mad.

Merlin stayed on her heels as she walked into the police station and the desk sergeant buzzed them through. Jimmy slung his coat over the back of his chair and slumped in his seat.

"What's up with you?" Stella asked him.

"He's unhappy that we can't go and arrest Rupert Sands," Kate said.

"Do we have something on him?" Stella asked.

"Yeah. He's got motive, no alibi, and he can make the shot that killed her," Jimmy said.

Stella frowned. "Am I missing something?"

Kate quickly brought the three of them up to speed. Stella and Tom quickly agreed with her decision to wait until the test results and other information came in. Collier stayed quiet.

"As much as we might want to, Jimmy lad, we can't just arrest everyone who we don't like," Tom said.

"But he's got no alibi."

"At least half of the village didn't either."

"Yeah, but none of them are on this list. They couldn't have made that shot."

"How do you know? Just because they don't go to one of the gun clubs you went to, doesn't mean someone can't practice elsewhere. It doesn't mean that someone else doesn't have the skill."

Kate listened to them argue the point backward and forward while she stared at the code on the board again. *LN353, 03.06.14, MK52UXB, 54.4, -3.03, 20.* "Have we got the vehicle details on those registrations yet?"

"We do, indeed." Stella stood up and walked over to the board. "MK52 UXB is a Mitsubishi pickup registered to one Matt Green."

"Shit," Jimmy said.

Tom grinned. "See, lad, you gotta wait for all the information to come in."

"KL51 KLD is a Peugeot Estate registered to Leah Shaw." Stella went on writing the information on the board. "And MN02 MRS is a Toyota Hilux registered to...any guesses?"

"Tom or Ally Robbins," Kate said.

"Neh." Stella made a rather rude buzzer sound, signalling the incorrect guess. "Close but no cigar, kid. Cedric Robbins." She added the final name to the board.

"So nothing to do with Rupert Sands or Edward Sands," Kate said.

"Nope." Stella sat back in her seat.

"Doesn't mean it wasn't him," Jimmy said stubbornly.

"No, but it does mean that something about these people was of interest to our victim. But Sands wasn't."

"Matt Green works for Sands," Jimmy said stubbornly.

"Move on, Jimmy." She pointed to the board. "What? What was it that Connie was logging here, people? What do those numbers mean? The prefix at the very beginning? What is it?"

Tom shook his head. "Given that she was a photographer, I thought it might have something to do with images, so I've been looking through her photograph library that we found on her laptop."

"Good thinking," Kate complimented.

"Don't be so quick to congratulate me, boss. So far I haven't found anything catalogued under any of these codes. But I did find something interesting."

"And that is?"

"I can't find any pictures for the dates on the board. Nothing."

"So?"

"She took pictures every day. I've got backup hard drives, and everything on this machine. I mean, she took a couple hundred pictures every single day."

"Wow."

"Yeah. She didn't always edit them. Some of them are just sitting on there, either waiting for her to get around to them, or just practice shots. I don't know. If nothing else, she took picture after picture of that dog." He pointed to Merlin.

"But nothing on those dates?"

"Nada."

"That is strange. Does she store images anywhere else?"

"I wondered about that too, so I asked Miss Temple. She said that anything taken specifically for the site was stored at work, so I went down and took a little look around the server."

"Find 'em?" Kate asked hopefully.

"Zip." Tom grinned. "We got another little mystery."

"I think we've got more than enough of those."

"True, but these are all pointing somewhere."

"Does Miss Temple have a calendar or diary for Connie's appointments? Was there anything happening on these dates that meant she couldn't take pictures? Let's rule that out before we start to assume it means more than it does."

Tom nodded and picked up the phone.

"Anything on that key?" Kate asked Stella.

"It's definitely a boat lock, but it was sold from the manufacturers in a batch about five years ago."

"Where did the batch go?"

"To the chandlery at Brandale Staithe, but they don't have any record of who that particular lock was sold to. I already phoned."

"So we can't trace it?"

"Not unless we start randomly sticking it into boat locks and seeing what happens."

Kate grunted. "If there weren't so bloody many around here, I might take that idea seriously."

Stella chuckled. "In lieu of that, Matt Green and Rupert Sands." She pinned a picture of each of them on the board. "Both sketchy in the alibi department. Green told Tom he was working at seven. Ed Sands says he didn't get there till almost half past. That makes him missing at time of death. Rupert says he was home alone. Both these guys are a dab hand on a target range. These are our prime suspects."

"But Sands isn't identified in Connie's diary?"

"No, his licence isn't on there. We don't know what the rest of it means, and when we figure it out, who's to say it won't point to him? Like Jimmy said, Green does work for him." She shrugged. "Either way the other two points still mean we need to look into him. I want everything we can find on both of them. If they've not paid a parking ticket, I want to know about it."

Kate shook her head and decided to focus on Green. As far as she was concerned, Rupert Sands was an arse, but like all bullies who think they're something, when it comes right down to it, they're just full of shit. She fired up her computer and pecked away at the keys, but her eyes continued to drift back to the board.

Missing pictures. Key to an unknown boat. Mysterious code that implicates Matt Green, Leah Shaw, and Cedric Robbins in…something. And one dead campsite owner. What the hell was going on in Brandale Staithe?

CHAPTER 13

Gina stared out of the window and across the fence that separated her garden from Connie's. The last of the leaves had fallen from the sycamore tree at the edge of Connie's property, and the debris blew haphazardly on the wind. She'd made Sammy rake up the mess in their garden earlier that day. She knew her daughter needed to be outside, and she needed to be kept out of trouble. Putting her to work seemed like a good idea. Now the pile of fallen foliage that she'd tossed onto the composting heap was blowing across the garden again and collecting against the fence. The never-ending battle with Mother Nature.

She considered asking Sammy to clear Connie's garden too, but given the way she'd stayed at least five feet from the fence and refused to look into the neighbouring garden the whole time she was out there, Gina couldn't do it. She supposed she'd have to do it herself at some point. Who knew what was going to happen to the place now. She knew Connie had owned her own property, and she assumed it would now go to Leah. Unless Connie had changed her will after they split up. If she even had one. Jesus, it was a mine field. She shook her head and put the kettle on. Her hands were still cold and the only thing that seemed to thaw them was holding on to a hot mug.

She'd just poured water into the cup when she felt tears on her cheek. She swiped at them but it wasn't enough to wipe away the memories of all the times she'd shared this simple ritual with Connie. How many times had she made them both a brew? Tea for her and coffee for Connie. "You won't catch me drinking that gnat's piss," Connie had said to her time and again, usually as she gratefully received her mug and reached for a biscuit to dunk. Gina sat back at the table, stared over into Connie's garden again, and smiled sadly.

She'd wished over the years of their friendship that the house had been her own. One she was buying rather than renting. One that offered her and Sammy more security than a year's contract at a time. But there was no way she could afford a mortgage on a place like this. Instead, she had to rely on wealthy landowners like the Sands for a roof over her head as she lined their pockets with her hard-earned cash and they sat in the lap of luxury. Bastards.

"Don't let 'em get you down, kiddo," Connie's voice whispered in her head. The phrase she'd said to Gina more times than she could count. "Don't let the bastards get you down."

"I won't." Gina whispered. "And I won't let everything you worked for go to waste, Connie. You have my word on that." Her hands felt warm for the first time in days. The sun shone through the window, casting bright swathes of light across the scarred wooden surface and over her hands. She smiled. She'd never considered herself a believer in God or religion, or life after death, or anything like that. She was more concerned with living from day to day and making the best life possible for herself and Sammy. But the warmth across her hands as she thought of Connie at that moment, well, she could have sworn she was being given a message. A positive one. Perhaps even one of forgiveness.

She felt lighter than she had since Sammy had spilled her secret and thrown them into a panicked tailspin. She felt as though maybe, just maybe, everything was going to work out all right. Connie had always been able to do that. Convince her that everything would be okay, with that quiet competence that was so often overlooked. Connie had never felt the need to go around shouting about what she did, or how good she was to anyone who would listen. She just quietly got on with it and let the results speak for themselves. Something she'd encouraged Gina to do more than once.

Gina sipped her drink and watched the sun set on another day, and a thought struck her. Who's arranging Connie's funeral?

It had been three days now since the body had been found, but she had no idea what was going on with the arrangements, or who was taking care of them. She knew that Connie had no family left since her grandmother had passed away eighteen months before. As far as Gina could see, that left only Leah and she seriously doubted Leah could arrange her own bed anymore. A funeral was likely to be well beyond her current capabilities. Given that it was her daughter who had killed her, surely arranging a funeral was the least she could do, right? It was the right thing to do, right? To say her goodbyes properly, to show Connie the respect she deserved. That made sense, right?

She hadn't noticed the sun sink beyond the horizon, or the darkness descend as she sat wondering, worrying, trying to work out what she could do for her friend. She'd never been closely involved in a death before. She didn't know what needed to be done, or arranged. What would she be allowed to do, since the police were conducting a murder enquiry? So many things she didn't know the answers to. She retrieved the card DS Brannon had given her and dialled the number before she had the chance to talk herself out of it.

"Hello?"

Oh, her voice sounds just as lovely over the phone. "Detective? It's Gina Temple."

"Well, hello, Miss Temple. What can I do for you this evening?"

"I, erm, well, I was wondering who was organising the funeral for Connie?"

"Oh, I see. At the moment, no one is. The body hasn't been released and won't be while the investigation is ongoing."

"Oh, right."

"After that, it depends on who comes forward to claim the body."

"And who is that normally?"

"Relatives, a partner, children, parents, or sometimes close friends."

"And if not? What happens then?"

"The local authority would organise it."

"The council?"

"Yes."

"So she'd just be carted off from the hospital and thrown in some sort of pauper's grave?" Gina was aghast.

"Well, not exactly. Most councils do go above and beyond their legal duty which would be to bury or cremate the remains. Most arrange a simple service and hire one of those professional mourners so that there's someone there to see the person off. It's done with as much dignity and respect as they can."

"A professional mourner?"

"Yeah, I know. Sounds like a really morbid job, doesn't it? But I spoke to a woman who was one once, and she said it wasn't morbid at all. She said it was respectful and offered a little something to the poor person who was being buried that they wouldn't otherwise have. She said she remembered the name of every person whose funeral she attended and mentioned them in her prayers every night. She felt that by never forgetting them, she gave them what the family of most other people gave their loved ones. The gift of not being forgotten."

Gina's tears rolled down her cheeks again and she hoped that they couldn't be heard in her voice when she asked, "Would I be able to organise Connie's funeral? When the time comes."

"Yes, of course." Her voice was gentle, compassionate. "I'll give your details to the coroner tomorrow and have them inform you when they can release Connie's body for burial. I have to warn you, though, it really could be a while yet." There was a familiarity to the way she spoke. Gina felt as though she was trying to convey far more to her than the words she said. It felt comfortable and comforting at the same time. Like hugging someone and forgetting who was doing the holding and who was being held.

"I understand." Gina heard the break in her own voice. "I just don't want Connie to be left to people who didn't know her. She deserves better than that."

"Everyone does."

Gina heard the catch in Kate's voice and wondered what she was thinking about. Kate didn't know Connie enough for this to have affected her so. "Do you have someone to remember you, Detective?"

The silence stretched between them until it became brittle, like glass, one wrong move and it would shatter, splintering the fragile intimacy that had grown between them. She wondered if she should just hang up, pretend she hadn't asked the question, and move on.

"No," Kate whispered. "There would be no one to mourn or remember me." She cleared her throat. "Good night, Miss Temple."

"Gina," she said, "please, call me Gina." She heard a short intake of breath down the line and then the words were almost too quiet for her to hear.

"Good night, Gina."

Kate hung up the phone and tried to swallow the emotion that clawed its way up her throat. *Damn you, Gina Temple. I was doing all right.*

Merlin sat beside her and put a paw on her thigh. She stroked her head as the first of the tears tumbled down her cheeks. The dog whined, slowly crawled onto Kate's lap, and tucked her head against her neck, offering comfort to the crying human in the only way she could. With her whole self.

Kate wrapped her arms around her warm, furry body and cried as she hadn't since she was seventeen and had buried her grandmother. The woman who had raised her after her father died on that terrible night that *Piper Alpha* had burned. The night her father had died alongside the other men working on the rig.

Loneliness was a word she hated, but most nights, sitting alone after she'd finished work, it was the only one that applied. She tried to hide it, or rather hide from it, by staying busy at work, going to the gym or the swimming pool, running, anything that kept her out of the house longer. It kept her sane, it kept her functioning, it kept the long winter nights from becoming too dark. It gave her a vent for the anger that sparked now and then. It gave her a rhythm, a reason, a purpose. She worked hard, but not for those she helped, and she hoped no one ever found out that she worked hard only to help herself. Selflessness for selfish reasons didn't really count as far as she was concerned. The reason, the intent, was more important to her than the act. She didn't help others to make them feel better, she helped them to stop herself from feeling so bad. For those few seconds, she felt a sense of belonging, a feeling that someone else did care about her, about what happened to her.

But it never lasted. It was there one moment, and then, with a fractional shift, less even than a breath, the sensation changed. From inclusion to intrusion. Like the twist of a toy she'd had as a child, a kaleidoscope, where a tiny twist of the lens made everything move and the picture changed. That was what happiness was for her. Fleeting. Intangible. Elusive. Gone in less time than it takes to blink an eye.

Would anyone remember her when she was gone? Would anyone mourn her? No.

Tonight, Gina's simple question and the unconditional love offered by a grieving animal were her undoing.

CHAPTER 14

The harbour was quiet and dark. The green and red lights of the boats grew smaller as they headed out to sea. A head torch illuminated the path for her while she stretched out her hamstrings by the side of an A2-sized plaque. Sixteen and a half inches by twenty-three, extolling the renascence of the Brandale Staithe Harbour in the last five years. A small line drawing of a near-derelict harbour, run-down boats, and discarded fishing gear. A mess, basically. Until 2010 when investment was secured by C. Robbins and family to reinvigorate the tiny, struggling port and all those who relied on her for their survival. C. Robbins. Cedric Robbins and family. A photograph at the bottom of the board showed Cedric, Ally, and Adam with the other fishermen, arms slung about each other's shoulders, smiles on their faces, and a caption beneath: "Cedric Robbins and twins, Adam and Ally, showing there's life in the old sea dog yet."

She lifted her arms over her head and twisted to get a good stretch on her back. "Twins, huh?" She shook her hands out and set out with Merlin.

Running was her release, her thinking time. She was lost in her own thoughts and she drifted from one subject to another. From Gina and her phone call last night to the blasted code that was driving her mad, and the key that seemed to belong to nothing. She knew that she needed to crack them both in order to solve this murder and the more time that dragged on, the less likely catching the culprit became. Mud squelched beneath her feet with every step and she finally looked out instead of in and realised how far she and Merlin had travelled. Merlin barked.

"Shit." She started to turn around, to head back towards the car. "Merlin, come on girl, let's go back this way."

The dog clearly had other ideas and took off in the direction they'd been headed. Straight towards the area where Connie had been killed.

"Bollocks." She ran after the dog, calling her name. As she got closer, she saw that Merlin had stopped and was growling at something a little way off in the distance. She squinted, still finding it difficult to see through the dim early morning light and the fog that rolled in off the North Sea. Momentarily, the fog cleared and she saw a smouldering heap of wood slowly being surrounded by the incoming tide. "Oh fuckity fuck fuck fuck." She clipped Merlin's lead onto her collar and attached her to a post close enough so that Merlin could see her, but far enough away to prevent her contaminating another crime scene.

She pulled her phone from her pocket and dialled Wild. She waded through the thick mud and cold water to the remains of the houseboat she'd seen on the creek two days earlier. The roof and most of the walls were gone. She presumed the floor had only remained due to the water underneath it, but she'd be amazed if that lasted much longer, as the water rushing into the creek would surely claim the rest of the wreckage soon enough.

"It's not even six in the friggin' morning. Something better be on fire."

"Wild? Are you psychic? It's Brannon. I've got another crime scene out here on the marsh. I need you to get here ASAP."

"Are you kidding?"

Kate could hear him climbing out of bed and the rustle of fabric. He was no doubt hurriedly dressing. "No," she replied.

"Another body?"

"No, you were right first time. Houseboat on fire. Well, it was. Smouldering now. And sinking."

"The big one that was just the other side of where the body was?"

"Yes."

"Shit. What's the tide doing?"

"Coming in."

"Bugger."

"I know. I think we're going to need something to try and keep it from sinking."

"No time. Just get up there and collect whatever you can."

"I'll contaminate the scene."

"Contaminated or lost. Your choice."

"Shit."

"Yup. Just get hold of whatever you can and I'll be there in fifteen with my kit. The fire would have most likely destroyed any physical evidence of whoever set it anyway. The fire boys will do what they can with whatever remains that we manage to save."

Kate reached the gangplank and started to walk up. "Right. See you when you get here." She ended the call, opened her camera app, and took pictures from as many different angles as she could. She emptied her pockets and used her driver's licence photo card in each shot to establish scale. She wasn't sure how much use they'd be, but it was surely better than nothing. She sifted through the ashes, using the stick Merlin had brought her earlier, and found the remains of paper, plastic, and some porcelain crockery. Just one plate, one cup, and a metal bowl on the floor. Like a dog's bowl. She frowned. The metal was covered in soot but there was a raised name that was now slightly warped. Kate wiped the soot from it and several pieces fell into place as the letters "M", "E", and "R" were clearly discernible.

She fished through the ashes close to the gangplank and eventually found the hunk of metal that would have been the lock mechanism. Gut instinct—also known as Merlin's water bowl—told her that the hunk of steel was the key to her key mystery.

"Why the hell did no one know about this?" As Kate continued to leaf through the ashes, water rose around the hull. She worked her way through the debris as methodically as she could, taking pictures every couple of inches, and looking closely at every scrap she could find. There were pieces of paper that looked like photographs, burned beyond recognition. The only thing that remained of them were centres or corners, neither of which helped Kate make out what the hell the images were supposed to be. They looked like cages of some sort. Twisted bits of metal, maybe rope, or string with something inside them. What they were, she wasn't sure, but she was certain that these were the missing photos that Tom had been looking for. Why were they here and what the hell were they pictures of?

But the hull began to sink and the front end of the wreckage dipped abruptly before stopping. No doubt it was hitting the creek bottom, and Kate was very grateful that it wasn't deep. But the water was still rising and the bow of the boat was still floating, throwing her balance way off. She started to grab more and more scraps of paper, certain that these were the remains of Connie's photos. Photos that would tell them something about why she was killed. It was the only thing that made sense to Kate. Why else would someone have burned this down? And the only person who would have any reason to do that was the killer. No one else seemed to even know this boat was connected to Connie in the first place. So how did the killer know? And why draw attention to it by burning it down? We'd have never figured it out if they hadn't done that.

Kate's mind was whirling as Wild pulled up as close to the remains as he could. He grabbed a shovel and metal bucket.

"Here, the easiest and quickest thing is going to be getting it all into these buckets and sorting it out back at the lab." He passed her the metal shovel. "Normally I'd say bags, but this stuff's still hot enough to melt my evidence bags."

She nodded and started scooping up the evidence she'd sorted—the scraps of paper, the hunk of lock, the metal bowl—and then started on the ash and whatever evidence it was hiding. She dropped it into bucket after bucket while Wild took them and poured them into bigger containers. She looked closely and saw that they were metal rubbish bins. *He had those in the back of his car? What the hell does he drive? A lorry?*

She found a couple of larger scraps and handed them to him. "These are cool enough for evidence bags. And I'd like to see if we can figure out what the pictures are of." She handed him another full bucket and took an empty one from him. The sound of rushing water filled her ears and the back end of the boat sank to the creek bed.

"Quick as you can, Brannon." Wild grinned at her.

"Piss off." She mumbled and shovelled faster. The water around the outside was rising and almost level with the floor she was scooping contents from.

She handed him the last bucket, the floor as clear of ash and remains as it was going to get and she stepped towards the rail where the gangplank remained. A sharp crack below her foot made her look down. The damaged wood splintered under her weight.

"Oh, fuck! Jump!" Wild shouted.

Without questioning his instinctive order, she jumped towards the edge and realised her mistake as soon as she landed. The forceful impact of her landing caused the floor that was left to fracture and give way completely beneath her.

"Ah, crap." She landed with a splash into the icy cold water that had collected in the innards of the boat. Splintered wood scraped painfully at her legs and she could feel where a nail, probably a rusted one, had cut into her calf when she'd fallen and she could feel herself starting to shiver. The bone-chilling cold penetrated her soaked jeans and surrounded her toes. "Bloody hell that's freezing." She braced her hands on the floor that was now at her hips.

Wild looked over the edge of the charred wood. "Perhaps not my brightest suggestion."

"You think?"

"I didn't make you follow it," he said with a huff.

"No, but I didn't have time to think of anything else either." She held a hand up to him. "Pull me out."

He held his hands up and shook his head. "No way. There's nails and all sorts in that mess. I'm not getting involved in shish-kebabing you."

"Oh, give over." She pushed against the floor but something dug into the back of her thigh. She tried to pull her leg forward in the hopes that it would dislodge it, but she found she couldn't move far enough and a sharp pain shot up her thigh. *Bugger.* "On second thought, might be an idea to call for some other help. Something's stuck in me that doesn't seem to want to move."

"Already called." He waved his phone. "Shouldn't take long."

"Great. In the meantime, have you got a first aid kit in that car of yours?"

"Yeah, of course. Why?"

"I'm bloody freezing. You got one of those space blankets or something? I'm gonna die of hypothermia otherwise."

"I'll go see."

It felt like two hours of shivering before he came back with the bad news that he didn't have one in his kit. "Must have been used and not replaced. I'll go and get one from across the road. Hold tight."

Her teeth were chattering so much that he was gone before she could respond. "Bring two," she shouted after him, in the hope, he might have been able to hear her. Merlin barked. She mustn't have been able to see anyone anymore and thought she'd been abandoned. "I'm here, girl. Sorry I tied you up before. But we'll get out of this in a few minutes. Just you wait and see." The barking became a piteous howl. Kate laughed despite her shivering jaw. "Oh, that's pathetic, Merlin."

The pain in her leg subsided. Numbed by the cold, no doubt. She kept checking her watch to see just how much time had passed. After precisely three minutes and twenty-three seconds, the dog began to yip and bark excitedly.

"Who's there?" Kate asked.

"A friendly first aider," Gina said, peering over the edge of the hull. "Looks like you're in a bit of mess."

"Yup. And freezing."

"So I see. Your lips have gone blue. I'm guessing that isn't a new lipstick you're trying out."

"What? You don't like the frozen-arsed, punk look?" The banter took her mind off her predicament for a few moments and helped ease her embarrassment. Well, sort of.

"Well, I can think of a few looks that would suit you better." She shook out a silver foil blanket and wrapped it around Kate's shoulder.

"Can you now?" She smiled and gripped the edges of the foil. "Thanks."

"Several, in fact. And no problem." She pointed to the sharp edges digging into Kate's hips and buttocks. "I'm not going to stand on that as I'm afraid I might drive something into you farther. The ambulance is on its way, and I've got William coming over with some tools on the quad in a couple of minutes. We should be able to figure something out and get you out of this mess."

"Thanks."

"So what happened here?"

"Fire."

Gina laughed. "Yes, I can see that bit. I meant, how come you're stuck in the hole?"

"Trying to collect evidence before it got washed away." She nodded towards the water.

"Ah." She peered down into the hole, clearly trying to see what was going on underneath the charred planks. "And how high has the water gotten now?"

"It's hard to tell, as the water's soaked into my jeans and my legs are pretty much numb now."

"Can you get a hand in there without causing any damage?"

"Erm, yeah, probably. Why?"

"Well the water out here's pretty high now, and it's going to make it harder to work if we have to keep you standing. The higher the water level in there, the quicker you're going to get hypothermic."

"Right." Kate slid a hand down her thigh and leaned to the right until she felt the water level. "Half way up my thigh."

Gina's eyebrows rose. "Bleeding?"

Kate glanced down. "The waters the colour of coffee. How could I tell?"

"Fair point. Pain?

Kate shook her head. "At first, but now it's just numb."

"How bad?"

"Sharp stabbing pain. Maybe a four or five. Nothing bad."

"Okay. I'm going to try and pry away some of these boards that I can reach here and see if we can make a little more room to work. Can you brace your arms either side?"

"Yeah. There's something sticking in the back of my right thigh. I tried to pull it forward but I couldn't get free."

"Something like a piece of wood or a nail?"

"Not sure. I can't reach to feel what it is."

"Okay." Gina reached forward and tugged gently at the short plank between Kate's belly and the edge where she was leaning over.

"Aren't you getting cold in the water?" Kate asked.

"I'm on the gangplank."

"Oh, right." Kate shook her head. "Sorry."

"Don't be." Gina pulled harder until the length of wood rose slowly against the force of the nails holding it against the support struts. It took many attempts to finally free the short plank from its hold, but she was then able to toss it towards the front of the boat and she could see that the water was now level with the supports.

"Jesus, that's rising fast," Kate said, nervous.

"Yeah, it's a spring tide right now. High, fast, and strong."

"Great. My lucky day, it seems." She cocked her head. "How are you keeping Merlin quiet?"

"Sammy's taken her over to the information centre. I had your Mr Wild see them safely across the road."

"Thank you."

"How come you've ended up with Merlin?" Gina asked as she pulled at another plank.

Kate shrugged. "I'm fostering her. I couldn't see her go to a dog shelter or something. It just didn't seem fair." A Mona Lisa smile spread across Gina's lips before she went back to tugging on the next plank. "What's that for?"

"What's what for?"

"That smile."

"Nothing. Pull that blanket tighter, your fingertips are going blue."

"Yes, Mum." Kate did as she was told. Her hands were numb and the shivering was easing. As much as she hated the shivering, she knew it wasn't a good sign that it was stopping now. Later, when she was in front of the fire, or tucked up in bed, sure. But not now, while she was only getting colder. "So what's with that smile?" she asked again.

"I told you," Gina said, and freed the next plank, "nothing." She tossed it towards the front again and dipped her hand into the cold water. "Shit that's cold."

"I know."

Gina swept her hand around obviously trying to find whatever was obstructing Kate's movement. "I'm just going to see if I can feel what's stuck in your leg." She reached around Kate's thigh and swept her hand from the knee upwards.

Kate was sure she could see a rosy glow over Gina's cheeks and wondered if it was the cold and wind or her leg that had caused it. Mostly she hoped it was her leg. Gina glanced up as her fingers paused, her grip on the muscle tightened and another of those smiles spread across her lips.

"If you keep smiling at me like that, I will have to employ interrogation techniques."

Gina chuckled. "I don't think you're in any position to be making threats right now."

Kate nodded. "You might be right." She noticed how her words sounded a little slurred. "But I maintain the right to interrogate you later."

"You do that, Detective."

"Kate."

"Excuse me?"

"My name's Kate. If you want me to call you Gina, then you have to call me Kate."

"Kate it is." Gina had continued her quest up Kate's thigh until she found what she was looking for. She frowned and the consternation on her face made Kate worry.

"What is it?"

"I think the wood that's sticking in your leg's one of the support struts. It feels pretty big and it won't budge."

"Wonderful," Kate said.

"Oh, it could be worse, Kate."

"How's that?"

"You could be in danger of slipping under the water and drowning."

"Well, aren't you just a regular Pollyanna?"

Gina laughed. "That's me. The eternal optimist."

"Gina, I've got everything I thought could be useful. What do you need?" A male voice came from behind Gina.

"One second, William. I'll be right there." Gina looked at Kate again. "Don't run off now." She winked and shuffled out of sight.

"Where would I go?" Kate chuckled. She knew that this playful side of Gina was her way of taking Kate's mind off her predicament, but she had to admit that she really liked it.

"Hey, don't fall asleep on me," Gina said.

"I didn't."

Gina frowned but didn't say anything more about it. "William's going to come up the plank in a minute and then walk around the edge to the other side."

"What if he falls off and goes through the floor too? Then we'll both be in trouble."

"He won't. He's got balance like I've never seen. Apparently, he was made to do gymnastics when he was a kid. Probably one of the reasons he's refusing to go back home."

Kate sniggered. "Can't say I blame him. Where's the ambulance?"

"They're on the way, but you know how long it takes to get here from King's Lynn."

Twenty minutes in the best of conditions, thirty on average, and over forty if you get stuck behind a tractor or a lorry. "Yeah, I do."

"So, William's going to try and lift the planks behind you and get at that strut so we can get you out. He may have to try and saw the strut through the water."

Kate gulped. "Is that even possible?"

"Yes. But it sure as hell won't be comfortable. Be glad that your leg's gone numb, my friend."

"Why don't we just pull my leg off the wood?"

Gina cocked her head. "You've done first aid training, right?"

Kate nodded.

"Then we'll blame that question on the cold. If we pull your leg off the wood, I'm concerned about what it's hit inside your leg. It may be nothing, but there are also some pretty big veins and arteries in there, not to mention tendons and muscles. I don't want to do any more damage to your leg, Kate."

"I get it. Leave the spear in place and let the doctors make the call."

"Exactly."

"Chicken."

"Yeah, and?"

"What if he can't saw through the strut?"

"Hopefully, the paramedics will be here by then." Gina grinned. "And I won't have to be the one to do any damage to that gorgeous leg of yours."

"Are you flirting with me just to take my mind off this?"

Gina laughed. "You're the detective, Kate. You work it out." Then Gina was gone and William scurried up the plank and around the rim of the boat like it were a mile wide. Kate could feel tugging and pulling behind her as he removed board after board, the hammer and crowbar allowing him to work much faster than Gina had.

"Okay, I'm going to see if I can feel where this thing attaches, Gina," William shouted over her head.

"Got it." Gina shuffled back up the plank, saw in hand, and a warm smile on her face. "How're you doing, Kate?" She handed the saw to William.

"Never been better." The words were little more than a whisper and slurred almost beyond recognition.

"Excellent. Listen, I hope you don't mind, but I sent Wild to your house to get you warm clothes. We've got blankets and stuff out here waiting for you, and I've set up a sort of screen using part of the car. Once we get you off this boat we need to get those wet clothes off you and start warming you up, regardless of whether or not the paramedics are here then. Do you understand me, Kate?"

"Yeah. You're gonna strip me naked on the marsh, you wild woman, you."

Gina threw her head back and laughed. "Yes, I am. Aren't you a lucky woman?"

Kate looked into those blue eyes that she hadn't been able to get out of her head and whispered, "Yeah, I think I just might be." Gina's cheeks coloured and she dropped her gaze.

William's shuffling had caused the boat to rock. Kate glanced down at the water and a piece of paper floated across the rippling surface. She fished it out and turned it over with fingers that barely did as she told them. The image on the reverse showed a cage-like structure next to the numbers "53" in white paint. The cage hung on a rope with a grey block inside it. It was the date in the bottom right-hand corner that caught her eye though: 12.06.15. Twelfth of June. The date struck a chord in her memory but she couldn't remember why. All she could remember was that this was important.

She handed it to Gina. "Give this to Wild."

"Why? What's important about a lobster pot?"

"A lobster pot?"

"Yes, that's what that is. Why's it important?"

"I think this is why some arsehole took a sniper rifle and murdered Connie."

"A sniper rifle? Not just a .22 or something?" Gina frowned.

"No, definitely a sniper rifle. A big one, from a long way away." She tapped the photo. "And this has something to do with why."

Gina's face was pale as she scurried down the ramp again, but Kate couldn't think why that would be. Then her brain caught up with what her mouth had said. "Oh, fuck." She'd just given away details of the case to a civilian. She felt a tug on her leg as the strut was pushed against it. *Damn it. Two civilians.*

"William, did you just hear any of that?"

"Every word."

"Fuck."

"Don't worry. I want you to find out what happened to Connie. Like I told you, she was fair with me. I didn't want anything bad to happen to her. I won't say a word."

"Thanks."

"Gina'll be cool too. Now I'm going to start sawing. This is going to take a while probably, and it's most likely going to hurt."

"I understand."

Hurt wasn't the right word. Her skin and muscles had numbed with the cold. But her bones hadn't. She felt every stroke of the saw in her bones. Every knot he struck resonated throughout her entire body. She screamed, but she didn't care. Then a hand gripped hers and Gina spoke words she couldn't hear. Then the world grew colder still.

CHAPTER 15

Gina stretched as far from the edge of the plank as she could and supported Kate's weight while William continued to saw through the two-inch by six-inch wooden beam. The combination of the cold, the pain, and the undoubtedly strange sensation of the sawing had all conspired to knock Kate out. Gina could feel the vibrations of the saw through Kate's body and it felt damn weird to her. She heard voices from behind her, but she couldn't move to see what was going on. Kate's head rested over her shoulder, and she had her arms wrapped around her body. Together they were doing a good job of counterbalancing each other and stopping either of them falling into the water. "How are you doing, William?"

"Halfway. Sawing through the water isn't exactly easy. You okay with her?"

"Yeah, I'm fine."

"She shouldn't have said what she did about the investigation, you know."

"I know. She only said it because she's hypothermic and not thinking straight."

"I promised her that I wouldn't mention what she said to anyone." He looked Gina in the eye. "Connie was good to me. You know everything she did for me. Helping me get myself straightened out when I got here. Giving me a chance. I don't want anything to screw with her finding out what happened to Connie."

"I understand, William. You don't have to worry about me. I won't say a word." She was still trying to make sense out of what Kate had said. A high-powered sniper rifle shot from long range. That meant that there was no way Sammy could be responsible. That it was purely coincidence. She was simply in the wrong place at the wrong time. It made so much more sense than her little girl's unlucky shot being able to kill her best friend. It made so much more sense than a random accident. Well, not sense, exactly. But it was much easier for her to believe that some bastard had taken Connie from their lives rather than her little girl being responsible. She closed her eyes and leaned into Kate's body a little farther. She wished she could thank her for the information that would release both her and Sammy from the prison of guilt they had been constructing around themselves. Now all she had to do was convince Sammy that it hadn't been her shot that had killed Connie. She snorted. That was easier said than done.

"How're you doing there, love?" A man in a green jumpsuit and high visibility coat asked over her shoulder.

"I'm fine, thanks. About time you guys got here."

"We were on another job when this call came in. How's she doing?"

"Hypothermic and her leg's still trapped under the water. William's almost done releasing it."

"You sawing her leg off, lad?"

"You're a funny guy," William said. "I'd have brought a chainsaw for that. This shit's way too slow."

Gina sniggered.

"How long's she been unconscious?" the paramedic asked.

"Since I started sawing."

"About two minutes," Gina said.

"And we're through." William pulled the saw out of the water and dropped it to the deck beside him. He reached back into the water and pushed Kate's leg forward, visibly pleased when it moved unrestricted. "Great. Does she have any other injuries?"

"None that we've been able to see," Gina said to the paramedic.

"And she was moving freely, no spinal injury, no neck pain?"

"No, just stuck because of her leg."

"Okay, I think the guys have sorted some more planks to set up a kind of bridge to lift her out. I won't be a minute. Are you okay there with her?"

"Yeah, I'm fine," Gina said. She was actually not looking forward to the moment when she would have to let go of Kate. Thick planks landed either side of her and she heard heavy boots stepping towards her. Two large pairs of hands slid under Kate's arms and lifted her weight from Gina.

"Okay, love, you slide off that plank. We've got her."

Gina didn't want to let go, but without Kate's weight, her back and stomach muscles were straining to keep her torso from tumbling into the water.

"Quick as you can, love. She's pretty cold now."

Gina used her arms to shove herself away from Kate's body and inch down the gangplank. As soon as she was at the bottom, a lightweight metal frame was slid along the plank and held in position by Wild. The two paramedics lifted Kate out of the hull of the boat and the guy on the right lifted her right leg forward to keep it elevated. Wild pushed the frame farther up until they could get Kate onto it. Between the three of them, Kate was quickly off the boat and being lifted onto a proper trolley. Within seconds, she was in the back of the ambulance and her clothes were being cut off her. Gina saw them cutting her jeans away and the grey coloured flesh was the last thing she saw of Kate as the doors were slammed shut and the ambulance drove away.

Wild put his hand on Gina's shoulder and squeezed gently. "Don't know what we'd have done without your help today, Miss Temple. You and that lad of yours." He nodded to William. "Reckon she owes you both a drink when she sees you next."

William dropped his tools back into the trailer attached to the back of his quad. "Sir, I think I'll settle for not getting a ticket for driving this here quad on the road when I'm not legally supposed to."

Wild grinned. "I think we can make an exception under the emergency situation rule."

William nodded. "Thanks." He put the quad in gear and set off down the passage and back to the campsite.

"Will you be going to the hospital?" Gina asked.

"I'll drop off these things for her." Wild replied.

"Would you give her a message from me, please?"

"Sure."

"Just tell her that it wasn't just the situation."

"I'm sorry, I don't understand."

"She will."

He nodded.

"Tell her we'll look after Merlin for her too."

He chuckled. "Anything else?"

She smiled. "No, that should be all for now, thanks."

He tipped his finger to his forehead and climbed into his car. Gina made her way back to the information centre, where a nervous looking Sammy petted Merlin while Sarah was on the phone.

"Is she okay, Mum?"

Gina held open her arms and hugged the girl when she willingly fell into her embrace. "She'll be fine, sweetheart. She's going to hospital to get checked over, and I said we'd look after Merlin for a little while for her. Is that okay?"

Sammy glanced at the dog. "I think Merlin hates me now," she whispered.

"It didn't look like it when I walked in. She looked very comfortable and relaxed with you."

Sammy shrugged and pulled away.

"Sammy, I know why you don't want to look after Merlin, but I can promise you, this is the right thing to do, and we need to talk about the other thing later."

Her shoulders slumped. "Okay."

"Get Merlin on her lead and we'll go up to the office. You can help William clean and put away the tools if you like." She knew Sammy enjoyed spending time out of the way in the tool shed, doing something that she enjoyed and was useful to help her mother while not getting into trouble. It was a rare activity for Sammy, and Gina embraced and utilised every single one she found. What Gina really wanted to do was to go home, get in the shower, and fall back into bed. But there was a mountain of paperwork growing in her office and there wasn't anyone else to help her with it anymore. There was stock that needed ordering, bills that needed paying, and the payroll to complete. Joy.

CHAPTER 16

"Oh, for God's sake, stop fussing." Kate shucked the blanket and swung her legs out of bed. Sure, they still felt a bit rubbery and cold, but she was fine. Perfectly able to get back to her desk and get some work done. They should have tons of evidence now for her to go over and figure out who killed Connie Wells.

"Detective Sergeant Brannon, you have just had ten stitches in the back of your leg. You can't feel them right now because of the local anaesthetic, but believe me, you will before long. You were brought in with hypothermia, and you are still cold."

"I'm fine. I'll put on extra layers."

"You can put on your blanket and lie back down. You're not going anywhere until the doctor's looked at you again." The nurse tugged the curtain closed behind her as she left. "Who made you God?" Kate sneered at the curtain.

"The Royal College of Nurses," came back the unexpected reply. Kate blanched, swearing under her breath as she lay back against the pillows and clasped her hands over her stomach. Her phone had been in her jeans pocket and consequently it was now ruined. As were her jeans, her boots, fleece, and T-shirt. The only thing they hadn't cut off her was her leather jacket, but that was going to take some drying out too. The bottom of it was sodden and stained.

"I come bearing gifts." The curtain slid back and Wild stepped into her curtain enclosed space. He dumped a plastic bag on the bed by her feet. "Trainers, sweatpants, T-shirt, and a sweatshirt."

"That's great, thanks." While Kate was glad he hadn't gone through her underwear drawer, she dearly wished there had been at least a bra in the bag.

"Oh, and socks."

She smiled. "Perfect. Thank you." She waited for him to go so she could get dressed and leave.

"I've got a message for you from Miss Temple."

So leaving was out of the question. "What message?"

"She said, she's got Merlin and will look after her for you for a while."

"Oh, right." Kate couldn't help but feel a little disappointed, but she supposed it made sense. Sammy had taken the dog with her when Gina had first arrived.

"She also said to tell you that it wasn't just the situation." He crossed his arms over his chest. "She said you'd know what that cryptic little message meant."

Kate frowned, then the meaning hit her.

"I take it from that shit-eating grin that you not only know what she means, but you like what it means." He perched on the edge of the bed. "So, spill."

Kate shook her head. "I don't know what it means." She tried to wipe the smile off her face.

"Sure you don't."

"I don't," Kate protested. She was lying and they both knew it.

"Fine. Just remember one thing."

"What?"

"She's a witness in your ongoing investigation."

"Yes, a witness, not a suspect."

"You don't know that until you've caught the person or persons responsible."

She looked him in the eye. "I do know."

He sighed. "I saw the way you were looking at her, and the way she looked at you. Just be careful. That's all I'm saying." He nodded to the bag. "I'll leave you to get dressed. I'm guessing you've been cooped up long enough."

"Yeah."

"How many stitches?"

"Ten."

"Need a lift back to your car?"

"I'd appreciate it."

He backed out of her space.

"Sergeant, I don't even know your name."

"Len."

"Kate," she said. "Nice to meet you."

He chuckled and closed the curtain behind him. She quickly pulled on her clothes. Extremely grateful for the baggy sweatpants that didn't touch the back of her leg at all. The local was starting to wear off and she knew that pretty soon she was going to be feeling very sore. Ah, well. That's the price for getting vital evidence in the case. She was certain of that.

A lobster pot with a brick in it and "53" in white paint beside it. 12.06.15. The code. A sniper rifle-toting murderer. And the pool of suspects that just wasn't getting any smaller.

Okay, so maybe vital, but not the most illuminating of evidence. At least now she knew what the key was all about. It was a shame the murderer had gotten to that evidence before they did. She was sure that if she'd been able to see everything that was in there, she'd know who the killer was by now. But the question remained, how did the killer know about the houseboat hoard, when it seemed that no one else in the village knew Connie had any connection to it? Did Connie own it? If so, why did no one else know about it? If not, why did no one else know about her using it?

It's a tiny little village for God's sake. Everyone knows everything, right? So who was lying to her? She'd shown the key to Leah Shaw, Ally Robbins, Gina, and William. Gina and William, no way. They're the only ones who cared about Connie. Leah Shaw's implicated with the coded list, the ex, money motives. *Fuck, Leah's got a motive list as long as my arm but that still doesn't make her capable of this crime.* Ally's got a good rep on the range, but she was on a fishing boat at the time of the murder, so no go. One of them must have mentioned it to someone else who knew about the houseboat and Connie's connection to it. It's the only thing that made sense. But who? Matt Green or Rupert Sands?

She pulled the curtain open in time to come face to face with the doctor who had examined her when she'd first arrived.

"Off so soon, Ms Brannon?"

"I'm in the middle of a case. I need to get back to work."

"Case?"

"I'm a police officer."

He glanced down at the notes. "Of course. Sorry. Busy day." His smile was impersonal. "Well, let me take your temperature and write you up for some painkillers. I think you'll need them later with those stitches. Any allergies?"

"No."

"Excellent." He stuck a sensor on the end of her finger without even making her sit down and scribbled across a pad. "I take it you'll collect these from off the premises?"

"Please."

"Very well. You'll need those stitches out in seven to ten days. You can get them done by the nurse at your GP's office rather than coming back to wait here. If you have any puss or smelly discharge, come back straight away. If you find the pain doesn't settle down in the next forty-eight hours, see your GP."

"Got it." The machine attached to the sensor beeped and displayed its results.

"Still a little cold, but nothing that causes me to worry." He tore off the script. "Lots of hot drinks, and keep warm. No more swimming in the North Sea."

"Don't worry. It's not something I plan to repeat." She folded the prescription in half and stuffed it into her pocket. "Thanks."

Len was chatting to the receptionist when she walked into the waiting area.

"Ready to go?" he asked.

"Yup. You?"

"As I'll ever be." He nodded to the receptionist again. "This is my wife, Val. Val, this is Kate Brannon. DS on this Brandale Staithe case."

"Nice to meet you, Kate." She shook Kate's hand. "I hope you aren't hurt badly."

Kate laughed. "Nothing but my pride."

Len chuckled. "I pulled the lasagne out this morning, as ordered, love." He leaned over the counter and kissed her on the cheek. "See you tonight."

"Let me know if you're going to be late."

"Yes, dear."

Kate slapped him on the back and followed him out the door. "You're a lucky man, Len Wild."

"I know." He winked over his shoulder. "I know."

"Timmons has ordered me to make sure you take the rest of the day off. So where are you parked? I didn't see your car when I pulled up to meet you," Wild said.

"I'm fine. I don't need the rest of the day off," Kate replied.

"Tough. I'm making sure you get home. After that I'm going home to have a nice evening with the wife. You can do whatever you bloody well want."

Kate got it. Code for shut up and let me follow orders, and then you're on your own. "I parked at the harbour and ran from there with the dog. Can you believe it's been there for seven hours? It's almost three o'clock. The day's almost gone."

"Actually in the harbour?" Wild asked.

"Yeah, why?"

"And you were parked there before five this morning?"

"Yes, why?"

"It floods at high tide."

"You're joking?"

"'Fraid not." He pulled out onto the A149. "Not all of it, though. If you were over at the back, or right by the crab shack, you should be fine."

Kate groaned.

"I'm guessing you weren't near either location."

Kate shook her head. "I parked out of the way of the little boats so I wasn't blocking them."

"So effectively right where the water's going to flood in?"

"Right next to the reed bed."

"Yup. That's it. Right in the flood plain." He tried valiantly to hide his laughter. He didn't manage it, but he did try. "Not your day, is it?"

Kate cast him a withering look. "Seems not." *Please let him be winding me up.*

"Well, at least it'll take your mind off your leg for a bit."

"Yeah, till I have to walk everywhere and end up crippled because my car can't swim."

"Want me to get Val to bring you some crutches down to the station?"

"Ha bloody ha." She covered her eyes and leaned her head back. "Well, nothing I can do about it now."

"True." He quickly changed lanes and sped around the roundabout. "So I was looking at your picture. The one you risked life and limb for."

"You're the one who told me to jump."

"And it's a good job I did. Or we'd have lost that vital evidence."

"No need to be sarcastic, Len."

"I'm being serious. Did you happen to have a good look at that picture?"

"I'm a little hazy on the details but Gina said it was a picture of a lobster pot."

"A lobster pot with something in it."

"Isn't that what the fishermen want?" She gripped the grab rail over the passenger door. Whatever they'd given her to help with the pain in her leg was wearing off and the pain was really starting to kick in.

"Indeed. But they're usually hoping for lobster in their lobster pots. Not blocks of something shiny and grey."

"So what is it?"

"You're the detective, Brannon. You tell me."

She sighed and reminded herself to breathe through the next wave of pain.

She pulled her prescription out of her pocket. "Can we stop at the chemist?"

"There's a pharmacy on the high street in Hunstanton. Will that work?"

Another wave of pain hit her as Wild rounded a bend. "Let's blame it on my leg and the pain and all that good stuff, Wild, but how does this break the case?"

"Like I said, Brannon, you're the detective not me. When you figure out what that photo means and why she was hiding it, you'll crack this case and figure out who killed Connie Wells."

She leaned back against the head rest. "So you don't know what the grey, shiny block is either."

"Nope, but it's another piece in a fascinating puzzle."

"Yup." She sighed and closed her eyes. "Fascinating."

He woke her up when they got to the harbour, a small paper pharmacy bag sat on her lap as he shook her gently awake. "I'd have taken you straight home but I figured you'd need to deal with your car first."

She came around slowly, groggily, and followed his pointing finger.

"Fuck me." She pushed open the door and stepped out of the car on rubbery legs. "You weren't winding me up?"

Her car sat almost where she'd left it. Almost. It was slightly more on an angle, but not much. Water was still dripping from the crack between the passenger door and the car body. The taillights were flashing quickly, while the headlights were flashing slowly, and the alarm sounded like a bull frog that got strangled into silence every minute or so before finding release to start again. Her lovely little mini was drowned.

"I called a guy from the garage down the road. He's got a tow truck and he'll be here soon. He can tow it straight to the scrap yard for you, if you like."

"What? Scrap yard? Surely he can just dry it out and it'll be fine, right?"

Len shook his head. "Salt water. Even if they manage to dry out all the components the salt's what does the real damage. It dries up and sticks to the components. Look at the way your lights and alarm are going haywire. The salt water's got into all the computer parts of the engine. Excuse my language, Brannon, but it's fucked."

"Bugger."

The guy from the garage turned out to be a lot nicer than the chap on the phone from her insurance company. It took several threats to his manhood, his life, and eventually with Twitter before they agreed to a courtesy car even though the incident was clearly her fault. Apparently, ignorance of the tide doesn't make one exempt from the "Act of God" clause in an insurance policy. She was not looking forward to her renewal next year but the car would be dropped off at her house later that afternoon. Both the insurance Nazi and the mechanic agreed with Len, the car would be written off, and she was now in the market for some new wheels. Yay. Not.

She pulled the few remaining personal items from her car and tossed them into the black bag the mechanic had handed her. Then she fished the keys from her pocket and watched him load the car onto his truck. She swallowed a couple of the pain pills Len had picked up for her and leaned against the fence rail, wedging the foot of her injured leg onto a lower rung to watch. She needed to get the weight off her leg for a bit.

She stared out to sea. It was bright today. Barely a cloud skidding across the sky. The October sun offered little in the way of warmth, but it was more than enough to make you believe it had plenty more in the tank. She looked across at Scolt Head Island—a barren, desolate place, reserved for the breeding of birds and illicit trysts for those with the knowledge of how to navigate the tidal waters of the harbour. And access to a boat.

Len sauntered over.

"You didn't tell me how you got on with Dr. Anderson and your geek yesterday," Kate asked.

He smiled. "Well, our shooter's either better than I estimated, or I'm on the wrong track all together."

"Why?"

"I was right about the gun. The metal slivers confirm it was a 7.62 by 51 millimetre NATO round. I sent Goodwin a list of potential guns last night. But the distance is deceptive here." He pointed out across the water. "Grimshaw programmed the computer to show where the marsh was covered due to the tide. Land was a lot farther away from our vic than I'd estimated. Our shooter had to be at least eleven hundred yards away from her."

"I'm guessing that making a shot like that is pretty much impossible?"

"Well, no. Not impossible. But not likely either."

"So what is likely?" Kate asked, still staring out at the water.

"I don't know."

"Could she have been facing the other way? There were a few houses in that direction and you said yourself that the sun was rising that way."

Len sucked on his teeth. "Well, yes, it was, but from the position of the body, she was looking towards the harbour, not away from it. She had to be up on the embankment or her body wouldn't have gone so far towards the creek and the camera wouldn't have made it to the water." He folded his arms. "No, she was definitely on the embankment facing the harbour with the camera held to her face."

"There are houses there too, Len. Could the shooter have been in one of those windows maybe?"

"Then surely the whole village would have heard it. The round definitely came from a big rifle. Someone would have heard it. Besides, the angle's all wrong. She'd have had to be taking pictures into someone's *bedroom* window to make that scenario work. Which would mean she'd have landed with her feet towards the village, not her head. The way she landed, she was facing the harbour but slightly towards the sea. Maybe ten degrees off straight, and the shot had to come sea to shore to push her head back towards the village rather than shore to sea." He pointed as he spoke. "Seems like it came from the island except it's too far away to really be feasible." He shook his head. "Doesn't add up."

"Silencer? On the path farther ahead of her?"

He barked a laugh. "This is Brandale Staithe, Brannon. We're in the middle of nowhere. A silencer?"

"Is it really any more absurd than a pinpoint accurate shot from, what? Over half a mile away?"

Len opened his mouth looking ready to argue, and then he stopped. "I guess not, but that would still put the angle off. She'd have stayed on the path, then, rather than being pushed down the embankment. I wish there was some way of being able to tell exactly how high the water was and where someone could have been positioned."

"I thought Grimshaw's computer program did that for you."

"Yeah, well, all that whizz-bang shit gives me a headache. I want to see it in front of me now." He pointed out at the marsh. "I want to see it out there."

Kate smiled and felt like kicking herself for not thinking of it before. "You live close by, Len?"

He shook his head. "No, Lynn born and bred, me."

"Ever been sailing?"

"No way. Fish crap in that water. You won't get me in there if I don't have to."

Kate chuckled and pushed away from the fence she leaned against. "Well, I grew up on the water in one way or another." She dusted off the back of her pants cautiously. "Come on, then, let me show you how they do all that tidal crap. Let's see if we can figure out what was covered and what wasn't."

She limped her way across the harbour and up the short road, and crossed the A149 to the chandlery. She went in. There was a selection of sailing clothes, wetsuits, and life vests to the left, deck shoes, sandals, and boots straight ahead. A selection of ropes hung from a board over the back of the till and were strung up in the rafters neatly, making use of the otherwise wasted space. A small room off to the right was packed full of boating spares and repair equipment. Pulleys, cleats, metal rings, adhesives of all kinds, marine filler, and buoys filled the room. On the window sill was a neat selection of nautical books and charts. She quickly searched through and located the one she wanted. *Imray's Y9 Nautical Chart of The Wash* and a chart table. She handed over her card to the guy behind the counter and asked to borrow his marker pen.

"So, Len, how high was the tide?"

"Anderson puts TOD at seven a.m. on the twenty-ninth. High tide was at seven zero seven and nine point six metres."

Kate whistled and checked over the tide chart noting the prevailing tide directions, the height of the land masses on the marsh, and increment depth of the creeks. Using the blue marker she'd borrowed from the cashier she marked a dotted line around the marsh, including the Coastal Path at several points, and then cross-hatched the enclosed area.

"I take it you do sail then, fancy pants?" Len griped.

"I've been known to set foot on a boat or two in my time." She smiled. "Not for a long time, though, and I haven't sailed around here."

She handed the marker back and led Len back to the harbour. She held up the nautical chart so they could both see, and pointed to two areas—Long Hills on the south side of Scolt Head Island, and the eastern point of the dunes of Brancaster beach.

"Those are the closest points of land that weren't covered with water," she said.

"Everything else was underwater?"

"Everything. Nine point six metres is a huge tide. It was a tide like that along with a wind storm that caused the flooding up and down the coast in December 2013. Don't you remember?"

"I do. But I thought you were new to the area."

"I was working in Norwich, but they sent me over to help out over Cromer way." She shook her head. "Houses were falling into the sea when the cliffs gave way."

"I thought that was meant to be a fluke?"

"The circumstances all colliding to create the breach were a fluke, but the tides can get that high regularly." She pointed to the man-made dykes all along the edge of the marsh. "That's why they've spent time putting in those flood defences. Without that, most of this village would have been underwater that night, I'm sure."

"Good job it's there, then."

"Yep. But we do have a conundrum, Len."

"We do. Can any of your suspects make that kind of shot?"

"Theoretically, two, maybe three. But none of them were without an alibi long enough to be on either of those spots at that time, and then back." She thought of Rupert Sands and his father confirming his whereabouts from eight in the morning and Matt Green's location from just before seven-thirty. "Can you access this from land at that time?" She pointed to the dunes at the end of Brancaster beach, the island obviously having zero land access at any time.

"Yes, but you've got two big problems with that route."

"What?"

"That's a good three-mile hike over the sand. Not an easy walk to do quickly. I think you're looking at around forty-five minutes, maybe an hour. But that's not the end of it. That road," he said pointing, "is a road that is notorious for flooding when the tide goes over eight metres. We call it car killer lane around here." He grinned smugly.

"Not endearing yourself any, Len."

He sniggered. "Sorry."

"Yeah, yeah. So if our shooter was there, he was stuck there until when?"

"We're told to give it an hour and half or so after one that high. Or walk the mile along the dyke from the golf course to the main road on top of the beach hike."

"So at least eight-thirty."

"Best case, whether the shooter walks the whole way or waits out the tide."

"Doesn't work."

"What about them coming in by boat? Either option could have taken a small motorboat out, landed it on the beach at either position, and then come back by water. Would that be possible?"

"There's a six-knot speed limit, they're no more than a mile from the harbour, less than half at the dunes. Yes, that would be possible. Let me borrow your phone."

"Use your own."

"I can't, it went swimming."

"Damn it." He fished his phone from his pocket and handed it over to her.

"Thanks." She punched in Stella's number from memory and waited for her to answer. "Stella, can you find out if Matt Green or Rupert Sands has a boat?"

"What kind of boat?"

"Something small, fast, and manageable alone."

"Like a tender for a sailing boat?"

"Yeah, exactly like a tender, actually."

"On it. Where are you anyway? Timmons said you were out of commission for the day."

"I'm at Brandale Staithe Harbour at the moment. I'll tell you all about it when I see you."

Stella laughed. "Right. I'll look into those boats and see what I can find. Want me to text you the details?"

"Best not. I'm in the market for a new phone."

"Why?"

Kate sighed heavily. Sometimes it was best just to do these things quickly. "I parked my car at the harbour this morning while I took the dog for a walk. I found a houseboat on fire and went to rescue evidence, got stuck on the houseboat, went to hospital for stitches and hypothermia, and came back to find my car had been swimming in the North Sea. Only it didn't fare as well as I did. She's a write-off."

Stella whistled down the line. "You've had a busy day."

"And the day's not over yet."

Len sniggered beside her.

"Want one of us to pick you up tomorrow?"

"I've got a courtesy car coming this afternoon."

"Good. Need anything?"

"My pride restoring?"

"No can do. Piss taking, that I can do, mate."

"Thanks. I look forward to it." She chuckled and hung up. "They were incredibly sympathetic," she said as she handed the phone back to Len.

"I just bet they were. So who's Matt Green?"

"He's the Sands' foreman, and dad to Gina Temple's little girl. He also shows up in Connie Wells' diary, made it onto our sniper list, and his alibi—if he has a boat—is a little thin on the ground."

"Any motive?"

"Nothing that's come up so far. Just his licence plate in Connie's diary."

"Which could mean absolutely nothing."

"Exactly." She folded the map up and tucked it under her arm. "You busy or do you want to come and see what we can find out about Mr Green?"

"Well, I'm always busy, but you seem to need babysitting, so where are we going?" Len fell into step beside her.

"So far, the only people I think are telling me the truth in all this are Gina Temple and William Clapp. Gina had his child. She's got to know something about the guy, right?"

"If she's his ex, how do you know she'll tell you the truth about him?"

"He turned up at her house last time I was there. I wouldn't go so far as to say she hates him, but I don't get the impression that she's in any hurry to cover his tracks for him."

"Fine. But then I'm taking you home."

"Best offer I've had in years, Len."

CHAPTER 17

Gina put the glass of milk on the table and called up the stairs. "Sammy, get your little butt down here. We need to talk."

The crashing and thudding she'd heard up to that point suddenly ceased and she could practically hear Sammy swallow. Slow, heavy footsteps resonated over her head and Gina could imagine her heavy-footed child walking as though she were heading to the gallows. She waited with the kitchen door open, and put her hand on Sammy's shoulder when she neared.

"I'm sorry, Mum."

Gina frowned. "What for?"

Sammy shrugged. "Whatever I did now."

Gina laughed. "You didn't do anything now, sweetheart." She pulled her close, wrapped her arms around skinny shoulders, and kissed the top of her head. "This is good news, I promise." She pushed her gently towards the table. "Go sit down."

Sammy slumped in her chair, obviously still not convinced that there could be any good news.

Merlin walked at Gina's heels and curled up under the table by Sammy's feet. There were patches of fur that had been shaven away, obviously during the evidence collection and the anaesthetic she'd had to undergo.

"Sammy, I need you to tell me again what happened when Connie died."

"Why? You said I wasn't to talk about it again."

"I know, sweetheart, but I don't think you did it. I think it was someone else who shot Connie. So I want you to tell me again what happened."

Sammy glared at her sulkily.

Oh those teenage years are going to be so much fun. "Please."

"Fine." Sammy kicked at the table leg, startling poor Merlin from her comfortable spot. "Dad gave me his rifle so I could shoot him a hare or something for his tea. He said he had to go up to Top Wood for Mr Sands."

"Right. Then what happened?"

"I was sat on the grass just off the path."

"Whereabouts?"

"Outside the fence of Mrs Webb's garden."

Gina pictured the house, the first one along the cul-de-sac with a huge garden that backed onto the marshes. Sammy was probably less than ten yards to the left of the entryway. She could see her scruffy, dirty denim-covered knees tucked under her chin as she waited in the dark. *I could fucking kill him.*

"What happened next?"

"I could see Connie. She was throwing a stick for Merlin and taking pictures of the fishing boats like she always did. I made sure she didn't see me 'cos I knew if she did, she'd take me home and you'd shout at Dad."

"Was Connie on her own?"

"Yeah. Just her and Merlin."

"Was there anyone else on the path? Any other walkers?"

"No. Just Connie and me." She sniffled.

"Okay. What happened next?"

"I saw a hare or a rabbit or something so I was going to shoot it. I got the rifle and aimed it, and I tried to keep my breathing soft like dad said, and tried to keep the barrel dead still, but I was excited. I closed my eyes when I pulled the trigger and it went all over the place." She wiped her nose on her sleeve.

"Don't do that, Sammy."

"Sorry, Mum."

"What happened after you let off the gun?"

"I looked up and tried to find the rabbit, but I couldn't. I could hear Merlin howling, and when I looked up I couldn't see Connie any more.

Merlin just kept barking and howling. And running up and down on the same spot. Back and forward. Over and over. So I went to see what happened and Connie was on the grass on the other side of the dyke. But her face wasn't there no more. I shot it off."

Gina wrapped her arms around Sammy. "No, you didn't, sweetheart. The police said that there's no way the gun that you were using could have done that to Connie. It wasn't you."

"But I shot and she died, Mum."

"Where was she?"

"I just told you, on the grass—"

"No, I mean was she near the houseboat or farther away?"

"Oh," Sammy said, clearly thinking about the question. "They were up near the sluice."

More than half a mile along the path. "And you were using the gun your dad gave you?"

Sammy nodded.

"Sweetheart, I'm not an expert in this, but I don't think that gun could have shot that far even if you had been unlucky enough to have been so accurate with your eyes closed. The sluice is more than half a mile from where you were sitting. It just couldn't have done it." She kissed her cheek. "You couldn't have done it." She wished she'd realised it when Sammy had first told her. She wished she'd had the clarity of mind to think it through clearly, but she hadn't. Shock. Shock over Connie dying. Shock at Sammy's confession. Anger at Matt for being so bloody stupid. All those hours of panic could have been spared if she'd just thought it through.

"I really didn't kill her?"

"No, kiddo. No way." She squeezed her tight. "That rubbish gun of your dad's couldn't have killed her." Gina wanted to run around screaming and shouting, free of the terrible burden, but she was still pretty damn sure that Social Services would look less than favourably on the whole incident, regardless that they were all innocent of murder.

"Does that mean I can see him again?"

"What? No!" She pulled Sammy back from her so she could look into her face. "Just because you didn't kill her doesn't mean that what happened was any less dangerous or stupid on your dad's part. He should never have been letting you handle that rifle, especially not on your own, and he should never have left you alone on the marsh like that. Not to mention that he didn't meet you like he said he would and left you to deal with the gun on your own. No. This does not mean you can see him again now."

"But he's my dad."

"I know he is, but that doesn't mean he's fit to look after you."

"I don't need no looking after."

"Oh, how I wish that were true. You're nine years old, and as far as I'm concerned you're my little girl and you will always need looking after. It's my job to do that. And letting him be a part of your life is not doing that to the best of my ability."

"I hate you."

"I know." Gina shook her head sadly. "Go to your room."

"I won't." Sammy pulled away and started to open the front door.

"If you step one foot outside that door, Samantha Temple, I will ground you until you're at least thirty. Now get up to your room and don't come down again until you're willing to apologise."

The door slammed and heavy feet echoed up the stairs as she ran to her room and slammed yet another door.

"Bloody kid'll be the death of me." She sat down in her chair and leaned heavily against the back rest. Merlin put her head over her thigh and whined. "You too, hey girl?" She stroked the top of Merlin's head and took comfort from the simple act. A sharp rap of knuckles on the door startled them both from their moment of relaxation. Merlin barked, and Gina slowly dragged herself from her chair. "Yes?" she asked as she pulled open the heavy old door.

"Sorry to bother you, but could I ask you some more questions?" Kate smiled at her.

"No problem." Gina smiled back at her, genuinely pleased to see her again now that she didn't have to hide anything.

"Have you met Sergeant Wild?"

"We met this morning. Good to see you again," she said to Len.

"And you," he said.

"How's your leg?" Gina asked.

Kate winced and followed Gina to the kitchen. "Sore, but they said I'll live."

"Unlike her car." Wild offered with a wicked chuckle.

"Your car?"

Kate shot him a withering smile. "Thanks, pal. Yes, my car was at the harbour. I didn't know it flooded."

Gina laughed heartily. "I'll bet one of the locals has posted it on Facebook. It's the local spectator sport around here for some folk."

"You're joking, I hope."

"Nope. They have a pool running at the sailing club to guess how many cars get killed over the season. Fiver to enter, winner gets the pot."

"Why don't they put up signs or something?"

Gina shrugged. "Where's the fun in that? Tea? Coffee?"

"Coffee, please," Kate said.

"Tea. Black with two sugars," Len said.

Gina fussed over the mugs and kettle, then joined them at the table and waited for Kate's questions. She wondered what they needed to know now, but she'd find out soon enough.

"Gina, we're trying to narrow down the suspect list and given what we know of the way Connie was killed, we've got a few people who have the skill necessary to pull off a shot like that who are connected to Connie. Most will be completely innocent but we need to rule them out."

"Okay. Who do you need to know about?"

"Can you tell me about the relationship between Rupert and Connie?"

"Oh, God. They hated each other. Rupert and Edward wanted the campsite. Badly. Still do, I assume. Probably Leah will sell it to them eventually."

"I thought she didn't want to sell it."

"She doesn't. But she can't run it either and she'll need money sooner rather than later."

"Why did Connie refuse to sell to them?"

"Stubborn bloody mindedness."

"Pardon?"

"She had no business reason other than she couldn't stand the thought of Rupert lording it over everyone even more than he already does. It was truly personal. She despised him."

"Why?"

Gina shrugged. "A whole load of little things that grew in her head until they were totally insurmountable. He shows no respect to anybody. No one at all. She used to say that just because he was born with money didn't make him better than anyone else. After all, those of us who had to work for it have proved our worth in the earning. And that he'd proven his lack in the three businesses he's already driven to bankruptcy."

She took a sip of her tea. "Anyone can make a mistake once and get caught in a bad place. Bad health, recession, etc. But to make it three times showed a distinct aura of stupidity in Connie's opinion." She smiled. "She thought, and I quote, he was a weasely little pissant who lived in daddy's shadow and would do nothing but destroy the legacy that Edward had to leave behind."

"Best of friends, then," Len said.

"Indeed."

"What about Matt?" Kate asked.

Gina frowned. "What about him?"

"How did he and Connie get on?"

Gina's frown deepened. "They didn't really have anything to do with each other as far as I know. He had no ties to the campsite other than he drove past to get to the farm."

"So he didn't work for her at any point?"

"No."

"He didn't have any kind of personal relationship with her?"

"Like what?"

"They weren't friends? Drinking buds down the pub?"

"Connie didn't go down to the pub. She didn't want to socialise with them all."

"Them all?"

"The locals. It's one of the reasons they all think she was stuck-up. She just didn't feel comfortable in that kind of environment. Not her thing. She'd rather be at home with a good book, Merlin, and a mug of hot chocolate. I know it sounds boring, but that's what she liked. She didn't like loud, noisy, cramped places. She didn't really like crowds. They gave her migraines, so she avoided them." Gina shrugged again. "So she didn't make friends with them." She sipped again. "And, yes, *them* includes Matt." She chuckled slightly. "In fact, the only time I ever remember them speaking was one time when Connie got into an argument with him about Sammy."

Kate cocked her head to one side. "What happened?"

Gina waved her hand dismissively. "It was ages ago. Christmas last year. He'd bought Sammy a pellet gun as her present and when he turned up that night, pissed, I wanted him to leave. Sammy was already asleep and Connie was in the house with me. We were having a little drink and chatting. She'd been on her own for Christmas so I invited her around."

"No Leah?"

"No. She was out with them."

"Ah." Kate waited for her to continue, then prompted Gina. "So what happened?"

"Matt was his usual self when he's had a few. A bastard. Said he wanted to see Sammy, his kid, and all that. I told him to come back in the morning when he was sober, she was awake, and they could have breakfast together. Apparently, that wasn't good enough for him. He grabbed my arms and tried to pull me out of the doorway."

"Did he hurt you?"

Gina shook her head. "Connie shot a pellet from Sammy's little pellet gun over his head. The noise made him back off. She told him to do what I'd said and bugger off."

"What did Matt do?"

"He said he wasn't, and I quote, scared of no rug muncher, and that that little pellet gun couldn't hurt a person and that Connie should stop trying to corrupt decent folk and leave me alone." Gina chuckled. "So Connie aimed it at his crotch. Seems he wasn't quite so sure it wouldn't hurt at that point."

"So she humiliated him?"

"I don't think he even remembered. He never turned up the next day and he never made any mention of it again."

"Did he think there was something going on between you and Connie?"

Gina shrugged. "If he did he never asked."

"But he thought she was trying to corrupt you?"

"Look, he was pissed and she scared him. He was just mouthing off to cover up the fact that he'd pissed himself." She chuckled. "He really was that far gone that he wouldn't have remembered his own name let alone Connie showing him up."

"Has Matt always been a gun enthusiast?"

"Well, I suppose so. His dad bought him his first gun when he was about Sammy's age. That's why he thought it was an appropriate thing to do."

"Does he spend much time practicing?"

"I've no idea. I don't tend to know what he's doing on a day-to-day basis."

"What about while you were in a relationship with him?" Kate asked.

"There wasn't much of a relationship. We dated for a few months, as soon as he got what he wanted he stopped calling. Three months later I found out I was pregnant with Sammy. She's the only reason we have contact now."

"I'm sorry," Kate said.

"I'm not. I was seventeen and stupid, but I wouldn't be without Sammy for the world. Matt, however, I could live without."

Kate nodded and finished her drink, placing the mug back on the table. "Thank you. If you think of anything else, you've got my number."

"I do," Gina said and watched them both. She followed them to the door. Len exited first.

Kate turned back to her as Len pulled open the gate. "I'm still sorry he treated you the way he did, and if he turns up here and hurts you ever again, please call me."

Gina narrowed her eyes against the bright sunlight and looked at Kate. There was an aura to her, a strength that radiated out of her just as bright as the sun glinting off her copper hair. Her green eyes were so earnest and open that she wished she could stare into them all day.

"I'm fine."

The right-hand corner of Kate's mouth lifted in a flirtatious little twist. "Oh, I know you are, but that doesn't change the offer." She ran her fingers through her hair. "Please?"

Gina nodded, and then Kate turned and followed Len out of the gate with a slight limp.

"I'm taking you home. Timmons made me promise," Wild said.

"Fine." Kate crossed her arms over her chest. "I'll need the courtesy car anyway."

"Bloody hell." Wild checked his watch. "You know it's almost five, don't you?"

"And?" She lowered herself gingerly into the seat. "The case demands, Len. I am but a puppet on its string."

"Oh for God's sake."

"Take me home, Jeeves."

"What the hell are those bloody pills they gave you?" he asked, then pulled away from the kerb.

CHAPTER 18

Tom was holding the door open for her when Kate got back to the station. The funny bugger was wearing a snorkel and mask.

"Everyone's a comedian."

"Well, Sarge, what can I say? A man's got to have a hobby."

As soon as she walked inside, she was welcomed by a rousing chorus of "Hot Legs" by Rod Stewart. Jimmy pulled her chair out for her with an exaggerated limp.

Bastards. Leave it to a bunch of coppers to show nothing but sympathy and compassion for a colleague with an injury or a misfortune. *Only one thing to do in a situation like this—play along.* She exaggerated her limp and sat heavily in her chair, perched her feet on the edge of the desk and waved her hand like a conductor. The laughter felt good. Really good. Almost as good as that look Gina had given her when she was leaving. The one that had taken in all of her and seemed to want more. The one that would have had Kate asking to go back inside, if not for Len Wild standing on the other side of the gate.

"How you doing, hoppy?" Stella asked.

"And they just keep coming. Any more piss-taking quips you all feel the need to get off your chests?"

"Nah. We'll save them for an appropriate time, thanks," Tom added.

She sighed heavily and pinned the picture she'd rescued from the boat to their crime board.

"Is this the one you risked life and limb for?" Tom asked, sniggering.

She sighed again, resigning herself to a life of ridicule for at least the duration of the case. "Yes, that one." She folded her arms over her chest and stared at the board, just letting her eyes drift from one piece of information to the next, well aware of how sulky she looked, but willing to play her part. Good for morale and all that bollocks.

Tom was still chuckling as he stowed his snorkel in his desk.

"You do know it's worrying that you have that in there, don't you?"

"Never know when you might need help getting out of deep water."

"Oh, bloody hell. Someone say something intelligent before my brain leaks out of my ear and I end up like him."

Stella cleared her throat. "Sands has a boat moored out in the harbour. Name of *His First Love*."

She nodded, trying to suppress the smirk she could feel on her lips. "Classic."

"It has a tender with a four-horsepower outboard on it."

"More than fast enough to get to six knots against the tide. What about Matt Green?"

"Nothing so far, but we thought Sands was the priority check."

Kate sat down and wriggled, trying to find a comfortable spot for her leg."Yeah, maybe. But Green and Connie had a set-to a while back. She showed him up pretty bad and it doesn't sound like he's the kind of bloke that takes too kindly to that."

"What happened?"

Kate quickly covered the gist of the confrontation and Tom whistled.

"So he has the skill to pull it off, alibi is on the dodgy side, he's got motive, all we need now is a boat and he's your man."

"He could have borrowed a boat even if he doesn't own one."

"Would people round here lend a boat out like that?"

Kate shrugged. "Probably. A small one anyway. Maybe not a sailboat but a tender. Yeah, most likely."

"How do you know that?"

"I grew up in small communities like this one. A little farther up north. My dad worked on the rigs, and me and Gran tried to stay close to wherever he was working. Small villages like this are close-knit communities. They help each other out when they need it, and they lend things out because they never know when they might need something in return."

"Sounds like a good policy."

"Yeah."

"Until you're trying to catch a murderer."

"Exactly. So the question of the day now is, does Matt Green have access to a boat?"

"Don't beat about the bush, hey?"

"No point. Who knows what other trouble I could get into today, given enough free time."

"It's a fair point. And in answer to your question, yes, he does. He's got a motorboat."

Kate grinned. "I think, ladies and germs, we have a lead suspect."

"Not Sands?" Jimmy asked.

"Nope." Kate got up and walked towards the board. She pinned the nautical chart up and pointed to the cross hatchings she'd filled in earlier. "Wild, Anderson, and Grimshaw have confirmed that from the body position, our victim was facing the harbour when she was shot. They've also identified the round and Len said he'd sent you a list of rifles. Is that right, Stella?"

"Yup. I've been trying to track down permits for any that are on the list or anything that matches and has been reported missing in the last six months."

"Good." She pointed to the dunes and Long Hill. "These are the two closest spots that a person could have been lying in position for Connie to take her morning walk at seven a.m. All this," she said circling the blue zone, "was under water."

"Scolt Head Island's cut off," Collier said.

"As is this section of beach at a high tide like this," Tom said. "The beach road floods."

"Hence the boats," Stella said. "So we've got Sands and Green with shaky alibis, access, and ability. Only Sands we know has motive—"

"No, Green does too," Kate said.

"What motive?"

She quickly updated them on her latest conversation with Gina. She grabbed a pen and circled Matt's name. "Matt Green. Tom when you questioned him, where did he say he was?"

"At work."

"Edward Sands said he was almost half an hour late. Didn't get there till almost seven-thirty."

"So it could still be either of them," Jimmy said. "Green or Sands."

"She had Green's licence plate number in her diary," Collier said.

"Exactly. Nothing in the diary indicates Sands. It's the one other thing that connects her to Green, not Sands," Kate said.

"Still, not solid evidence," Stella said.

"No, but surely enough to bring him in for questioning?"

"Questioning about what?"

"Where he actually was when he was late for work. Why his licence plate number is in her diary."

"And if he isn't the killer and you bring up the diary, it's out of the bag. I think it's too soon," Stella said.

"You're also ignoring the other two suspects on the capable list," Tom said. "Adam and Ally Robbins. They also have a boat."

"They were out on the fishing boat," Jimmy said.

"Yes, giving each other an alibi," Tom said.

"Along with their father," Jimmy replied. "Kate took a photo of the log book."

"Have we got a print of that?" Tom asked.

"No. I can do that now, though. I wasn't sure why I wanted it, to be honest. I think just to make her prove that they were out on the boat." She searched her photostream for the image, while sending a silent prayer to her OCD about backing up her phone everyday. "I didn't like her at all." The printer was slow, and the hum and screech as it ran through its warm up routine was, well, annoying. When the photo finally rolled out of the machine, she pinned it up on the board.

"Do those things have to get verified anywhere?" Stella asked.

"No, but they have to register their catch or they can't sell it. They also have a quota that they can't exceed, so we can check those records," Tom said.

"And where, pray tell, would one search for that little nugget of information?" Stella asked.

"I don't know. Fisheries commission, maybe?"

Stella shook her head. "I'll find it." She picked up the phone and started her hunt.

Kate stared at the board and tried again to figure out what the numbers meant. 52.764. 52.289. 52.233. What the hell were they?

Through her musings, she heard a phone ring. Tom picked it up.

They had to mean something. The other parts of it all meant something, she was sure of it. And she was equally sure that as soon as they figured out what they were, they'd probably kick themselves because the answer would be obvious. Her Gran had always said it was easy when you knew the answer. *Got any for me now, Gran?* She looked up at the ceiling.

"You're on speakerphone, sir," Tom's voice brought her attention back to the present.

"Good. I understand that you've identified a viable suspect in the case?" Timmons asked.

"Well, sir, it's possible," Stella said.

"I understand he has motive, means, opportunity, and the skills to pull this off. Is any of that wrong?"

"No, sir, it isn't, but there are other factors."

"Such as?"

"There are other suspects that meet the same criteria."

"Really? Brothers said this one had a connection that the others didn't."

Stella scowled at Tom. He held his hands up in surrender. "Green is mentioned in her diary by way of a number plate in a code. The other suspect with the same means, motive, and opportunity wasn't mentioned there. But others were. I'm working on their alibis now to see how solid they are."

"And how are they looking?"

"Unfortunately pretty solid."

"Brannon?"

"Yes, sir?"

"Go and pick up this Green. We need to know where he was when he should have been at work, and why his licence number is in her diary."

"Yes, sir." She glanced over at Stella, and mumbled an apology, before tapping Tom on the shoulder and nodding towards the door. He grabbed his keys and jacket before meeting her at the door, eyes widened a little. They both felt bad for Stella. Being overruled by your CO in front of your team was not a nice feeling and Kate knew she wasn't the only one glad to get out of there.

The sky was turning from blue to grey as the afternoon turned to evening and her painkillers started to wear off again. She wished she'd thought to bring them with her.

Out to sea, she could just make out the tall, white masts of the offshore wind farm against the clouds. Row upon row of white steel glinted in the sun, created new havens for wildlife on the seabed, and turned the near constant wind into vital power. She wondered how many homes each one powered as Tom drove past. Probably took half a dozen to power a laptop if you asked most of the critics.

"Do you think he's our guy?" Tom asked.

"Green?"

He nodded.

"Don't know. Let's see what he's got to say for himself." She looked back out the window. "Maybe he just overslept, or he's got a new girlfriend he was bonking."

"Ask before we take him in?"

"Probably best."

"Any idea where he'll be?"

She pointed to the clock on the radio. "Half six. Let's drive by his house and see if he's home. If not, work?"

Tom carried on until they reached the village. Matt Green's house was on the main road. The lights were out, but Kate climbed out of Tom's car and knocked. No one home. She got back in her car, Tom drove the mile to the other end of the village, and turned directly into the farmyard. The gravel crunched beneath her feet when she got out of the car and followed Tom to the Sands' door. Rupert opened it this time.

"Oh, for God's sake, what do you want now?"

Kate raised her eyebrows at him. "Not very friendly, Mr Sands, but we're actually looking for one of your employees. Matt Green."

"Why? What's he done now?"

"We just need to ask him a couple of questions. Do you know where he is?"

"He's working late. We've had a breakdown and he's supposed to be at the irrigation plant. There's a blockage."

"Can you direct us?"

"It's over—"

Tom's phone rang. He held his hand up apologetically as he reached for it.

"Sorry, you were saying?" Kate prompted.

"It's the field across the road. Backs onto the Coastal Path. You need to go—"

"That was Stella. Gina Temple was trying to get hold of you. Apparently, Green's round at her house causing problems."

"Right. Thanks for your help, Mr Sands, but it looks like I don't need those directions after all." She walked back to the car.

"Tell him I'm docking his wages!" Rupert shouted.

"My pleasure," Kate muttered under her breath.

"So where am I going?" Tom asked. Kate gave him directions and they arrived within two minutes of peeling out of Rupert Sands' gravel farmyard. Matt Green was banging on the door with his fist, shouting, and demanding to know where his gun was.

Kate and Tom looked at each other as they rounded the car and walked up the garden path.

"Mr Green?" Kate said. "I'm Detective Sergeant Brannon and this is Detective Brothers. We'd like to ask you a few questions if you don't mind."

"Fuck off. I'm busy." He pounded on the door again. "Gina, open the fucking door. If you're not gonna let me see my kid again, at least tell me where my fucking gun is. I need it."

"Why do you need a gun, Mr Green?"

"I told you to fuck off."

"And I've been asked by the homeowner to tell you that you're not welcome here."

Matt Green laughed. "She's not the fucking homeowner. She just rents, like every other fucking lowlife in this shithole."

"Rupert Sands has also instructed me to tell you that he's docking your wages. I'd guess how much he docks them by is up to you at the moment."

"What do you mean?"

"Well, if you answer my questions right here, right now, then you can probably get back to work and he'll only dock what you've skived."

"Or?"

"Or you can refuse to answer my questions and I'll take you to the station and decide how much time you're going to spend down there. By which time, I doubt Rupert Sands will be in favour of continuing your employment, given his, well, charitable mood when we left him a few minutes ago."

"You fucking bitch."

"Me?" Kate pointed at her chest. "You shouldn't shoot the messenger, Mr Green. That's not very nice. So the twenty-ninth of October, seven o'clock in the morning, where were you?"

"Working."

"Not according to Edward Sands. He said you were almost half an hour late for the daily morning meeting and he had words with you over it. Remembered it very clearly, didn't he, Detective Brothers?"

"Very clearly," Tom said.

"So where were you?"

"I was with the kid." He nodded in the direction of the house. "She stayed with me the night before and I was with her. She slept in and I was late."

"Bullshit."

Kate turned to see Gina standing in the doorway, her fists balled on her hips, her eyes red rimmed, but her cheeks flushed with anger. Green blanched as she stepped out of the house towards them.

"Yes, I was. You know she stayed with me that night."

"She stayed at your house, but she did not oversleep, and she wasn't with you at seven o'clock."

"She bloody was," Green said, a hint of desperation in his voice.

"No, she wasn't, she was sat on her own, on the Coastal Path with your stupid fucking gun when Connie died. You weren't with her. You told her that you were working at Top Wood and sent a nine-year-old off with a rifle to catch you something for dinner. You fucking idiot."

Green blanched. "That's not true."

"Calling your own daughter a liar now, Matt? You're pathetic." Gina stared at him and Kate watched him squirm like a maggot on a hook.

She wished she could enjoy the squirming some more but there was a story to get to the bottom of, and it seemed Gina hadn't been as forthright with her as she'd thought. "What are you telling me, Miss Temple? Sammy shot Connie with his rifle?"

Gina shook her head. "No. He gave her a .22. You said it was a bigger gun that killed Connie."

Kate nodded slowly. "So?"

"Sammy was on the marsh when Connie died. She was trying to shoot him a bloody rabbit and thought she'd killed Connie."

"Is that why you got blind drunk and Sammy was so upset?"

Gina nodded, her eyes pleading with Kate to understand.

Kate did. "And you weren't going to tell me."

Gina shook her head. "But then you were stuck in the sinking boat and got hypothermia and told me that she couldn't have killed her with that gun."

"And you still didn't tell me that she was there. That she's a witness."

"I'm sorry," Gina whispered.

Kate didn't say anything. She'd trusted her. She'd trusted her and almost from the very beginning she'd been hiding information, lying, misleading her.

"Well, I guess I'll just leave you to it," Green said and tried to step around Kate.

"I don't think so, Mr Green. You still haven't answered my question. Instead you've given me two lies and a third about your daughter." She didn't take her eyes off Gina as she spoke to him. "You're coming with me to the station. I need the gun he gave to Sammy, and you and she both need to give us a statement."

Gina nodded. "Of course. I'll get them both now." She ran into the house, apparently glad to be away from Kate.

Kate turned back to Matt Green. "Get in the car."

He shook his head. "I haven't done anything wrong. You can't do this."

Kate tipped her head to the side. "Sweat's beading on your top lip and it's not exactly hot. Your cheeks are flushed, but the rest of your face has gone grey, Mr Green. Your body is telling me that you've done something very wrong." She opened the gate and pointed to the back seat. "Now you can either come voluntarily or I can arrest you. Either way, you're going to the station."

Gina and Sammy stepped out of the door and she handed a long, thin something wrapped in a towel to Tom. The gun, presumably. Tom took it and carefully put it in the boot of his car. Gina ushered Sammy into the car while Matt Green shot her a withering look.

"Now, Mr Green." Kate pulled open the back door to Tom's car and waited. She didn't have to wait long. He sauntered over and put a hand on the door frame, a valiant attempt at a cocky attitude now fixed in place. So that was how he wanted to play the game. She mentally sighed and counted to three before he grinned at her and winked.

"I'm more than happy to help you with your enquiries, Detective." He ducked into the car. She slammed it shut behind him and hoped the loud bang had deafened him. Well, a girl can dream, right?

CHAPTER 19

"Want me to interview her and the kid?" Tom asked quietly.

Kate shook her head. "No, it's fine." She smiled at him as he pulled out onto the main road and headed back to Hunstanton. "I'll send Stella a message. She'll need to get things ready for when we arrive."

"Okay."

Kate pulled her phone from her pocket. Her text was brief and to the point. Stella's reply matched. Kate glanced through the wing mirror and saw Gina right behind them. She'd seemed so scared. Kate gripped the handle above the passenger door so tight her knuckles turned white. She tried to put it into perspective. She went over each conversation they'd had as she tried to figure out how deep the lying and betrayal went. At their first meeting, Gina had been helpful, and there had been nothing that indicated she'd been anything less than 100 percent honest with her. The next time, she'd been drunk and in the morning she still hadn't lied to her. She hadn't told her about Sammy, but she hadn't lied, and there had been no attempt to lead her in the wrong direction. Either she hadn't figured out whom to try to blame, or she wasn't going to try and pin it on someone else. Perhaps just hoping that it would remain unsolved. The next time they met, Kate had been in the houseboat, hypothermic, and let slip the information that cleared Sammy of any wrongdoing.

Well, other than being out hunting rabbits at the age of nine. I should lock him up for that alone. Surely that's reckless endangerment or something.

"You're quiet," Tom said.

"Thinking."

"About what the kid might have seen?"

"And about locking him up for giving a child a gun and leaving her on her own."

"She knows what she's doing with a rifle," Green said from the back.

"Clearly not or she wouldn't have thought, for even a second, that she could have killed someone with that thing." Kate looked at him through her mirror. "If nothing else I'll make sure you never have unsupervised access to that child again, pal."

"You can't do that. She's my kid."

"Exactly. She's a kid. Kids and guns are a very bad combination."

"I had a gun at her age."

"I rest my case."

"Bitch."

"Pillock."

"Come on now, kids. Let's all try to play nice," Tom said, trying to hide his smile.

He indicated to the left, and pulled into the car park. Gina, right behind them, pulled in as well, and then she and Sammy climbed out of the car.

Tom got out and opened the boot while Kate opened the door for Green.

Stella, Jimmy, and Collier were all standing at the door waiting for them. Collier took the rifle and headed away. Kate knew he was going to bag it and run it straight over to King's Lynn for analysis. Although it wasn't the gun that had killed Connie, who knew what else they might find. Stella ushered Green into one of the interview rooms, and Tom guided Sammy and Gina into the other before closing the doors on them all and reconvening with the others in the hallway.

"How do you want to do this?" Stella asked.

Kate squeezed the bridge of her nose. "One at a time. Two in the room, two watching. We'll start with Gina and Sammy. I want to hear what the kid saw and didn't see, and be clear about exactly how long Green needs to account for before I tackle him."

Tom nodded. "Who do you want with you?"

Kate looked from one to the other. "Jimmy. I think he'll be least threatening to the kid. Then, Tom, you and I can take Green. I want him to feel as threatened as possible."

"Right." Tom grinned. "I look forward to it."

She pushed open the door and saw Sammy sitting next to Gina. Her face was grey, and her hands shook in her lap. Instantly, she felt sorry for the child. And protective. She understood why Gina had reacted as she had. She didn't like it, but she understood.

She crouched down beside Sammy and took hold of her hand. "You all right, kiddo?"

Sammy looked at her. Her eyes were red rimmed, her nose running, and there was a smear of dirt across her cheek. Kate couldn't help but smile at her a little. She was one of those kids who could get dirty just looking out of the window, and she just wanted to tell her that it would all be okay.

"Now, I need you to know that you're not in any trouble. I just need to know what happened, and what you saw."

"I'm not in trouble?"

"Nope."

"But I'm going to jail."

Kate laughed. "No, you're not. I promise. As long as you tell me the truth, all of it, then you won't be going to jail."

Sammy let out a huge sigh. "Okay." She held out her little finger. The nail was torn and jagged.

Kate frowned.

"Pinky swears." She wiggled her finger.

Kate hooked her little finger around Sammy's, shook on it, and took a seat opposite her at the table. She pointed to the recorder on the table. "I need to tape all this to make sure I get it right. Is that okay with you?" Sammy looked at it and nodded, then Kate pointed to Jimmy behind her. "This is my friend Jimmy Powers. He's going to listen too."

"Why?"

"To double check the tape. Make sure we both get everything right."

Sammy scowled at her. "We pinky swore, that means you have to tell the truth too."

"It is the truth. There needs to be two of us to make sure we get everything right. But I suppose it's also in case he thinks of a question I don't."

Sammy seemed to think about it. "That makes sense, I guess."

"My boss thinks so." Kate smiled and turned on the tape. "The time is seven-fifteen p.m. on Sunday, the first of November, twenty-fifteen, I'm Detective Sergeant Kate Brannon interviewing Samantha Temple and Georgina Temple. In the room is also Detective Constable James Powers. The purpose of this interview is to collect witness testimony from Samantha Temple, a minor. How old are you again, Sammy?"

"Nine."

"Thank you. Her mother is present. So, Sammy, can you tell me what time you woke up on Thursday morning?"

"Same as every day. Oh-dark-thirty." She giggled. "Mum always says I get up too early."

"And what time is that?"

"Five," Gina said. "She wakes up at five in the morning, every single day."

"Ouch. Your mum's right, kiddo. That is too early."

Sammy shrugged.

"So what did you do then?"

"I'd stayed at Dad's house the night before, so I got up and dressed, then went to make breakfast."

"Where was your dad?"

"Sleeping."

"What did you eat?"

"Cereal."

"I like frosties best."

"Coco pops."

"Bunny poops."

"Ew."

Kate laughed. "So what time did your dad get up?"

"Half past five. He said he had work to do at Top Wood, but he needed my help."

"And what did he want you to help him with?"

"He was supposed to be scaring the birds off the fields, and he said I could kill two birds with one stone if I used his gun and tried to catch him a rabbit or something for his tea while I was scaring the geese off the fields."

"Had you done this with him before?"

"What? Scared the geese?"

"Yes."

"Well, yeah. We normally do it with rockets, though. We all have different places to go and let them off depending on where the geeses are."

"Do you normally do this on your own?"

"Not normally."

"But you have done?"

Sammy nodded.

"For the purposes of the tape, Sammy nodded yes. What about the gun? Does he normally let you shoot his gun?"

"Sometimes."

"On your own?"

"No. This was the first time he let me on my own."

"Have you killed a rabbit before?"

Sammy shook her head.

"For the purposes of the tape, Sammy shook her head no."

"I don't like killing fings. It was just 'cos he asked me to that I was gonna try."

"That's okay, Sammy. Thank you." She smiled and waited for Sammy to relax a little. "So what time did you and your dad leave the house?"

"Erm, I think it was about six o'clock." She scrunched up her face trying to remember. "No, it must have been before because the church bells rung six times while I was in my place waiting to scare the birds."

"The bells at Brandale Church?"

"Yeps. I heard them ring six times and then I heard them ring seven times too."

"And you were on your own the whole time?"

"Yeppers. Dad dropped me off at the trees and told me to find him a nice, big, fat one."

"So where did you go and wait?"

"I went and waited against the fence at the bottom of Mrs Webb's garden."

"Where's that?"

"From the houseboat," Gina said, "look towards the harbour. Mrs Webb's garden is the first house along that side of the Coastal Path. She was sitting about twenty yards from the sign post at the junction."

"Thank you. So you didn't go too far onto the path?"

"No. It was dark, and the gun's heavy."

"Yes, it is. So you sat there and waited. Can you tell me what you saw?"

"Well, it was dark to start with."

"Yes, I'm sure it was."

"So I didn't see very much. But then it started getting light and I could see some birds and some rats and a hedgehog."

"When it got lighter, where was the water?"

"Everywhere." Sammy's eyes opened wide. "I normally sit on the edge of the path and dangle my feet over the marsh, but I couldn't this time. The water was all there. Right up to the edge. That's why I was against the fence. Mrs Webb doesn't like people on her fence."

"So the water was all around you already?"

"Yep. All the little broken old boats were all floating. The fishing boats was out too. I could see the lights on them first and then I could make 'em out later. The *Jean Rayner* was over the mussel beds and everything."

"That must have been exciting?"

"Well, I suppose."

"What else did you see?"

"Well, I saw Connie and Merlin, of course. She's always out in the morning taking her pictures."

"And you saw her that morning?"

"Yep. She came out of the houseboat and her and Merlin started walking away from me. Towards the sluice on the Norton side."

"You knew she used the houseboat?"

"Yeah. 'Course. She used it for taking special photos, she said."

"Did she tell you what photos?"

Sammy shook her head. "She just said it was a special project for Leah. Like a leaving present. She said she was going to help her whether she wanted her to or not."

Kate nodded. "Do you know what she meant by that?"

"No. But she said it was mega important and a big special secret so I shouldn't tell anyone." Realising what she'd said she put her hand over her mouth.

Kate smiled. "It's okay. I'm sure she'd want you to tell me about it."

Sammy frowned. Obviously not convinced.

"Did you see anyone else, Sammy? Maybe someone behind her?"

Sammy shook her head. "No."

"No one coming from the opposite direction?"

"No. Just her and Merlin. And me."

"Okay, so what happened next?"

"I saw a big, fat, rabbit and I tried to shoot it."

"Did you miss?"

Sammy nodded again. "I tried to remember everything Dad told me about shootin', but I got excited and scared all at the same time and I closed my eyes when I pulled the trigger." Tears welled in her eyes. "And then Connie was gone and Merlin was going mad."

"Did you go and see what happened to her?"

"Yes," Sammy whispered. "I thought I blewed her face off, but Mum said it wasn't me and you said I wasn't going to jail 'cos I didn't do anything wrong."

"You're not, kiddo. It wasn't your fault. But this is very important. When you shot at the rabbit, did you hear anything else?"

"Like what?"

"Anything?"

"I just heard my gun. It was right by my ear."

"Okay."

"It sounded like it was echoey, though. It was longer than I remembered it being when Dad showed me it."

"How do you mean?"

"Well, instead of it going *bang*, it kind of went *bang-ang*." She frowned, clearly not sure how to articulate what she'd heard.

But Kate understood it all right. A second shot. No way could they have predicted that Sammy would have been firing at the same time, even if the shooter was her father. He'd sent her after rabbits. Coincidence? Surely, if he wanted her shot to be his cover, he'd have told her to fire at a certain time. Maybe to scare the geese. *Scare the geese. I'm an idiot.*

"Sammy, while you were out on the marsh, did you hear any other bangs, to scare the birds?"

"Yeah, 'course. They were going off every few minutes. The birds are always hungry in the morning."

The shooter was using the everyday sounds that people no longer heard to mask the killing shot. *Ingenious. And I'm a fucking idiot.*

"So what did you do next, Sammy?"

Sammy quickly told her how she ran to school and waited for her dad to show up and collect the gun from her. When he didn't, she'd walked home, running across the main road and into the farm fields on the other side. She didn't want to go near Connie again, and she didn't know what to say if someone had seen her on the path with the gun. So she'd gone home and tried to hide the gun in a gutter, which Gina confirmed.

"Miss Temple, why didn't you bring this information to the attention of the police?"

"I—I think I was in shock at first. I wasn't thinking clearly. Connie was my best friend. I was still reeling from the fact that she was dead and when I learned that Sammy thought she was responsible...I panicked. I didn't think about it clearly. I didn't think that it was impossible for the little rifle she was carrying to be able to shoot as far away from her as Connie was. I didn't think about anything rationally. I just panicked."

"And then lied to us?"

"No. I didn't lie. I didn't tell you about this, but I didn't lie to you. Every question you asked, I answered honestly." She stretched her hand across the table and then pulled it back. "When you asked about Leah and the drugs, I could have pushed you in that direction. I could have easily led you to believe it was her. But I couldn't do it. I couldn't direct you falsely and let someone else rot for a crime they didn't commit."

"So what did you want?"

"I guess I was hoping you weren't very good at your job and that it would never get solved."

Kate tried not to let the comment get to her. People had said far worse over the course of her career. But for some reason it really did.

"Then when you were hypothermic and you let slip that it was a much bigger gun than she was carrying, I knew it couldn't have been Sammy's fault."

"So why didn't you come forward with the information then?"

"It's a good question."

"And the answer?"

"I don't have a good one for you."

"I'll settle for an honest one."

Gina blanched and Kate almost apologised for the hurtful comment. But she didn't. She held her tongue.

"I asked Sammy to go over it again. She didn't see anything that could help you. She didn't see anyone. How could going over it again and again help her? She's having nightmares about what she saw."

Kate looked at Sammy. "Are you?"

Sammy shrugged, her chin hitting her chest, and she nodded.

"We can get her help with that," Kate said to Gina. "I'll get you the number of a counsellor from victim support."

"She isn't a victim."

"No, but she's a witness. They help those too and they have people who specialise in helping kids." She looked at Jimmy, wondering if he had any questions. He shook his head. "Interview terminated at seven forty-four p.m. Thank you for your time, Miss Temple. Sammy, thank you. You were a big help."

She shook Sammy's hand and held hers out for Gina. Her touch was electric. Fingers sliding against hers, palm to palm, Kate swore she could feel Gina's pulse hammering against the thick pad at the base of her thumb. Her skin was soft, smooth, velvety, and welcoming. She pulled away quickly. "Detective Powers will show you out. Please, don't go anywhere without letting us know, as we may need to speak to you again."

Sammy and Gina followed Jimmy to the door. Before she left, Gina turned back.

"I'm sorry, Kate. I didn't want to keep things from you, and I never lied to you."

Kate didn't look at her. Now was not the time to think about why that hurt so much, never mind talk about it.

"I'll pick up Merlin when I finish this evening."

There was a long pause, then Gina whispered, "Fine." She walked out without another word.

Kate rolled her head from side to side trying to ease the tension in her shoulders. She heard the door open again.

"Want the other good news?" Stella asked.

"What's that?"

"Matt Green has a Kimber 8400 patrol .308 rifle registered to him."

"Other than the word rifle that means nothing to me."

"It's one that takes 7.62 by 51 millimetre NATO rounds."

Kate turned to look at her quickly. "And he has one registered to him?"

"Yes."

"Why?"

"Why don't you ask him?"

"I will." She stood up and tugged on her shirt.

"Oh, now there's a look of determination," Stella said.

"He has no alibi, a weapon that takes the round we found evidence of, and motive. He's lied to us and I don't like him. And he's an idiot of a father. I want to charge him for that stunt with Sammy."

"I'll add it to the list."

"Good." She pulled open the door of the interview room. "Where is he again?" Stella pointed down a short corridor. "Right. Are we ready?"

Stella handed her a thin file. "Tom's in there already."

"I thought he was going to wait for me?" She glanced through the file. Everything she needed.

"He is. You also said you wanted him intimidated."

"So what's he doing?"

"Staring at him."

"And?"

"And nothing. He's just standing in the doorway, staring at him." Stella shuddered. "It's bloody creepy. He narrows his eyes and stops blinking. I'm telling you, it's creepy. Green's already shaking in his boots."

Kate pictured the tall, stocky man standing still, just watching her. Doing nothing, not even blinking. She shuddered too.

"See? Creepy."

Kate shook it off. "All right, let's get on with this. I've got a home to go to tonight."

"You do?"

"Well, a house."

"Empty one?"

"Won't be once I pick up that mutt."

She opened the door and went inside. She didn't speak but sat down, opened a pad, and set a pen on top of it. Then she started the recorder.

"It's seven forty-nine p.m. on Sunday the first of November, twenty-fifteen. I'm DS Kate Brannon and in the room with me is DC Thomas Brothers. Please state your full name and address for the tape."

"Matthew Green, Pebbles Cottage, Brandale Staithe."

"Thank you, Mr Green. For the benefit of the tape, Mr Green has not been arrested, he is at this stage helping us with our enquiries."

Tom still hadn't moved, still hadn't blinked. Stella was right. It was bloody creepy. Green could barely keep his eyes off him.

"Where were you between six a.m. and seven-thirty a.m. on the morning of October twenty-ninth?"

"I was with my daughter, and then I went to work."

"I have a statement from your daughter that you left her alone on the marsh, in possession of a fully loaded firearm before six a.m., and you weren't seen at work until almost seven-thirty. Hence the specific times I refer to. So I will ask again, Mr Green. Where were you?"

"They're lying." His eyes were still glued to Tom.

"Both of them? I doubt it. Besides, your daughter was more worried that she was going to be in trouble. Your actions left her convinced for three days that she'd killed Connie Wells."

"What?" Matt's eyes fixed on her with laser-like focus. "What did you say?"

"She fired at a rabbit. Like you asked her to. Then Connie was dead. She thought she'd done it. She saw it." Kate placed a photograph of Connie on the table. The grass was green and trampled all around what was left of her head.

"That's fucking gross. Get rid of it."

"Your little girl saw this because you left her alone with a gun." She tapped her fingers on the table beside the picture.

"You're lying. She didn't. She'd have said something."

"She's having nightmares because she saw this." She started drumming her fingers. Ring, middle, index, little finger. Her little finger landing on the picture each time, drawing his focus back to what was left of Connie's head.

"She didn't."

"Oh, I'm afraid she very much did. She saw this because you left her alone before six o'clock in the morning. She remembers because she was sitting in the grass, in the dark, when the church bells rang six times."

He swallowed hard.

"Your boss didn't see you until almost seven-thirty, Matt. Where were you?"

"I was busy."

"I'm sure you were. Busy doing what?"

"Just stuff."

She drummed her fingers again, ending with her pinky on Connie's hair. "Busy doing this?"

"What? No!"

"Prove it. Tell me where you were."

"I don't know."

"You don't know?"

"No."

"Right." Kate left the picture where it was and pulled another from the slim file. She placed it next to the first. "Registered to you is a Kimber 8400 patrol .308, just like this one, correct?"

He nodded.

"For the purposes of the tape, Mr Green."

"Yes."

"Thank you." She put a third picture down. "I'm showing Mr Green a picture of a 7.62 by 51 millimetre NATO round. Is this the correct ammunition for your Kimber rifle, Mr Green?"

"Yeah, that's what I use. That's what works best with that weapon. Why?"

She tapped the picture of Connie again. "We found traces of a 7.62 by 51 millimetre NATO round in the wound track, Mr Green. Do you know what that means?"

He said nothing.

"It means that a 7.62 by 51 millimetre NATO round," she said touching the picture of the cartridge, "killed her." She pointed to Connie again. "A bullet that is fired from a weapon just like the one you own. Does that help jog your memory, Mr Green?"

He said nothing.

"We know that you had a run-in with Connie at Christmas."

No response.

"She told you to fuck off and pointed an air rifle at your little todger, didn't she?"

Nothing.

"Is that why you decided to do it?"

Not one word.

"Did you kill her?"

"No."

"Did you kill Connie?"

"No."

"Did you murder Connie Wells?"

"No, I didn't kill her."

"Then prove it, Matt. Tell me where you were."

"I was nowhere fucking near the marshes. I was nowhere near Brandale Staithe. I wasn't even in fucking Norfolk."

"Where were you?"

"I was meeting a guy at Sutton Bridge."

"What guy? Why?"

"Just a guy."

"Why?"

"I just was."

"You don't just leave your daughter and drive—how many miles is it to Sutton Bridge from Brandale Staithe?"

"I dunno. About thirty, maybe."

"About thirty?"

He shrugged. "Yeah, about that."

"So you left your daughter, your nine-year-old daughter, alone on the marsh, with a loaded gun, to drive thirty-ish miles to meet "some guy" just because?"

He dropped his head to his chest.

"Doesn't sound good when I put it like that, does it, Matt?"

He shook his head.

"For the purposes of the tape, Mr Green shook his head no." She folded her fingers together. "So what were you doing in Sutton Bridge?"

"I told you, I was meeting some guy."

"Why?"

"Just...just because..."

"Not good enough, Matt. You really need to convince me or I can probably convince my boss that you did this." She tapped the picture of Connie again. "And if I can convince that cynical old bastard that you did it, trust me I can convince the crown prosecution service and a jury that you fucking did it."

"I didn't kill her." He slammed his hands on the table. "I didn't do it."

"Prove it. Give me something I can corroborate that puts you anywhere but holding that gun."

"I can't." He shook his head.

"Why not? If you weren't there, all you've got to do is show me where you were. Give me something that proves it."

"I can't."

"Who was the guy?"

"I don't know."

"Why were you meeting him?"

"I was selling him something."

"Selling him what?"

"Nothing."

Kate laughed. "That's not how this works, Matt. Either you were selling something to a guy or you weren't. Either you can prove you were there or you can't. If you can, we can clear this up, and I can keep looking for Connie's killer. If not, well, you're looking at a long stretch, Matt."

"I want a lawyer."

Kate laughed. "This isn't America, Matt. You get a solicitor over here, a brief, but not till you've been arrested. And I haven't arrested you." She gathered up the pictures and slid them back into the folder. "Yet."

"It wasn't me. I didn't kill her."

"Then tell me who you were meeting."

"I don't know his name. It's just a delivery driver."

"A delivery driver." She sighed. "Okay, Matt, I'll play. Were you dropping this nothing that you were selling off at his depot?"

Matt shook his head. "No."

"His house?"

"No."

"Come on, Matt, you've got to give me something or I can't help you."

Matt laughed. "You don't want to help me. You think you've got it all worked out." He looked her up and down, a sneer twisting his face. "You haven't got a fucking clue." He held his hands out on the table, wrists together. "Arrest me, bitch, and get me my brief 'cos you ain't getting another word out of me."

He did have an alibi. She could feel it. But unless he gave it to her it didn't matter. Unless he proved it, it made no difference to what they had on him. What was it about the alibi that he was so scared of? What could be worse than facing a murder charge? Didn't matter—until he gave them the information, she didn't have anywhere else to go.

"Matthew Green, I'm arresting you for the murder of Connie Wells. You don't have to say anything, but your defence may be harmed if you do not mention, when questioned, something that you later rely on in court. Anything you do say can and will be used as evidence. Do you understand your rights?"

Tom helped him to his feet and waited for him to respond. Matt spat on the table.

"Do you understand your rights as I've explained them to you?" Kate repeated.

"Yes."

"Thank you."

Tom guided him out of the room and to the custody sergeant, where he was quickly booked and led to a cell. Kate watched with detached curiosity. At least now they could get a warrant to search his house and car. Maybe they would tell them more than Matt Green was willing to.

CHAPTER 20

"Mum, can I have some chocolate?"

"No. It's too late."

"But—"

"I said no."

Gina knew Sammy was going to sulk all the way home, but she had other things on her mind. The fact that Kate had refused to look at her when she was leaving. She'd taken it so personally. *Oh, for God's sake, why now? All these years and now I find someone that I really like and she's never going to talk to me again, well, not in a personal capacity anyway.*

"I said, can I have a hot chocolate, then?" Sammy shook her arm.

"Oh, erm, yeah. That works."

Sammy smiled.

One mini disaster averted. Shame about the bigger one. *Should I have kept my mouth shut about Matt not being with Sammy? No. Definitely not. No matter what else happened. Why was he lying about where he was? Did that mean...?*

She didn't want to think about the prospect of what that lie could mean. She really didn't. Thinking about her daughter accidentally killing Connie was bad enough. To think Matt, someone she had a history with, someone who she had a daughter with, might have murdered Connie was too much. It was a crime that had taken planning, patience, care. It wasn't a spur-of-the-moment, heat of anger thing. It was a cold, calculated crime, and one she didn't want to picture anyone she knew committing.

"Mum, why was Kate angry at you?"

"DS Brannon to you."

Sammy frowned. "She told me to call her Kate."

"When?"

"The other night when you slept on the sofa."

"Oh, right."

"So why was she angry?"

"Because she feels I should have told her what happened to you earlier. About what you saw."

"But you said I wasn't to tell anyone. Why were you supposed to tell her?"

"Because she's the police and she trusted that I was helping her to find who killed Connie. I think, she thinks I betrayed her."

"Did you?"

Gina sighed. "I suppose I did. I had to. I had to protect you."

"But you didn't need to. I didn't do anything to go to jail for."

"True. But we didn't know that at the time."

"Hmm." Sammy looked out of the window. "Would you still have kept it secret if I had?"

"Sammy, even if you had killed Connie it would have been an accident. You wouldn't have gone to jail."

"Then why did we betray Kate?"

"Because I was scared that I'd lose you."

Sammy frowned. "I don't understand, you said I wouldn't go to jail."

"Your dad giving you that gun and leaving you alone was a very, very bad thing. So bad that Kate and her boss will have to make sure that he can never see you on his own again because he can't be trusted to look after you properly. Do you understand?"

Sammy shook her head. "His dad let him shoot guns when he was my age."

"That doesn't mean it's the right thing to do. You could have killed someone. You could have killed yourself. He can't be trusted to look after you." Gina pulled into a lay-by and tugged the sobbing child into her arms. "It's so bad that I'm scared they might not think I can look after you either. That's why I didn't tell Kate what you saw. Because I'm scared they will take you away from me."

"I don't want to go away."

"I know, sweetheart, I don't want that either. That's why I'm so scared."

"I'll be good, Mum, I promise. Please, don't let them take me away."

She squeezed tighter and kissed the top of her head over and over. "Not if I can do anything about it."

"I'll be good, I promise."

Gina laughed and knew the little scamp would try dearly, but she equally knew she'd fail. Sammy was a magnet for trouble. Always had been. If there was one child you could guarantee to be in the wrong place at the wrong time, it was her. She may have only been doing the same as every other child, but you could bet your life that she was the one who'd get caught.

"We'll see, sweetheart."

CHAPTER 21

Pebbles Cottage was definitely an apt name for it. The entire outer render was made of the local flint pebbles. Most of the local houses had a small amount of it between decorative brick columns, but Pebbles Cottage was entirely covered with pebbles of all different shapes and sizes. It was set in the middle of a small housing estate, little more than two hundred yards from the campsite and less than a hundred from the Coastal Path. The harbour was half a mile to the west.

There was a short drive that led to a carport with corrugated plastic roofing and thick telegraph poles sunk into the ground. The car was a three-year-old Mitsubishi Barbarian, bearing the licence plate number MK52 UXB. The hard-covered load bed of the pickup was empty, save for some dead pine needles, off an old Christmas tree, no doubt. The back seat was also empty and the car had recently been professionally cleaned. The closest place where that could have happened was ten miles away in Hunstanton. Not something done on a whim for a guy who lives within a five-minute walk of where he works.

She sat in the passenger seat, Tom was in the driver's side fiddling with stuff on the dashboard.

"Want to know something interesting about the Barbarian?" Tom asked.

"What's that?"

"They've got built-in satellite navigation."

"And that's good because?"

"It also tracks where he's been."

"Really?"

"Yup." He touched the screen and brought up a log book of sorts. "This was where the car was at six forty on the twenty-ninth." He pointed to a spot on the map close to a large river and some sort of bridge.

"And where is that?"

"On the outskirts of a town called Sutton Bridge."

"And what's there?"

"At Sutton Bridge?"

"Yeah."

He shrugged. "Big power plant, not far away."

"And?"

"Houses, countryside. Normal stuff for round here."

"So it gets us nothing."

"Well, Sarge, it corroborates what he was saying about not being the doer."

"Just because his car wasn't here, doesn't necessarily mean he wasn't."

"Grasping at straws."

"Maybe, but we'd better be damn sure because he sure as shit is hiding something or he'd just tell us where he was and who he was meeting to give us his alibi."

"True."

She got out and went into the house. A laptop and tablet were being bagged. A rifle, two other firearms, and an assortment of ammunition were already packed and in a box, waiting to be carried away for forensic testing. The house was much tidier than she'd expected a bachelor pad to be. It was tidier than her own place. There was no clutter at all, no dirty dishes on the coffee table, no magazines strewn about. Just one mug was on the side, the TV remote was on the TV stand, and, while worn and threadbare, the sofa was clean and serviceable. There were photos all over the walls. Pictures of Sammy and Matt. Not one of them was in a frame, just printouts that were stuck to the wall with Blu-Tack in each corner. But every one showed him in some stupid pose with her—pulling faces at each other, Sammy grinning at the camera while he watched. It was clear that he loved her. Adored her. Shame he hadn't thought of that when he put her in danger. She shook her head and continued to look around.

The same clean and tidy theme was continued throughout the house. One bowl and one spoon sat on the drainer to go with the single mug in the front room. The fridge held nothing but a half pint of milk, a pat of butter, and a beer can with the plastic around the rim, indicating it was the remaining survivor of a four-pack. Microwave meals packed the shelves of the freezer compartment. The remaining half of a loaf of bread, two tins of beans, a box of Coco Pops, a jar of coffee, and a boil-in-the-bag rice packet sat in another cupboard. More than she had sitting at home. She had more dog food than human food in her own cupboards.

In the master bedroom, the bed was made and clothes hung neatly in the wardrobe or were folded tidily in drawers. Everything in its place. The second bedroom resembled a bomb site and she knew it had to be Sammy's. The third room was appointed as an office of sorts. Computer, printer, etc. Again, organised, clean, and tidy. The SOCO team were carefully bagging the contents for removal and analysis, and she didn't want to get in the way. She turned to leave and spotted a map stuck on the back of the door. It was a huge map of East Anglia with circles in seemingly random locations. But then she spotted one just to the left of Sutton Bridge.

She tapped the nearest chap on the shoulder. "You got a bag for this?"

He quickly removed it and sealed it in an evidence bag before handing it to her. She took it out to the car.

"Tom, bring up the log from where he was," she said when she'd reached the car again. She held out the map as he did so and she pointed to the circled location. "It's the same." She got in and stabbed her finger at the arrowhead marking a spot near the river. She touched the screen without meaning to and the image changed. Instead of the map, she was faced with a series of numbers: 52.764, -0.192.

"Shit, don't touch it. We don't want to delete anything." Tom reached towards the screen. She grabbed his hand to stop him from changing anything, and pointed instead.

"I'm an idiot," she said. "Look."

"What am I look...fuck. You are an idiot."

She slapped him across the arm with the back of her hand. "You are too."

"We're all idiots," he said.

She pulled her phone out of her pocket and dialled. "Stella, we know what the numbers are that start with fifty-two."

"What?"

"GPS coordinates."

"You're shitting me."

"Wish I was. I've got a map with about a dozen locations circled. I'm betting that each one of them is going to link up with one on that list."

"You're a friggin' genius."

"Hold off on the praise. If he was in the car, he was at one of these locations on the twenty-ninth. He couldn't have been the shooter."

"It gets worse on that score."

"How?"

"Wild called. He's been doing more research on the round and this weapon, now that he has something to start with."

"And?"

"There is no way on God's green earth that gun and that round could have made a killing shot at a distance of more than eight hundred metres."

"Shit."

"Exactly."

"So what kind of gun do we need to be looking for?"

"Here's the real kicker, kiddo. That bullet in any gun it fits, has a maximum range of eight hundred metres. There is no way, without changing the laws of physics, that the bullet that killed her could have been fired from either of the positions identified."

"So, what's Wild saying? He made a mistake with the bullet?"

"Not possible. He said there's a database for that kind of thing and the molecular structure of the fragments were definitely from that bullet."

"Could he have been wrong about the shot coming from the houses?"

"He says no. Said he's run the scenarios a dozen times now. For her body to have landed where it was, she had to have been looking out due west. Not west by southwest or anything else. Due west. The shot could have only come from the houses if she'd been facing south by southwest. A difference of more than thirty degrees, he assures me. So I'm taking his word for it."

"So there must have been a bit of land closer?"

"Not according to your map."

"Stella, something along the way is wrong. If the bullet is right, the direction is right, then the map can't be. We're missing something."

"I know, but what?"

Kate sighed. "Don't know. Listen we'll bring this map back and see what we can match up."

"I've been running the coordinates on Wells' list through Google Maps and I've got locations on each of them."

"Okay. We'll be there soon."

CHAPTER 22

Gina held a mug under the tap and rinsed the soap away. She heard a knock at the door and Merlin started to bark. She glanced at the clock. It was well after midnight. She dried her hands and looked through the peephole before opening the door.

"I'd just about given up on you."

"I'm sorry it's so late. It's been a busy day," Kate said. "I'll just get her and go. Sorry if I kept you up."

Gina shook her head and grabbed Kate's hand to tug her inside. "Don't be silly. I just thought it might—" she waved her hand. "Never mind. Did he do it?"

"I can't talk about the case with you."

"Of course not, I'm being daft. Can I get you a drink? Tea? Coffee? Glass of wine?"

"Thank you, but I'll just get Merlin and go." She looked around, clearly looking for Merlin's lead.

"Kate, please let me explain."

"You don't need to. I understand what you were trying to do. I don't blame you for trying to protect your daughter when you thought it was an accident."

"And do you understand why I still didn't say anything when I realised she hadn't?"

Kate looked at her for a long moment then shook her head. "I—I mean—we—the police—could have made sure he didn't put her in danger again. We are doing that. I don't understand why you don't want that. Surely you can see he's a danger to her?"

"Of course I can. I'd already told him he wasn't going to see her anymore."

"Then why?"

"Have you informed Social Services yet?"

"Of course. We have to let them know that she's at risk with him."

"And me?" Gina felt the tears welling in her eyes. It was too late now, nothing she could do.

"What? Why would they...oh. I see. You're worried that because he was stupid while she was in his care you'll be, what? Tarred with the same brush?"

"Yes."

"You think they're going to take her away from you?"

"Yes." The tears coursed down her cheeks and she swiped them away. "I'm sorry but she's all I have. She's my daughter." She buried her face in her hands and let the tears fall. She leaned into the wall and didn't even try to stop them. A moment later she was pulled into a strong embrace. Soft hands curled around her shoulders, gentle fingers caressed the back of her head, and Kate's low voice in her ear whispered soothing words as she cried out all her fear and frustration.

"They won't take her away from you."

"What? How do you know?"

"I had to write a statement this evening. It's one of the many reasons I'm so late."

Gina wrapped her arms around Kate's waist and clung on. "Please tell me."

Kate sighed. "They'll want to talk to you, probably tomorrow when they get the statement through. And Sammy too, of course."

"Okay. Then what will happen."

"They'll talk to Matt when we let them, but we're charging him with reckless endangerment of a child. He hasn't denied giving her the gun, or leaving her alone to wield it, so the case is pretty clear. He'll be convicted of that and in the future he'll only ever be granted supervised visitation. As you assisted the police, and were taking steps to ensure her safety the moment you discovered what happened, you'll be fine. They may want to do a couple of home visits or something, just to make sure everything's really okay, but they won't take her away from you. They've got enough kids out there with bigger problems than this."

She felt the crushing weight lifted from her and took her first free breath in days. She gulped in one lungful after another, shuddering and swaying as each breath rejuvenated her. She leaned heavily against Kate, her hands gripping her tighter. The rush of oxygen around her body brought with it the awareness of sensations she hadn't felt in far too long. Everywhere her body touched Kate's, she tingled. Her arms were awash with the feel of Kate's coat, and beneath it the skin that she was sure was soft and velvety. She turned her head and caught the scent of Kate's neck. The scent was warm, like cinnamon, vanilla, and chocolate with a citrus aroma that mingled from her hair. Like a chocolate orange. She wanted to move her hair to one side and taste that scent on her tongue. To breathe it in, breathe her in, and let it wash over her, fill her up.

"And what about you?" Gina said, her voice scratchy and raw.

"What about me?"

"Can you forgive me?"

Kate shrugged and pulled away. "Like I said earlier, I understand."

"But?"

"But nothing, Miss Temple—"

"What happened to 'Gina'?"

Kate spotted Merlin's lead hung up on the coat rack and picked it up. Merlin came at the sound of the clasp being flicked. "I trusted Gina." She clipped the lead to her collar and pulled the door open. "Thanks for looking after her. Good night, Miss Temple."

The soft words, the frosty politeness, and the withdrawal of the friendliness that had been growing between them—it couldn't have hurt more if Kate had slapped her.

CHAPTER 23

Kate parked in the car park of the sailing club, despite the warnings that non-members' vehicles would be towed. Better to be towed than write off another car. It was eight o'clock in the morning and the tide was out, but she'd learned already that it paid to be careful around here.

She opened the door and Merlin followed her out of the driver's door, offering her a doggy grin when Kate unclipped her lead to let her wander wherever she wanted and sniff to her heart's content. Kate looked around her. The sun had not long since risen and the muted colours of the marsh were cast in shadows, making the greens murky and drab, and the mud look grey. The vast plain would soon be under water. Not as much water today as on the twenty-ninth, but enough. Every plant that grew was adapted to growing in the salt water of the ocean. Every creature that lived on it had a way of going with the flow. Home was different from one tide to the next, with nothing more permanent than a few hours.

The husks of forgotten and damaged boats littered the heather and samphire-strewn landscape, offering a speck of variety against a backdrop of flat sameness. In the distance, she could just make out what was left of the houseboat. They were still waiting to see who it had actually belonged to. Perhaps today, they'd get that information and it would lead to a breakthrough.

She watched as the first trickle of the tide started to slink into the channel. A flutter of wind rippled the steel cables and set them rattling against masts all along the harbour. It was pretty, in a desolate, barren kind of way. She could see the appeal. The seemingly endless sky made her feel small, insignificant, and it helped her put things into perspective. Her mind drifted from the endless sky to the sky blue eyes that had tormented her last night. Blue eyes and long dark hair that smelled of coconut. Shampoo she presumed, or maybe it was body lotion on her skin rather than in her hair. *Oh for God's sake, stop it. It's never going to happen.* There had been something in Gina that had appealed to her on a level that made her want—no, need—to keep going back. Gina eased the loneliness that always lingered, and sometimes overwhelmed her. She seemed to fit into the space that Kate couldn't fill, no matter how hard she worked, or how fast she ran. It was ridiculous to think that. She knew it was. She'd only met Gina four days ago, and circumstances had been less than ideal. But somehow Kate knew that there could have been something wonderful between them. Could have been. Three words that only made her feel lonelier than ever. Had she been too hard on her? She really did understand Gina's reason for doing what she did. Love. "What do you think, Merlin?" she asked. The dog pricked up her ears and came to Kate's side. "Was I too hard on her? Should I go and say sorry, see if she'd have coffee with me?"

Merlin tipped her head to the side, whined, then yipped a short bark.

"Simple as that, hey girl?" She stroked her head. "Maybe you're right." She sighed. "Maybe I will. Other people find happiness, why shouldn't I?"

Could it really be as simple as that? Just like turning on or off a light switch? Could she really just shift her thinking from expecting to be unhappy, expecting to be lonely, to something else? Just a little twist in perception, right?

She took a seat on the bench between the sailing club launch and the harbour proper, squirming when the hard wood pressed uncomfortably against the stitches in the back of her thigh. She didn't sit because she was tired or it was a long way. It wasn't. No more than fifty yards. She just wanted to watch. To stare at it all. To see if any spit of land jumped out as being a possible position for the sniper. Nothing did. The only things she could make out were the two spots they'd seen before. The ones that were too far away for the bullet to have been shot from.

Something about their theory was wrong. Something about their assumptions stopped the facts from allowing them to make the logical conclusion and find the killer. *So take it right the way back to the beginning. What do we know?* Connie Wells was shot with a bullet that couldn't have been fired from more than eight hundred metres away. She was facing the harbour when she was shot. And the only thing in that direction eight hundred metres away or less was water.

Water.

Just a little twist in perception and whole different picture collides into place. Just a few degrees.

She glanced to her right and watched as the fishermen loaded lobster pots onto their boats. There were three in the harbour loading up. The *Jean Rayner*, the *Shady Lady*, and the *Anglian Princess*. The *Jean Rayner* was a pale sky blue with white paint neatly indicating her name and her registration number. The *Jean Rayner LN353*.

"I really am a fucking idiot."

CHAPTER 24

She straight-armed the door to the squad room and waved her phone in the air. "I've got it. I know what the other numbers are."

She tapped on the picture she'd pulled from the wreck of the houseboat. It was still covered in its plastic evidence bag, tagged, sealed, and ready for them to study. She pinned it to their board.

The grainy image had obviously been shot at long range using a lens at its maximum focal length. It had been blown up as much as possible to show whatever it was she was now looking at. The rope and steel frame of a lobster pot, water droplets dripping off the rope. The numbers "5" and "3" were clearly visible in the background, even though the leading edge of the "5" had been cut off slightly. It made it look uneven. The background was a pale sky blue with irregular white shapes here and there. The shapes weren't smooth. There was a granular texture to the edges.

She checked around her to make sure they were all paying attention. "That's a boat in the background." She pointed to the splotches. "The shapes are the remains of sea spray that has dried and left a salty residue on the hull of a pale-blue boat. A pale-blue fishing boat hauling its lobster pots." She pointed to the list of numbers from Connie's diary. "It was right there in front of us. LN353. It's a fishing boat called the *Jean Rayner* owned by—"

"The Robbins," Tom said.

"Exactly."

"How does that help us?" Collier asked. "We still can't make the shot that killed her, kill her."

"What do fishing boats do?" Kate asked.

He scowled at her, obviously aware that there was a trap ahead but unable to see it to avoid it. "They fish."

"Uh-huh. How do they do that?"

"In this case, they pull pots out of the water."

"That they do." She tugged the chart off the board and located the picture she'd taken of the *Jean Rayner*'s log book when she'd first questioned Ally Robbins for her whereabouts. Tom, Stella, and Jimmy crowded around her and looked over her shoulder. Carefully, she transposed the coordinates in the log book onto the chart and drew a cross with a circle around it. "To do that, they have to be on the water and, according to the log book, that is where she was hauling pots on the day Connie Wells was murdered." She tapped the end of her pencil on the mark she'd made.

"From the boat?" Stella asked.

"It's the only way the evidence physically makes sense."

"But surely you couldn't make an eight hundred-metre shot from a moving boat?"

"You wouldn't have to." Kate used the pencil and her thumb as a ruler to measure the distance from where Connie's body was found to where the boat was logged. "Just because the bullet can make eight hundred metres doesn't mean it was shot from that far." She held the pencil to the scale marker. "That boat was less than two hundred yards from where Connie was shot. Given what we know of the skills of the Robbins siblings on the range, either of them could have made that shot."

"Especially given the weather conditions at the time," Tom said pointing to another piece of paper. "It was raining by nine but at seven, there wasn't a breath of wind. It was like a mill pond out there."

"Sands has a boat too," Jimmy said. "As does Matt Green."

Kate nodded. "True, but Sands isn't logged in Connie's diary at all, and the satellite navigation info from Green's car puts him at Sutton Bridge just ten minutes before she dies. It's forty minutes away from here. Physically impossible."

"Why would either Robbins want to kill her?" Stella asked. "Have we heard anything about a grudge between any of them?"

Kate and Tom both shook their heads.

"And that's strange, really," Tom said.

"Why?"

"Because the rest of the village either loved her or hated her. There's no one really indifferent like they seem to be. Doesn't fit with what we know of the woman."

"I don't know," Kate said. "Ally seemed to dislike her pretty well."

"For Leah's benefit," Jimmy said. "Nothing else."

"That's true, actually. And it struck me as odd at the time. I actually thought she didn't really care about Leah and would rather she was somewhere else. The outrage towards Connie seemed like bluster to me." Kate shrugged. "I assumed Leah'd worn out her welcome with the drugs and all and she was just playing her role as good friend or something."

"But her licence plate's on the list too," Collier said. "Leah's, I mean, while neither Ally nor Adam's is."

"Did you find any CCTV footage of those coordinates, Stella?" Kate looked at her.

"No. Each location is just a lay-by on a major A road." She grabbed Matt Green's marked map off her desk and spread it out. "No cameras anywhere close. I only know that they're lay-bys because I looked them up on Google Earth."

"Green said he was selling something. That he met a bloke who was a delivery driver and he didn't know his name." Kate looked at the lobster pot picture again, then back at the diary page. She tapped the map and let her gaze drift, trying to see beyond what was in front of her to what was actually happening.

"What're you thinking?" Stella asked.

"That I really want to know what's in that." She tapped the grey block in the lobster pot. "And that we need to bring Timmons in. I think this is a whole lot bigger than one DB."

Timmons looked at the evidence they had lain out for him, moving one page to the back of the stack before carrying on.

"So these Robbinses? Do we know if they have registered firearms?"

"Still awaiting the confirmation," Stella said.

"Okay, don't arrest either until we know for sure."

Stella nodded.

"So what are you thinking?" He looked at Kate.

"I'm thinking that I might have watched too many action films with drug runners in them, but I think that," she said, pointing to the block, "is a brick of something and that these locations are transfers of drugs from the Robbins and cronies to the sellers or dealers next up in the chain."

"Are you winding me up? We're talking about a tiny little village on the friggin' coast here. This isn't the Costa del Crime, or Florida, you know?"

"I know. And, no, sir, I'm not winding you up. I think Connie was trying to break this."

"Why?"

"Those drugs took everything she had and turned it to shit. Her partner got hooked and wouldn't come off them." Another piece of the jigsaw dropped into place. "Sammy said Connie was determined to help Leah. She said she was working on a project to help her, and I quote, whether she wanted the help or not, as a leaving present."

"Okay, but why not come to us with it? Why not tell us what's going on in Norfolk's new crime capital?"

"I don't know."

"She did," Collier said.

"Excuse me?" Timmons looked at him.

"She did, sir. She came here in April and made a statement that she suspected drugs were being smuggled in and out of the harbour by persons unknown and that we needed to look into it."

"How do you know this?"

"When we arrested Green, I was talking to the custody sergeant. He said he was surprised we'd gotten anywhere looking for the murderer of a slandering bitch like her. Said she'd made a number of scurrilous complaints about several people in the village. He told me about the one where she claimed they were big drug smugglers. The interviewing officers laughed at her."

"Why didn't you mention this before, Collier?" Stella asked, her cheeks reddening with visible anger.

"I thought it was just a bit of time wasting, like he did. Didn't think anything of it." He had the good sense to look like a puppy being kicked. "He thought she was just some crazy busybody out to cause trouble. It was a bit of a laugh, that's all."

"It wasn't looked into at all?" Timmons asked.

Collier shrugged. "He said a couple of PCs went down to the harbour and had a look round, spoke to a couple of people, but there was nothing to it."

"So they wrote it off." It wasn't a question, just a statement of fact. "Christ." Timmons tossed the sheaf of papers back on the table and ran a hand over his face. "Good work putting this together, Brannon, but we need concrete evidence that this is a drug smuggling ring before we bring them in for this. I need more to charge anyone with the murder of Connie Wells, given this new information."

"What about Matt Green? We have him in custody," Stella said.

"Pursue the reckless endangerment of a child charge and then we can continue to question him about this other evidence. He's clearly implicated. Let's see if he'll talk, now we have better questions to ask." He stood up. "Good work, team. Keep me up to speed."

"Sir, you don't want to take over?" Stella asked.

"You've got it under control for now. I'm at a critical stage with the other murder hunt. Gather the evidence. Hopefully, by the time you're ready to move on this, I'll be through there and we can finish this up." Then he was gone. The door banging shut behind him.

"Well, that was different," Tom said.

"Yeah." Stella looked at Collier. "I should arrest you for impeding a police investigation, you idiot. Why the hell didn't you tell us all that?"

"I didn't think it was relevant."

"Well, clearly it is."

"I'm sorry."

"Not good enough. You can go down and talk to your new mate and get all those not-relevant statements that Connie made." Stella curled her fingers in the air, indicating just what she thought of that response. "And feel free to tell your buddy that she was most probably murdered because none of them did their jobs properly. Let's see how that little nugget sits with them." She pointed towards the door. "Actually, you know what? I want to see their faces when they find that out. I'll come with you. I could do with cheering up right about now." She marched to the door. "Well, come on," she shouted as she pushed open the door. Collier skulked away behind her.

Tom chuckled. "Not sure who I feel more sorry for, Collier or the sergeant."

"Collier," Kate said. "He's inexperienced and it really was too late for him to help at that stage. The sergeant could have saved her life."

"Maybe."

Kate just stared at him.

"Okay, almost certainly, but we still don't know for sure."

"I know."

"Well aren't you just the little genius. But we still need evidence to convict. Suspicion isn't enough."

"I know."

"So, good cop, silent cop again?"

She nodded. "Yeah, let's see what Mr Green has to say about this little lot." She scooped up her files and followed Tom down to the custody suite. She could hear Stella's voice over the normal din of the working station and was really glad she wasn't on the other end of that tongue lashing.

CHAPTER 25

They had to wait twenty minutes for his brief to appear before they were sat in the interview room, recorder running, facing a truculent Matt Green. His arms were crossed over his chest, hair in disarray, and his clothes very dishevelled. Kate didn't feel like wasting any more time.

"Matty, Matty, Matty, you've been up to no good." She laid a copy of the diary entry in front of him, followed by the marked map, a picture of his licence plate, and one of the *Jean Rayner*. She watched his reaction. Each one elicited a marked response. A growing number of sweat beads formed first on his forehead, then on his upper lip, then a trickle ran down his neck. His breathing picked up, getting steadily shallower, closer to a pant than a steady breath. She could see his pulse at his temple increase, a steady sixty when he walked in, now climbing towards the hundred mark.

But she wasn't done. She'd used the twenty minutes to get the grainy shot she'd pulled from the houseboat blown up to A3 size. Forty-two centimetres by almost thirty of pale-blue hull, steel, two colours of rope, a white painted "53", and a grey block in the bottom, right-hand corner. A grey brick, shiny and slick with water. As grey as Matt Green's face had just turned. Another trickle of sweat ran down his neck, leaving a wet stain on the collar of his T-shirt, and his pulse went way over a hundred.

"We can do this the easy way and you can confess to what you've been up to at Brandale Staithe. And maybe, just maybe, you'll get out of jail in time to see your grandkids get married."

He didn't respond.

"Or we can do it the hard way and you'll never see Sammy again." Nothing.

She pointed to the marked map. "Recognise this?"

He said nothing.

"We got it from your house. It was in your study, and I'm guessing that someone isn't going to be very pleased that you marked up all your transfer locations."

He still said nothing.

"Okay, we'll come back to that. This is a page from Connie Wells' diary." She pointed to the top line. "This is your licence number and these GPS coordinates correspond to a lay-by just outside of Sutton Bridge. The one you have circled," she said, pointing to the map, "right here. And this number. The number twenty. Is that the number of bricks you exchanged or how much you were paid? I'm guessing the number of bricks. I don't think Connie would have been able to get close enough to count pound notes. Do you DC Brothers?"

"Don't think so," Brothers replied.

"I've got a friend in SOCO who's using this picture to figure out the quantity of drugs that will be in that little block. He did explain how he planned to do that. Something about scale of the lobster pot and the extrapolation of the data and some other bollocks, but I've got to admit, it went over my head. The bit I did understand was that he could prove how big those blocks were, and, therefore, how much shit you're dealing in."

"I'm not a drug dealer," Green said between clenched teeth.

"No?"

"No."

"Then what's in the bricks?"

Silence.

"Come on, Matty, you can't say you're not a dealer and then pull back. You're a tease." She leaned forward. "I know this is about drugs. I know it for a fact. Do you want to know how I know that?"

He said nothing.

"I know it because Connie loved Leah."

He snorted a laugh. "Bullshit."

"She did. She couldn't live with her. Couldn't trust her. But she still loved her. This," she said, sweeping her hands across the contents of the table, "was her last attempt to help her. Her going away present to the woman she loved." She pointed to another registration number. "That's Leah's car. Was she working off some of her tab? Lent her car to one of you?"

"It wasn't like that." Matt spat and his brief touched his shoulder to get his attention.

"Really? What was it like, then?"

He stared at her.

"Are you going to tell me again that you're not a drug dealer? Because I don't think anyone in this room's going to buy that."

"I'd like to consult with my client," Green's brief said. "In private, DS Brannon."

Kate nodded. "A wise precaution. But remember, this is where he can help himself."

He nodded and Kate led Tom out of the room.

"Think he's going to 'fess up?" Tom asked as soon as the door was closed behind them.

She shrugged. "He's said enough for me to be sure it's drugs at the root of this. But that opens up so many more questions."

"What kind of drugs?"

"More than that. Where are they coming from? My marine biology isn't exactly top notch but I'm pretty sure the sea bed doesn't sprout grey bricks full of whatever that shit is. So where are they coming from? Who are they selling them to? Are they working for someone bigger or are they in business for themselves as couriers of sorts? The variety of GPS coordinates seems to lend itself to that theory for me. But if they are, where are they getting the drugs in the first place?"

"You couldn't just start with the easy stuff?"

She chuckled. "I think we're already way beyond the easy stuff. How big a problem is the drug issue round here?"

Tom sighed. "Probably as big as in the city to be honest. Boredom and little in the way of entertainment during the winter, and bloody long hours during the tourist season. A lot of the kids, in particular, dabble, as my niece calls it. Apparently, it's not serious, just a bit of fun."

"Not for Leah. Not for Connie."

"No."

"And what's the drug of choice?"

"Same as everywhere else. There's tourists coming in from London and every other big city in Britain every weekend. Getting hold of stuff really isn't hard."

"Okay, but this isn't coming in from elsewhere in Britain. This is coming in from abroad. Why else would they be pulling it out of the water?"

"Maybe they're storing it down there? It's not like we can easily see what's down there if we're walking around on land."

"That's actually a really good point."

The door to the interview room opened again. "My client wishes to talk to you now."

"Excellent news."

They went back inside and Kate restarted the tape, introducing everyone in the room before she looked at Matt Green. "You wanted to talk to me?"

"I have information that will be important to you, but I won't say anything until I know my daughter is safe."

"Excuse me?"

"They've killed already."

"Have they threatened you or your daughter? Is that how you got involved in this?"

Matt slumped farther in his chair. "Not initially, no. But it was too much. When Connie started poking around, then those two PCs turned up at the dock, well, I told them I'd had enough. I wanted out. They told me there was no out and that I'd better keep my mouth shut and behave or they'd make sure Sammy ended up like Leah, or worse."

Kate swallowed hard. She didn't want to picture Sammy, impish, willful, and so full of life, become the husk of a person that Leah had become. "I'll make sure she's out of danger. You have my word."

"I need to be sure. I need to know that they can't hurt her."

Kate pulled her phone from her pocket and dialled. "Miss Temple, this is DS Brannon, I need you and Sammy to come to the police station at Hunstanton."

"Why?" Gina asked.

"I have something I need to discuss with you both."

"Fine. When?"

"Now."

"What's so important? Is it Social Services?"

"I can't go into it over the phone. I will tell you when you get here."

Gina sighed heavily. "Fine."

"Thank you." Kate hung up. "When she gets here, I'll keep them here until I can find somewhere safe for them."

"Where?"

"I don't know yet. You've only just sprung this on me. Give me a couple of hours and we'll come up with something." She offered what she hoped was a reassuring smile. "I'll do my part to keep your daughter safe. Now you need to do yours. The more you can tell me, the better. Names, dates, places, quantities, everything."

"I need a laptop."

"Your laptop is in custody."

"Doesn't have to be that one and you won't get anything off it. I delete the history all the time and reformat the hard drive once a week. I've got data on a cloud server. I just need a laptop or computer to access it."

"Given everything you've just said to me, you can't honestly think we're going to let you have access to a police laptop in here. You need web access to get on a cloud server. I didn't understand half of what you've just said, which means you getting a laptop in here is too much of a risk to our security."

"Fine. Bring me anything that can get onto the internet and will let me send an email. That'll give you everything you need. You can watch every keystroke."

"I'll get something sorted," Tom said. "Back in a minute."

"While we're waiting, start talking."

"Did you know that the Robbins were in the army?"

"No," she said.

"Hmm. Served ten years apiece, then came home to work the boat with dear old dad."

"Heart warming."

He chuckled. "Yeah. Pair of saints, them two. Ally was in logistics. And Adam, well, he never talks about what he did. He just gets this creepy little smile on his face when you ask him. Like he's keeping a secret you're glad you don't know. You know what I mean?"

Kate nodded and let the silence do its work.

"Someone said he was Special Forces. Anything nasty that needed taking care of, he was your man." He picked at the skin beside his thumb nail. The little bit that comes away and tugs painfully at the tender skin a few millimetres below. He didn't seem to feel it. "I believe that."

Kate waited and watched as he tore the skin away and a bead of blood started to form beside his thumbnail.

"When they came back, the harbour was on its knees. I mean it was fucked. Everything was falling down, the boats were dangerous. The harbour needed dredging so they could get out. They were all fucked. Cedric couldn't have been more than three months from losing it all. The boat, his house, everything. They all were."

"When was this?"

"Five years ago."

Kate whistled. "Five years?"

He nodded.

"They came out of the army together?"

"Out, in. All of it. Twins. Not identical, you know."

"Right."

"Can I have some water?"

She nodded and waited for him to carry on. She knew Tom would bring it back with him.

"Anyway, when they came back, it was like a miracle. Robbinses boats was earning again. They secured funding to do up the harbour, helped the other guys get loans to fix their boats. It was like they single-handedly got the fleet working again. You know what they say about good things?"

"Too good to be true?"

"Yeah. Before we knew it we were all in it up to our necks."

"How did you get involved? You don't work on the boats."

"No, but my old man did. When I needed money for Sammy, he used to bung us some cash. Then he told me I could earn a ton just by driving for a couple of hours. Easy money."

"He didn't tell you what you were delivering?"

"I didn't ask. Didn't care, if truth be told. Like I said, easy money."

"What changed?"

"Leah."

"I don't understand."

"No one else in the village was really bad with the drugs. I mean, we had a few spliffs from time to time, maybe a couple of Es at a party, but not the really hard stuff. Not the stuff that's coming out of the pots."

"Which is?"

"Heroin. One kilo per brick."

"And that's what Leah's using?"

He nodded.

"For the purposes of the tape, Mr Green nodded his assent."

The door opened and Tom came back in. He placed a plastic cup of water in front of Green. "It's going to take a little while but we'll have something here this afternoon."

"Thanks." He picked up the water with shaking hands and downed it quickly.

"So Leah using made you, what? Grow a conscience?"

He shrugged. "Something like that, I suppose. I didn't really know what it was before. I didn't really think it was any worse than a bit of weed. I started asking questions after that."

"And when was that?"

"Maybe two years." He shrugged again. "I can't remember really, but something like that. I'm pretty sure she was using before that, though."

"So you started asking questions?"

"Yeah."

"And what did you learn?"

"Not a lot, to be fair. They're pretty close lipped and don't want people poking their noses in where they don't belong. As Connie found out. So I asked, and didn't get very far. Instead, I started listening. And I learned a lot more."

"Christ, this is like pulling teeth. Spit it out."

"The Robbinses don't exactly sell or smuggle drugs. Well, not really. They offer a specialist service. Almost like a storage service."

"I don't follow." But Kate was beginning to.

"Those big container ships that pass by on the North Sea, every so often one of those containers falls off. Accidently on purpose, you know? So Adam dives down and breaks them open. They transfer the contents to lobster pots and keep them on the seabed until they get the delivery instructions. Then they haul the pots, unload the quota, reset the pot, and send out a delivery driver to one of a dozen predetermined destinations. We just stay in the car with the boot unlocked, and the guy at the other end takes it out and moves on. I've never seen, or spoken to, the person who collects from me, and I don't know what happens after that."

"I hate to burst your bubble mate, but that's exactly what smuggling is. Bringing illegal substances from foreign shores onto British soil. Smuggling defined," Tom said.

"Just back up a minute. You said container vessels drop these containers overboard so he can break them open, right?"

"Yeah."

"How does that work exactly? It's a huge body of water, Matt, how do they find them? Where are they coming from?"

Matt swallowed. "I've got all the details I could find saved to my cloud server. But the upshot is that there are two ports Robbinses clients use to get their merchandise off mainland Europe. Tallinn in Estonia and Isdemir in Turkey. The ships are heading for Hull. I don't know how it works on their end. I never saw anything or heard anything to give you any specifics. I presume some customs official is paid off and an extra container with the bricks makes its way onto the ship. But like I said, don't quote me on that."

"Okay. But you know more about the operation on this end?"

"Yeah. The bricks are in a container with a GPS locator. They get the transponder numbers so that finding the containers is easy. They take a detour en route to Hull and drop the containers over the side."

"How many bricks per container?"

"I don't know. But based on the number I shift in a week and how often they drop them, I'd say several hundred."

"What?"

"I'm not the only driver they use. I can't be accurate and I never saw anything with a number on it."

Kate's mind spun. The operation was huge. How the hell had this gone unnoticed? "Go on."

"Well, there's not much more to add. Adam dives down with underwater cutting gear and they empty the containers and store the shit in lobster pots on the sea bed. They pull them when they get instructions and deliver on request."

"Is he some sort of deep sea diver or something?"

"What? No. You don't have to be. The North Sea's not that deep off the coast here. They drop the containers when they've got about twenty metres under the keel."

"Don't those huge container ships need deeper water than that?"

He shook his head. "The massive ones, like one hundred and sixty feet long, only have a draft of six to eight metres. Allowing twenty below the keel gives them tons of clearance."

"And a twenty-metre dive isn't a difficult one?"

"No, not at all." He shrugged. "Well, not if you know what you're doing."

"And he does?"

"With bells on."

"How is Leah involved?" Kate asked

"She stole a brick from Ally. Ally let her keep it because it was already opened but she's still working it off."

"And what is this information you've got in the cloud?"

"Dates of containers being dropped. The name of the ships dropping the containers. That sort of stuff."

"How did you get this information?"

"I didn't just listen. I looked too. I took photographs of invoices and notes I saw in Ally's office. I kept copies of emails that I'd been told to delete."

"Emails from Ally?"

"And Adam."

"So how much did Connie know and how did they find out she was on to them?"

"Connie told them. She told them she had enough evidence to go to the police and get us all locked up. She told them that she didn't really care what they were doing, she just wanted them to release Leah and let her take her to a rehab centre. She said if they did, they'd never hear from her again."

"Naive?"

"Oh, yeah. They laughed at her and said the police had already been around to the harbour once and wouldn't take her seriously. She told them she had pictures. Ally said she'd better make sure that whatever pictures she had showed her best side or she'd walk away and come for her."

"Where was this?"

"At the harbour."

"When?"

"The day before she died."

"Do either Adam or Ally own a sniper rifle?"

"They both do."

"Surely that gives us enough to go and pick them up?" Tom said.

They all stood in the incident room, arms folded over their chests, and staring at the speakerphone.

"If we move now we'll get one of them for murder." Timmons' voice sounded slightly robotic out of the speaker. "Maybe we get the other two for conspiracy. If even half of what Green says is true, then we need this whole operation brought down. I want more before we move on this."

"Sir, we're putting civilians at risk," Kate said.

"You said you've got them in a safe place."

"For now. They're here in the station. Where do you want me to keep them while we find you more?" Kate knew the sarcasm in her voice was easily discernible. She thought he did a pretty good job ignoring it, to be fair. But she didn't care if he'd pulled her to task on it. She was worried about Sammy and Gina. She hated the thought of them being at risk in any way. To have them at risk because her superior officer wanted a bigger bust...well, that just grated on her last nerve.

"I don't care where you keep them. Stick them in a cell, give them your own bed, whatever. Just keep them safe."

Stella cleared her throat. "Do we have any resources to put them in a hotel, sir?"

"No. A hotel would be risky," Kate said. "Locally, everyone knows everyone else, and moving them out of area puts them at risk, as we can't be on hand to help."

"Then where?" Stella asked.

"Like the man said," Kate said, pointing to the speaker, "I guess they'll have to stay with me."

"Settled," Timmons said. "Keep me updated." The speaker went dead.

"Great. Just fucking great," Tom said. "How do you plan to keep them secret at your place?"

"Leave her car here, park round the back, and hope no one sees them." Kate shrugged. "The houses on either side are empty now, and I've got blinds. Any other bright ideas?"

Shaking heads and mumbled words of good luck were all she got.

"Thanks." She dropped her arms and tugged on the front of her shirt. "Since I get to share my house, would anyone else care to tell them what's going on?"

Suddenly everyone was really busy.

"That's what I thought."

CHAPTER 26

"Look, DS Brannon rang and specifically asked me to come as soon as possible. So here I am. Now what the hell is going on here?" Gina leaned against the reception desk and hoped she looked slightly menacing, since the nice approach had gotten her exactly nowhere.

"I'm sure she'll be along soon to talk to you, then, Miss. Until then, why don't you take a seat?" He pointed to the row of hard plastic chairs secured to the wall.

"I could just walk out, you know?"

"I'm sure you could, Miss."

"She'll be very unhappy with you if I do."

"I'm sure she would, Miss."

"Yeah, you sound it." Gina turned her back on him and caught Sammy grinning at her. "And you can wipe that smile off your face, young lady. She probably changed her mind and decided to put you in jail after all." The smile slid off her lips and Gina instantly regretted her words. "More likely she's putting me in jail."

"What for?" Sammy asked.

"For foisting you on the world. That's got to be a crime, right?" She ruffled Sammy's hair and sat down heavily beside her.

"What do you really think she wants, Mum?"

"I really don't know. Only that it sounded really important and urgent on the phone." She said the last sentence loud enough for the desk sergeant to hear and looked over to see if it'd had any effect. Nada.

Sammy lay across the row of seats, put her head in Gina's lap, and tucked her feet up close to her bottom. Gina stroked her hair softly and smiled as she started to snore. Gina looked out of the window. Not that she could see anything but light and a few coloured splotches through the heavily distorted glass, but the only other options were the desk sergeant or a poster advocating women to stand up against domestic abuse. Good advice, but not something she wanted to stare at for however long Kate—sorry, DS Brannon—decided to keep her waiting. She rested her head back against the wall, played with Sammy's hair, closed her eyes, and tried to take a nap herself. She hadn't exactly been sleeping well, after all.

"I'm really sorry to have kept you waiting." Kate stood in front of her, her green eyes soft, and a gentle smile on her lips. She reached out and Gina waited—longed—for Kate's touch. It never came.

"Hey, kiddo," Kate said, shaking Sammy's shoulder, "time to wake up, sleepyhead." She smiled at Sammy. That full, beautiful smile that Gina had wanted to see. But it wasn't for her.

Kate turned her head and spoke to the guy at the desk. "Can you bring Miss Temple a cup of tea and a hot chocolate for Sammy, please? I need a couple of minutes with Miss Temple." She nodded towards Sammy, letting the officer know that he was to watch her.

"Will you come with me, please?" Kate led Gina into the same interview room they'd been in before.

Was it only yesterday? It felt like a lifetime ago and all Gina wanted to do was sleep. "What was so important that I had to drive down here like a bat out of hell only for you to keep me sitting on those bloody uncomfortable chairs for nearly an hour?"

"I'm really sorry to have to tell you this but we have reason to believe that Sammy's at risk from the people who killed Connie. I wanted her here to make sure she's safe. To make sure you both are."

"Oh, God." She felt as if a pin had been pulled from her knees and she dropped to the floor. Kate held her arms out to try and catch her, but instead Gina managed to pull them both to the ground as she landed heavily on her knees. "Oh, God." She wanted to throw up. She could feel the bile rising in her throat, burning and spitting, churning like the fires of hell wanting to rise up and swallow her whole.

"It's okay. We know what's going on now, we'll have it all sorted really soon, and then they'll be in prison. They won't be able to hurt her then."

"Who?" Gina's heart hammered in her chest, determined to escape and find Sammy on its own. To protect her no matter what.

"The Robbinses."

Gina tried to push away from Kate. She pushed at her chest trying to lever herself up and away, but her legs wouldn't support her weight. All she managed to do was push Kate far enough from her to look into her eyes. Those grass-green orbs that looked damp, as though kissed by the morning dew. Compassion, understanding, and fear shone out in equal measure as Gina tried to breathe. But her lungs weren't working. They pulled air in but seemed to refuse to push it back out again. In, but not out, over and over. She felt Kate's arms close around her but she couldn't see what was happening. Black spots swam before her but she could hear her blood in her ears. Not her heartbeat, no, that had already left to find Sammy. Just her blood drowning out Kate's voice telling her that she would be okay, that Sammy was going to be fine, that she would make sure of it herself. Then it stopped and everything went quiet.

"When will she wake up?"

"I'm not sure, Sammy. Has she had a panic attack before?"

"Don't know." Sammy's voice sounded small and scared.

"I'm fine, sweetheart," Gina said, but her voice sounded far from fine. It sounded hoarse and thick, but it broke and went squeaky halfway through the sentence. "Christ, I sound like a pubescent boy."

Sammy lay down next to her and wrapped a skinny arm around her waist, touched a soft kiss to the tip of her nose, and giggled.

"What?"

"You've got morning breath."

Bloody kid.

Kate chuckled. "Welcome back. I'd offer you some tea, but I think it's long cold."

She was on the floor in a pretty good version of the recovery position. There was a thin pillow under her head, presumably from one of the cells, and a silver blanket over her. But she was still lying on the floor and the cold was seeping into her bones. She suppressed a shiver and asked, "How long have I been here?"

"About half an hour."

"Oh, hell."

"Do you suffer from panic attacks a lot?" Kate asked.

Gina shook her head. "I had a few when I went through puberty but nothing really since then. Except the other day, when you told me about Connie, but that wasn't exactly a full-blown episode."

"True."

"Would you like me to call a doctor for you? He could prescribe something—"

"No."

"It might help. It's got to be pretty stressful for you right now."

"I said, no. I'm fine now. It was just a shock."

"Mum, why is it a shock to go and stay at Kate's while the police have to do stuff at our house?"

"Excuse me?" Gina looked over at Kate.

"Sammy, your mum didn't really give me chance to explain the situation to her properly. That might be why it's such a shock. She doesn't really know that you're going to stay at my house for a few days until this whole thing is sorted out."

"And where will you be?" Gina asked.

"Working. To sort this whole thing out."

"And what are we meant to do at your house?"

"Stay there. Look after Merlin. Stay out of sight."

"Locked in the house?"

"Well, not exactly. But you know how rumours are. It would be better if no one knows you're there."

"So, yes, locked in the house."

"Give me a break, Gina. This was dumped on us in the last hour. I'm doing the best I can here."

She called me Gina again. "What alternatives did you work through before you came up with this plan?"

"Staying here."

"In jail! No way," Sammy shouted.

"Not in jail, just here. But you see what I mean. We don't exactly have a ton of options. My house is off the main road. As long as you stay inside, no one will know you're there. Hell, the houses on either side of me are empty holiday lets, and I live alone. It's the only option that makes sense."

"To you," Gina said.

"Yes, to me. Do you have a better idea?"

Gina shook her head. "But I've had less time to think about it."

"Well, if you come up with a better plan, you just let me know."

"You called me Gina."

"I'm sorry."

"I'm not."

Kate opened her mouth to speak but stopped herself. She shook her head and hauled herself up from the floor. "Come on, let's go and get you two settled. We'll need to go shopping first. I've got no food, and I believe kids need to eat a regular supply of junk food or they shrivel up like raisins."

Sammy laughed as Kate tugged her to her feet. "I'm starting to wrinkle. Mum, I need pizza."

"You had pizza last night."

"Then I need hotdogs or something. I'm going raisiny."

"That's not a word."

"It should be," Kate said, "it's a good one."

"See?" Sammy grabbed one of her mother's hands and helped Kate tug Gina gently to her feet.

"I think I'm going to have to work that one into a proper bad-guy insult someday."

Sammy giggled and whispered in Gina's ear, "I like Kate."

Me too, sweetheart. She ruffled Sammy's hair and followed Kate out to her courtesy car.

"If we leave yours here, then no one will spot it at my place and start snooping."

Gina nodded and climbed in. *Okay, Kate Brannon, let's see what happens next.*

CHAPTER 27

Gina twisted her hands in her lap as Kate drove them away from the police station and into Docking. She had so many questions she wanted to ask Kate. But she had no idea where to start.

Kate's house was the second in a row of four and the only one occupied full time. The other three were second homes and a holiday let, which meant that between September and Easter, they sat empty, collecting dust, and eating money. It was dark when Kate parked at the rear of the house, a small gravel-covered area looking out onto arable fields that would grow wheat, barley, and oilseed rape through the season. In the distance, Gina was sure she'd be able to see the tall, white turbines of the onshore wind farm that had been so controversial in the last few years. She'd see them tomorrow, no doubt. All she could see now was endless, inky blackness.

It looked like a small cottage. The standard brick with lime-and-flint render covered the outer walls, and the small square of grass that made up the back garden led to a set of patio doors.

"Are you sure you have enough room for us?"

"Yeah. I only have the one bed in the spare room. But it should be big enough for the two of you, if you don't mind sharing?"

"No, that's fine." Gina resigned herself to a night of tossing and turning as she shared a single with Sammy. Not a fun experience in the past. Her daughter had a tendency to wriggle, and often Gina woke her in the morning to find feet on the pillow rather than a head.

Kate fumbled with the key, struggling to get it in the lock in the low light and with her hands full of bags. "Sorry."

Gina smiled and took the key from her, slid it into the lock and opened the door. It was much bigger inside than she'd expected. The whole downstairs was a long, open-plan living and dining room, with a good-sized kitchen looking out to the front of the house. There was a set of stairs on the left as she looked forward, and on the wall beside the patio doors was a large wood-burning stove with a huge glass window. She could imagine sitting on the comfy looking leather sofa watching the flames, reading a good book, sipping hot chocolate.

"There's a toilet just through there, by the front door," Kate said as she put the bags on the kitchen counters. "Let me show you upstairs. My room's at the back, but this one should be okay for you." Kate pushed open the door to a room with a king-sized bed that was already made up. Sammy bounded in and tossed herself on the mattress bouncing up and down on her back.

"Sammy, behave."

"I'm just testing it," she said. She sat up and dangled her feet over the edge.

"Master bathroom's here, just at the end of the landing. I've got an en suite, so you can have this to yourselves."

"You don't have to do that," Gina said.

"It's what I normally do anyway." She pointed to the basin. "See? My toothbrush isn't even there." She smiled. "I'll go unpack those bags and leave you two alone for a while."

Gina started to tell her again that she didn't have to do that but Kate was already gone, skipping lightly down the stairs. Within seconds, Gina could hear the plastic shopping bags rustling and doors being opened and closed. She shook her head and turned to Sammy.

"Now you listen to me, young lady. Kate is being really, really good to us, letting us stay here, I need you to promise me that you'll be on best behaviour."

"'Course, Mum."

"I mean it. No shoes on the sofa, no back chat, mind your manners, and don't, for the love of God, tell her anything embarrassing. I've shown myself up enough today. Got it?"

"Like what?" Sammy grinned impishly.

"You know what, madam, and don't pretend you don't." She tapped her on the nose, then patted her bottom. "Go wash your hands and I'll go and get some hotdogs ready."

"Okay." Sammy bounced off the bed and raced across the landing.

"Walk. No running in the house." She heard a snort of laughter coming from downstairs. She followed the sound. "I swear, sometimes I open my mouth and my mother comes out." She hit the bottom step and smiled. Kate was bending down to put some fruit in the fridge. *Oh, I was so right, that's a gorgeous arse.*

"The hotdogs and finger rolls are just on the side. I'd cook, but I can't be sure I wouldn't burn them." Kate offered her a smile over her shoulder.

"You can't burn hotdogs."

"*Au contraire, mon amie.* If there's heating involved, I can burn it. Trust me."

Gina shrugged and opened the cellophane on the buns. "Knives?"

"In the drawer in front of you. Pans are in the cupboard underneath it, and the tin opener should be in the drawer with the knives."

Gina quickly found what she needed and smiled in thanks when Kate handed her plates.

"Does she only drink milk?"

"At this time of night, it's milk or water. Nothing that will keep her awake. Sammy on a sugar high is not a pleasant experience."

"And you?"

"No, I can drink other things and still sleep just fine, thanks."

"Ha ha." Kate held up a bottle of red, eyebrow quirked in question.

"Oh, yes, please. That definitely won't stop me sleeping."

"I thought as much. It's also a great vintage for hotdogs. Goes great with mustard and ketchup."

"Multipurpose."

"I like all things in my life to multitask."

Gina chuckled and put plates on the table. "I could've guessed that about you. Sammy, Kate's about to eat your hotdogs if you don't hurry up."

"You better not," Sammy shouted, running down the stairs. "I'm starving."

"I wouldn't dream of eating one of your hotdogs, kiddo. Your mother's on the other hand, well, they look mighty tempting, don't you think?" Kate winked at her.

Is she flirting with me? I think she's flirting with me. But she said she didn't trust me anymore. But that was definitely flirting, right? Oh my God, I don't even know what flirting is anymore. Gina shook the bottle of ketchup trying to properly dress her hotdog but her lack of attention led to serious overkill. And a splotch on her chest. Maybe two. Sammy burst into giggles while Kate had the good grace to hide her snigger behind taking a bite at least. *End of flirting. If it was flirting.*

"How come you live in this big house on your own?" Sammy asked Kate. Gina could have kissed her for diverting attention away from her and her stain and for asking a question she really wanted to know the answer to.

"Well, I don't have a Sammy to share it with."

"You don't have to have a kid. You could have a husband or a girlfriend or a mum or dad."

"Hmm." Kate swallowed another bite. "Are those my only other options?"

Sammy shrugged. "'Fink so."

"In that case, I'm out of options. Don't want a husband. I decided when I was your age that boys smell and I haven't met one yet to convince me otherwise. I don't have a girlfriend because the last one ran off with my best friend. Which means I don't have one of those anymore either. And I don't have a mum or dad. They both died before I was your age."

"I'll be your best friend," Sammy offered, holding out her hand.

"Okay." Kate held hers out to shake, only to have Sammy whip hers away, put her thumb to her nose, and wiggle her fingers.

"Too slow."

"Right, well I see. It's going to be one of those BFF relationships, is it?"

Sammy nodded and started on her second hotdog.

"No one?" Gina asked.

Kate shook her head.

"I'm sorry."

Kate shrugged and reached for her glass. "Long time ago."

From the look in Kate's eyes, Gina thought that the length of time didn't matter. The pain was still raw, and she wished she knew which part of her story was responsible for that look. The idiot girlfriend, the stupid friend, or the orphaned little girl. She found she really wanted to know. Maybe she'd ask later, when Sammy was in bed. She wasn't sure how much more Kate would say in front of Sammy. She was clearly protective of her and didn't want to upset her either. Gina sighed. Good with her daughter, gorgeous, intelligent, and funny. Perfect. And she hates me...and flirts.

She watched as Kate paid attention to Sammy's every word, refilled her glass for her, and flicked through the TV looking for cartoons for her. They, whoever "they" is, say that the way to a man's heart is through his stomach. Well, the way to this woman's heart was definitely through her kid. Gina could have happily watched them together all night. When bedtime came, Sammy begged Kate to read her a story.

"I don't have any kids' books, I'm sorry."

"Doesn't have to be little kids' books."

Kate frowned.

"It's okay, Kate, Sammy can live without a story tonight."

"Aw, but, Mum—"

"Actually I might have something." She patted Sammy on the bottom. "You go and get ready for bed and let me see if I can dig it out."

Sammy didn't need to be asked twice. She was up the stairs before Kate had finished her sentence.

"You don't have to."

"I know." Kate stood up. "But I enjoy her company, and I'd like to."

"What book are you going to read to her?"

"*The Anatomy of Murder*. I started it when I was her age. I figure she'll grow up to be a police officer or a criminal. Either way it'll help her."

"Ha ha."

"I was thinking *Stig of the Dump*. It's one my gran read to me when I was about her age."

Gina smiled. "Lovely."

Kate smiled and left. A shy smile, one that seemed incongruous with the strong, confident woman Gina knew her to be. Yet it seemed so natural, and Gina couldn't help but respond. She knew her own smile was growing and there was a flutter in her belly that had been missing for far too long.

Gina could hear them both upstairs. Giggles and explanations, Sammy reading as often as Kate, and Gina shook her head. Sammy loved to hear stories, but getting her to read was difficult, to say the least. Yet Kate had managed it seemingly with ease. Sammy really was on her best behaviour.

Gina busied herself washing the dishes but eventually drifted upstairs to find Kate still reading aloud, Sammy curled fast asleep beside her.

"Your kid snores."

"I know." Gina grinned. "Like a train."

Kate closed the book and slowly extracted herself, tucked the covers around Sammy, and left the room. "I'll leave you to it."

"I was coming up to see if you fancied a coffee."

"Oh, sure. I'll stick the kettle on."

"I can do it."

"Don't be silly, you're a guest and you already had to make food so I didn't kill us all. I can make coffee."

"But there's hot stuff involved. You sure you won't burn it?" Gina offered with a look of fake concern.

Kate frowned. "Out of my way, woman. My honour is obviously at stake." She held up her hands and flicked them towards Gina like she was shaking water off them. "Shoo."

Gina laughed and followed her back downstairs. She watched as Kate managed to make them coffee, sans burning, and then held up a bottle of Bailey's Irish Cream.

"Would Madam like a little tipple in her coffee?"

"Wine with tea, Bailey's with coffee. Are you trying to get me drunk?"

"Merely offering sleeping aids to those who must sleep with a freight train this evening."

"It's a fair point, and it's well made. Make mine a double, barmaid."

"Yes, m'lady." Kate drew the word out with a pretty good impression of the butler from *Downton Abbey*, and a shiver ran up Gina's spine.

"Oh, I could get used to that."

"What? Having Bailey's in your coffee?"

"No. M'lady." She tried to imitate the way Kate had said it, and giggled at her very poor attempt.

Kate's lips quirked in a slightly lopsided grin. "And why's that?" She handed the mug to Gina and led her to the sofa. She turned the sound down on the TV to almost nothing but left *SpongeBob SquarePants* playing in the background.

"I'm pretty sure you know why, Kate." She sat down and took a sip of her drink, hoping that Kate would sit next to her. She felt like dancing in her seat when she did. "I think you're flirting with me."

"Me?" Kate tried to look innocent, but her eyes gave her away.

"Yes, you."

"Do you want me to stop flirting?"

"That depends."

"On what?"

"Whether you stop flirting and run away again, or you stop flirting and kiss me."

"What if I want to keep flirting?"

"Then keep flirting. It means you aren't running away."

The green of Kate's eyes was darker in the dim light, the colour of dark oak leaves at dusk. Her pupils were huge, and Gina knew she wanted to kiss her just as much as Gina wanted her to. She wanted to thread her fingers through those copper strands and cling to her while her mouth and tongue explored Kate's. She wanted to feel her whole body pressing closer to hers, to feel the warmth of her through her clothes, then feel her skin with her fingertips. She wanted to start at the top of her head and work her way down. Slowly.

Kate cleared her throat and looked away. "Sorry," she whispered under her breath.

"Don't," Gina's voice cracked as she spoke, "don't go."

Kate shook her head. "I'm not. I don't want to."

"But?"

"I'm not very good at any of this."

"You seem to be doing just fine to me."

Kate wrinkled her nose so Gina decided to try a different approach. "What aren't you good at?"

"Relationships."

"Why do you say that?"

Kate sipped her drink and leaned forward, bracing her elbows on her knees. "I wasn't kidding earlier when I told you both that there's no one in my life. Literally, there's no one." She put her mug on the coffee table. "My mum died just after I was born. Gran said she held me and passed away. Dad never forgave me for that, but he made sure Gran and I had everything we needed. He worked on the oil rigs. Moved us to wherever was closest to the rig he was working on, so we moved around quite a lot. Lots of little seaside towns and villages. We were just outside of Boston, towards Skegness, when he was offered a job on a rig in Scotland. Last-minute thing, so he went up and started before we found somewhere else to live. We were three weeks from moving to Aberdeen when it happened. July 1988."

"Oil rigs? Do you mean the *Piper Alpha* disaster?"

Kate nodded. "One hundred and sixty-seven men lost their lives that night. My dad was one of them." She clenched her hands between her knees. "It's an awful thing to say, but I really don't remember him. I see the pictures in the albums that Gran took, and those are the only images I have in my head of him. I remember the pictures of my dad, but not my dad. Do you know what I mean?"

"How old were you when he died?

"Is that a crafty way of asking how old I am?"

Gina nodded. "Maybe. But you couldn't have been very old."

"I was eight then, thirty-five now." She sniggered. "In case you were wondering."

"It wouldn't matter to me if you were fifty-five. But then you were a child and I'm guessing he was away a lot, right?"

"Yeah, he was. But still, a kid should remember her parents. All I remember is my gran."

"She was your mum and dad."

Kate sat back again. "She was."

"When did she pass?"

"When I was seventeen. Cancer. She was a stoic old woman and by the time she admitted there was something wrong, it was too late. Riddled with it. They gave her six weeks. She lasted eighteen months."

"Wow."

"Like I said, stubborn."

"It's genetic."

"Hey, I've been very well behaved with you."

"I'm sure." She reached out, unable to resist touching her anymore. She placed a hand gently on her arm and rubbed her thumb softly back and forth. Kate stared, seemingly mesmerised by her fingers and where they touched her skin. Gina had been right, soft and velvety. So, so soft. "Did she really run off with your best friend?"

"Oh, yeah."

"She was an idiot."

Kate shook her head and turned her arm over giving Gina easier access to the sensitive skin of her forearm and wrist. "Nah. We weren't right for each other. Don't get me wrong, at the time I thought we were perfect together. We worked together, liked all the same stuff. It was good. We differed on one really big detail, though."

"What was that?"

"Fidelity. She seemed to think that sex outside the relationship was okay. As long as it was just sex. No feelings, so not a threat."

"And she could do that?"

"Apparently."

"But you couldn't?"

"No. Not that I even knew it was what she wanted while we were together. She just did it. Whatever Melissa wanted, Melissa took. Or let it take her." She shrugged. "Whatever."

"Wow." Gina used only her fingertips to run along Kate's skin. Slowly memorising each little bump, every tiny hair. The little white scar about halfway down caught her attention and she wondered what had caused it. Her veins stood out at her wrist, pale blue beneath milky white skin. The corded tendons down to her hand and the crease line at the junction of wrist and hand were all fascinating to her. She couldn't ever remember feeling so enthralled by such a simple touch before. The more she learned, the more she wanted to learn.

"Yeah."

"So how did the whole running off with your best friend thing happen?"

"From what I gathered at the time—and I might add that an argument is not generally the best time to gain reliable intel—they had the same outlook on dating. This was news to me from both of them, and they informed me that they were in love and going to make it work."

"Sounds like you're well clear of them."

"I think so too." She chuckled. "Now I do."

"Are they still together?"

Kate shook her head. "They didn't last three weeks according to reliable sources. Unreliable ones said two. Scuttlebutt in the force is second to none."

"When was this?"

"Three years ago."

"No one since?"

Kate shrugged. "Not really."

"Like I believe that."

"It's true. Anyway, enough about my sad and lonely life. Tell me about you."

"Not much to tell. As you know I got pregnant at seventeen, by an idiot, and I'm a closeted village lesbian. There really isn't anything to tell." She stroked over the pulse point and watched, rapt, as all the hairs on Kate's arm stood up and goosebumps rose along her flesh.

"Surely there must be something. At least one skeleton in that closet with you."

Gina laughed. "Okay, I've been out with a few women, but nothing exactly developed into a relationship."

"Why not?"

"You've met Sammy, right?"

"So?"

"As soon as Sammy knows something, the rest of the world does too. If I brought someone home to meet her, I knew I had to be ready for everyone to know."

"I think you're doing a disservice to Sammy there. And yourself. Sammy was keeping secrets for Connie, she was keeping the secret of what happened on Thursday, and if you told her how important it was to you, I'm certain she would have kept a secret for you too. But I don't understand why it would have to be a secret. Connie and Leah were lesbians and even though I've heard plenty of bad stuff about people hating Connie, only one person seems to have had a problem with her because she was a lesbian. What makes you different?"

"Nothing. I know all of that, but I still hadn't met anyone I was ready to upset the applecart over."

"You speak in a lot of clichés. You know that, don't you?"

"Yes. Doesn't make it any less true, though."

"So just to be clear here, when you say you went out with a few women but they weren't relationships...?"

"So curious, DS Brannon."

"A hazard of the job, I'm afraid."

Gina laughed. "I guess I'm a try-before-you-buy-kind of girl."

Kate's eyes widened. "Are we talking one-night stands? Little flings?"

"Definitely not. I'm not into one-night stands. A long weekend's more my kind of thing."

"I see."

"Do you?" Gina ran her finger down the inside of Kate's arm, again leaving another series of goosebumps in her wake.

"Definitely."

"Are you going to kiss me?"

Kate swallowed and shook her head.

Gina stopped. "Really?"

"Really."

"But—"

"I like you."

"I like you too."

"I like you more than just a long weekend." She wrapped her fingers around Gina's and gently squeezed. "And I want someone who doesn't need a test drive to know that I'm right for her." Kate stood up, gathered their mugs, and ran a finger down Gina's cheek. "Good night, Gina. Sleep well."

Gina sat until all she could hear from upstairs was Sammy's snores. Her skin still tingled from where Kate had held her hand. Her breathing and heartbeat had finally slowed back to normal, but she could still feel the heat from that last look. The one that had scorched her flesh and melted her insides. The one that had spoken of a passion she'd never felt but had read about in every love story she'd ever read. A passion she longed to feel.

Why is it every time I open my mouth to speak to her I manage to say the wrong thing?

CHAPTER 28

"I have a plan," Stella shouted. "I got one."

"Enlighten us, Master," Tom said.

"Funny. For that, you're on stake-out duty."

"Fuck."

Stella grinned smugly at him. "That'll teach you."

"So, the plan?" Kate asked.

"Right." Stella laid out a length of printer paper. The old-fashioned kind that ran off in long uninterrupted lengths of white and peppermint green stripes and with perforations down each side to keep it running through the cogs. "I've been looking over the data that Matt Green provided us with and corroborating that against Connie Wells' diary list. There are fluctuations in delivery drops on all but one day. Every single Thursday, there is a drop to the Sutton Bridge location. Matt Green runs it and if it's an evening run, he takes the kid with him. Supposedly he takes her for a Maccie's at the next roundabout along the A17."

"Bastard," Kate said.

"I know. I really want a Maccie's now too," Tom said.

"I meant taking his kid along on a drug drop."

"Oh, yeah. That too. Bastard."

"So the plan," Stella said, "is to stake out the lay-by this Thursday. All day, as Green doesn't get to know the drop-off time until the morning. That's why he was in a hurry on the twenty-ninth. He didn't find out until his phone woke him up."

"Why didn't he take her for breakfast? Why leave her on the marsh?"

"After the night before with Connie confronting the Robbinses, he didn't want to take the chance of having her in the car if he got picked up."

"So instead he left—never mind. So we stake out this lay-by. Green's in custody. He won't be doing the Thursday run."

"If he can't make it, the Robbinses will make someone else do it. Probably Leah, Matt said. So we'll have one team following her and one team at the lay-by, just in case it isn't Leah. If it is, great, we'll pick her up and bring her in for questioning. Lay-by team needs to get pictures of the pickup driver and, if possible, to follow and see what we can get on that."

"Okay."

"If we can get one of the Robbinses supplying Leah with the drugs that get picked up, we'll have enough for a warrant for the boat, the office, the shack at the harbour, and the houses. We need the logs to get locations of the storage pots. Then Timmons can send in divers to recover."

"And we'll have the Robbinses for the drugs, as well as murder," Kate said.

"Belt and braces," Stella said.

"So which one of them did it?"

Stella shrugged. "Doesn't really matter who pulled the trigger, does it? They both did it, or should I say all three of them did it."

"Three?" Jimmy asked.

"Dad drove the boat. He had to be the one holding it steady so one of his kids could pull the trigger. That makes three of them going down for either murder or conspiracy to commit murder, as far as I'm concerned."

"Yeah, but who did it?"

"Adam," said Collier.

"Yeah, my money's on him too," Tom said.

Stella nodded. "You heard what Green said about his time in the army. I bet he was a sniper. Bet he's killed loads of people before this. What do you say, Kate?"

"I'll bet a tenner it's Ally."

"Why?"

"I've never liked to follow the crowd."

"And?" Jimmy prompted.

"I don't know. Just something about her. Too competitive, I think, to let her brother take care of a problem for her if she could do it."

"That's it? Sibling rivalry?"

"Gut feeling."

"All right people, pay up." Jimmy held out his hand with a coffee mug in it. Kate didn't want to guess if it was clean or not. At least it was dry and the winner wasn't going to have to towel off soggy tenners in a couple of days.

"So, Thursday's planned. It's Tuesday today. What's the plan between then and now, Stella?" Kate asked, leaning her chair back on two legs and hooking her foot around the desk leg to stabilise herself.

"Tidying up all this bloody paperwork. We're still waiting on the gun registrations for the Robbinses. We need to see whether or not those geniuses over in tech managed to get anything off that memory card in the camera or not, and I could use some help going through this data to track missing cargo containers."

"Right, so I'll go see the geniuses," Kate said, then quickly righted her chair and grabbed her coat.

"I've got a mate over in the gun reg thingy place," Tom said.

"Not even close to being good enough, Tom," Stella shouted at their backs as they escaped out the door. "And you two don't even think of making shit up. Sit down and grab some paper." The door closed on the desperate groans of two junior officers being forced into a day of hell. Paperwork.

Tom picked Kate up from home that morning. As much as she wanted Gina and Sammy to stay put, she didn't want to leave them stranded if they really did need to get out, so she'd left the rental in the car park.

"I really need to sort out a new car," she said and sat back to enjoy the scenery on the way to King's Lynn. The scenery she got was grey clouds, trees, and cars with their headlights on in the middle of the friggin' day. What was that all about?

"So, Miss Temple and Pippi Longstocking stayed with you last night."

"Huh?"

"Gina and the brat."

"What about them?"

"They stayed with you?"

"Yes, and?"

"Well, you know?"

"I know what?"

"You and Gina, you know?"

"Tom, have you lost the ability to form coherent questions in the last two minutes?"

"No."

"Then spit out whatever it is you're trying to ask. I'm not a bloody mind reader."

"Well, she's...you know. And I have a mate who works in your old nick and he said you were, you know. So, I...oh forget it."

"Good, God, man, what are you? Twelve?"

"Yeah, eleven and a half, actually."

She glanced down at his feet. Yeah, that looked about right. "Yes, I am, you know. How do you know Gina is?"

"We went to school together. I was a couple of years ahead, mind, but she was always cool. Till that fucker got his hands on her."

"So how did you know? About Gina?"

"Oh, well, I suppose I didn't when we were kids. I don't think she did either, really. Hence that prick and Sammy. But I think everyone around her probably knew before she did. She never hung around with lads. Well, not in the way girls do who are interested in them. You know what I mean, right?"

Kate nodded. She did. There was a flirtatiousness and a sense of experimentation that seemed to surround them. Something she'd never felt until she went to college and discovered a gay bar and the world just opened up before her very eyes.

"Well, I like to consider myself a man of the world and, well, she went out with a copper in Lynn once. Didn't last very long from what I hear, but this woman said she was a real heartbreaker."

"Gina?"

"Yeah, seems she's a fan of my dad's motto for laying tiles."

"You're losing me, Tom."

"Lay 'em once, lay 'em well, and never return to the scene of the crime."

She stared at him a moment. "For a semi-intelligent guy, Tom, you really do come out with some shit."

"I'm just telling you what Carly told me."

See, force scuttlebutt—an intelligence, or rather semi-intelligence, network like no other. "And what does that have to do with me?"

"Well, is she walking away from another crime scene, my friend?" He chuckled at his own joke.

"I'm glad you find yourself amusing, pal, because I don't."

"Aw, c'mon. You got to admit that was a little bit funny."

"No, it really wasn't."

"The way you're dancing around answering makes me think you and li'l Shirley did the nasty."

"Li'l Shirley?"

"Yeah, you know? Shirley Temple."

"Tom, mate, these are getting worse."

He shrugged.

"And, no. There was nothing nasty going on at my house last night. Except maybe Sammy's snoring. The kid's like a bloody train. Kept me awake until three." She refused to acknowledge that it was actually the remembered touch of Gina's fingers on her arm and the burn it had caused inside her that had really kept her awake.

"Really?"

"Really."

"But, I mean, she was there, and you were there, and you're both... you know...so why not?"

"Just because two lesbians are in the same room together does not mean they will automatically fall into bed with each other."

"It doesn't?"

"Oh, for God's sake."

"Now you're just trying to ruin all my fantasies."

"If I ever even suspect I feature in one of those fantasies, Tom, I'm going to borrow Sammy's air gun and do what Connie threatened to do to Matt Green. Are we clear?"

"Crystal, Sergeant, ma'am. Crystal."

She suspected that if he'd been able to drive in such a position, he'd have had his legs crossed to protect himself. She smirked. Too easy.

"Does everyone know about Gina?"

He shrugged. "Most, I'd guess. Why?"

"She thinks no one knows."

"In a village the size of Brandale Staithe? Give me a break. Her neighbours know what size bra she wears and when she changes the batteries in her vibrator. Nosiest old biddies in the bloody world."

"Do you only think about sex?"

"Pretty much."

"Is that a male thing, a cop thing, or a you thing?"

"Yes."

She laughed. "Small villages. Hot beds of iniquity and scandal."

"Bring it on," he said and pulled up outside the King's Lynn station. "Let's go see what we can get our hands on."

In truth, it was nothing much. The memory card was too damaged for them to retrieve anything despite their whizz-bang, shit-hot new software. And the list of guns registered to the three Robbinses was extensive, almost as big as the armed response unit's armoury. These were not people you wanted to be on the wrong side of. Len Wild confirmed what Matt had told them of the approximate size of the brick in the photograph, but had found little else that would have helped to further their investigation from either the original crime scene, the houseboat fire, Connie's house, or Connie's office. Matt Green's computer was of little value. Same with his other electronics. They had downloaded the data from his car's satellite navigation and retrieved corroboration of his attendance to at least four of the other drop sites in the last four weeks. Data didn't go back any farther than that.

"Looks like we have to just sit and wait and go along with Stella's plan," Tom said.

"You see a problem with her plan?"

"Yes."

"What?"

"It means we've got to do paperwork for the rest of the day and all day tomorrow."

"It's a fair point, well made, Tom. Don't we need to talk to someone again about something?"

"I wish I could say yes, but I can't think of anything."

"Shit."

"Precisely."

They sighed in unison and walked slowly towards Tom's car. Very slowly.

CHAPTER 29

Sammy was colouring at the table when Kate walked through the door. Merlin lay patiently at her feet.

"Hi, Kate. I drew this for you." She made one last mark and held up the paper for Kate to see. The picture was clearly supposed to be of her and Merlin with Gina and Sammy in the backyard. The eyes weren't symmetrical, and if she were honest, Sammy's version of her was a bit tubbier than she liked. But in general, it wasn't bad at all. Merlin definitely came off best.

"That's really cool. Want to stick it on the fridge for me?"

"Okay." Sammy used the magnets that Kate had collected on holidays to keep it in place. The ones of the bare-breasted sunbather she'd gotten in Lesbos, if she wasn't mistaken. She hoped she wasn't going to get in trouble with Gina about those.

"Where's your mum?"

"Upstairs having a sleep. She said I was terrible last night."

"Terrible? You didn't get up once."

"I know. She said I snored and wriggled so much she nearly came down to sleep on the sofa."

Kate laughed. "Oh, dear."

"I think she's going to ask you for spare blankets tonight so she can."

"What if I haven't got any?"

"Then I have to sleep outside on the washing line."

"Why on the washing line?"

"So she can peg me on it then I can't sleepwalk off onto the road."

"In that case, it's a good plan. Better get yourself ready for it, Mrs Woo."

Sammy frowned. "Who's Mrs Woo?"

"She's a lady from a song about a Chinese laundry that George Formby used to sing about."

"Who's George Formby?"

"An old singer."

"Oh, Mrs Woo, what shall I do? I'm feelin' kinda Limehouse Chinese laundry blues," Gina sang from the stairs.

"We have a winner." Kate pointed.

"That's daft," Sammy said.

"You won't say that when you're hanging on the washing line."

Sammy pushed her hair out of her face. "You won't let her do that to me. You're police."

"Hey, I know better than to get between a mother and daughter when sleep is involved. You're on your own, kiddo."

Gina looked at the clock. It was barely four-thirty. "You're earlier than I thought you'd be," Gina said.

"Got an early start tomorrow so I thought I'd make it an early finish today."

"Can we take Merlin for a walk?" Sammy asked.

"I guess so. Where do you want to go?"

"Beach."

"Okay, but we'll have to go to Wells-next-the-Sea beach then. I don't want to be easily spotted."

"'Cos of the mess?" Sammy asked, nodding her head seriously.

Kate fought valiantly not to laugh and mirrored Sammy's folded hands and sage nodding. "'Cos of the mess."

Gina wasn't nearly so successful at holding the laughter at bay.

"Come on, then. How about fish and chips on the beach?" Kate asked.

"Aw, yeah. Can we, Mum?"

"I don't see why not."

"Yay."

"Put your wellies on," she said to Sammy. Then she turned to Kate. "Do you have torches or head torches? It'll be dark by the time we get there."

"I do, and I've got a glow-in-the-dark ball for Merlin to chase."

"Wicked," came the cry from upstairs.

Five minutes later they were bundled up and in the car at the back of the house, Merlin and Sammy happily playing in the back seat while Kate pulled out onto the road. She stopped at the chip shop, then looked for a place to park as close to the beach as possible. It was already dusk and it wouldn't be long before it would be full dark.

The tang of vinegar on their chips and the salt in the air was invigorating. Merlin and Sammy ran back and forth, Merlin barking, Sammy laughing. Kate, carrying a full plastic bag, watched them climb the dunes and drop onto the beach proper. The long row of beach huts ran along the back of the beach to her left, to the right she could make out the red and green lights on the signal buoys, directing boats down the channel and into Wells harbour.

The last of the light finally dropped out of the sky, and Kate handed head torches to both Gina and Sammy. She helped Sammy to tighten hers while Gina unwrapped their food. When Sammy's head torch was lit, Gina handed her a paper cone stuffed full of battered fish and crispy chips.

Kate perched herself on the step of one of the little huts and stared out at the water as she ate. She could hear the waves, and slowly her eyes adjusted to the low light level. Sammy had barely finished eating before she started throwing the ball for Merlin. The lights inside the ball sparkled red, green, and blue every time it struck the ground. Sammy giggled every time Merlin tore after it and brought it back in her teeth, her face lit up like a Christmas tree.

"This is nice," Gina said.

"Yeah." Kate replied.

"Last night—"

"Don't." Kate cut her off. "You don't have to say anything, Gina. You're entitled to conduct your love life any way you choose. I'm sorry if I came across as judgemental or anything. I had no right to do that."

"You didn't."

"Oh. Then that's okay."

Gina balled up her used paper and crammed it into the bag. "I wanted to say thank you."

"What for?"

"It's been a long time since someone's wanted more from me." She laughed. A laugh that sounded bitter to Kate's ear. "If they ever did."

"I'm sure plenty of people did—do—why wouldn't they?"

"I'm a package deal. That's hardly an attractive proposition, Kate."

"You really think Sammy's going to chase away a woman you want to date?"

"You've met her."

"Yes, I have. And I'd ask you out for a date right now if I thought you'd say yes."

"You would?"

"Didn't I make that clear last night?"

Gina didn't say anything.

"I don't understand why you would ever think no one would want you. With or without a great kid like Sammy."

"She's a pain in the backside sometimes."

"Aren't we all?"

"And she swears."

"Like mother, like daughter."

"And no one's ever stuck around."

"What do you mean?"

"When I found out I was pregnant, my dad told me to get rid of it. Of her. I wouldn't. Couldn't. He told me if I didn't, I was never welcome in his house again. They live four miles from where I do, but Sammy's never met her grandparents. Matt didn't stick around, obviously, and when Sammy was little I started to get close to someone. Claire. I thought she was the one, you know? I was eighteen, with a newborn, and had no one to help me look after her. Claire didn't stay much more than a month. Looking back now, I'm actually amazed she lasted that long. But that was that."

"So you gave up."

"I didn't give up."

"Yes, you did. You gave up on finding someone special because you got burned. Once. When you were eighteen."

"And Matt."

"Oh, sorry, and Matt who you would never have been happy with anyway."

"It sounds pathetic when you put it like that."

Kate laughed. "It is."

"Thanks a lot."

"It's true."

"So she wouldn't put you off?"

"At the risk of repeating myself, no, Sammy would not put me off dating you." Kate stood up. "She would not put me off getting involved with you." She held her hand out. "She would not put me off being in a relationship with you." Gina took her hand. "So I'm going to ask this one time." She tugged Gina to her feet. "Will you go out on a date with me?" Kate wished she could see better because she was sure Gina was smiling. She wished she could see it.

"Yes."

Kate didn't need to see to hear the smile in Gina's voice.

"Okay. Dinner, this weekend."

"I need to find a babysitter."

"Leave it to me. I think I know someone."

"She can be a nightmare for babysitters."

"Like mother, like daughter."

"Hey."

Kate chuckled. "Don't worry, I guarantee this person can handle Sammy."

Gina linked her arm through Kate's and led her down the beach.

Kate just hoped she could handle Gina.

CHAPTER 30

Kate flipped through the pages of the *Autotrader*, idly scanning for new cars. She glanced up every few seconds to see if there was any movement. They'd rented one of the many holiday lets in the area that overlooked Ally Robbinses house. After all, it was November and there were no tourists left. Stella had gotten a stonking deal on it. So now Kate and Jimmy were sitting in the car under the carport. It was the only way they'd been able to think of remaining mobile, while inconspicuous. Ally's house was on the main road, and there was nowhere they could sit in the car on the street and not be spotted within a few seconds. The carport had a good growth of shrubs and trees around it, enough to keep them from being easily spotted anyway.

Matt had told them the drop could happen at any time from seven in the morning onwards, and when they couldn't get a hold of him, they were going to be pissed. And worried. He hadn't told them he wouldn't be able to make a drop and he'd been missing all week. Messages on his phone told them this was very true. Both Robbinses had left increasingly threatening messages, questioning his whereabouts, and no one seemed to have any idea where he was.

That could be good. Concern could make them careless. It might make them pay a little less attention to what's going on. It might make them make a mistake.

Or it could be bad. It could make them nervous and hypervigilant. Maybe even a little bit paranoid. It could make them change the drop. If they were paranoid enough, it could even make them cancel it.

Matt hadn't been sure. He said it depended on who was calling the shots. If Ally suspected that the cops knew something, she'd try to beat them by changing the drop point. If Cedric made the call, it would get cancelled. Adam, he couldn't predict. Matt said that was what made him scary. You just never knew if he was gonna laugh with you, or lay you out.

Kate drew a circle around the advert for a black Astra going for less than two grand. Possible.

"Are we gonna be here all day?" Jimmy asked, pouring coffee from a flask and handing her a small cup.

"Thanks. Probably." She took a sip.

"My cousin's selling his car. Eleven hundred."

"What kind?"

"Beemer. Five series."

"For eleven hundred? What's wrong with it?"

"Nowt. Diesel engine."

"How many miles?"

"A hundred thousand."

She laughed. "No thanks. I'll do it the old-fashioned way."

"Half of that lot are stolen."

"I'll check VIN numbers before I buy. Don't worry."

Out of the corner of her eye, she saw something move. She glanced up.

Leah dumped a black bag in the boot of her car and slammed the lid shut. She glanced up and down the road like she was looking for something, a frown marring her face.

"Heads up, Jimmy," Kate said. "We could be on the move."

Ally appeared in the doorway and said something.

"Can you read lips?" Jimmy whispered.

"They can't hear you, numbnuts. And, no, not from this distance. Pass me those binoculars you've got there." When he handed them over, she fiddled with the focus until she could make out Ally telling Leah that it was "a limit, not a target" and "I won't pay the fine for you again." Speed limit. Had to be.

"What's she saying?"

"Telling her to stick to the speed limit."

"Do you think she knows we know?"

"Jimmy, I have a number of skills, but mind reading is not one of them."

"Yeah, but you know how women think."

"And why's that?"

"Well, 'cos you are one."

"So I know how this woman thinks. Do you know how all men think?"

Jimmy scratched his head. "Most of 'em, yeah. Birds, footie, birds, beer, birds, work, and birds."

"You're a Neanderthal."

"No, I'm a canary. Norwich City all the way."

She chuckled and handed him back the binoculars. "That explains it all."

"Hey, I think I'm offended."

Leah began pulling out of Ally's driveway, so Kate tossed the magazine onto the back seat and turned on the engine. Leah turned right towards King's Lynn. Kate didn't put the car into gear, though. She waited. She let Leah increase her distance and waited.

"She's getting away," Jimmy said.

"She's still watching." Kate pointed to the doorway where Ally Robbins stood, looking up and down the road.

"Why?"

"To see if Leah's being followed."

"Does she always do that?"

"No idea. But she's doing it today."

Thirty seconds passed.

"What should we do?" Jimmy asked.

"We wait."

One minute.

"She's getting away."

"We know where she's heading and the boys are waiting at the lay-by."

"She might be going to a different place."

"She might, but each set of GPS coordinates in that direction go through Lynn. If we cut through Docking and then past the construction college, we'll catch her up at the Knights Hill roundabout."

"You sure?"

"I'm sure."

Three other vehicles and a bus sped past them and two long minutes dragged by before Ally Robbins went back into the house. Kate edged out of the carport and turned right onto the main road, away from King's Lynn.

"Wrong way."

"Shortcut."

She cut a right beside the Jolly Rogers and flew around the tight bends, shortening the distance between them and Docking by four miles. Jimmy clung to the handle above the passenger door as she skidded around a tight left and slowed at the perimeter of the village. No sign of Leah's car. She drove on, taking a right by the primary school, then a left a hundred yards later, and flooring it as she headed towards Bircham. A deceptive right-hand bend made her hit the brake when a tractor came barrelling towards them, taking up too much road. Jimmy crossed himself and whispered a Hail Mary under his breath.

"Didn't know you were Catholic, Jimmy."

"Neither did I."

She ran over a hillock that led to a hidden dip and caught air under the tyres.

"Oh, Christ."

She chuckled. "You'll have to go to confession for that."

"Do I go to confession for pissing myself too?"

"No. You go to the cash point and pay for the car to be valeted."

"There," he said, pointing out of the windscreen. "That's her."

Kate hit the brakes and slowed them down to fifty miles per hour. Enough under the speed limit to prevent them gaining on Leah anymore, but fast enough not to lose her.

"Phone Stella. Tell her where we are."

Jimmy did as he was asked and Kate continued to hold her distance from Leah. Traffic onto the A148 slowed Leah to a stop and Kate could do nothing but join the queue behind her and hope she didn't recognise either of them. Leah turned right and Kate followed, pulling out in front of a huge lorry to make sure there was nothing too big between her and Leah. Nothing was going to come between her and wrapping up this case. She had a weekend ahead that she planned to enjoy.

Passing through the town, she managed to pick up three cars between them, a Kia Picanto that couldn't have reached seventy if it had tried, a BMW X3, that seemed just as frustrated with the Kia, and a VW motorhome that equally couldn't have made seventy if it had tried. A section of dual carriageway on the flyover let her and the BMW pass their struggling friends, and Leah was once again in easy view as they started down the A17. Ten minutes more and they'd be at the lay-by where Tom and Collier were waiting in a car park to pick up the collection vehicle and follow it to wherever it went.

Traffic ahead of them slowed to a crawl. A string of drivers ahead weaved to the right to see what was up ahead. Judging by the way speed dropped from sixty to twenty-five, it didn't take too much effort to figure that a tractor was holding them all up. So much for progress.

Five minutes later, the queue in front began to speed up and she saw a tractor idling in a parking place fifty yards ahead. "Let Tom know she's almost there. Five, six minutes tops."

The lay-by in question was brilliantly placed between two roundabouts. One at the end of a swing bridge over the River Nene and the other fifty yards farther on, which offered a convenient turn-off to Tydd Gote power station. Or, for their purposes, to turn round on themselves. Leah was two cars ahead of them and they could see her pull off into the lay-by while they were still on the bridge. She stopped twenty yards along a tarmac road beside the river. A road that went nowhere. Not even back up to the main road. It was simply a dead end. And Leah just sat there. Waiting.

Tom and Collier were sitting in their car on the opposite side of the road to the lay-by. There was a small shed builder's yard and the car park led out onto the power station roundabout. Kate drove all the way around the roundabout and went back over the bridge. She pulled in to a parking area across the river from Leah. She had a better view of Leah's car than Tom did, but he was better placed to follow the second vehicle they were expecting. Kate was perfectly placed to pull Leah over after the exchange happened.

She pulled her new phone out of her pocket and dialled Tom. "She's there."

"Any sign of another vehicle?"

"None. Stella tell you about Ally watching out of the door?"

"Yeah. You think she's set us up?"

"Don't know. Possible."

"Time will tell. Ring if you see anything."

"Will do." She tossed the phone into the drinks holder between the seats. "Eyes peeled, Jimmy."

He handed her the binoculars. "I did bring two pairs, you know."

"Good."

"Do you think it's a setup?"

She shrugged. "Like I said, it's possible. Time will tell."

"It was odd, though. Her waiting at the door like that for so long?"

"Maybe. Or maybe that's her routine. She's gotten away with this for a long time, Jimmy. You don't do that by being stupid or careless."

"I guess not."

"So we just have to wait and see."

CHAPTER 31

"Hello?"

"Gina, it's William. One of the pipes has burst for the upstairs bathroom. There's water pouring through the ceiling in the dorm room and the whole place is flooding."

"Damn it. Have you turned the water off?"

"I've turned the isolation valves off but it made no difference."

"No, you need to turn it off at the stop cock."

"Where?"

"Boiler room."

"Okay, there's a lot of pipes in there. Which..."

Static filled her ears. "Oh, for God's sake. Bloody signal." She knew from past experience that as soon as you went in the boiler room, all mobile signal was lost. Connie had said it was to do with all the copper pipes in there. She didn't know if that was true, but the signal disconnection certainly was. "Bollocks."

She stuffed her feet into her shoes and looked at Sammy.

"I have to go to work. Get your shoes on."

"But I'm not supposed to leave the house." Sammy made her voice all deep and stern.

Gina fastened her laces. "I'm serious, Sammy. We've got to go. We won't be long."

Sammy tutted but started to hunt down her shoes. "Fine."

Gina went to grab her keys and remembered that her car was still at the police station. "Shit."

"Mum!"

"Exceptional circumstances." She grabbed the key to Kate's courtesy car, clipped Merlin's lead to her collar, and hustled Sammy out the back door. She glanced around to make sure there was no one around before unlocking the car and ushering Sammy and Merlin into the back seat. "Put your seatbelt on."

"I know."

"When we get there you are to go into my office and stay there. Right?"

"Right."

"I mean it, Sammy. You go in there, put the telly on, and you do not leave. Understood?"

"Can I watch a film?"

"Only a kid's one."

"Okay."

Gina pulled up at the campsite, unlocked her office door, handed Sammy the remote, and pushed her onto the sofa. "Do not—"

"Leave this room, I know. But, Mum, what if I need a wee?"

"Do you?"

"No."

"Then we'll worry about it later." She kissed the top of Sammy's head and went straight to the boiler room. William stood with his phone to his ear and a red wheel about four inches in diameter in his hand. He stuck his phone in his pocket as soon as he saw her and ran over.

"It said 'water stop cock to hostel' on a tag so I turned it." He held up the red wheel. "Then it broke off."

"Right. Because this just wasn't bad enough. We need to turn it off at the mains, then. It's under one of the manhole covers in the driveway." She went straight to the tools hung up on a board at the back of the barn and selected a hammer and a crow bar. "It's the oblong-shaped one that says 'water' on it." She handed William the tools. "Put the hazard triangle out and pry up the cover. I'll be there in a minute."

William took the tools and ran out, obviously glad to be able to do something. Gina started rummaging around for the tool she needed. She knew from experience that the stop cock in the main was too far down for either of them to be able to reach and get enough leverage to turn the valve off. It had happened once before and they'd had to improvise a turning device out of a piece of board that had snapped halfway through. Afterwards, Connie had found a specialised tool for just this kind of job. They'd never had cause to use it. Until today. It was a three-foot-long steel rod with a cross piece on top and a V-shaped notch at the bottom. It simply slipped over the tap head of the valve and allowed them to turn it from a distance. Perfectly simple. Would work a treat. Just as soon as she could find the damn thing.

In the end, it took five minutes to locate the tool. It had fallen behind a metal locker filled with gas canisters and all she could see was the blue painted steel V-shaped notch sticking out. A quick shove, a kick, and a few more curse words later, she managed to retrieve it and the water was turned off in a few seconds.

"Come on then, show me how bad it is."

Bad was being generous. The ceiling above two of the rooms was badly damaged. In one, it had already come down, which had let all the water escape. But the plasterboards in the other were beyond saving. The whole ceiling would need to be taken down and replaced. The floor boards in the upstairs room were badly damaged and probably half would have to be replaced. The insulation, the underfloor heating system, the joists, all showed a lot of damage and would have to be replaced or repaired before any of the rooms could be used again. But they needed to get the water capped before they could turn it back on for the rest of the building.

She pulled her phone out of her pocket and dialled the plumber. She begged and pleaded with him to come out and help her. He said he'd be there before the end of the day. She checked her watch. It was barely lunchtime. She shook her head. Helpful.

"Do we have anyone in?"

"Yeah. Three couples."

"Move them to the other building. We should be able to get water back on for them today. This one's going to be out of commission for a while. Any idea what happened?"

William shook his head. "The woman in that room came into reception and said water was coming through the roof." He shrugged. "Don't know anything else."

She sighed. "Right, thanks. Can you talk to the guests and get them resettled while I go and call the insurance company?"

"No problem."

"Thanks. Oh, and can you also start taking some pictures, will you? I'll need those for the claim."

"Already got some. While the water was pouring out."

"Thanks, William."

It was three hours before the plumber arrived. He sucked on his teeth and crossed his arms over his chest, whistled, then got to work. Gina decided that was plumber speak for "it's going to be expensive." Wonderful.

Two hours later she was ready to get Sammy and make her way back to Kate's. She opened the door, stepped out of the information centre, and walked up the lane.

"Hey, Gina, thought it was you I saw earlier playing about in manholes."

Shit. "Hi, Ally. Yeah, we had a burst pipe in the hostel. Had to get it turned off."

"Ouch. Lot of damage?"

"More than I'd like, that's for sure."

"Shame Connie isn't here to sort it out." Ally closed the distance between them and Gina wished she'd thought to just wave and keep on walking.

"William and I coped."

"I'm sure. Haven't seen you around for a while. How've you been? Nasty business all this. Murder, in our little village, hey?"

"Yes, terrible."

"But you're coping, right? And little Sammy too?"

"Yes, thanks, we're fine. I need to get off now. Need to make tea and all that."

"Sure, sure. Haven't seen you around much lately."

"No, I've been busy. Between this place and Sammy, I feel like I never have a minute to myself."

"I'll bet. Haven't seen Matt around for a while either. Not been in the pub or anything."

"Really? That's not like him."

"You're right it's not. You ain't seen him, have you?"

Gina shook her head.

"Well, that's even stranger. He's like clockwork with that kid of yours, ain't he?"

"Most of the time."

"But not lately."

"No. Maybe he's sick or something. I've had more on my mind to worry about than Matt's social life." She moved to edge around her. "Like my daughter being upset because Connie died."

Ally leaned in and stared at her. "I think you're telling me porky pies, Gina."

Gina could feel the sweat bead on her brow, her heart thundered in her chest, and she drew in a deep breath to try and steady her nerves. "No, I'm not."

"I think you are."

"Why would I do that?"

"Hmm. Interesting question. Why would you do that?"

"Exactly, I wouldn't. I'm not his keeper, and I don't care what he does if it doesn't relate to Sammy." Gina's palms were slick and her fingers trembled. She lost her grip on her keys and leaned forward to pick them up. "Now if you'll excuse me, I've got stuff to do."

"I'm sure you do. But I think we need to have a little chat, Gina." She leaned closer and wrapped her fingers around Gina's bicep. "I don't like it when people lie to me."

"I'm not."

Ally smiled menacingly at her. Her dark eyes looked almost black in the fading light and Gina could see nothing in them. They looked flat and lifeless, there was no spark of humanity in them. Soulless. Gina shuddered.

"I guess we'll see about that." Ally tugged and pulled until Gina was moving away from her office and the information centre. She started to scream but a large hand covered her mouth and pressed hard. "Enough of that. Let's go say hello to that little scamp of yours. See if she knows where dear old dad's hiding."

Gina stopped resisting so much. Ally was dragging her away from her office and towards her house. She didn't know where Sammy was and that was just fine with Gina. She didn't stop resisting altogether, she wanted Ally to believe she didn't want to go to home, but home was a far better option than where Sammy was. Whatever Ally had in mind, she didn't want to give Sammy any more ammunition for her nightmares.

CHAPTER 32

Kate checked her watch. Five o'clock. The light had already started to fade and everyone had their headlights on. The lights were bright and distracting and the sheer quantity of them coming and going was going to make it difficult to see what was happening at the lay-by. She realised now why the earlier time had been chosen last week. Early morning rush hour and low light—even if someone was watching, they'd have a hell of a job seeing what was going on, and following a vehicle driving away would be difficult. It made her glad she hadn't pissed off Stella and was tasked with picking up Leah instead.

"There," Jimmy said, "you see it? There's another car pulling up behind her."

Kate looked through her binoculars and stared across the river. "Licence plate Charlie Bravo five five Bravo Romeo Tango. White Ford panel van. Not a transit van, the one down."

"Got it."

"Pass me the camera, I've got the better angle for the licence."

He handed her a DSLR with a large zoom lens on it. She used the steering wheel to help hold the heavy lens still and zoomed in tight on the back of the van. Then she clicked off a few shots, and swivelled a few degrees over to get the driver as he climbed out and went to the back of Leah's car. Exactly as Matt Green had described. He didn't talk to Leah, he didn't even indicate he was there. He looked right and left, but obviously saw nothing of concern. He just opened the boot, lifted out the black bag, and closed it again.

"Description?" Jimmy asked.

"White male, maybe late twenties, maybe six-foot, judging against the height of the vehicle. Jeans, dark coat, beanie hat."

"In other words, every white van driver in England."

"Pretty much. Is Tom ready to roll?"

"I'm on speakerphone, your majesty," Tom said.

"Hmm. I like that one, Tommy boy. You can keep using it. He's getting back in the car now, the bin bag's in the back."

"Gotcha."

"Good luck."

"See if you can get an ID on this guy before I have to stop him, will you?"

"Uploading his picture to Wild now. We'll let you know if we get anything from facial recognition or off the plate. He's rolling. Waiting for a break in traffic to join the A17, indicating left," Kate said.

"It's a one way. He wouldn't be going right."

Kate ignored him. "He's pulled into the right-hand lane, should be visible to you now."

"I see him," Tom said.

"All yours. Leah's still here. Looks like she's asleep in there."

"Be careful, Kate."

"Worried about me?" Kate asked.

"You ruled Leah out as the murderer because she hasn't got what it takes to plan this murder or hold her hand steady enough to make the shot, not because you don't think she's capable of killing. A junkie with their back to the wall. You've seen it more often than I have. Be careful," Tom said.

"We'll be fine, dad."

Jimmy sniggered.

"Don't lose him." She hung up and handed Jimmy the camera to pack away. "Wanna wake up sleeping beauty or wait and see what she does?"

"Wait. If she wakes up, checks the boot, and finds it empty, we've got her dead to rights that she was waiting for the drop-off. If not, she could argue she was robbed while she was asleep."

"She still might try that one."

"Won't stand up unless she calls the police straight away. She's got a mobile on her," he said.

"Fair point. We just might make a fair investigator out of you yet." She winked at him.

Leah didn't wake up for another hour. Six-fourteen, to be exact. Traffic was thinning, and it was fully dark. The red lights on top of the power station could be seen for miles around. Kate stared at the reflection they made in the water. Two little red dots shimmering and dancing on the ebbing tidal river. It amazed her how a slight shift in perspective changed things so much. One slight shift of the head and you see something different. Like the world tipping on its axis and the picture you're looking at changes. Only it doesn't change, and you don't change, but in that instant everything changes.

It was her phone that had woken Leah up. Kate could see her holding it to her ear. She watched her get out of the car and check the boot. Just like Jimmy had predicted. Then she slammed it closed, got back into her car and started the engine. Kate's phone rang.

"Damn it." She clicked "answer" and turned on the engine. She pulled closer to the road, ready to pull out after Leah. "You better not have lost him, Tom, or I swear I'll—"

"Kate?"

"Oh, hey, Sammy. What's up?"

Leah pulled onto the road and made her way down to the roundabout farther away from them. Kate watched, waiting for her to turn back on herself and head for the bridge.

"My mum had to go to work, and she's been gone ages, and she's not answering her phone."

"Hold on, Sammy, one sec."

Leah crossed the bridge and flashed past them. They were heading back towards King's Lynn. Kate pulled out two cars behind her and followed.

"Sorry, kiddo, I'm with you now. What do you mean she went to work? She was supposed to be with you today. Staying in the house."

"There was an emergency at work. William phoned her and she drove your car. She told me to stay in her office and not come out, and said I could call if I needed her. But she's not answering."

She watched Leah overtake a lorry and cursed, knowing that she wouldn't be able to do that without killing them in the oncoming traffic. She had to settle for overtaking the cars in front and waiting for another opportunity to take the lorry. She pulled wide in the lane to look for the opportunity and make sure Leah wasn't getting too far ahead. "Okay, we'll call the campsite and see what's going on, kiddo. Want me to give her message for you?"

"I haven't left the office, but I need a wee. I'm hungry and bored and lonely and I want to know when's she coming back."

Kate smiled. "No problem, I'll pass it on."

"Thanks, Kate."

Kate passed the lorry and ducked back into her lane, putting her foot down. She closed the distance to Leah. "When did you both get there?"

"Before lunchtime."

Kate glanced at the clock on the dash. "That's more than six hours. Does she usually leave you alone this long?"

"No. She says I can't be left for five minutes 'cos I get in trouble. But I've been good, Kate. I've not done anything bad."

"That's okay. I'm sure you've been really good."

"Merlin's been bad, though."

"Has she?" Kate smiled knowing that Merlin was getting the blame for whatever Sammy had gotten up to.

"Yeah, she's eaten all the cereals and spilled milk on the desk and on Mum's keyboard."

"I didn't know she drank milk."

"It was my milk. But she spilled it over."

"Well, I'm sure we can sort it out."

"Phew. She's been worried."

Kate chuckled. "I'm sure she has. Okay, I've got to go and call your mum now. She's probably just got really busy and didn't hear her phone or something." Sammy hung up and Kate glanced at Jimmy.

"I'm already dialling," he said. "You just keep watching the road."

"Thanks, Jimmy." Kate caught up to Leah's car and decided to wait until they were on a quieter road before pulling her over. Perhaps after the turnoff at Hillington.

Jimmy hung up. "Shit."

"What?"

"Gina left William in the information centre after sorting the problems at five o'clock."

"An hour and a half. It doesn't take an hour and a half to walk from there to my house, never mind fifty yards to her office."

"The car's still there. At the campsite. William found it on the campsite."

"So where's Gina?"

"He doesn't know, but the last time he saw her she was talking to Ally in the car park."

"Shit."

CHAPTER 33

Gina rubbed her arm, trying to coax the circulation back. She tried to ignore the fact that Ally was standing in the middle of her sitting room after shoving her on the sofa. "Look, Ally, I already told you. I don't know where Matt is. Why would I? I'm not his wife. I'm not his girlfriend. The only thing we talk about is Sammy."

"Then why are you sweating?"

Gina couldn't deny it. She could smell it herself. The pungent aroma of fear mingled with sea salt, diesel, and dead fish that had permeated Ally's clothes a long time ago. Gina was glad she was in her house and not on Ally's boat. A fishing boat was not a nice thing to be on. Especially when you're scared. "Because you dragged me off the street and you're scaring me. Acting like some gangster badass. This is Brandale Staithe, not some fucking gangster movie."

Ally laughed. "Matt was right about you, wasn't he?"

"What are you talking about?"

"He always said you were fucking clueless."

"About what?"

"Everything."

Gina's pride squawked loudly but her sense of self-preservation managed to muzzle that bitch. She was trying to goad Gina into letting something slip. *Oh, you're so not getting anything out of me.*

"Vague, Ally. You'll have to be more specific if you want me to know what you're talking about. I'm clueless, remember?" *There, that should satisfy my pride and keep me safe. Ish.*

"Well, did you ever wonder why he ran off after you fucked him?"

Gina cocked her head to one side. "Briefly. But then I figured out I'm a lesbian so I didn't let it bother me." She lied. About the bothering her bit, not the lesbian bit.

Ally grinned. "Well, well, well. Perhaps not so clueless after all." She looked Gina up and down. "Just gutless, then."

"Where do you get that from?"

"Never done anything about it, have you? Just sat in this little cottage drying up."

"Now who's clueless?" *Shut up!*

"Oh, really? Well, let's see if I can figure it out." She drummed her fingers on her lips. "Oh, yeah. You and Connie were always pretty close. How did it happen? Did she take you under her wing, as it were?" Ally sat beside her and leaned in close. She wrapped her arm around Gina's shoulder. "Did she get you drunk and lean in like this?" Ally rubbed her head against Gina's hair. "Did she make you think she was going to leave Leah for you?"

"You haven't got a clue. Connie and I were only ever friends. She was in love with Leah. Even after she threw her out, she loved her."

"You don't abandon the people you love, Gina. You do whatever it takes to help them. Whatever it takes."

Something in her head shifted. Gina thought of how she'd been more than willing to lie for her daughter, she'd have told Kate she shot Connie before letting anything happen to Sammy. Ally was right, whatever it took. The wrong things for all the right reasons. "You did it."

"Did what?"

"You killed Connie."

Ally laughed but there was something in her eyes—a flicker, a shadow, a ripple in the dead pools that glinted out at her. Fear. "You shouldn't be going around slandering people like that, Gina. It could get you into all sorts of trouble."

"Why, though? You don't love Leah. You treat her like crap."

"I wouldn't spit on that useless piece of shit if she were on fire."

"Then why? You said you don't abandon the people you love."

"And I never have."

"I don't understand."

"All the better for you. Now tell me where Matt is and we can get this shit over with." Ally pulled a gutting knife from her belt. Gina froze. "Come on, Gina. Where is he?"

Gina just shook her head.

"Think about it like this, you can tell me now and I'll go home before your kid gets here, and leave you with nothing more than a little piss in your pants." Ally stood up tall and towered over her. "Or you can refuse to say anything and I'll start practising my knife skills. Then there'll be crying, and blood, and talking and maybe your kid sees you with a few nasty scars from now on." Ally put the tip of the blade to the corner of Gina's mouth and scraped the cold steel along her cheek, hard enough to feel, but not hard enough to draw blood. "Or you can be real brave and tell me nothing at all. And do you know what's going to happen then, Gina? Do you? Can you imagine?"

Gina shook her head.

Ally wrapped her fingers in Gina's hair and twisted her head to look her straight in the eye. "We wait a few hours for the tide. And then I'll take you out on the boat." She smiled and Gina saw spittle collect at the corner of her mouth. "Ask me what comes next, Gina," she said quietly.

Gina couldn't work up enough saliva to make her voice work.

"Ask me!" Ally shouted.

"What comes next?" Gina whispered, her voice shaking, crawling past her lips with barely enough force to be audible.

"Bait." Ally whispered the word into her ear. Slow and low, dragging it out so it sounded like "Bay" and "T".

Gina shivered. Her breath was coming thick and fast but it wasn't right. In, and in, and in, but no out. The muscles in her hands locked, her fingers stiffened into talons and her vision shrank. The focus of her world shifted until all she could see was the bait station she knew was on every fishing boat. She could see the steel table covered in chopped fish, guts, and dried blood. She could see the wicked grinder bolted into place. Effectively it was a massive blender designed to chop up frozen fish leftovers to use as bait. The noise was horrendous, and the bite of the grinder unforgiving. Bones, sinew, muscle—it all broke apart beneath the power of it. And that was all she could see. That and the dead eyes of the fish at one corner. Mouth hanging open, slimy, and its black, dead eyes covered in a film of mucus.

"I can't...I can't tell you what I don't know."

"No? Really, Gina, is that the best you can come up with?"

She tried to slow her breathing down, she tried to listen to her heartbeat, but it sounded more like a flutter than a beat. Like the wings of a hummingbird, fluttering too fast to see, too fast to hear distinctly, just a hum. A hum in her ears that still didn't manage to drown out Ally's voice as she toppled over.

"Oh, for fuck's sake, that's pathetic."

CHAPTER 34

"Stella, you need to get someone—"

"I've already got a WPC going to the campsite to stay with Sammy. She'll be fine. Timmons is on his way here. He wants you to pick up Leah as per the plan. We may need her for information."

"But—"

"No buts. Orders. I'm on my way to speak to William now and find out what happened and when. Arrest Leah and put her in a cell. Let her stew, let her get antsy. She'll surely be needing a fix soon. The more she's on edge, the easier it will be to interrogate her."

Kate knew Stella was right, and that it was the best plan. But the time it would take to pick Leah up, get her booked in, and then get out to Brandale Staithe as well...it was too much.

"If they were going to kill her, why take her somewhere else?" Stella asked.

"I know, I know."

"We'll find her."

"I'm sure we will. But will it be in time?"

"We're doing everything we can, Kate."

"Don't make me tell Sammy her mother isn't coming back, Stella. Don't make me do that."

"Drive safely, Kate. But drive fast."

Kate had no intention of doing anything else. She followed Leah off the A148 and through Flitcham village. She overtook the car that separated them and flashed her lights at Leah. A three-flash burst, then a second burst. Leah's car slowed. She flashed again, one burst, then a second. Leah's car slowed more and she indicated left. As soon as they stopped, Jimmy jumped out of the car and ran to Leah's door. She rolled down the window and he reached inside and pulled the keys out of the ignition. Leah tried to grab them back and Kate could hear her shouting but couldn't make out the words. She watched without seeing as Jimmy pulled open the door and helped Leah out of the car. He cuffed her wrists behind her back, walked her to Kate's car, and pushed her into the back seat.

"I'll drive her car back to the station. Forensics will want it. There's stuff all over the passenger seat. I wouldn't want to leave it here to be picked up," Jimmy said. "Have you got a set of coveralls and shit in your boot?"

Kate nodded and pushed the button that released the lock. "Help yourself."

"You go on ahead. By the time you've booked her in, I'll be with you."

She nodded and waited until he'd closed the boot again and set off.

"I haven't done nothing. You can't do this," Leah said.

"Leah, I've got pictures of you participating in a drug smuggling operation," Kate replied. "Do you really want to start out playing the innocent victim role?"

"What are you talking about?"

"Did you know?"

"What?"

"Did you know what they were going to do to Connie?"

"What?"

"The Robbinses. Did you know they were planning to kill Connie?"

"They didn't kill her."

Kate looked at her through the rearview mirror, the stubborn set to her jaw, the tilt of her head. She hadn't known. She still didn't know. Kate wondered for a moment if Connie might accomplish in death what she probably wouldn't have achieved had she lived. Would Leah get help now when she finally realised that Connie had died trying to help her? Would she help herself when she saw what her supposed friends had done? She saw how Leah twitched on the backseat, trying to itch her arm against the seat back. Probably not.

It took more than thirty minutes to get Leah back to the station and booked into her accommodation for the night. Jimmy had just finished booking Leah's car into evidence when Kate found him.

"Ready?" she asked.

He simply nodded and followed her back out to her car. They didn't speak during the drive. No need. Stella would have answers for them when they got there or she wouldn't. They'd have a plan in place or they wouldn't. No point in trying to guess until they got there, until they knew, then they would do whatever needed to be done.

Stella and Timmons were outside Ally Robbinses house. Patrol cars blocked the road from the Jolly Rogers to the beach turn-off. No one was getting past the house. Blue lights thrummed and Stella nodded when they hauled themselves out of the car.

"House is empty. We've already arrested Cedric and Adam. They were at the harbour getting the boat ready for a run tonight."

"Gina and Ally?" Kate asked.

"They weren't there."

"The harbour office?" Jimmy suggested.

"Empty," Timmons said. "All empty. We have no idea where Ally is and those bastards have gone quiet."

"The tide's out and the boat's in dock," Kate said, looking down the harbour road.

Timmons nodded. "We'll find them."

Kate checked her watch. Almost nine o'clock. She needed to think. She needed to stop reacting and think. She ran her hand cross her face. "Okay. What do they know? What are we sure Ally knows?"

Jimmy frowned at her, then smiled slightly. "She knows Green is missing, but not where. She knows Connie is dead and that they burned whatever evidence she had in the houseboat."

"How did they know about the houseboat?" Stella asked.

"Ally was there when I asked Leah if the key was hers. She must have recognised it. Does she have some connection to the houseboat?" Kate asked.

"None that we've been able to trace," Stella said. "The owner was a Mrs Webb. Lives in one of the properties that back onto the marsh."

"Cedric's sister. She was married three or four times. They don't talk much now," Jimmy said. "Had a falling out about five or six years ago. Never knew what about."

"Why didn't you mention this before?" Kate asked.

"I didn't know the houseboat was Mrs Webb's or I would've done," Jimmy said.

"Okay, what else do they know? What could they want from Gina?"

"They know Matt's not been seen for days," Stella said.

"And?"

"They don't know where he is."

"And?"

"If they suspected he was in custody—well, you heard what he said. They'd have changed the drop location or cancelled it altogether, right?"

"That's what he said. Doesn't mean he's right."

"He's worked with them for a long time now. Let's assume he does know what he's talking about. They didn't switch locations or cancel it. So they don't know we know."

"They're looking for Matt," Kate said. "They just want the intel."

"Only thing that makes sense."

"So where would Ally take her?" Jimmy asked.

"Information gathering can be a messy business," Timmons said. "She needs somewhere private, but they left the campsite on foot."

"They did?" Kate said. "How do you know that?"

"Ally's car's here. Adam and Cedric's are also accounted for. Gina's vehicle is still at the campsite."

"You've checked Gina's house, right? That's less than two minutes from the campsite," Kate said.

They all looked at each other.

"Oh, for God's sake." Kate turned her back on her colleagues and shouted to the nearest PC. "You, assign PCSOs to watch all locations and get every other available officer to the other end of the village.

Move these bloody cars, and get the nosey friggin' neighbours back in their houses."

"Yes, ma'am."

Jimmy was revving the engine while she screamed orders. Timmons was on his phone. Everyone else was jumping in their vehicles and heading one mile east. From one end of the village to the other.

"What will Ally do to her?" Jimmy asked when Kate climbed into the car and ignored the *bong-bong*, telling them both that she wasn't wearing her seatbelt.

"Depends what Gina tells her. If she tells her Matt Green's in custody, she'd be smart to run. If she doesn't," Kate said, "Ally Robbins has a lot to lose. Her base is here. Her haul, her network is here. She's worked long and hard to put this into place. It's not something she'll be happy to give up on."

"If Gina doesn't tell her what she wants to know, what will she do to her?"

Kate didn't answer as she tried not to picture what was happening to Gina.

"What will she do to her?"

Kate indicated her turn out of habit.

"Will she kill her?"

"I don't know, Jimmy," Kate finally said. "Might be best not to think about it right now."

Kate couldn't stop herself. She pictured Gina battered, bruised, and bloody. She imagined all the potential torture devices that were available in the everyday home. It all depended on how creative Ally wanted to get and how much she wanted to know where Matt was. Given everything that Matt knew, Kate guessed she wanted to know a whole lot.

CHAPTER 35

"See, the thing about knife wounds, Gina...no, no, no, stay with me now. No passing out again." Ally tapped Gina's cheek quite softly and Gina slowly opened her eyes.

She wished she hadn't. She was in her hallway, a picture of Sammy right in front of her on the wall. Her hands were tied at the wrist and held over her head. The rope lashed over the banister rail and pulled tight. Her coat was open and Ally was slicing the buttons off her shirt.

"Oh, hello again. As I was saying, the thing about knife wounds, is that they hurt the most when they're fairly shallow." She drew her knife across Gina's stomach scoring a thin line across the soft flesh. Blood pooled in its wake and ran down her skin in a trickle. Gina expected it to hurt and was shocked when it didn't. Instead she felt the cold steel, the tickle as blood ran, the heat that radiated outward and along her nerves. Then the heat grew teeth and gnawed at those same nerves.

"See?" Ally continued. "The idea is to cut at the nerve endings to maximise the pain but not wound so badly that your, erm, subject loses too much blood and passes out." She grinned. "You're more than able to do that without any help, aren't you, chick?" She grabbed Gina's cheek between her finger and thumb and squeezed in a mock gesture of affection, then followed up with a swift slap that split her lip and filled her mouth with the rich, salty tang of blood.

Gina held her breath, determined not to cry out.

"So, where's Matt?"

Gina shook her head. "Did you check your bed?"

Ally slapped her again and grinned when Gina was unable to suppress the grunt of pain. "Not funny. Where is he?"

"No idea." She spat blood out of her mouth. "What's this all about? I know you and Matt are friends, but seriously, Ally, this is too much."

"Nothing to do with friends. This is just business, chick. And no one gets in the way of our business." She tapped the blade of her knife to Gina's nose. "Now, where's Matt?"

"I've told you, I don't know."

"And I know you're lying. So I'll mix a little business with pleasure." She slashed the blade across her chest, the red welt appearing just above the fabric of her bra. Her left breast felt as though it was burning. Gina gritted her teeth. She couldn't stop the tears seeping from her eyes, but she sure as hell wouldn't scream. If she did she knew she wouldn't be able to stop. And she couldn't let Ally win. She closed her eyes and wished someone had noticed she was missing by now. She hoped Kate was looking for her. And she prayed. She prayed that she was strong enough to keep her mouth closed and her daughter safe.

"I don't know where he is," Gina said quietly.

The third slice mark went down her belly crossing the other mark, as if Ally were slicing open a potato jacket. "This is fun for now, but it will get boring soon."

She bit her tongue to stop herself shouting out and tried to breathe through the agonising pain. She counted through wave after wave of cold, heat, and teeth as they attacked nerve after nerve. One through ten, then again. And again. She had to remind herself to breathe out. She didn't want to hyperventilate and pass out. Again. "I can't tell you what I don't know, Ally, no matter how much you torture me."

"You know, that's a very good point." A fourth welt appeared over her right breast. "But I'm sure you do know. Now, tell me where he is?"

Gina squeezed her eyes closed trying desperately not to give in. The urge to end the pain was incredible. The knowledge that she could end this was powerful. If she hadn't been certain that her revelation would result in her death, she knew she would have talked. As it was, she knew there was only so much more she could take. "Perhaps he went on holiday." *Please, Kate, please save me.*

Ally sighed and made four more slashes in quick succession. "Maybe I'll play noughts and crosses? I could make a grid on your back. That might stop me from getting bored."

Gina let the tears fall freely now. She didn't fight them. She couldn't fight them and the pain all the same time. Her silence was more important than her dignity now. "Please, Ally, stop this. Please. I don't know where he is, I swear."

"Hmm, or snakes and ladders."

The malevolent glint in Ally's eyes was terrifying. Gina swallowed hard. Survival. That was the best she could hope for. Just survive. For Sammy. "Please, Ally," she sobbed, "Please don't do this. I don't know where he is."

"Liar. Maybe a chess board." She twitched the knife back and forth like she was practicing the strokes.

I'm going to die while she makes me look like a fucking board game. "Please, Ally. Please. You don't have to do this." She looked her in the eye. *Oh, God, it's like she's dead inside.*

"No, I need something that's more fun on my own." Ally grabbed Gina's hair and spun her around. Her shoulders were twisted painfully as Ally started to cut away the cloth from her back. "Solitaire. I'll just mark out the board first." She measured where she was going to cut. Gina could feel the soft practice strokes against her skin.

The tears tumbled down her cheeks as she sobbed. The first true slice had the now familiar sensation of cold then warmth, followed by the teeth chewing on the nerve endings down her spine, and Gina shivered. Partly from the cold, partly from the pain, but mostly from fear. She'd reached her limit. She couldn't talk her way out of this. She couldn't save herself. The realisation turned her knees to jelly and she slumped against the rope holding her upright. Another slice across the base of her back bit. Then she threw back her head and screamed.

CHAPTER 36

"Armed response is on the way. ETA thirty minutes," Timmons said.

"Let me guess," Kate said, "they're coming from King's Lynn."

"Yes."

"Great." She closed her eyes and tried to calm herself down. "Are we certain that they're in there?"

"Lights are on and Stella heard a scream when she first arrived. Since then, we've heard some mumbling when we were close to the door, but nothing distinct."

Kate nodded. "So what's the plan?"

"Like I said, armed response is less than thirty minutes away."

"And until then?"

Timmons shook his head. "We wait."

"You're kidding?"

"No."

"We don't make contact at least?" Kate stared at him incredulously.

"No, we wait."

"Sir, I think that's a mistake. We should at least try to negotiate with her."

"I said, we wait."

Kate stared at him but knew she wasn't going to get any further talking to him. She turned away from him and stared at the house. The lights were on and the curtains in the living room were open. She could see right in. She could see light coming from the upstairs windows too, but it was too weak to have been on in that particular room. It was more diffused, like it was having to travel a long way before it reached the window. *It's coming from downstairs. Which means they're probably in the kitchen.*

Kate started walking, ignoring the whispered demands that she stop and get back to her colleagues. She was going to be in deep shit later.

She didn't care.

She walked along the side of the house, careful to tread on clumps of grass or in the border rather than crunching across the gravel. She didn't want to be heard. Slowly she rounded the back of the house, the lean-to and shed providing adequate cover for her to see through the kitchen window without being seen. She peeked around cautiously. A very quick look. A fraction of a second. Just enough to see that there was no one sitting at the table and convince her that a longer look was possible.

She inched a little farther forward and peeked between the ivy leaves. The room was empty. The lights were on, but there was no one in the room. Where the hell—

A loud scream focused Kate's attention to the left of her view. To the hallway. The scream sounded inhuman. The indistinguishable cry of any animal in pain and Kate wanted to smash her way through the glass and rush to Gina's aid. She wanted to bring her suffering to an end and beat the living shit out of Ally Robbins for daring to lay a hand on her.

She heard a knock on the door and a woman's voice. Stella.

"Ally Robbins, this is the police. We know you're in there, and we know you have Gina with you. Come out now and no one has to get hurt." Stella's voice sounded muffled and far away. Too many closed doors between them.

"Fuck you." Ally shouted back through the door.

"Ally, the armed response unit is on the way. They'll be here in twenty minutes. Right now, it's just us. We can work this out."

"I said fuck off."

"That's not going to happen. I can't leave while you're holding a hostage."

Kate used the noise to step closer to the window.

"I'm going to open the letter box so we can talk better."

"Don't. Don't you do it."

"Ally, put the knife down," Stella said. Her voice slightly clearer to Kate's ear. *She must have opened the letterbox.* "You don't need to hold it to her throat. I'm not coming in. Keep looking at me." *Thank you, Stella.* She grinned and pictured the scene that Stella was seeing. How she was filling in the blanks that Kate couldn't see from behind them.

"I said don't."

"I'm not doing anything else, Ally. I just want to talk to you. All right? I'm just going to talk."

"I've got nothing to say."

"That's okay. I've got plenty. I'll just keep talking and you can keep that knife away from Gina's throat, okay?"

"I don't want to talk."

Kate tried the handle to the lean-to and breathed out as it gave under her hand and the lock opened.

"That's okay, Ally, like I said, I've got loads to talk to you about. Like Matt, and Adam, and your dad, and Connie, of course. That's what started this whole mess after all and it was you, wasn't it? With the rifle?"

Ally said nothing.

"I'll bet it was. All the guys that I work with, well, they all reckon your brother was the only one who could do it. But DS Brannon—you remember her, right?"

Kate eased the door open an inch. Praying that it didn't creak.

"Well, she actually put money on you being the one who did it. She was right wasn't she?"

The door opened another inch in silence. Kate took another breath. She could hear a pained whimper. *God only knows what that bitch has done to her.* Stella kept on talking.

"The boys all said it had to be another bloke to pull off a shot like that. But she said no. You would've done it."

Kate edged into the doorway, eased the door open another inch, and then slipped inside. The light was dim and her eyes were slow to adjust. Kate waited. Stella just kept on talking.

"We've arrested your brother."

Shapes began to form in front of Kate. Tins of paint stacked on a shelf. A tool box under a coat rack that was filled with kids toys and waterproofs.

"And your dad. He's a feisty old bugger, isn't he?"

There was a shovel and a rake in the far right-hand corner.

"Don't worry, we didn't hurt him, though. Your brother, on the other hand, was resisting arrest so he may have a bruise or two when you next see him. Mind, they'll have probably faded by the time that happens."

"Fucking bitch."

"No need for that, Ally," Stella said with a small chuckle. "It wasn't me personally."

"I'll kill her."

Kate picked up the shovel and tested its weight. Too big and heavy to be effective. If she missed Ally she might catch Gina with it.

"No, you won't. Even you can't think that would be a clever idea while I'm here watching."

She put it back down as quietly as she could.

"You can't stay there forever."

"No, you're right I can't."

Kate looked at the kids toys again. There was a rounders bat sticking out of a bag filled with soft balls and tennis balls. Perfect.

"But I don't need to. Armed response are on the way. Once they get here, well, I wouldn't want to be in your position, let's put it that way."

Kate gripped the handle of the short bat and slid it out of the bag, one inch at a time.

"They'll probably surround the place, and get cameras and shit in there. And they've got those cool night vision goggles and heat sensor stuff. It's all high tech now, you know."

Kate held the bat in her hand, getting used to the weight and feel. Two feet of solid, rounded wood. Thirteen ounces of clubbing power. Absolutely perfect.

"We arrested Matt too, you know. That's where he's been all week. With us."

Kate pushed her shoes off and slipped into the kitchen in just her socks. No point giving herself away before she was in position to do something.

"He's been very helpful, I've got to tell you. Helped us make sense out of the evidence that Connie left behind."

"What evidence?"

Kate crept farther across the linoleum floor until she was at the doorway between the kitchen and the hall. Ally's broad back obscured everything in front of her.

"From Connie? Well, she left us some pictures, her body, of course, and some stuff in her diary that was really interesting."

"You're full of shit."

Kate closed the distance. Six feet. Five feet.

"No, no, I'm really not."

"What did it say, then, this diary entry?"

Four feet.

"Well, it tells us that you're a drug-dealing, fucking scumbag and that you should really give yourself up."

Three feet.

Ally laughed. "See? I knew you were full of shit."

Kate lifted the bat and set herself to swing it at Ally's head. "Drop the knife and step away, Ally."

Ally twisted towards Kate and time slowed. In the next half second, Ally lifted her knife from her side and thrust towards Kate. Kate cocked the bat backwards and swung. They each made contact at the same time. Kate's momentum spun her away from Ally's knife as the bat crashed into Ally's skull with a resounding thunk just above her left eyebrow. Ally slid down the wall and slumped on the ground. Kate looked down at her stomach and was shocked to see that her shirt was sliced open but even more shocked to see that her flesh beneath wasn't.

She glanced up. Gina hadn't been nearly so lucky. She was hanging from her wrists.

"You're okay now, Gina," Kate said. "You're okay." She touched Gina's shoulder as she passed to open the door and let in the cavalry.

Stella came in clutching a silver foil blanket. Tom ran up the stairs and cut through the rope that was holding Gina's arms above her head. Paramedics ran in and checked for a pulse in Ally's neck, then shouted for equipment. She was breathing fine.

Timmons tugged Kate out by her arm and pushed her against the car. "Stay put this time."

The paramedics had Gina on a trolley. She clutched the foil blanket around her like a shroud, clinging to it as though it could protect her.

"Gina!" Kate shouted and started towards her.

Gina's eyes met hers and she simply asked, "Sammy?"

"She's fine. I'll bring her for you."

"Thank you," she whispered. The trolley was wheeled into the back of the ambulance and then she was gone. Again.

The ambulance tore out of the cul-de-sac and turned left, heading straight for King's Lynn, and slowly everyone drifted back to doing what they needed to do. Kate stood where she was. Staring at the empty road where the ambulance had been.

Stella bumped her on the shoulder. "Hadn't you better get going?"

"Huh? What?"

"You told her you'd pick up the kid and meet her at the hospital."

"Oh, right. Yeah."

"We need her statement too."

Kate spun and looked at her.

"When she's ready. But the sooner the better, right?" Stella said.

Kate nodded.

"Don't scowl at me. It's my job."

"Sorry. Sorry, I know. Mine too. Will Ally be okay?"

"Concussion. They're taking her in for an X-ray just to be sure she can't scream police brutality, but she'll be fine. And so will you. Go on, get out of here. Tonight you can go be a relative."

"I'm not."

Stella laughed. "Maybe not, but you sure as hell act like it."

"Oh, crap."

"Only if she's not interested."

Kate groaned.

"And I've seen her look at you." Stella patted her shoulder. "Go pick up the kid."

"Thank you."

"Just doing my job."

"How did you know what I was going to do? I didn't even know."

Stella shrugged. "I didn't. But once you broke ranks, I wasn't going to sit on my arse. Besides, that bad stuff's always harder to do with a witness there. Now go on, get out of here. I'll see you bright and early tomorrow, and we'll get started on the paperwork."

Kate groaned and walked stiffly towards her car. Paperwork. Lovely.

CHAPTER 37

Gina shivered under the blankets, her teeth chattering, pins and needles biting at her flesh. Every firing of every nerve ending stung as sensation returned to her numb body. Especially every thin line that Ally had torn across her skin. Ally had been right, though. Not a single one was deep enough to warrant stitches. Just row after row of those little white strips holding her together. *Bitch.* She was equal parts glad and pissed off that she couldn't see her own back. Ally hadn't finished her solitaire board, but she'd made a decent start on it.

She closed her eyes and cried. The nurse had claimed she'd be back in a minute with a painkiller and a sedative to help her sleep. That must have been twenty minutes ago, but she knew without a doubt that she wouldn't be sleeping that night without either pill.

The only reason she was glad she hadn't returned yet was her need to see Sammy. And Kate. Kate said she'd bring her. She shifted on the thin mattress and one of the wounds pulled. Maybe more than one. *They'll scar. Like a patchwork quilt. No. More like Frankenstein's fucking monster. No way will she want that date now. Who would?*

Gina swiped at the tears. Angry that something with so much promise was gone before it even started. "Bitch."

"Mum! That's a swear," Sammy said as she entered the room.

"I'm sorry, sweetheart," she said reaching out a hand to her, "I just moved and caught one of my little cuts."

"Did it hurt?"

"Yes, little bit, that's why I swore." She wiggled her fingers at Sammy and tried not to look at Kate. "Now come here and give me a hug."

"Be careful though, kiddo. You don't want to hurt your mum," Kate said as she helped Sammy climb up on the high bed. "You okay?" she asked Gina.

Gina closed her eyes as she wrapped her arms around Sammy. "I'm fine now. Thank you." She didn't care that Sammy was probably helping to pull off all the little white butterfly strips. This was what she needed to help her heal. She clung tight.

"You scared me," Sammy whispered.

"I scared myself, sweetheart." She squeezed and pulled back to look in Sammy's eyes. "Don't worry. I won't do it again."

"Promise?"

"Pinky swear," she said, holding up her little finger. Sammy threw herself back into her mother's arms and sobbed against Gina's neck.

"I'll leave you to it," Kate said quietly.

Gina nodded. So that was how she planned to do it. Just quietly walk away. No big, teary goodbye. No, we'll-catch-up-soon. No, it's-been-nice-but-blah-blah-blah, just "I'll leave you to it." She swiped at another tear.

"Want me to bring you something back with me? Coffee? Tea? If I remember right, the coffee here sucks."

"What?"

"Oh, is that not okay to say? Sorry. The coffee's really bad, I was going to go to the cafeteria. There's a Costa machine. It does hot chocolates for her royal highness there, and I thought coffee might—why are you looking at me like I've grown another head?" Kate glanced over her shoulder, and raised a hand to her hair. "Have I got something in my hair?"

"No, it's just," Gina said, "I thought that, well, I just thought, erm, that you'd have stuff to do." *Genius. That's going to be helpful.*

Kate shook her head. "Stella told me to come and be a relative tonight."

Gina frowned. "What does that mean?"

"Well, when we found out you were with Ally, I was, erm, a bit..." Kate sighed. "I lost it. Bawled out my DI in front of everyone, disobeyed a direct order not to do anything till the specialist unit arrived, and then went and did, well, what I did. I was really worried about you." She chuckled. "I think I might have given away the fact that I'm ever so slightly crazy about you." She reached out and grasped Gina's hand, smiling at Sammy as she turned to look at her too. "Yes, both of you." She ran her hand through her hair. "So, she told me to take the night off and just be here for you, with you." She shrugged. "I can go if you'd prefer."

"No," Sammy said. "You can stay. Can't she, Mum?"

"Kate's probably got lots of other things to do, Sammy. She doesn't have to stay."

"But she's got the night off. Her Stella said so."

"Yes, but Kate's spent a lot of time with us lately, I'm sure she has lots—"

"I'm sorry, I didn't mean to intrude." Kate turned to leave but stopped by the door. Sammy was sitting up on the bed, frowning, with her hands balled into fists on her hips. She looked just like a miniature Gina.

"I want Kate to stay," Sammy said, sulking. "Kate said she wants to stay—"

"She didn't actually say that, Sammy," Gina said.

"But I do," Kate said. "Sorry, I don't want to butt in, but if you're sending me away because you think I don't want to be here, you're wrong. I do. Can't think of anything I want more right now."

"See?" Sammy said pointing to the chair. "Sit down, Kate. Mummy's grumpy."

Kate sniggered. "I see that. I'm not sure I understand why, though. I thought I'd made myself clear. More than just a long weekend, remember?"

Gina nodded. "That was before."

"Before what?"

Gina swiped at yet more tears. Angry and frustrated at herself. "Before Ally."

Kate frowned. "What about her?" Kate stuck her hand in her pocket and fished out some coins. "Sammy, do you know where the vending machine is in the hallway?"

"Yeah."

"Cool. Go get some sweets or something would you? I need a few minutes to talk to your mum. See if I can make her a bit less grumpy."

Sammy took the coins and hopped off the bed. "Good luck," she said, and pulled open the door.

Kate sat on the edge of the bed where Sammy had been. "Gina, what did she do to you?" Kate's voice was little more than a whisper as she took hold of her hand and brought it to her lips. "Please tell me. Whatever it was, it can't be worse than I've been imagining." She kissed her knuckles again. "What did she do to you?" Kate's eyes were damp as she gazed at her. "Please?"

"She..." Gina couldn't bring herself to say it. She couldn't think of the words to describe how Ally had marked her. She pushed the blankets away from her shivering body and showed her instead. She lifted the edge of the hospital gown enough to show Kate line after line of cuts across her abdomen, then she shuffled around until she was showing Kate her back. "She wanted to know where Matt was. When I told her I didn't know, she decided it would be fun to play solitaire with my back as the board."

Soft fingertips swept across the back of her neck and her hair was pushed over her shoulder. Then she felt a touch so light she wasn't sure of it until it was gone and a tiny wet spot was left behind. A kiss. A tiny kiss on the nape of her neck.

"And you didn't think I'd stick around."

"No one ever has."

"I'm not them, Gina." Kate touched her cheek and pulled gently until she could look into her eyes. "You are beautiful. You're stunning, and I can't wait to get to know every single inch of your body. Warts and all. I have my own collection of scars that I've picked up over the years." She pushed up the sleeve of her jumper and ran her finger over a crescent moon of jagged dots. "Dog bite. Does that stop you being attracted to me?"

Gina shook her head.

Kate pulled the collar away from her neck and pointed to a thin white line towards the back, almost over her left shoulder. "Bottle, from breaking up a bar fight when I was new to the job. Does that change anything for you?"

Gina shook her head again.

"Then why would this change anything for me?" Kate ran her hand over Gina's shoulder.

Gina said nothing. She knew that if she did she wouldn't be able to stop herself from crying again.

"If you want me to go, I'll go," Kate said again. "But if you want me to go because you don't think I want to stay, you're very much mistaken, Gina." She placed a tender kiss on Gina's shoulder. "I can't think of anywhere else I'd rather be."

"Please hold me," Gina whispered.

Kate leaned down and gently tugged Gina into her embrace. "With pleasure."

Epilogue

Kate smoothed a hand down her black blouse and tucked the back into her jeans again. She checked her hair in the reflection of the car's window, then quickly bared her teeth, looking for anything amiss. Good to go. The gravel of Gina's driveway crunched under her feet, and the wood of Gina's door made such a loud bang under her knuckles, she felt the need to stare at her hand. Chill, it's just a date. Just a little dinner.

Gina opened the door in a knee-length, halter-neck, black dress, and all thoughts of playing it cool ran away screaming. Her hair was piled up on top of her head, leaving her creamy white shoulders with the barest hint of freckles showing.

"You look amazing," Kate said.

"Not too overdressed?"

Kate shook her head.

"Because I can go and change. You're in jeans." She fidgeted with her bag. "I'll just be a minute. Wait there."

Kate grasped her hand. "Don't change. Please. You look incredible." She lifted Gina's hand to her lips and she heard Gina gasp. The scent of coconut, oranges, and jasmine lingered on Gina's skin. "Are you all set? Stella and Sammy all set up?"

Gina nodded and closed the door behind her. "They've got pizza and a night of action movies planned. Thanks for talking her into babysitting."

"No talking required." Well, only a tiny bit, but it was well worth it.

"You didn't tell me where we're going."

"No?"

"You know you didn't."

"It's a surprise."

Kate had booked a table for them at The Neptune, along the coast road at Old Hunstanton. A Michelin-starred restaurant specialising in fresh local produce, they seated only a very small number of tables in a beautifully intimate and romantic setting. The food was delicious, the company more so, and Kate was very sorry when it was time to leave.

She held Gina's hand as they walked to her door. Gina slid her key into the lock and smiled. "Coffee?"

Kate shook her head. "Not this time."

"Something wrong?"

"Not at all." Kate stepped in close. "It's been perfect." She leaned in farther until her lips were less than an inch from Gina's. "I've been wanting to kiss you since the moment I met you."

Gina's breath caught. "Then stop waiting." Her voice was breathy, but low. Her hands slipped around Kate's waist and she moulded herself to Kate's body.

Kate didn't want to rush. There would only ever be one first kiss, no matter how many others there would be. And she planned on many, many thousands, if not more. But this was the only first kiss they would get, and Kate wanted it to be the last first kiss she ever gave. She hoped Gina knew how important it felt to her. She hoped she was appreciating and savouring it just as much. She closed the remaining space between them as slowly as she could. Moving a fraction of a millimetre at a time until she felt Gina's lips give beneath her own.

Kate wrapped her fingers in Gina's hair and held her, cradling the back of her head as she worshipped Gina's mouth. Her tongue flicked against moist, yielding lips, delved into her mouth, and explored every inch of her. She pressed her back against the wall beside the door, and steadied them both. Gina twisted one leg around Kate's, hooking her calf behind Kate's knee. Kate traced her fingers down Gina's jaw from her earlobe to the tip of her chin, then slid them down her throat and along the shoulder she had admired earlier.

Gina's hands clutched at Kate's sides, ran up her back, and cleaved their bodies together until there was no space between them at all.

Kate couldn't get enough. She wanted it all now, but she wanted to savour the anticipation. She wanted to taste her, breathe her in, and feel everything all at once. But there would be time for that. She slowly began to gentle the kiss and they eased apart enough to breathe. Smiling against Gina's lips when she moaned a growl of frustration.

"Don't go," Gina whispered and pulled her head forward for another kiss. This one was more passionate, more hungry, more demanding. The needs of their bodies shouting loud and clear. Gina's hands slid down her back, grasped her arse, and squeezed. "Oh, God, that feels good," Gina mumbled. Then she closed her lips around Kate's tongue and sucked.

Kate ran her hand down Gina's side, across her backside, and tugged her thigh higher up her own leg.

"Ahem." Stella stood in the doorway looking out at them. A grin on her face.

Kate and Gina turned their heads to look at her.

"Your phone's going off." Stella pointed to the phone clipped to Kate's belt.

"And?" Kate asked, one hand still holding Gina's leg, the other at her throat. Their cheeks touched, Gina's hands squeezed her arse, and they were both breathing heavy.

"It's Timmons. We've got another one."

Until Next Time...

About Andrea Bramhall

Andrea Bramhall wrote her first novel at the age of six and three-quarters. It was seven pages long and held together with a pink ribbon. Her Gran still has it in the attic. Since then she has progressed a little bit and now has a number of published works held together with glue, not ribbons, an Alice B. Lavender certificate, a Lambda Literary award, and a Golden Crown award cluttering up her book shelves.

She studied music and all things arty at Manchester Metropolitan University, graduating in 2002 with a BA in contemporary arts. She is certain it will prove useful someday…maybe.

When she isn't busy running a campsite in the Lake District, Bramhall can be found hunched over her laptop scribbling down the stories that won't let her sleep. She can also be found reading, walking the dogs up mountains while taking a few thousand photos, scuba diving while taking a few thousand photos, swimming, kayaking, playing the saxophone, or cycling.

CONNECT WITH ANDREA:

Facebook: www.facebook.com/AndreaBramhall

Other Books from Ylva Publishing

www.ylva-publishing.com

Driving Me Mad

L.T. Smith

ISBN: 978-3-95533-290-7
Length: 348 pages (107,000 words)

After becoming lost on her way to a works convention, Rebecca Gibson stops to ask for help at an isolated house. Progressively, her life becomes more entangled with the mysterious happenings of the house and its inhabitants.

With the help of Clare Davies, can Rebecca solve a mystery that has been haunting a family for over sixty years? Can she put the ghosts and the demons of the past to rest?

Blurred Lines

(Cops and Docs - Book #1)

KD Williamson

ISBN: 978-3-95533-493-2
Length: 283 pages (92,000 words)

Wounded in a police shootout, Detective Kelli McCabe spends weeks in the hospital recovering. Her only entertainment is verbal sparring matches with Dr. Nora Whitmore, the talented and reclusive surgeon.

Two very different women living in two different worlds. When the lines between them begin to blur, will they run from the possibilities or embrace the changes they bring to each other's lives.

The Red Files

Lee Winter

ISBN: 978-3-95533-330-0
Length: 365 pages (103,000 words)

Ambitious journalist Lauren King is stuck reporting on the vapid LA social scene's gala events while sparring with her rival—icy ex-Washington correspondent Catherine Ayers. Then a curious story unfolds before their eyes, involving a business launch, thirty-four prostitutes, and a pallet of missing pink champagne. Can the warring pair join together to unravel an incredible story?

Conflict of Interest
(2nd revised edition)

(Portland Police Bureau Series - Buch #1)

Jae

ISBN: 978-3-95533-109-2
Length: 466 pages (135,000 words)

Detective Aiden Carlisle isn't looking for love, especially not at a law enforcement seminar, but the first lecturer isn't what she expected. After a failed relationship, psychologist Dawn Kinsley swore to never get involved with another cop, but she immediately feels a connection to Aiden. Can Aiden keep from crossing the line when Dawn becomes the victim of a brutal crime?

Coming from Ylva Publishing

www.ylva-publishing.com

Under Parr

(Norfolk Coast Investigation Story – Book #2)

Andrea Bramhall

December 5th, 2013 left its mark on the North Norfolk Coast in more ways than one. A tidal surge and storm swept millennia-old cliff faces into the sea and flooded homes and businesses up and down the coast. It also buried a secret in the WWII bunker hiding under the golf course at Brancaster. A secret kept for years, until it falls squarely into the lap of Detective Sergeant Kate Brannon and her fellow officers.

A skeleton, deep inside the bunker.

How did it get there? Who was he...or she? How did the stranger die—in a tragic accident or something more sinister? Well, that's Kate's job to find out.

Collide-O-Scope

© 2017 by Andrea Bramhall

ISBN: 978-3-95533-849-7

Also available as e-book.

Published by Ylva Publishing, legal entity of Ylva Verlag, e.Kfr.

Ylva Verlag, e.Kfr.
Owner: Astrid Ohletz
Am Kirschgarten 2
65830 Kriftel
Germany

www.ylva-publishing.com

First edition: 2016
Second revised edition: 2017

Credits
Edited by R.G Emanuelle
Cover Design by Adam Lloyd
Cover Photo by Andrea Bramhall

Printed in Great Britain
by Amazon